DAMP LEGACY

'ENGLISH VILLAGE LIFE SERIES'
Volume one

DAMP LEGACY

Part One

This story was influenced by, and is based upon actual events, it also contains a high proportion of fictional characters and material.

Trevor Sproston

AuthorHouse™
1663 Liberty Drive
Bloomington, IN 47403
www.authorhouse.com
Phone: 1-800-839-8640

Published by AuthorHouse 05/24/2012

ISBN: 978-1-4685-8269-7 (sc)
ISBN: 978-1-4685-8270-3 (e)

This book is printed on acid-free paper.

Chapter One

A good three hours would need to pass before dawn could break on that cold Saturday morning in early January. Frost glistened on the dimly lit cobbled street winding through the village of Augers Bank, the pools of light cast by the few gas lamps shimmered as the tramp of steel studded boots and wooden clogs progressed from one pool of light to the next. The early shift miners were making their way towards 'Tilly Pit', they would not witness the dawn today, dark as they were caged down the pit shaft, in darkness underground most of the day, with the possibility of a few hours daylight after their eight-hour shift ended.

Evie Swindon stirred in her bed, disturbed by the heavy plod of the miners feet, although almost seventeen years old, she had the good fortune to have been employed 'in service' as a kitchen maid with the family of a wealthy business man in North Staffordshire for the past year, as a result, she was used to rising early. This being the eighth week of the servant's rota, she had been allowed to return home last night for the weekend. Sharing the bed was her younger sister Fanny; if all the Swindon girls had been at home the bed would have slept four. Their two elder sisters also worked away from home, holding positions as domestic servants.

Fanny, the youngest member of the family was ten years old, and in comparison with the other girls considered to be of a rather sickly constitution, true or not, her mother allowed her to take many liberties the other girls were denied. Fanny was a good-looking child, stout of build and well developed for her age, to any outsider she would appear to be the picture of health; however, too often for her parents or her siblings liking, she still exhibited a tendency to escape into that world of fantasy usually associated with much younger children.

Evie turned towards Fanny, and to wake her gave her shoulder a shake.

"Come on Fanny, wake up," she murmured, "Mother said you were to black-lead the range and light the fires this morning."

"But it's still dark," whimpered Fanny, "And it's cold."

Recognising Fanny's familiar technique of dodging housework, Evie retorted, "Of course its cold, it's the middle of winter, and this house will stay cold until the fires are lit, you have to learn how to do these things Fanny; you will be eleven in six weeks."

Fanny mused for a moment, "Evie, can you do it; I've got a terrible headache this morning."

Evie, never regarded as being the most tolerant of people began to lose her patience.

"That may work on mother, but not me," she snapped, "I have to light fires every morning, this is my weekend off."

"Please Evie;" insisted Fanny, "You can do it much better than I could."

The older sister began to regain control, "I am not going to do all the chores that mother gave to you so that you can stay in bed again, if you get up now I will help, I'll black the ranges for you, and you can light the fires."

Fanny realising that further argument would be fruitless, agreed. Evie struck a match and lit the bedside candle; Fanny reluctantly raised herself out of bed.

"Brr it's cold," she complained, "What time is it Evie?"

"Just gone five thirty," replied her sister.

Disgruntled, Fanny muttered under her breath, "Too early."

The sisters were soon dressed, downstairs and moving about quickly to combat the chill, young Evie had the kitchen range blacked and shining in about twenty minutes, the brass oven handles gleamed. Fanny's second attempt to light a fire in it failed, with a sigh, Evie relinquished her resolve and lit the range fire herself; it was far too cold to wait for her young sisters fumbling efforts to provide warmth. Once the kitchen fire was going well, Evie turned her attention to the back kitchen range; this one housed a fire at its centre, flanked by an oven and a deep, cast-iron boiler. She lit the fire and filled the boiler; this boiler served to provide hot water for the family, which, when required could be drawn out through a convenient brass tap set at bucket height from the floor.

The large smoke blackened kettle Evie filled with water and hung over this fire to boil; an early morning pot of tea Evie always considered an absolute necessity. The girls seated themselves on the hearth as near to the just kindled fire as they could get, they, like the water in the kettle were cold, and desperately in need of the radiating heat as the coals took hold and began to burn well.

"Evie, why do you think mother wanted me to clean the range and light the fires this morning, she usually does it herself . . . and why so early?"

Evie smiled as she replied, "Early for you maybe, but this is my usual time to start work, anyway, the day shift men at the pit woke me this morning with their delph clogs tramping past the window. I don't hear things like that at work, the master's house stands in its own grounds, there is very little noise to be heard."

Fanny persisted, "Yes, but why did she ask me?"

Evie reflected for a moment, "Maybe because I am home, Lizzie, Emily and I were all able to do these household chores by the time we were eight, you're nearly eleven and still struggle to light a fire, or do anything else for that matter."

Fanny could be bright enough when it suited her purpose, she snapped back.

"She needn't teach me, I'm not going into service, I'm better than that, I am going to be a concert pianist, so there!" Evie was hurt by these implications, and annoyed by the peevish attitude of the ten year old.

"Oh really Miss Perfect, you may be having piano lessons now that our brother Lijah has brought a piano into this house, but it certainly does not make you better than us, you will find that out one day young lady."

Fortunately, before the argument could develop further, their mother, Eve, from whom Evie inherited her name, came downstairs.

"Oh! It's nice to get up and not have to light the fires, what a good job you have made of the kitchen range Fanny, and tea is made as well, well done Fanny."

"Thank you mother," Fanny responded with a smirk, and with a roguish flick of her skirt, turned and went back upstairs. Evie glared after her young sister as she left the room, but said nothing.

Eve Swindon, a well-built woman in her late forties caught sight of Evie's glare as the younger girl left the room.

"Oh! I see, she didn't do the grate, you did it Evie, I'm sorry."

"Yes and everything else, as usual," mumbled the girl.

Eve realised that some controversy had taken place.

"Evie, I know you all think I am too lenient with Fanny, your father tells me off about it sometimes, but we should be grateful she is still here with us, I am," Evie nodded signifying she understood her mother's inferred meaning.

The six and a half year age gap between the youngest Swindon children in the early twentieth century villages would have been uncommon. Eve Swindon had in fact given birth to eight children, five daughters and three sons. Unfortunately, in 1905 an outbreak of 'Consumption' as many called it, a disease more correctly named tuberculosis. To this killer disease of those times, the Swindon family had lost four-year-old twin sons, and an eleven-month-old daughter. The loss of a child to any parent is an ordeal, but to face the prospect of having to bury three of your children on the same day as Samuel and Eve Swindon did was unbearable. Sam, Eve, and the older children, each in their own way now grieved their loss in silence, rarely if ever speaking of it, especially in Eve's presence, by so doing endeavouring to lessen the pain they all felt. Eve, a very strong willed, level headed woman able to cope admirably with almost any situation, but this, the loss of her three children cruelly taken from her within the space of twenty four hours, she held deep in her heart.

With the arrival of Fanny on the first day of March 1907, fearful that history should repeat itself, the remaining family vowed to unite and take prestigious care of the new baby.

It is common knowledge now in the twenty first century that babies learn quickly from their environment, so it was in the case of young Fanny, she soon came to realise that the slightest noise, cry, sniffle or cough would bring one of her parents, or siblings running in haste to her aid. All the Swindon children received the utmost care their parents could bestow, but Fanny arriving as she did late in the child bearing age of her mother, and following the families loss to the dreaded 'consumption' two years earlier, had been pampered by everyone far too much for her father Sam's liking.

Sam Swindon was a fair minded, God-fearing man who loved and cared for all his children equally. However, the love he felt for Eve was strong, and the reasons she had doted on the new baby was not beyond his understanding. Nevertheless the ensuing favouritism on his wife's part towards Fanny disturbed him more often than he would ever fully admit.

As the infant developed Sam could see she began to exploit this excessive attention, however, trusting his wife would know best the ways of rearing a child, reluctantly, he observed in silence. With the passing of her early years, Fanny slowly but surely became ever more pretentious. Elijah, the only surviving male child, remained totally true to the initial family commitment of taking special care of her, this promise he continued to keep his entire life. In contrast, the three older sisters, to varying degrees eventually developed a sub-conscious, veiled resentment towards her, Fanny was so often excused the general household duties, they, and every other girl in the village learned and carried out during their own early years.

Sibling loyalty in the Swindon household was undisputed, Evie being the youngest but one remained at home for some time after Lizzie and Emily found placements away 'in service'. Subsequently, with events that transpired during this period, she came to nurture a strong belief that Fanny should, with some small allowances made for her age, contribute much more within the home, all too often Fanny's fair share of chores had fallen to Evie.

From the time Fanny was seven years old, their mother Eve, just as she had taught her other daughters endeavoured on many occasions to set Fanny various small tasks, simple household duties, from which she could gradually learn the normal life skills of a woman of their status. The loss of three of her children remained so painfully embedded within Eve, the slightest intimation of illness from Fanny would result in the allocation of her set task to one of the other girls, or Eve would finish it herself, thus, allowing Fanny to do just as she pleased, often escaping into her beloved world of dreams.

Three years earlier, Lijah had purchased an old redundant piano from their Wesleyan Chapel at Augers Bank, a new one having been donated by one of the more affluent members of the congregation. Fanny now considered 'piano practice' as she called it, far preferable to housework, and skilfully substituted this for any tasks more arduous.

Lijah, ten years Fanny's senior had willingly undertaken to pay Fanny's tuition fees in addition to his own, however, despite his good nature, on occasions he became irritated to find Fanny seated at his piano, flatly refusing to move for him to use the instrument himself. Elijah Swindon's nature and commitment to his pledge at her birth, always weighed in Fanny's favour, and more often than not, he gave way to her.

Eve and her daughter finished their breakfast of toast with beef dripping washed down with a strong cup of tea.

"Evie, the kitchen range's oven should be getting warm enough now, will you reach me the shopping basket off the stillage in the pantry, it's got flour and things in it."

The girl complied.

"Have you had a new basket mother?" Evie queried.

"Why no child, it's Mrs Moore's basket, she asked me to make some pies and cakes for the 'Prims' old folks party tonight, she called in with those ingredients yesterday before you arrived home."

Evie could not help herself, she let out a little giggle, "Oh mother, you never could say no could you? The Primitive isn't our chapel, but your pastry is always so light they are always asking you to make things for them, hold on, ... will there be enough stuff in here?" she observed, investigating the contents of the basket and its request note.

"Probably not," replied Eve, "Maybe my working as a cooks assistant at your age was not such a good idea, Eh!" they both laughed and began to gather the cooking utensils onto the kitchen table.

Mother and daughter worked together, transforming the contents of the basket into delicate pastries, Fanny re-emerging from her room, seeing this activity in the kitchen, hesitated a moment and catching her mother's eye quickly interjected.

"Mother, it's very cold this morning, can we have a fire in the front room as well so that I can do my piano practice?"

Evie's eyes darted straight to her mother, Eve smiled back at her, "Perhaps a small one as it is Saturday," she winked at Evie and continued, "You made such a good job of lighting this one, I'm sure you can light another fire for yourself, you know where everything is, we are busy at the moment."

As she carried on with her baking, a smile of satisfaction crossed Evie's face at her mother's response, Fanny, for her part had anticipated a different reaction to her request, but having owned to lighting the kitchen fires, even she realised her little deception would be discovered if she said anymore, gathering up some kindling she returned into the front room.

"Mother, that was impish of you," Evie tittered, "I was expecting you to tell me to light it for her."

"Perhaps it was, a little, but not as impish as Fanny allowing me to think she had done the ranges this morning," replied Eve in resolute tone. Evie felt a little guilty for unintentionally imparting the truth of earlier events,

"She didn't actually say that she had mother."

"No, she didn't, nor did she admit that you had done them, it's time Fanny did more around this house, it will do her good."

From the front room came the monotonous sound of piano scales being played.

Eve muttered in dismay, "Oh bother! I had hoped to have these cakes in the oven well before your father and Lijah came down."

"Don't worry mother, Fanny can't have lit a fire yet, once her fingers get cold she'll be out of there pretty sharpish, hoping that you or I will light it for her," consoled Evie.

"Yes! You may be right," agreed her mother, "But this time we won't, what do you say?" Evie smirked; she enjoyed her mother consulting her as an equal adult.

"Agreed," she replied.

Evie was right; Fanny was back in less than three minutes.

"Something wrong Fanny?" inquired her mother.

"Yes," fanny replied, "I just remembered I haven't had any breakfast."

"I know," Eve smiled back, "There are two slices of bread cut for you in the back kitchen, the toasting fork is hanging up, and the dripping is still out, oh, and there should be tea left in the pot on the hob, can you manage on your own?"

Evie noted with amusement the scowl on her younger sister's face as she replied.

"Of course I can mother."

Evie followed Fanny into the back kitchen, ostensively, to wash the baking bowl and their other tools, out of habit she also intended to keep an eye on Fanny, aiding her if needed as she endeavoured to prepare her simple breakfast. Meanwhile, Eve nipped back upstairs in order to make certain Sam had not been disturbed by the piano, he had not, he was still dozing. Once Evie was satisfied that Fanny was all right, she returned the clean baking utensils to the kitchen table in readiness for her mother to start the last batch of cakes for Mrs Moore.

Seeing everything ready to start again when she returned to the kitchen, Eve smiled.

"Is Father alright?" asked Evie, "It's unusual for him to be still in bed at this time, its well gone eight."

Eve reassured her daughter, "Why of course he is child, he and Lijah are on late shift today at 'Tilly', I suggested they have a lie in this morning so that I could get this baking done," Eve's face was alight with an expression of satisfaction.

Evie began to sort the remaining ingredients but stopped suddenly, "Oh now I get it, you didn't want them down here under your feet, smoking their pipes of twist while you are baking did you?

"No, I did not! You will find its wise not to let men know we have are own reasons for suggesting they do anything you know, they can be obstinate creatures if they think women are in charge."

Evie, delighted to have her mother to herself for a change, changed the subject but continued chattering.

"I suppose it is better for them now, they only have half the distance to walk to the pit since we moved out of the cottage in 'Little Row' into this new house."

Eve stopped her baking for a second, "Yes, I suppose this is about half way, but 'Little Row' was still only twenty minutes or so walk to the pit head across the fields, that's not very far either is it?"

Evie decided to press a point she had been curious about for sometime.

"Mother, I never really knew how it was that we were able to move into this bigger, almost new house, may I know?

Eve pondered a moment; "I think you're old enough, yes I will tell you, after all, it was rather strange how it came about."

Fanny, who had overheard some of this conversation, being as inquisitive as ever came out of the back kitchen at this point.

"May I hear as well mother?" she inquired.

Eve was not entirely sure that Fanny should be told, in the company of her young friends she had a tendency to chatter, but eventually replied, "Very well, I can hardly believe it myself sometimes."

With that, Eve began to relate the chain of events that had led to their good fortune.

'Little Row' comprised of eight cottages in a cul-de-sac set at right angles to the main road, at a less steep section of Augers Bank, these cottages veered down from the road in the direction of Heals End. These were typical of those in which, excluding the pit officials, the bulk of the mining community lived. Small rooms approximately ten feet square, two upstairs, two down, doorways

and ceilings very low, invariably cottages of this type were damp and musty.

At 'Little Row', and most other houses of the time, the only soil drain access comprised of one grid in the back yard of each cottage, the bulk of wastewater had to be carried and emptied into this. Fresh water supply was communal, one outdoor pump to serve the whole row. Although it was not obvious from the outside, each cottage inside was of an alternating narrowing shape, the first being wider at the front whilst the one next door was wider at the rear, and so on. Narrow staircases led off from the wider downstairs room, comprising of ten ascending steps, ending, at the right-angled doorways to the upstairs rooms. Kitchens used for cooking, dining, and laundry were the occupant's main area of habitation, the other downstairs room had varying uses, often a sitting room, or, dependant on the number in a family, doubling as an additional sleeping area.

Basic kitchen fitments consisted of a 'Range Fire Grate', a shallow brown stoneware sink from which a narrow lead waste pipe normally fed outside through the wall from which wastewater was open gullied to the yard grid. Wooden framed windows in all rooms were small, letting in very little light, and like all the internal doors painted in a universal brown with a topcoat of varnish, this varnish as it aged always exhibited a deeply cracked appearance, after sundown, the only light available was provided by oil lamps or candles.

Outside every back door, hung on a large nail driven into the mortar between the bricks could be found a tin bath. This bath would be dragged into the kitchen when the miners returned home after their shift at the pit, their bodies and clothes thick with coal dust. Behind a makeshift screen, they would wash and change from their delph clothes.

Brick built structures, approximately five feet square were situated at the bottom of each yard, these housed a large thick wooden chest, inside, sunk into the earth was a very large earthenware barrel sized pot. Cut into the hinged lid of the chest was a circular hole averaging about one foot in diameter; these structures, Earth closets', were the toilets, quite commonly referred to as 'The Privy'.

Samuel Swindon had rented one such cottage from the time of his marriage to Eve, until four years ago. Sleeping arrangements as a family increased followed the accepted mode of the time, babies and children less than five years old slept with their parents in the larger of the two bedrooms, normally in cots along one wall hidden behind an old blanket slung on a length of clothesline across the length of the room. The older children shared the second room, again divided by a blanket to separate genders.

The Swindon's current house was considerably larger than a cottage, being, as it was, a double fronted, three bed roomed 'L' shaped semi detached house, built in 1900, downstairs, the rooms were a good four yards square. This house, being one of three pairs was situated half way down, and at the steepest part of Augers Bank. To compensate for the steep incline of the bank and the lay of surrounding land, the foundations for these particular houses had been dug out in such a way that the adjoining ground level at the rear was between five and eight feet higher than floor level. This higher ground, retained by the house walls themselves proved to be a constant source of penetrating damp. The remaining higher ground was held back by retaining walls which continued from the gable end to form the small back yards.

In comparison to the cottage, this house was luxurious, having in the back kitchen above the shallow brown stone sink, one tap of cold running water, plus the advantage of illumination by gas light in all rooms instead of oil lamps.

The door at the front of the house was central, and accessed from the road by climbing seven steps situated at the left hand side; and by following a short path to the right. This door opened onto a small porch from which the staircase of thirteen steep steps rose to a small landing. To the right of the landing, a passageway which had two bedrooms off it, the master bedroom being to the left of the stairs. Downstairs, to the right of the front door was the kitchen, to the left a sitting room, generally, despite the house being double fronted referred to as 'the front room.' At the rear of the kitchen was, the 'back kitchen,' which completed the 'L' formation. A rear door opened from the back kitchen onto a yard, and in turn, a path led from this around the house back to the steps at the front.

One bedroom of mirrored dimensions above each of the downstairs rooms, whilst under the staircase, being the coolest place in the house was a pantry.

The bathing facilities were the same as the cottage, the tin bath hung in its traditional place outside the back door, The Earth Closet toilet at the farthest point from the door, opposite this, and taking its line from the back kitchen window, a brick built fuel store..

Broughton Parish consisted of seven villages of which Augers Bank was one. Due to the bank's gradient, previously, in the interests of simplicity housing and most other buildings had been restricted to any moderately level plot of land nature offered. However, by the early nineteen hundreds, infill building following the contours of the roadways, and the use of the less obvious plots linking existing structures, had become fashionable.

The three pairs of semi-detached houses, of which the bottom one was now the Swindon home evolved from this new trend. The site itself, though steep and difficult to excavate in order to lay foundations, chosen, and the houses built facing due west to afford as they did, a magnificent view over the Cheshire Plain towards the mountains of North Wales.

A social class structure existed within the villages, ordinary miners families, though not at the very bottom were considered to be quite near it. There were even those in the higher and mid classes who held the belief 'Poor people are unimportant, dirty they live, and then they die.' For a common 'pit man's' family to aspire to live anywhere but their conventional cottage hovels was rare indeed.

Eve began to answer her daughter's query as they worked, "Fanny, you will not remember this, but Evie might, can you remember Mr and Mrs Scrivens who used to live here, they were members of our chapel, I used to take in their washing when you were younger?"

"I can remember Mrs. Scrivens," Evie replied racking her memory, "She was a widow, went to live away somewhere with her daughter didn't she?"

"Yes, that's right, Mr. Scrivens was a manager with the coal and coke company, but he passed away in his early fifties, the same time as—," Eve began to choke slightly with emotion.

Evie responded swiftly, “I know, Lijah has told me about that, the same time as our loss, his funeral was on the same day.”

Eve took a few moments to compose herself; Fanny opened her mouth to speak, but upon receiving a swift rebuking glare from Evie, closed it again and sat on the hearth in silence.

Eve continued, “Yes, well, Mr. Scrivens was a ‘Methodist’ but Mrs had been an ‘Anglican’ before they married, she changed over to ‘Methodism’ to please her husband.”

“That’s not usual,” Evie chirped.

Eve retorted, “Do you want to hear this or not?”

“Sorry mother,” Evie responded quickly, mentally resolving not to interrupt again, casting a desperate glance towards Fanny and hoping she would not either, from Fanny’s expression Evie concluded that for once her young sister would hold her chatter.

“Very well then,” Eve resumed, “It was just after Christmas four years ago, I received a note from Mrs Scrivens inviting your father and me to tea. Your father thought it was strange, and as you would expect he did not want to go. We hadn’t seen Mrs Scrivens at chapel for over three years; she reverted back to the ‘Anglican Faith’ after her husband passed away. However, I was curious, we had never, ever, been invited to mix socially with those sorts of people before, eventually, I persuaded your father to accept the invitation. Your Father was still not sure about going even on the day, but after sufficient nagging from me he went, we got all dressed up in our Sunday best for the occasion.”

Fanny and Evie exchanged a look of bewilderment, although congregations exhibited congeniality within the Chapel walls, there was always an underlying evidence of an air of superiority from those whose condition in life was above average.

“Mrs Scrivens herself answered the door to us, her daughter Molly and her husband the Reverend Mr Cummings were there as well, can you guess how that made your Father feel.”

Evie cautiously replied, “A fish out of water?”

Her mother smiled as she continued, “He did feel out of place, but, to our surprise they were all politeness and made us feel very welcome. Eventually, Mrs Scrivens informed us that Molly had asked her to go to live with them at their ‘Parsonage’ in Shropshire, and that she had accepted. She told us that she did not want to sell her house, but being on her own it was too big for her now. Then came the shock, Mr Cummings turned to your father and said, Mr Swindon, as you probably know Anglican Parsons have a residence provided for them within their parishes, I have over thirty years before I am due to retire. We three have discussed Molly's mother's feelings and are in agreement to let this house, provided, we can find a tenant we consider trustworthy.

Your father and I couldn't understand why they were telling us their family affairs; Father felt very uneasy and sat fiddling with his collar. Mrs Scrivens said she and her late husband, knowing us at chapel, had developed a great deal of respect for your father and I, and she had suggested that the tenancy be offered to us." Eve paused briefly, looking to her daughters, inviting a response.

Evie, wide eyed with astonishment could only manage.

"Unbelievable, how did father react?" whilst Fanny, who had not fully grasped the implications of her mothers revelations, nodded in agreement.

"We were both speechless," continued Eve, "Mr Cummings went on to explain that they would naturally expect a higher rent than we were paying for the cottage, but if we were interested, they would let this house to us after Mrs Scrivens moved".

Evie became too confident, "How much is the rent mother?"

"That's none of your business, lets just say more than double what the cottage was, but with Lizzie and Lijah both working and contributing, your father and I eventually decided that we could probably just about afford it, the rest, of course, you know."

Fanny raised herself from her perch on the hearth.

"I knew it" she exclaimed, "We are special people who our Lord looks after."

Eve sighed at her young daughter attributing events solely to the Deity.

"Fanny!" Evie snapped forcibly back at her, "we are not special people, but in this instance we have been very fortunate indeed," to which rebuke Fanny shrugged her shoulders and replied.

"I know what I know, even if you don't."

The baking now completed, Evie washed and stowed away the utensils, Sam and Lijah, appeared downstairs, their senses having been aroused by the delicate cooking aroma drifting aloft.

"Sam," said Eve, "Fanny has asked for a fire in the front room so that she can do her practice, is that alright?"

"We are getting a bit low on coal," he replied.

Lijah in response to Fanny's frown proffered the suggestion, "Let her have one father, I might use the piano myself later, and I can get some more coal next week," Sam nodded in agreement.

Evie noting the lack of movement from Fanny, swiftly added, "She says she will light it herself, didn't she mother."

The younger girl scowled at her sister and went back into the front room.

Evie, smiled to herself in satisfaction, "Shall I get you some breakfast Father, and for you Lijah?" she asked, without waiting for any reply made her way into the back kitchen.

Sam settled down in his easy chair by the kitchen fire with Friday night's paper, and Lijah glanced at the clock on the mantle piece.

"Good heavens," he exclaimed, "It's gone twenty to ten, we are late this morning, Mother, have you finished with the kitchen table? I haven't prepared the lesson for my Sunday School class tomorrow yet." Receiving no objection, Lijah laid out his Bible, class notes, and began to formulate the lesson.

Fanny, still in the front room, kneeling on the hearth lighting her fire, squealed, Eve rushed in, closely followed by Lijah and Sam.

"Whatever is the matter?" Eve asked, somewhat bewildered by her daughter's paled face.

"I don't know, I just struck a match, and the fire grate moved," replied her terrified daughter.

Eve retorted pointing to the grate, "Don't be silly child; the grate is part of that wall, tiled and cemented to it."

"But mother, it did, I was kneeling on the hearth, it moved underneath me, it did, it did," Fanny insisted hysterically, the match she had struck and dropped onto the tiled hearth still alight, went out.

Evie appeared in the doorway, "What is it, has Fanny burnt herself?"

"No Evie," her mother replied rather short of patience, "Fanny is being silly, she says the grate moved when she lit a match."

Evie hesitated before admitting, "Perhaps she is not being so silly this time mother," puzzled they all looked at Evie.

"I was leaning on the kitchen sink, it has just started to snow and I was watching a Robin on the back yard wall after the bread crumbs I threw out, and I thought I felt something through the sink."

Mother and daughter began to calm the terrified Fanny, Sam and Elijah's faces held the same look of dread.

"Father, all that dust and gob since old Ernie finished last September."

Sam whose thoughts, although he wished they were not, were comparable to his sons, pondered before responding.

"No it can't be, impossible, only three years next week since,—no, no it can't be."

Lijah wished, rather than believed his father to be right, shook his head and in a hushed tone added.

"Father, she's so unlucky though, isn't she?"

Totally baffled, Evie and Fanny listened to their father and brother, not understanding a single word.

Eve however with sudden realisation of their implications cried out, "Oh no, heaven forbid," and burying her head in her hands collapsed into a chair.

Chapter Two

Following Fanny's outburst and claims of movement from the immovable, a state of unease infected the Swindon household, although Fanny herself forgot the occurrence almost as soon as the others left her alone in the front room, where she was now happily hammering out scales on the piano. Eve, not wishing to betray her fears or show any emotion preferred to be alone, she had retreated upstairs, there were always things to do, beds to make, rooms to tidy. Elijah resumed his place at the kitchen table, and despite his insides churning in apprehension, attempted to concentrate on his lesson preparation. Sam, his pipe of twist well alight and sizzling merrily, once again ensconced in his chair appeared to be reading his paper, but in truth, his mind was engaged on other things than the trivia in this local rag.

Evie busied herself with household chores, pottering between kitchen and back kitchen, she sensed a peculiar atmosphere that she found ominous, something was going on, but what. Unobtrusively watching her father and brother, she noticed numerous furtive glances between them that spoke volumes, but no words were forthcoming from either of them. With the tension in the air, she decided it was probably best not to ask questions, earlier Eve had talked to her as an equal, but she knew, whatever was troubling her father and brother, there was little chance Sam or Lijah would do the same. Whatever the problem was, it all started with Fanny's claim that the front room fire grate moved, she tried to remember everything that followed. Lijah had said something about someone being unlucky, who is it that is unlucky? Fanny could be very silly at times, but insisting the fire grate moved was no reason for this kind of reaction, Fanny's claim could not be the cause; after all, she herself had thought she sensed a vibration through the kitchen sink. Evie had heard of things called 'earthquakes,' but not in England, so she decided that could not be anything to do with it. Elijah's words 'she is so unlucky' kept coming back to her, who was this person that is unlucky? Elijah, as far as she knew didn't know many girls well enough to know if they were lucky or not.

Suddenly it dawned on her, what if the she is not a person at all but something else attributed a feminine gender, she stopped what she was doing, her heart came into her mouth as a possible reason for the apprehension of her parents and brother hit her, her mother's words, 'Oh no, heaven forbid' added credence to this idea. Evie's initial thought was to ask her father and brother if she was right, but from the stony, grim expressions they both held, she thought better of it and continued with her chores in silence.

It is sometimes said that music hath charms to calm the savage breast, the hammering out of scales on a piano however as Fanny did now had quite the opposite effect on everyone else in the house, the youngster's belief that if the noise is loud then the music is good did not help. In addition to which, was the fact she always held down the right foot pedal, this habit not only had the effect of increasing the volume, but also merged the notes from one key onto the next, accumulating into a monotonous, nerve jarring blurred noise. Usually the family paid no attention to this aggravation, today however, the monotony served only to increase the tense expectations of ill fortune already felt by all.

An hour passed in this manner, Lijah, finally finishing his lesson preparation cleared away his notes, joined Evie, and their mother in the back kitchen.

"Any chance of a cup of tea?" he asked.

"Of course Lij," Evie replied, "I was just filling mother in on the latest gossip from work."

Sam remained by the fire in the kitchen, his third pipe of 'Twist' sizzling away in his mouth, by now every room in the house was filled with the distinctive aroma of his tobacco.

Fanny stopped playing just before there was the sound of a hurried, heavy knock on the front door; out of the corner of her eye, Fanny had caught sight of a young man passing the front room window.

Sam reacting to the piano's sudden silence called out urgently.

"I will answer the door Fanny."

Fanny resumed her piano practice without comment or concern, but to everyone's relief, now with the piece her teacher had set this week instead of more scales.

"That's unusual," observed Evie, "People usually knock at the back door, and father never answers it if anyone else is in," Eve nodded, both turned to Elijah to resume their previous conversation, his face drained of colour held a look of horror and his eyes were firmly fixed on the closed door to the kitchen.

Sam appeared in the doorway.

"Lijah lad, we have to change into our delph clothes, 'Tilly' has blown again, we are needed urgent, they are trying to get a rescue team together."

"Many down?" asked Lijah as they hurriedly opened the old kitchen cupboard in which their pit clothes were kept.

"Yes, full shift, two hundred and fifty odd."

"Jim Porter's on 'day shift this week I think, I hope he's alright."

Sam nodded, "Aye lad, so do I, everyone can well do without bad news, especially our Emily."

To allow the men to change Eve and Evie left the room and went into the kitchen, after a couple of minutes, Eve called through the closed door.

"Sam, will you need any snapping?"

"May do, yes we will, but we haven't time to cut any, young Frank said we are needed, and to come straight away."

"Alright, you go, I'll do some and get it down to you."

Fanny, hearing the commotion, and as inquisitive as ever, emerged from the front room.

Sam now dressed in his work clothes, opened the kitchen door, kissed his wife and daughter's goodbye, an uncharacteristic thing for him to do when dressed in pit clothes, he hesitated a second or two before turning to open the door. Lijah, full of apprehension found himself unable to speak, tentatively waved goodbye as he followed his father through the back door, and with that, the men were gone.

Puzzled, Fanny watched them go, "Mother, I thought they were on noon's today?" she said.

"They are, but there has been an accident at the pit, an explosion or something, men are being fetched in," Eve replied as she and Evie busied themselves cutting snapping for father and son.

"Shall I run down with this," Evie offered as they wrapped up the food, "Someone will have to stay here with Fanny."

"Can you love, you are probably fast enough to catch them before they get down there themselves, but be careful in this snow."

Evie grabbed her coat. "I will," she called back from half way down the backyard.

The immediate panic over, Eve and Fanny remained in the back kitchen; Eve slumped into a chair fully aware there was a distinct possibility that her husband and son might not return. Her mind now clearing after the hectic past few minutes, she recollected Elijah saying he thought Jim Porter was on the 'day shift,' she felt a little ashamed that Elijah's observation had not registered with her, but, during the haste in which the men had changed into their delph clothes, it had not.

Jim Porter, was a twenty-four year old man from Knolsend, a village two miles away, last August Eve's second eldest daughter Emily and Jim Porter had become engaged and intending to marry this coming June. Emily, twenty-three years old was also in 'domestic service' at Potterton, a town nine miles away from Augers Bank, if Jim was down 'Tilly' this morning, and if he was injured, or worse, how on earth could they break such news to Emily. Eve not relishing the prospect of this, and desperately hoping Jim was safe above ground put it from her mind.

Surprisingly, even Fanny realised something serious had occurred, mother and daughter were both silent for about five minutes; Fanny sat quietly at the table doing her best to remember earlier events of the morning, and of what had been said since her scare while lighting her fire, trying, as best she could to piece them together.

"Mother," she began, "An explosion is a sort of fire making a big bang isn't it?"

"It is," replied Eve now beginning to compose herself.

Fanny's train of thought gradually became more focused, "Was that what made our front room grate move?"

Eve paused before replying, apparently, the girl had made the connection, "I think Lijah and your father thought it might be."

"If they are right," continued the child; "Father said something about it only being three years next week since,—since what?"

Eve, knowing that Fanny could be annoyingly persistent when she chose to be, decided to try to help the girl comprehend the dangers miners faced on a daily basis.

"It was on a Sunday three years ago, January 17th, 1915, a maintenance crew were down 'Tilly,' twenty seven of them I think, there was an explosion of 'Fire Damp,' nine men were killed, and as many injured, some quite seriously."

"Fire Damp, what's Fire Damp? If fire kindling gets wet it won't burn, how can something wet burn?"

Judging by the too familiar stubborn expression now in evidence on Fanny's face, Eve knew this would not be an easy thing to explain; she now regretted answering the child's original question. There were two options open for Eve, and she knew it, either snap at the girl to put an end to the questioning, or despite her own inner turmoil, help the girl to understand. Eve chose the second option.

"It isn't wet at all Fanny; fire damp is just what the men call it, it's a kind of gas that burns very, very fast, something like the gas we burn to light our house but a lot more powerful, it has a fancy name, 'Methane' or something like that."

Po-faced, Fanny responded. "Funny of them to call it 'damp' mother if it isn't even wet."

"I suppose it does seem strange to a child, there is another one they call 'Choke Damp', that's another kind of gas that gets down the pits as well, but I can't remember its proper name, you'll have to ask your father or Lijah about that." Eve was about to add, 'if they come home', but thought better of it.

"What does 'Choke Damp' do, does that burn as well?"

"No, I don't think so, but I do know it's extremely poisonous, people soon choke on it and die of suffocation in a matter of minutes. Seems pit men call any kind of gas there is down the pit that is able to move with the air pumped down from the surface 'damp', I don't know why."

Fanny pondered a moment trying to make sense of this, gas which moves in the air, she looked at the fire burning in the range grate and went over to it.

"Mother, when Evie was showing me how she lights a fire this morning she moved this thing," she pointed to a lever on the grate, "She said it makes the air carry the flames under the water boiler to get it hot, and this one is for the oven, she called them both 'Dampers'. Are those gasses down the pit called 'damp' because they blow about in the air?"

"Fanny love, I don't know, I never thought of that, but those levers are called 'Dampers' all the same."

Fanny stood gazing into the fire as it burned, suddenly from a flat side of one large piece of coal, a tiny jet of white smoke emerged; the jet caught light pushing a yellow flame about an inch long outwards from the coals face towards the room. The flames tip turned into a wisp of jet-black smoke; this was pulled back up the chimney by the hot air as it rose. She had seen these side flames before but never paid any attention to them, so that's it, she thought to herself, it isn't just the coal that burns, but something trapped inside it as well.

The clock at the centre of the living room mantle shelf was just beginning to strike mid-day as Evie came in through the back door. Eve and Fanny greeted her, eager for news.

"Well? Eve asked as she helped her daughter out of her snow-covered coat.

"I caught up with Dad and Lijah as they were going through the pit gates," gasped the girl trying to regain her breath after hurrying up the steep bank through the cold snowstorm.

"I gave them their snapping, there are an awful lot of people down there, women, children, a couple of men in suits and posh coats, vans, ambulances, both motor and horse drawn, I felt really sorry for those poor horses having to stand out in this cold."

"A turn out like that is to be expected," agreed her mother.

Evie continued, "Some people said something about the 'Air Flow Fan Engine' has been running in reverse, and some said lots of black smoke had come up the main shaft," Fanny had no idea what Evie was talking about, her failure to understand was a frequent occurrence to which she was never prepared to admit.

"Anyway, the under manager has been sent down to try and find out what happened."

Eve asked, "Is he still down?"

"He was when I left; a rescue team are following him down."

"Your Father and Lijah?"

"I think so, I saw them go across to the cage from the 'Lamp House,' about ten men went down."

Eve clasped her hands and looked skywards, saying, "Heaven protect those men and those they seek."

Fanny not wanting to be left out, even though she had not understood very much of Evie's account of her errand, asked.

"Did you learn anything else Evie?"

"I heard people talking about things, someone said that the big 'Winding Engine' had stopped for some time, but it's working again now, some of the night shift miners are still on the pit bank, they had been waiting from six o'clock for their wages to arrive when the explosion happened."

Eve interrupted, "Do you know if any of them volunteered to go back down Evie?"

"Most of them I think, but the talk is, the pit manager, someone named Shaw I think they said, told them they could not until under manager Cleaver phoned up from the workings below ground to report how dangerous it is down there. He told the night shift men it would be better to send other men down who were not so tired, and that runners have been sent out to fetch rescue team men in. Some of the night shift while they waited have cleared out the 'Smithy' instead, you know the one, that small building where the pit ponies are shod, and they have turned it into somewhere for the rescue men, and other people to rest and eat."

"Of course!" exclaimed Eve springing to her feet, "Evie, will you look after Fanny for me, I'll go down and see if there is anything I can do to help."

Eve went to the pantry, surely, they could spare some food to take down for the rescue teams to eat, the consideration and generosity of the mine owners towards their workers was usually non-existent. Evie aware of her mothers generous nature helped pack the food, as she did she caught site of the cakes they made earlier.

"Mother," she said, "I almost forgot, I saw Mrs Moore going down to the pit as I came up, she wanted to know if you had made the cakes she asked for, she says the 'Old Folks Party' has been cancelled, and if you had made them will you send them down for the workers."

"If that is what she wants, I will, but sandwiches are more filling, still I suppose it would be a shame to waste these."

As soon as everything was packed into tins, baskets and bags, Eve put on her warmest boots, coat and bonnet and set out into the falling snow.

The two sisters now left alone in the house, Evie went into the pantry seeking something for their own lunch, Fanny spotting her sisters intentions, was, as usual, heading towards the front room door.

"No you don't," snapped Evie, "You can help me get something to eat."

Evie found some cheese, pickles, and a fresh loaf of bread; Fanny filled the kettle and hung it over the range to boil. When Evie had cut sandwiches, they sat at the back kitchen table waiting for the kettle to boil.

Fanny's brain was working overtime, some points from Evie's account of her errand had registered with her, but she had not understood them, still unable to understand fully what had actually happened at the pit, now they were alone, she hoped her sister could help her make more sense of what was happening down there this morning.

"Evie," she began, "When you came in you said something about a fan engine going backwards, what does that mean?"

Evie was no expert on mine workings herself, but living in a mining family, over the years, she had learned a little of the basics, but how to explain to a wilful silly little sister was another matter, she pondered a moment or two before an illustrative idea struck her.

"Fanny, you remember before I went to work away, we were up in the 'Bluebell Wood', you found a rabbit hole."

Fanny nodded excitedly, "I found more than one, fairly close together, I found five didn't I?"

"That's right, five holes in the ground, but underground they all meet, lots of little tunnels, with sort of caves where the rabbits live, no animal, or anything can live without air, can it?"

With the hint of a scowl on her face, Fanny shook her head, even to a ten year old this was an obvious fact.

Evie smiled as she continued, "The slightest breeze from any direction makes air travel through all those holes so that all the Rabbits that live there can breathe underground, well, as I understand it, the pits are like rabbit burrows, but much bigger and deeper. Lijah once told me Tilly's main shaft, that's the straight down hole, is about 360 yards deep, and then the workings where the coal comes from go away from the bottom of the shaft and much deeper, getting to them must be like walking down this bank we live on."

Fanny tried to picture these things in her mind, still puzzled she asked. "But where does the fan engine come in?"

Evie continuing with her illustration, tried again, "Rabbit holes are only a few feet deep, and like I said, a gentle breeze will carry air all the way round the burrow, but the pits are much deeper, with tunnels all over the place and going on for miles."

It was plain to see the younger girl still struggled with the concept, Evie persisted.

"Fanny, have you ever seen a picture of something called a 'Windmill' at school?"

The youngster thought a moment, "Is that the thing with four big sail things that turn in the wind?"

"That's right; now think of those sails lying flat across a wide hole in the ground, an entrance to a tunnel that reaches into the pit. Instead of the wind turning the sails, a steam engine turns them very fast, the sail things blow clean fresh air down, or is it sucks the old air up the tunnel, I'm not quite sure which way it goes. Like the rabbit burrow, all the mines have lots of other holes called Air Shafts in fields, and woods, at different places above the main workings, so that fresh air can blow through every tunnel and reach all the places underground the men work, anyway that is how the men down there get air to breathe."

"Oh! I think I see, the sails become a 'Fan' and the steam engine is called the 'Fan Engine,—yes?"

"Right," replied Evie breathing a sigh of relief, she made the tea and they began to eat their lunch. Momentarily, Fanny's chatter ceased, she had understood so far, but there had been a great deal more mentioned.

"Evie, why would the fan turning backwards be important?" continued Fanny.

Evie replied truthfully, "That, I don't know for sure, you will have to ask Father or Lijah, I think they have ways of sending air to where they need it down there by blocking off some of the tunnels or something like that."

"Oh! They won't tell me anything, they will just say I'm too young."

Suddenly a look of dread came over Fanny's face, "Evie, if that poisonous stuff is in the pit, Father and Lijah, they—, they will be coming home won't they?"

Evie gasped, such a thought had not occurred to her.

"Silly goose," she exclaimed, "Of coarse they will."

Relieved, Fanny continued quizzing her sister, "Evie, do you know what a 'Winding Engine' is? You said that had stopped."

"That's easy Fanny, the 'Winding Engine' is a big one that turns those huge iron wheels that stick up in the air on that square tower thing. The wheels have thick steel cables passing over them, the cable lowers and raises a big cage thing the men ride down and up in, it's the cage which brings the tubs of coal to the surface as well."

Eve hurried down Augers Bank, conditions under foot were slippery due to the falling snow, but she made good progress, well before she arrived at the pithead she heard the noise from the crowd of desperate people gathered there. Despite the weather conditions, three to four hundred people, men, women and children were milling around, and ambulance vans were parked in the roadway. A mere thirty minutes had passed since Evie had returned home; now thirty minutes passed mid-day and Eve herself became part of the crowd at Tilly Pit.

Every eye was focused on the winding gear wheels as they slowly rotated on the tower indicating that the main cage was returning to the surface, as they stopped turning, a cry of "The rescue team is back up." echoed from those people nearest the site gates able to see the cage return.

Eve eventually forced her way to the main gate, none of the crowd were being admitted onto the site itself, Eve however, laden with her bags of refreshments was escorted through to the 'smithy' with her food. Trellis tables, borrowed from Hales Brook Chapel had been erected, folding chairs from the same source were neatly stacked in one corner, the furnace was lit, but instead of burning white hot for the forging of metal, on it kettles now boiled.

The rescue team captain as ordered reported to the manager in his office, while the other men of the team found their way to the smithy for something hot to drink. Among them was Elijah Swindon, answering the inquiring look from his mother nodded once and said softly.

"Yes, it's bad down there; we will be going back soon."

Eve, and the other women who had volunteered to help, concentrated on their tasks. Three 'day shift' workers, who were working below ground near to the cage when the explosion occurred, had also returned to the surface with the rescue team. The miners who finished their shift at 6am but had remained on the pit bank, eagerly asked the men of the rescue squad about conditions below ground, it was a sorry tale they had to tell.

When their cage arrived at pit bottom, the rescue team had made their way in single file as far as they could. They found ventilation air lock doors had been destroyed by the force of the blast, these would need to be repaired or replaced to control the airflow circuits before any other work could be done, or indeed, more thorough searches made. Below ground, some bodies had already been found, both of men and ponies, it was hoped much further down in 'still chambers', deeper than the rescue team had managed on their first attempt many men were still alive. Mine workings went in every direction and at varying depths; the blast and 'Choke Damp' may not have reached every district of the mine. They went on to say their rescue team captain thought from his knowledge and experience of this pit, and by the limited evidence he observed underground, that the explosion may well have originated far away in the seven-foot seam. Fire damp had a tendency to congregate there, therefore, he had anticipated it would be a long job to establish a true estimation of losses or damage, and even longer to make Tilly safe again.

Speculation's flowed between the men, 'fire damp' which Tilly Pit was renowned to produce to an extent far greater than any neighbouring mine, had obviously caught light, maybe from a faulty lamp, maybe from a falling bulldog stone which had created a spark.

Besides the excellent quality of its coal, Tilly had another claim to fame, possibly due to the coal quality, and this being the copious amount of airborne coal dust that was always present. The dust had always been virtually impossible to control, always flying everywhere carried along by the circulating air. The minute particles the miners believed would have burned in the air fuelling the fire, in so doing also burning off all the available oxygen. Fire, having a life of its own would then search for more oxygen, and would have chased towards the fresh air intake, producing, and leaving in its wake 'choke damp,' more technically named 'Carbon Dioxide'.

It was quite possible, and indeed everyone hoped, many men could have reached safe air pockets in still areas the ventilation system could not circulate through due to there being no return shaft. Through the tunnelled cruts of the roadways however this was a different matter with all the airshafts facilitating the air's flow, out of the wind men may have survived both the blast and subsequent 'choke damp' it created. The rumour that for some minutes the powerful steam driven 'Fan Engine' had been operating in reverse induced wild theorising from the men. If the ventilation doors were set for the opposite flow of air to that which the engine was providing in reverse, even for a short time, fire damp if present would have been carried into the workings instead of being drawn clear and replaced with good air. The men below could have been confused, they would have sensed the different direction of the airflow, and they could have identified the presence of 'fire damp.' The probability of some men heading, as they thought for a safe place, instead could have been drawn unwittingly into worse danger because the air current was travelling the opposite way to that for which the flow doors were set. Without precise details of conditions below ground, many wild ideas flourished amongst the men in the smithy and the gathered crowd outside, it was not long before the mine owners were blamed for everything that happened.

It had not been that long since young children including girls were banned by law from working in the pits, at least now mineworkers had to be male, and over fourteen years of age. Tonnage of coal extracted as quickly and cheaply as possible had always been the order of the day for mine owners. The popular view held by most miners' families was that the life and safety of their workers was well down the owner's list of priorities, profit came first. For the men of these villages this lifestyle was inevitable, though mining coal was poorly paid, they had to work in the pit regardless of the dangers, or, their families would starve.

A new business venture by the Craighorne family in the year eighteen eighty-three had been the origin of 'Tilly Pit'. Matilda Craighorne, the family's eldest daughter, affectionately known by her family as Tilly dug out the first clod of earth to launch the excavation of the main shaft. Although at the beginning the mine was named 'Hales Brook Colliery,' this soon became obsolete because everyone referred to these new mine workings as 'Tilly's Pit', from whence the name 'Tilly Pit' eventually emerged and stuck. Speculative, high-risk investments and bad management had stripped the Craighorne family of all assets and interest in this mine over ten years ago.

In contrast to the joviality of the modest gathering thirty-five years earlier, when Tilly Craighorne first sunk her spade into the earth, today, the collected crowd at the pithead gates stood in anticipation of many lives being lost, and inside the manager's office, the mood was even more pensive.

Plans of the workings below ground lay out over the desk, and covered various folding tables erected around the room. Perusing these were Charles Heath Junior, and Henry Cotes, equal partners in, and sole owners of the 'Gas & Coal Company' which now owned Tilly Pit.

Henry Cotes, quite a tall man of about five foot ten inches, was in his early sixties, however, a fondness for good food and wine resulted in his general appearance now being portly in the extreme. He possessed a round face and a ruddy complexion, continuing over the top of his head, which shone like a billiard ball, not a single hair remained there, to compensate this, his remaining wavy grey hair at the sides and back of his head bushed out and rested on the astrakhan collar of his long dark coat. His overall manner and expression, purposely, and rigorously cultivated to leave no one in doubt that he considered himself a man of importance.

His partner Charles Heath, in contrast was a man in his late twenties, tall, well built, and extremely handsome with a fine head of reddish brown wavy hair. His clothing was immaculately styled and of the finest quality, his mannerisms and general deportment however exuded an air of conceited arrogance. Henry Cotes in addition to being Charles Heaths' Godfather was also the older brother of Charles's mother, widowed these past three months. Charles, being an only child and wanting for nothing, had led a life of dissipation. With the passing of his father, now being free of all restraint had yielded to the seduction he believed power and wealth should offer. His mother, however, realising too late her folly in pandering to her son's every whim, recently pleaded with her brother to try and instil into him some sense of common values.

In the presence of such company, the pit manager Mr Joseph Shaw nervously awaited an initial report from his deputy Arthur Cleaver, and rescue team captain Seth Fuller, whom, his illustrious guests on their arrival ordered must return to the surface for questioning before any further action is taken. Arthur Cleaver and Seth Fuller entered the office; Joseph Shaw introduced them to the owners. No handshake greeting was offered, nor expected by the men covered in soot and dust. Messer's Heath and Cotes merely nodded in acknowledgement of their presence.

"What are conditions like down there, how soon do you estimate before coal can be drawn again?" Charles Heath inquired coldly. Arthur and Seth exchanged a brief horrified glance.

"Sir," began Arthur Cleaver, "I cannot possibly answer that question, we only managed to proceed about a mile, or just over, before we received the order to return, there is a lot of 'Choke, and White Damp' in there, far too much to use the canaries, they will die as soon as, or maybe even before they hit pit bottom. We shall all need 'Nevito' units before the teams go any further in than we got this time. All I can say is what we did find I could only describe as total carnage sir."

The owner's gaze turned to Seth, Charles Heath snapped, "And your opinion?"

"With respect sirs, from what I saw, the pit has had its guts ripped out, the first thing needed down there is new timbers to replace the primary air-flow doors so that clean air can be forced in and controlled as we proceed. The blast seems to have knocked most of them out, that is to say, all those we saw as far as we got this time are badly damaged, some repairable, but most will need replacing. Both men and ponies are dead sir, but God willing some may have survived deeper, in 'Still Air Chambers' and the like."

Henry Cotes intervened, "Mr Shaw, exactly how many men were down the mine at the time of the accident?"

"A full shift sir, two hundred and forty eight men," replied the manager.

"And how many have come out?"

Joseph Shaw looked towards his deputy, who answered, "Three men sir."

"Charles" began Henry as he beckoned his young colleague to the far side of the room, "Coal cannot be extracted without men, two hundred and forty five still down there, alive or dead they must be brought out, agreed?"

"Agreed," said his partner, now comprehending the severity of the situation.

"Mr Shaw, how many 'Nevito Breathing Units' do you have on site?" Cotes asked.

"We have eight sirs, but three of them may be faulty," Another mini conference between the owners ensued.

"Gentlemen," continued Henry Cotes sternly, "Ring around, beg, borrow or steal enough units, contact other mines for volunteers, replace any air flow doors you need to, order as much timber as you need from my sawmill, but get those men out of there."

Re-assured that Henry Cotes appeared to have taken charge of the proceedings, all of the men congregated around the table on which lay the plan of 'Pit bottom' showing the area of tunnels nearest the main shaft. Seth explained that the whole area was covered with an oily black dust; his eyes had smarted as soon as he was underground, and it had been difficult to breathe.

"All symptoms of a 'Fire Damp' explosion," added Arthur Cleaver. The two men went on to explain, and illustrate on the plan where they had followed the roadway into the workings, as they past the tunnel to the stables the distressed ponies could be heard, and three of the team went down to investigate. The three ponies in the stalls nearest the entrance of the stables were dead; seven others at the far end of the stables had somehow survived. This, being a 'Still Chamber' with considerable breathable air, and more now flowing in, three stablemen had also survived, the stablemen chose to stay to calm and comfort the animals as best they could.

The remainder of the 'Rescue Team' followed the roadway in single file into the workings, post's had been loosened by the blast and there were some minor roof falls, they had continued in until their 'Davy Safety Lamps' indicated a dangerous increase in 'Damp'. Seth indicated the point they reached on the plan. The two telephones he had tested along the roadway were working, and it was on the second telephone's test he received the order to return. Four men had emerged along the roadway on their way out as Seth had tested the second phone; they had passed seven dead men on their way to this point, after giving full details of the location of these bodies to Seth. Two of these four insisted on staying at this place to operate the phone as long as possible, they would inform the surface of anyone else making their way out. The air now being cleaner by the first of the phones, the other two miners decided to stay here to operate this one, and to wait for their mates. Three of the four haulage men whose place of work was close to the bottom of the main shaft, having nothing to do below had returned to the surface with the rescue team. The forth man being the charge hand and the most experienced, remained below in order to call for the cage to be sent back down when needed.

Seth's report completed, Joseph Shaw immediately telephone the 'North Staffs Colliery Rescue Association' to relay details of the first inspection of conditions below ground, the association would arrange for additional skilled rescue teams and necessary equipment to be dispatched to the pit.

Tilly Pits own team went back down as soon as their breathing apparatus was checked, and as Joseph Shaw predicted, three units were faulty. It was decided that five men would venture further into the workings while the rest of the squad undertook repairs to the tunnel and ventilation system as far as normal breathing would safely allow.

The office, except for Henry Cotes and Charles Heath who were still studying the plans, had emptied.

"Uncle," Charles began, "Those men according to these plans did not get very far," pointing to the spot Seth had indicated, "And what was that he said about fire and choke damp?"

"Fire Damp is their name for methane gas, Choke Damp is carbon-dioxide, and carbon-monoxide is known as White damp or Afterdamp. Hopefully you will learn their slang Charles as you have more dealings with these people, both carbon-dioxide and monoxide is lethal if breathed in, they have the same effect, you choke on it and suffocation is almost instantaneous, which is why the men generally just refer to them both as choke damp."

"Methane gas, that is highly explosive, I bet someone was smoking down there and caused all this," Charles replied, his usual obnoxious character unmistakable.

"Charles!" his uncle snapped back in fury, "Sometimes you really are an insensitive pup, workers are not allowed tobacco or matches down a pit because of precisely that, not one of these men would risk his life and take them down, nor allow any other man to do so, except for the designated 'shot firer'. Your precious lifestyle is highly dependent on those poor wretches still down this pit, guard your mouth, and pray the damage and losses are not as bad as I fear. We have lost a great deal of money because of this, and could well be in serious trouble as a result of today's happenings."

Charles Heath reeled at his uncle's furious response, he was not used to being spoken to in this manner, however, his arrogance soon provided the courage to defend himself.

"Uncle Henry, I am now your partner in this venture, and your equal, what do you consider gives you the right to speak to me in that manner?"

"Charles, this is neither the time, nor the place to discuss the matter, Joseph Shaw may return to his office at any moment. Yes I agree, since the passing of your father you will own his share in this mine, but remember, I am the executor of his will and as for being my equal, I could dispute that most vigorously."

The younger man's temper increased, "Equal partners makes us equal uncle," Charles snorted.

Henry Cotes, remembering his sister's plea, and the promise he made to offer guidance to her son, paused a moment, took a long, slow breath in a conscious effort to cool his exasperation and rising temper.

"Charles, this mine has been highly profitable for your father and I, its produce is of the highest grade, and has always yielded the highest financial return. Unfortunately, safety standards to control the coal dust and extract the methane were operating at the very minimum, possibly below those now required by law. I have been able to diversify my funds into many other projects. Your father for reasons of his own would appear to have been less fortunate, not to mention against my advice to limit you to a regular allowance he always supported your extravagant lifestyle, your fondness for horseracing and card tables, the lavish parties you held, he paid for them all. Not to mention your fondness for the ladies, have you any idea how many children you have sired up until now, we, your father and I were aware of four, but of course, your mother is ignorant of that situation. Your father, being the man he was, set aside a considerable sum of money to provide for each child we knew of, the interest on which is helping their unfortunate mothers rear, feed, clothe and educate them, did you know that?"

"No I did not," his nephew replied indignantly, "I was not aware you even knew of the existence of the little bastards, anyway it's none of your business, you are only young once you know uncle, pretty little serving girls and barmaids can provide much enjoyment, my father must have been mad to settle money on them."

Henry could not resist smiling, he knew, prior to his death; his brother-in-law had made many other arrangements, of which his wife and son were ignorant.

Charles, still indignant blustered on, "No way should father have given anything to those stupid wenches, everything he had should now be mine. My inheritance is taking far too long, it should all be mine now, I have plans for it."

"Be that as it may, your father at heart was a good man, he considered it was his duty to provide for all his family, legitimate or not. Take my advice now Charles, this accident if it proves as bad as I fear, it could virtually ruin you, use your considerable charms with the ladies to find yourself a wife with the financial means to support you, and do so quickly."

At this point Joseph Shaw returned to his office, which abruptly ended the conversation between Henry Cotes and his nephew.

"We will speak of this again Charles, in private," Henry Cotes said quietly, "Time now for lunch I think."

On hearing this, it came as no surprise to Joseph that the two men took their leave of him, left his office, and the site, giving him an understanding they would return later. Food and drink was available on the 'Pit Bank' for anyone who needed it, but it would never occur to men like Henry Cotes and Charles Heath to eat with the workers.

Chapter Three

From the viewpoint of the gathered crowd, it must have seemed chaos ruled on the pit bank that morning. Night shift workers still waiting for their wages to arrive willingly joined forces with surface hands and office staff, everyone scurrying about in a mad frenzy, all endeavouring to mount the rescue of the men trapped below. Newspaper reporters from the local paper, 'The Sentinel' arrived shortly before mid-day, and were busy gleaning any scraps of information they could from within the waiting crowd, everyone there anticipating the release of an official statement. At precisely twelve thirty, the huge wheels on the top of the 'Headstock' began to turn; indicating the cage was on its way back to the surface.

A cry rang out, "The cage is coming up," everyone surged forward, massing around every vantage point that might facilitate a clearer view.

"The rescue teams back up," someone shouted from amongst those occupying space at the front and having sight of the returning cage. Late comers, wives, children, families who had travelled greater distances than the Heals End residents, being relegated to the back of the gathered observers were also hungry for news of their men below ground.

"How many in the team that went down?" echoed the question from those at the rear.

"Twelve," an almost unanimous reply came from the people with the best view through the pit bank gates.

Someone yelled from a different area at the back, "How many have come up on this cage?"

"Can't see yet, hold on, now I can, looks like fifteen," a woman answered in reply.

"Fifteen?" her reply was repeated in disbelief by the inquirer, "Are you lot sure there are only fifteen?"

Confirmation went back, "Yes, Yes fifteen."

General desperate murmurs of 'Oh, my God,' and the like travelled throughout the whole crowd.

The three additional men who returned to the surface on this first gage up had not been injured; they were only suffering from sore throats due to breathing small amounts of carbon monoxide. The youngest, fourteen years old Eric Wiseman being the worst affected, as soon as he had checked his lamp into the lamp house; was sent to the first aid room for examination; fortunately, his condition was not considered serious.

Temperature below ground since the blast, even near to the main shaft was much higher than normal. Now that he was safely back on the cold surface and released from the first-aid room, Eric lost no time in joining his mate in the smithy for a drink to wet and sooth his dry stinging throat. His workmate, seventeen-year-old Harold Wood stood waiting for him near the smithy door, inside; the rescue team were finishing their tea, whilst the other man who returned to the surface with them was facing a barrage of questions from men of the 'night shift,' and the ladies providing refreshments. As Harold and Eric entered, even before the pair had time to reach the tea table, they immediately became the centre of attention; their account of happenings below ground was sought, with his throat still very sore, Eric found some difficulty in speaking, so it fell to Harold to be their spokesman.

"We were working on the level about four hundred yards up in the haulage, unhitching wagons, pushing along, and hitching to the rope which takes them down to the pit bottom."

"By the manhole?" asked one of the men.

"Yeah," replied Harold.

Eve Swindon interrupted, "What is a manhole?"

Sam, who was sitting near to his wife answered, "It's a deep recess dug into the sidewall, there is a telephone and signal bell inside it."

"Oh, Thank you Sam," Eve and the other women gratefully acknowledged Sam's brief explanation, and returned their attention to Harold, encouraging him to continue his story.

"I had just asked Eric the time, he likes me to ask cause he's just been given an old watch and case," the younger lad, a little embarrassed by his mate's comment pulled the watch from his jacket pocket, showed it to the company, smirked shyly and helped himself to a cake from a plate on the table.

Harold continued, "Anyway, Eric said it was snap time, but the signal hadn't gone yet, then there was a whooshing noise, the air came the opposite way. Instead of going in it came out with a rush, same time, the signal for snapping time went but the haulage ropes didn't stop. Two wagons came down very fast, and then all at once it stopped. I said to Eric, we'd better get our snapping, so we went into the manhole to eat it. We'd just started when the telephone rang, I answered it and a voice said, Harry is that you? I said it was, and me and Eric was in the manhole, then they asked if we were alright, I said we was, and I was told to stay in there until someone came to us, they didn't say what the trouble was though. We did as we was told, stayed in the manhole until Mr Fuller fetched us out."

Three other night shift workers had entered the smithy just in time to hear Harold begin his story.

"Is that all you can tell us lad?" asked one of them.

"Don't know nothing else, cepting my wages will be down cause of coming back up now," replied the lad, who eagerly he took advantage of the impressive free food on offer.

Sam and Lijah, sitting opposite each other exchanged a knowing glance, which Eve spotted; she had lived with them too long not to recognise their mannerisms, she went over to their table, refilled their mugs with tea and sat with them.

"Well?" she said, "You two know more than that, what is really going on here?"

"We're not supposed to say anything," replied Sam quietly.

"Not even to your wife?" Eve scolded.

Lijah glanced around; no one was paying much attention to the three of them.

"There has been a big blast down there," he whispered, "Probably on the seven foot seam, there is always a lot of fire damp in there, we won't know how big until we can get further in, we were ordered out before we got very far this time."

"How far is it to this seam thing then, when will you know?" continued Eve.

"It's not just there, we have to check all the cruts and workings as we go, even the abandoned ones," Sam added.

"Cruts?" Eve asked, unfamiliar with the word.

Lijah smiled as he replied, "Tunnels mother, cruts are tunnels, going off in all directions like a spider's web, some are high and wide, some are narrow and low, they go on for miles and they are dug out at varying depths so that they can cross over each other. The workings, they are off these main tunnels following the coal seams and making a sort of big honeycomb effect down there."

"Are all the workings the same?" asked his mother.

Sam shook his head and joined in, "No lass, in some you have to crawl on your hands and knees to get coal out. 'The Rearers' district is under Bethel Lane Village, like the name says, the seam rears up and you take the coal from the side walls or blast it down from the roof."

"Bethel Lane is a fair distance, just how far do the tunnels go underground?" asked a bemused Eve.

Father and son thought a moment, Lijah offered, "In a straight line, about from here to Potterton, but like I said cruts go off in like a spider's web pattern, what do you think dad?"

Sam nodded, "About that, or maybe further," he agreed, Eve's mouth dropped in astonishment.

In disbelief, she added, "But that is well over six miles."

"That young lad said the air came whooshing the wrong way just before he went in that manhole thing, why was that?"

The rest of the people in the room were ignoring them, still engaged with their own little groups, Eve continued to pry. Sam was uneasy, he trusted Eve would not tell anyone else if asked not to, but if someone should overhear they might tittle-tattle about it outside and the wrong people might notice it, regardless, he answered his wife quietly.

"Can't really say, could have been the power of the blast being greater than the downdraft, could have been the downdraft stopped for some reason, anyway if they were in that manhole, anything coming up, damp, dust, or anything would have blown straight past them."

Seth Fuller appeared in the doorway, his men expectantly arose ready to accompany him back down and continue what they had started earlier.

"Take it easy lads," he said, "They are loading timbers onto the cage to repair the airflow doors, we have a few minutes, I could do with a drink before we go back into that hell hole."

When Seth was ready, the team followed him to the lamp house, handed in their tokens and checked out their paltry lamps again, each of these lamps capable of emitting only three quarter candlepower of light.

* * *

A little more at his ease now the influential visitors had vacated his office, Joseph Shaw, was now able to concentrate fully, once more he turned his attention to the plans laid out around the room. He was particularly concerned by the airflow that should have been in operation. He had had the foresight to scribble a few notes whilst Arthur and Seth were making their initial report. Referring to these and to the blueprints, in the safety of his office, he sought reason for, and solution to the events of the day.

By now, a twelve-man team led by Seth would have returned to the pit bottom, they were under strict instructions to keep the surface informed of conditions below at every opportunity, by using the underground telephone system. Whilst Arthur Cleaver, his deputy, would be fully occupied in his own office franticly telephoning, requesting help and equipment from neighbouring pits, and urgently tracking estimated times any additional trained rescue teams would arrive.

Joseph had earlier accidentally caught part of the private conversation between Messer's Heath and Cotes, now on recollection, its possible implications did not escaped Joseph's notice, and this niggled him. Pouring over the plans and his quick notes again, he also recalled the talk of the men in the smithy, in particular on a snippet of one of their theories he had also inadvertently overheard.

He turned briskly on his heel, left his office and strode down the short corridor to his deputies office, as he entered, Arthur Cleaver was replacing the receiver of his telephone.

"I was just coming up to your office Joseph; we have four rescue teams on their way as soon as they can be mustered."

"Good, are they bringing breathing equipment?" Arthur nodded in affirmative.

"I need you in my office now, we may have another problem."

The two men returned to the manager's office, "Close the door Arthur," Joseph said quietly.

"Another problem, what ever is it now?" asked the bewildered Arthur Cleaver; surely, nothing could be more important than bringing the men up in safety.

"Have you been anywhere near the smithy this morning Arthur, or heard anyone talking about that old fan engine?"

"No, one of the women brought me a cup of tea and a sandwich while I was ringing round for help, why?"

"There is a big crowd outside the gates including the press, correct?"

"Yes," Arthur replied, still confused.

Joseph continued, "That old fan engine can be temperamental, it was not new when it came here, nor was it the right machine for the job, it had to be modified."

"We know that, we have been asking for a replacement for years, but there lordships won't spend a penny on new equipment," Arthur agreed with some disdain.

"Exactly, and what would be your own estimations of conditions below ground, safety and maintenance wise?"

Arthur pondered a moment before replying, "At best, borderline with current regulations I would say, our late Mr Heath senior always said he would increase the maintenance budget when they could afford it, never happened though, less profit for them if they put money back in." Realisation of his colleagues point began to dawn upon Arthur.

"Ah yes, of course—and the fan engine, where does that fit in?"

Joseph began to expand his thoughts, "When you were caged down earlier, it seems some of the nightshift are claiming that smoke, soot and dust came out of the fan chimney and that the fan was in reverse. Obviously some of the nightshift men will have left the bank by now, those newspaper reporters are milling about outside the gates, and you can bet the press will have picked up all the things the men were saying."

Arthur soon caught on, "If it had been in reverse any length of time any 'Fire Damp' in the air could have entered the workings instead of being drawn clear."

Joseph nodded, "Precisely, Henry Cotes is nobodies fool, he was too quick to authorise unlimited spending to get the men out, he knows full well working conditions here were below safety margins. Men like him have very powerful friends, he knows there is bound to be an enquiry over this, and I would lay money that he is already looking for a way to ensure no blame lands at his door."

"I see where you are leading," mused Arthur, "Old Squire Heath senior may have shown a modicum of compassion, but Cotes, I think not, and that Charles Heath appears to be exactly the man I heard he was, not only a rake but an absolute bounder to boot, the way he spoke in here proves that. I couldn't help wondering if he is naturally that obnoxious or if he has to work at it, and I can't say I liked the way that Cotes puts on his show of self-importance."

"So, be that as it may," Joseph continued, "If they by hook, or more likely by crook are deemed not responsible, who are the next likely easy targets that can be blamed for loss of life due to negligence?—next in line will be the senior management of this pit, you and I Arthur."

"Don't you think you are taking this a bit far Joseph, we have always done the best we could to keep the pit running as safe as we could?"

"As safe as we could, yes, with the materials and funds they made available, and those didn't go far enough, you just said yourself that here we are probably borderline at best within the present safety requirements," Joseph replied in trepidation.

"I know what you are saying Joseph, but I still find it hard to believe all the blame for the explosion this morning can be put on us," Arthur insisted, "We have been pressing for improvements for years, old man Heath kept promising us he would see to it, get everything up to standard, didn't he?"

"Arthur, dead men cannot speak, we have no proof of any commitment on his part."

"Nothing at all?"

"Not enough to see us clear, he made sure he put nothing in writing."

Arthur Cleaver now fully understood the personal danger they could be facing.

The internal phone rang; Arthur answered it.

"Well?" asked Joseph.

"It's a report from Seth, he says they have found seventeen more dead, and nine survivors are on their way back up, the repairs to the first air flow doors are underway, but they will have to come up again soon, those 'Nevito Units' don't seem to be working properly." Joseph, his eyebrows raised, made a gesture with his hands by turning them palm upwards.

"OK, OK," conceded Arthur," Where do we go from here?"

"Our first priority Arthur is to get all survivors out as quick as we can, but we have to watch our own backs as we do it, any suggestions?"

"The rescue teams from the other pits should be arriving anytime now with decent equipment, that will help," replied Arthur, his mind again fully focused on the task to hand, he turned to leave the office.

"Arthur," Joseph called after him, the deputy returned to the office, "Who have we got working in the Fan House?"

"Not quite sure, the regular man for this shift is off sick, he hasn't been in since Tuesday."

"In that case Arthur I suggest you get the very best, most experienced man we have in there, that engine really belongs in a museum, fetch someone in if you have to, we cannot afford any more hiccups when we have outside teams down below."

"Good Idea, I'll see to that straight away," Arthur turned to leave again.

"Hold on a minute Arthur," Joseph called after him; a slim possibility to counter those dangerous rumours began to formulate in his head.

"When your best man takes over in the fan house, try to keep whoever he relieves away from everyone and bring him straight in here," Arthur acknowledged the instruction.

Joseph, had stumbled on irrelevant bits of information earlier, now they seemed more relevant, but before anything could be countered, he needed to know exactly what rumours were being banded about on the pit bank, and what the gossip was among the people in the smithy.

Joseph checked his watch, one forty five, he decided he could spare a few minutes away from the office. The only way for him to try to find out more of the gossip that was circulating, would be to go across to the Smithy under the pretence of satisfying his hunger, with a cup of tea and a snack of some kind. Hopefully, his presence would not stop those in there from talking between themselves, and he should be able to learn exactly what was being said. He was a few steps from his office when the outside line telephone rang, calling him back.

"Shaw," said the voice on the line, "Henry Cotes here, I shall be returning to the pit on my own in about an hour, my nephew, fortunately, has decided he has other engagements, nevertheless, I believe one of us should be on site at this time. There may be something I can do to ease the situation, has anything else happened I should know about since we left? Is there anything we should be doing,—if you follow my drift." Joseph did indeed follow his drift; he was convinced now more than ever his suspicions were right; this man on the phone was protecting himself.

Although his idea was still vague, Joseph replied, "There may be something sir, but I need to work on it a bit more before I say, and I would prefer to speak privately with you face to face."

After the briefest pause, Cotes asked, "Wouldn't have anything to do with airflow would it? Everyone's safety is paramount below and above ground, do what you can until I get back there, between us we may be able to contrive a reasonable rescue for everyone."

"Very well sir," replied Joseph with relief, 'rescue for everyone,' were Henry Cotes's words, Joseph took that as implying, the owners were alive to the probability of awkward questions being asked, and were looking for a way to guard themselves in the event of an official inquiry, but as yet had not thought of anything.

In the Smithy, Joseph faced many questions; he assured everyone all that could possibly be done, was being done. Joseph, although not as devout as many of the lower classes, many of whom belonged to the alcohol free 'Band of Hope' total abstinence brigade was of the 'Methodist' persuasion. A stiff drink may have been better, but he could not remember when a sandwich and a strong cup of tea as now served by Eve Swindon had been more welcome.

"Mr. Shaw, some people are saying that a lot of smoke came out of the fan chimney and it shouldn't, is that right?" asked Eve as she poured the tea.

"I don't know anything about that," lied Joseph, "but I will look in to it." Eve smiled graciously handing over the tea. If the women are asking about it, it must have been a hot topic in the smithy for quite some time; this particular suspicion needed quelling before being blown out of all proportion.

Returning to his office, Joseph spotted Arthur and a youngish man across the yard leaving the fan house and heading in his direction; he guessed whom this young man would be. All three reached the offices at the same time, Joseph indicated to Arthur to have the young man wait in his own office a moment while they updated each other on recent developments.

"We have Vern Ashton in the Fan House now, he knows that cranky old engine better than anyone," Arthur reported.

"Good," Joseph replied, "I think I was right earlier, Cotes phoned a while ago, he is worried, but he didn't admit it."

"Really, do you still think they will try to lay blame on us?" Arthur asked apprehensively.

"Hope not, I have an idea about a possible lifeline for us all, if it looks plausible I will need your backing."

Arthur, though not fully understanding nodded affirmatively. Joseph seated himself at his desk, cleared a little space and arranged the remaining papers to look authoritarian and impressive.

"If that young man you brought over was minding the Fan Engine this morning, better fetch him in."

Arthur ushered his charge into the main office.

"Mr. Shaw, this is Zack Morgan, he ran the fan engine this morning."

Joseph acknowledged the anxious young man before him. Joseph did not normally have dealings with anyone at the pit below management level, why would he, other staff would have employed this man, why then did his name ring a bell with him?

In an instant it came flooding back, some time ago Squire Heath had ordered him to find some light work for a man from his estate who had been injured by a Thrashing Machine trapping his left arm. The squire had gone on to explain, the doctors believed the lad would eventually regain most of the use in his arm, but at present there was no suitable employment for him on the estate, and the lad needed a wage.

When the lad arrived at the pit bearing a letter of introduction from the squire, Joseph had spoken to him briefly, before sending him to Arthur Cleaver to attend to the matter. He now recalled the lad had been disappointed because his injury had prevented him joining the army when his friends had.

Out of habit, the lad still carried the arm limply at his side, although it was evident, some use had returned to it.

The young man removed his cap, revealing a mass of wavy red hair, this coupled with his build and general demeanour struck Joseph with an air of familiarity that he could not place.

Arthur began to explain, "Zack has been with us for about two years now Mr. Shaw, he came to us from the Heath estate after his accident, Mr. Heath senior himself instructed me to find him work." Joseph nodded, signifying he recalled the incident.

"Zack has proved to be capable of many things despite his injury, he spent a little time working below ground, but he mainly works on the pit bank now. He had some knowledge of operating steam engines when he came to us; one of his jobs is to help in the fan house. He provides cover in there if any of the regular men don't turn in, he has been in charge of the fan quite a few times now with no problems."

Zack's face beneath the layer of dirt began to flush, emulating the same colour as his hair, he was intelligent, and the possibility of being held responsible for the days events by doing something wrong, which he knew he hadn't, did not escape him, he shuffled his feet uncomfortably. Joseph's mind was racing ahead, could he steer this situation to a conclusion beneficial to all, he studied Zack closely, aware of the lad's anxiety he paused before beginning to speak.

"Take a seat Zack," he began, the young man nervously took the proffered chair.

"Now, tell me in your own words exactly what happened in the fan house, before, during and after the explosion this morning."

"I followed the proper procedure sir, I didn't do anything wrong," Zack replied in a state of heightened emotion.

"I have not said you did Zack, but I need to know exactly what happened with the ventilation system, there is some talk of the fan running in reverse when the air flow doors below ground were set at flow. I presume you know what the effect of that would be?"

"I do know the importance of proper airflow sir; I worked underground in the stables for two weeks when I first started here." Zack looked toward Arthur Cleaver for support.

"That is true Mr Shaw, but Mr Heath senior came to my office to inquire how Zack was settling in on Zack's second week here, and he gave strict instructions that Zack was not to be allowed to work below ground," Arthur confirmed.

Joseph's train of thought was broken for a moment by this revelation, it was unusual for an owner to bother providing alternative work for someone of Zack's background, but to follow this up and insist he only worked above ground was very strange indeed. Joseph's gaze returned from Arthur to Zack, there it was again, that un-identifiable familiarity, he continued his inquiries, the prospect of a plausible escape for Arthur and himself from this situation fading at the young man's insistence that all proper procedures had been followed.

"Zack, are you saying that everything was as it should be with the ventilation?"

"Not categorically,—no sir, like the main haulage engine, sometimes the fan engine will stall, it's a temperamental old thing, occasionally when it's re-started it will kick up in reverse, it did that this morning but it only ran in reverse for three or four min . . . ."

"Seconds!" interrupted Joseph abruptly, "Surely you mean seconds, don't you Zack?" Arthur Cleaver who had been listening to the exchanges in a somewhat casual manner was now jolted alert by Joseph's sudden interruption, immediately; he grasped his superior's reasoning.

"Of course he means seconds Mr Shaw, Zack is very skilful with machinery, he would have had it running smoothly again in little more than five seconds, I'll bet, isn't that right Zack?"

The mid sentence interruption by the managers took the young man by surprise.

Zack looked slowly back and forth at one, and then the other of his bosses, his intelligence and education, unknown to his present company far exceeded that which would normally be expected of someone from the lower classes, his wits were as quick, if not quicker than their own. It was obvious to him that he was being led by these two men, the prospect of advancement in life and all the advantages it held presented itself here and now with his estimation of a lapse of time.

Considering the predicament he believed he was in a few moments ago, providing something they needed could rectify this, and also provide something to his own advantage. His courage rose at this attempted intimidation, his initial fears of retribution, together with his humility fled away, he replied thoughtfully.

"Yes sirs, I think you are probably correct, I don't own a watch, and it is far more likely to have been seconds only, as you say, definitely no more than ten."

Still under the mistaken impression he was directing these proceedings, Joseph asked in a firm but cautious manner, "You are sure about that are you Zack? You know of course that there will have to be an official inquiry into the reasons for today's accident, you may be called to give evidence."

"As I said Mr Shaw, I do not own a watch, more likely to have been a few seconds only," confirmed the young man.

Joseph Shaw was troubled, this had been far too easy, Arthur Cleaver could not believe his own ears, and both men felt the need to learn more of the young man who now sat in the office, exhibiting almost an air of equality with them.

"Tell me Zack, how do you like working here at the mine?" Joseph probed.

"It's a way to earn a living of sorts, but I much preferred working on Squire Heath's Highfield Estate," responded a now fully confident, relaxed Zack Morgan, "My mother was in service at 'Highfield Hall,' and my father used to work on the estate before I was born. Mother and I live in an estate cottage at Highfield."

"And your father?" inquired Arthur.

"No, Mr Cleaver, I was born out of wedlock, my father died of consumption before he and mother could be wed, after that my mother never married, she rarely speaks of my father, except to say he was a good, generous man."

Joseph probed a little further, "So, Zack, you were the family's breadwinner at an early age then?"

"In a way I suppose I was Mr Shaw. I worked at the Manor House, and in the stables, from when I was ten, but mother always made sure my schooling did not suffer, I always attended regularly, and Mr Brindley, young Mr Charles's tutor at The Manor, was able to give me extra tutoring at home three times a week."

The internal telephone rang interrupting the conversation, Joseph answered it, another rescue team had arrived on site, Arthur Cleaver was despatched to organise the new rescue operation with the team's leader. Joseph's attention returned to Zack, the young man's last statement seemed to him a little odd; however, he had his own different agenda to pursue.

"Zack, you said you would rather work on an estate than here, would that really be possible considering the state of your left arm?"

Before replying, Zack demonstrated he had regained the majority of movement in the arm and hand, which he assured Joseph, continued to increase week to week.

"Certainly not the sort of heavy labouring I did before, but I can read and write well enough, my numbers are good, and I can use a gun again, a gamekeeper, or something like that maybe, if I ever got the chance."

Joseph who, by his rank still believed he was in charge of this situation, never noticed that the young man had discretely, but definitely named the price for his cooperation, and by subtle suggestion had directed Joseph's course of action.

"Perhaps you could at that," was Joseph's reply, "Mr. Cotes will be coming back here very soon," Joseph continued, "He may want to ask you questions about what happened this morning, but for the time being, go back to the fan house, help Vern Ashton to keep the ventilation below ground at maximum. I will send for you if you're needed by Mr. Cotes."

Zack rose, replaced his cap, and with a slight smile of satisfaction, left the manager's office, and returned to his workstation in the fan house.

Chapter Four

Not even a cold, bleak January morning could deter the vigilance of people already gathered outside the pit, and still their numbers steadily increased. Every point of the boundary fence, which afforded a view of activities inside the confines of the Pit Bank was obscured by people. Seth led his team back across the yard to the waiting cage; the eyes of every onlooker followed the team's procession in silence.

An elderly, grey-haired man stood at the fore of this panic-stricken crowd, he was confident and compassionate in his bearing, a well used Bible clutched firmly in his right hand. The very presence of this man offered some comfort to everyone. He was a local man having been born and resided all his life at Heals End, this man was James Dale, a devout Christian and Methodist Lay Preacher of distinction, who, by his lifestyle, earned the respect of everyone who knew him. The Headstock wheels began to turn slowly lowering a cage of men once more into the bowels of the earth, the familiar, welcomed voice of James Dale rang out through the cold air, leading the assemble company in prayer.

A few minutes later, two vans arrived bringing the first rescue team from the nearest neighbouring pit, Larchwood, the new team's arrival helped to raise the watcher's hopes a little. No more than a quarter of an hour passed before this fully equipped visiting team made their way towards the cage housing. The huge Headstock wheels turned again commanding everyone's attention, their obvious expectancy was an empty cage returning to the surface for the new team to descend.

A cry of jubilation arose from the fortunate few having a clear view of the headstock and cage gates.

"There are men on this cage," someone called; this was welcomed news, which swiftly spread throughout the whole crowd.

"How many?" a desperate cry came from the rear of the assembled throng.

The response of, "Nine men, that's all I can see," to say the least, was disappointing.

Everyone strained to see, every watcher desperately hoping to recognise one of the men as their own. The nine made their way across the yard, first to the Lamp House and then to the First Aid station. All, except one of the nine appeared to be either only slightly injured or exhibiting some degree of discomfort.

The one exception was being led, half-walking, and half-carried by his companions; although his head was covered with a sack, he seemed quite young. The sight of this lad being led across the yard only served to increase the anxiety within the crowd, and one middle-aged woman near the gateway, unable to control her emotions any longer, cried out.

"My God, that is some poor mother's son."

This woman's friend standing next to her neither heard nor responded to her outburst, she had recognised her own husband safe amongst the nine, overcome with relief from fears of possible widowhood, she fainted and collapsed on to the snow-covered ground.

Amongst the nine survivors now returned to the surface, were the first four men who had been making their way out earlier, but had chosen to stay longer below ground operating the two signal telephones nearest the main shaft. Four of the others had been working in a spur tunnel comparatively close to Pit Bottom, the one casualty, whom they carried out must also have been working close to the main shaft. Only nine men up on this cage was disappointing, everyone of the crowd needed to hear how they made their escape and of the conditions below, but, they would have to wait.

Below ground, the air provided by the main and auxiliary fans at full speed, now, blasted its way into the mine at gale force along the main roadway. Without airflow doors correctly set to direct its flow through the miles of tunnels, there could be no way of knowing how deep, or in which direction this clean air could travel, or, if it was short circuiting through old return shafts and back out again. Before the blast, the old return shafts would have been set at minimum flow or closed off completely.

Choke Damp in the tunnels and workings just off the main roadway still remained in small quantities, not enough to be instantaneously lethal, but enough for prolonged exposure to be dangerous. Management had issued orders that no one without breathing equipment, would remain below ground near these areas longer than one hour at a time. Seth, as he returned below ground relayed these orders, and instructed the signal phone men in the roadway to return to the surface.

Approximately three quarters of a mile along the main roadway from the shaft, there was a small working, off to the left, the workplace of the other four men now safely out, this working, referred to down the pit as 'Webb's Place.' Because it was a spur, it would not have been directly in the path of the explosions aftermath. The senior men in this section, Charles Webb and Albert Beech were old hands and very experienced miners, who, on feeling the flow of air in reverse, had the foresight to close off their airflow doors providing them with a pocket of breathable air. This pocket, combined with air, which, now drifted in naturally from a small return airshaft excavated at the far end of their workings to take stale air out, kept their atmosphere breathable.

> *Within all mining communities, there was a well-established tradition, for easy identification purposes, of naming individual workplaces below ground after the 'Senior Man' in charge of the area. The custom of taking a surname and adding 'place' to it, therefore, with 'Webb's Place', the overhands name, plus, the suffix of 'Place' identified their working.*

By chance, Charles and Albert were very close to the crut end airflow doors when the flow interruption occurred; they changed the direction of their airflow immediately. Neither men had been informed of any scheduled change, therefore, Charles decided to close all their doors off completely for a while, rather than risk short-circuiting the main flow with too much air coming down their Return Shaft and entering the system, which would have drastically reduced the air supply to deeper districts.

This completed, they began to move back deeper into their working, as they did they felt the earth tremor.

"Good grief! Someone's using heavy shot," Albert observed, before his last word was spoken, an almighty roar went through the pit.

"That was no shot, that was fire damp and it's gone a right ripper by the sound of it," Charles replied, instinctively, they both raised their lamps to view the roof in anticipation of loose material being shaken free.

"What should we do now?" asked Albert.

Charles took his watch tin from his pocket, "Nearly ten to ten, we'd better stay where we are a bit, looks pretty sound in here."

They were soon joined by their 'loaders,' Jim Lewis, and Bob Broad, and together they made their way to a more comfortable spot, sat down and began to eat their snapping. The two loaders, Bob, sixteen and Jim eighteen, were anxious to hear from their colliers a reason for their current predicament, the tremor Charles had accredited to a firedamp blast, they knew Choke Damp always followed Firedamp, this supposition filled them with dread.

The older men offered no further comment, forcing Jim to ask, "Will we be in any danger if we try to walk out of here Mr Webb?"

Charles re-assured him, "That depends lad, I can't tell you yet, we have enough air in here to last us quite a while, I reckon we should give it an hour or so before we check for any choke damp the other side the doors,"

Young Bob was not convinced.

"But what happens if there is choke damp out there and we can't get through?"

Albert chuckled, "If there is Bob, and the worst comes to the worst, it won't be easy but we could climb out through our air shaft, we may have to dig a few footholds though."

"Albert, can you feel anything?" Charles asked,

"I can," was Albert's reply, the younger men looked at each other in bewilderment, Charles and Albert burst into laughter.

Charles explained to them, "It's alright lads, the air in here has got a bit chilly, they must have changed the fan's direction back again, and it's pulling cold air in down our shaft."

"And that means what?" Jim asked still bewildered.

"It means if we wait long enough, with luck the roadways will draw clear and we will be able to walk out."

There seemed little point of digging out more coal, there was no way of moving it out to the main haulage, the four men remained grouped together passing the time as best they could, the younger listening to stories from their elders of other incidents they had experienced during their lifetime below ground. Eventually, Albert moved over to his lamp that was hanging from a pit prop, took his watch tin from his pocket, opened it, and then sniffed at the air.

"It's ten to one Charles; shall we give it a try?"

"May as well," Charles replied picking up his own lamp, the lads did not move.

"Come on you two, if it's too risky we will come back and wait a bit longer," Albert cajoled, reluctantly the boys followed to the airflow doors, they listened a moment before Albert ventured the obvious question.

"You or me Charles?"

"I'll go," Charles replied opening the first door just enough to pass through, and closed it behind him. Entering the airbrake chamber between two sets of doors, he took his time checking for any sign of damage, keeping a constant watch on the behaviour of his lamp flame. There was nothing evident to give him any concern, excepting for a steady draught through the cracks in the doorway. Carefully he repeated the procedure on the outer chamber door, as he went through his eyes began to sting, he walked about thirty yards, the air was breathable. Returning to the others he instilled upon the youngsters to pay attention to their lamp flames, and to watch for any sign of the flames growing longer, cautiously, the four made their way towards the main haulage roadway.

Turning into the roadway, the strength of the down draft in their faces slowed their pace, carefully they avoided fallen timbers, roof falls, and partially caved in walls. Bob stumbled over a huge fallen rock; instinctively he put out his hand onto the wall to steady himself.

"Ouch, that's hot," he exclaimed in surprise, his hand was now covered in an oily black substance.

"Mr Beech," he queried, "What's this stuff? Where's the dust gone, none on the wall, and I can't see any driving in the air either."

They stopped, each man searched the air with their lamps, Albert answered the lad.

"That grunge on your hand is the dust, or at least what's left of it, as we thought firedamp has gone off, burned all the slack dust in the air, and what coal on the side walls it could before the air gave out, leaving—."

"Choke damp?" Jim completed the sentence.

"Correct," Charles smirked; these lads were learning the hard way.

From this point on they continued in single file, taking turns to lead, Jim, who was leading called out a warning.

"There's another roof fall coming up, whoa!—It ain't roof, its men."

The four men inspected this new obstruction in the roadway, which did indeed prove to be the remains of three men severely charred, and most definitely deceased. Never having seen anything like this before, the lads turned away, the sight of it made them feel rather sick.

"Can you recognise any of them Albert?"

"No, not even their delph clothes."

Charles checked again, "Maybe they're labourers off the main haulage, those chaps get everywhere, anyway, nothing we can do for them."

"Agreed," Albert concurred, "Better keep going, I'll lead."

With Jim and Bob, now sandwiched between the experienced men they carefully continued as before in single file towards the cage at pit bottom.

Albert called back, "There are a couple of tubs coming up, watch your step."

They moved over close to the sidewall in order to squeeze past the tubs, Bob, being the smallest of the four had no difficulty passing the tubs, he held back and shone his lamp around for a closer look at the obstruction as he passed.

"Mr. Beech," he shouted, "There's someone between these, I just saw him move a bit."

Albert wheeled round in disbelief, there was indeed someone lying in a pool of water hidden and trapped between the angled tubs. Two men pulling on each tub they were soon separated. The man trapped between them was semi-conscious. but alive, Charles, having a reputation as a fair 'Bone Setter' checked for any broken bones, turning the limp body over as he did. By the light from their four lamps, they could see the man appeared to be about twenty-three, or thereabouts, and he had a wet rag tied around his nose and mouth.

Dead men they could pass in good conscience, but somehow, this man had survived, his lamp had gone out but it still hung on the front tub, this they must carry out with them, for circumstances such as these each lamp was numbered as a means of identification.

Sending Jim slightly ahead with two lamps, one to hold out in front to light his own way, and one held behind him illuminating the way for the others. Charles and Albert lifted the semi-conscious man, took an arm each over their shoulders, and following Jim closely carried on up the roadway, Bob, carrying the remaining three lamps brought up the rear. After about a hundred yards, Jim stopped, there was someone else in the roadway at a haulage linkage point, it was a lad no older than Bob, but this one was dead.

Jim leading by about four yards now; at a junction to an old working again he paused; there was a heap of some kind in the junction, just visible in the outer glimmer from his lamp, there was something odd about it, and it caught his attention. To investigate he moved over towards the entrance, the full light from his lamp showed it to be three men sitting just inside the tunnel, their snap tins opened on their knees, sprawled across the legs of the seated men lay another, face down and motionless. The others caught up; Charles and Albert were just about to lay their burden down when Bob cried out from behind.

"Mr. Webb, my lamp flame is getting much bigger now," Charles whirled around; all the flames had grown slightly.

"Firedamp increasing," he yelled, "Get the hell out of here; keep moving, quick as you can Jim."

Three groups of flickering lamps converged near the deeper of the two signal telephones, stationary lamps belonging to the two men who remained operating this phone, Charles Webb and his group from below, and five more belonging to Seth's team on their way back in. Charles and Seth were close friends, Seth, pleased his friend was safe accepted Charles's report that no one was left in 'Webb's Place', one less tunnel for he and his team to check. Charles went on to describe how, and where they had found their semi-conscious burden. The rest of his findings, although expected, were not so well received by Seth, that others, working near to this man had not been so lucky. Jim, following instruction from Charles, eagerly relayed the location of the four men he found at the junction, while Bob, not wishing to be left out added; this was the place the length of his lamp flame had grown.

Seth smiled at the lad, "Nevito's from there in then," the older man humoured the youngster; everyone working in a mine had to learn how to act in these conditions.

Charles went on to speculate that although they were not able to check thoroughly with a firedamp on the increase there, the one who appeared to have tripped over the legs of the seated men looked young, and he might have lacked knowledge of the best action to take in such a situation. His lamp could have been extinguished by the blast, even if it had not, in the thick black smoke that was evident by its residue, he would have been unable to see and fallen over the seated men as he tried to reach safety, and apparently he had met with the same fate.

Ironically, as Charles observed, if he had gone the opposite way, further into those old workings, he would have entered a still chamber, and by so doing, considerably increased his chances of survival.

Seth noted Charles's comments, and as ordered used the telephone to report to the surface that six men were walking out carrying one injured from this point, and they would be joined by the two men still waiting by the first telephone, making nine in total.

The two groups divided, Seth and his team, Nevito Units at the ready continued deeper into the pit. Charles and his companions slowly made their way, negotiating around more sections of fallen roof, dislodged props, dead ponies, and men struck down by the fire and choke damp. Battling against the uncontrolled wind created by the fans at full speed, their progress was far from easy as they continued onwards towards 'Pit Bottom' and the cage to safety.

Before they joined up with the two men waiting by the first telephone, this group of seven survivors met Sam, Lijah and five men along the roadway; they had with them tubs full of tools, timbers, and canvass sheets making repairs to everything in need of repair as they went.

Working Nevito Units on site being limited to five, there had not been enough for the whole rescue squad; Seth, using the units they had, left his remaining team behind to clear the roadway, straighten and make safe the pit props and to repair airflow doors.

This task was well underway; section-by-section the airway system was being corrected, haulage tracks cleared and possible further roof falls shored up. Charles and Albert grateful for a break from their semi-conscious load discussed their findings with Sam and the others. Conditions below which Charles and Albert related were not good, even now the heat this near to the pit bottom was still far greater than normal, but from their knowledge of this temperamental pit the men agreed, the explosion had probably occurred in the seven-foot seam where 'Firedamp' normally gathered in abundance.

If this proved to be the case, as all the signs indicated, there could be many survivors in the newer 'Rearers Section,' which was well away from the seven-foot seam under Bethel Lane Village. There, similar to in Charles's workings there was another narrow airshaft surfacing in Bethel Wood. Therefore, they all believed clean air ought to be directed through the roadways towards any possible survivors in those still chambers, any men there, sensing the air coming in, could follow the direction it came from and make their way to safety.

The two groups parted, each going their separate ways, Charles and his colleagues reached the cage just as the signal sounded calling it back to the surface, the nine men boarded before the cage gates closed riding it safely to daylight.

In the first aid room, whilst the young man received treatment, Charles reported his actions and findings to Arthur Cleaver, Albert, being somewhat of a gossip and rebel, told their story to the men off the night shift who still remained on site eager for news.

The main casualty receiving treatment proved to be one Winston Turner from Heals End, his injuries and burns, once they were cleaned up proved far less severe than they seemed at first sight, now breathing the cool, fresh air he was fully conscious and lucid. Arthur, Charles and his companions in awe that Winston survived when those near him had not, were quick to press him for his account of what happened.

Winston began his version of events in the roadway.

> *"I was working at three road ends, bringing two loads out from the side workings to put onto the main haulage rope at the corner before knocking off for snap time, I was going up to the old workings to have my snapping with our Clem. There was a lot of dust in the main haulage, so I had tied my wet hanky round my mouth and nose. I had one arm on the front load, and the other behind me pulling one, and shoving the other, I'd just got to the corner when I saw this flash and I dropped down between the wagons, that's all I remember."*

Winston looked around the room, "Where's our Clem? What's happened?"

"Clem, who's Clem," asked Arthur.

"My brother, him and three others have started driving a road for airflow from the old workings through to the stables, they were meeting me to eat our snapping together at the old junction at snap time, where is he?"

Charles and his men knew exactly the place Winston spoke of, and what they passed there on their way out, turning away remained silent,

Charles however was a little quicker to defuse the situation, as cheerfully as possible under the circumstances he answered.

"He hasn't come up yet lad, apart from the bottom cage hands, we are the first out."

They left Winston in the first aid room and headed for the smithy, walking across the bank, Charles confided in his colleague.

"Albert, I've been thinking, perhaps I was wrong, that lad who fell across the other three could have been the last one out of those old workings, and he wasn't trying to head for safety when he fell but looking for his brother."

"Maybe so, but why did you lie to that lad in there?" asked Albert.

"I didn't," Charles replied, "I've never come across that lad or his brother, I spoke the truth, his brother hasn't come out yet."

Albert and the two loaders conceded Charles's point, Albert however, after some deliberation added.

"Aye, we were right, we checked them all as best we could with that firedamp about and found no sign of life in any of them excepting for young Winston in there," gesturing towards the first aid room.

"I couldn't recognise any of those men we came across either, most of their faces were in too much of a mess, but I thought perhaps I might have recognised one or two by the clothes they had on. No, if we're not absolutely sure, wouldn't have been right for us to have told that lad his brother is dead, they will have to do a tag and lamp number check later I expect, somebody else can break the news to him."

Before they reached the smithy, the four men agreed not to speculate regarding the identity of any of the deceased men they passed on their way out.

Seth's team soon located the four men at the old workings junction, Charles had been right, except that now there was no longer any indication of increased levels of firedamp present. Before the team left to go deeper, they discussed amongst themselves how it could have come about these three men were seated in that junction with their snap tins open in their laps. Two plausible theories arose, the force of the blast killed them outright, or choke damp took them by surprise, the first idea being instantly discarded, the positioning of the bodies, just sitting there, did not indicate any physical force from the blast at work.

These men would have felt the mine shake, but obviously not gauged its severity, they were in the entrance of a 'still chamber,' and most likely, the direction change of the airflow would not have registered with them. Hot air always rises, they were low to the floor, they would have assumed any smoke, soot or choke damp from the distant explosion would be carried away with the airflow, and cleared out of the mine through the many 'Return Shafts' further down. They would not have expected the poison gas to come this far up.

Understandably, having found so many bodies before they reached this point, and also having a report from an old hand, the five members of Tilly's rescue team presumed these four men had also perished. A thorough investigation at the junction was interrupted by a distant glimmer of many lamps following them along the roadway.

The advancing lamps belonged to the 'Larchwood' team, fully equipped with better lamps, breathing apparatus, stretchers, absolutely everything necessary. George Sanders, the 'Larchwood' captain, and Seth, had undertaken rescue missions many times before, each knew how the other worked. While the two captains decided the routes each should follow, thereby avoiding duplication the two teams would be able to investigate as many workings as possible, the members of both teams chatted, exchanging their own observation this far.

The captains decided that two of the Larchwood team would proceed up this tunnel into the old workings; they set off and passing the seated men, they lifted the sprawled man off his mates to put him in a more dignified posture. As they moved him, he groaned a little, immediately, everyman was upon him, by some miracle he was still alive. Two of the Larchwood team, and one of Seth's crew were soon delegated to carry him out. On closer examination and as far as their dim lights allowed them to see, he was naked from the waist up, and his skin under the normal pit grime did not appear burned.

Stretchered out and deposited unconscious in the first aid room, the news of another survivor soon spread over the pit bank, but not the identity. Winston Turner left the smithy and scampered back to first aid, until checks had been made on the condition of the new patient Winston was kept out, but he was a stubborn lad, when no one was looking, he sneaked inside.

With a joyful cry he yelled, "Clem!"

At the sound of his brother's voice, Clem Turner beginning to regain consciousness stared vacantly at his brother, with a hint of a roguish smile managed to utter.

"Win—thank God,—I came looking for you,—but I fell," and with the smile still on his face, lapsed back into unconsciousness.

Despite all efforts of the first aid staff, Winston refused to move from his brother's side until he awoke again after about half an hour.

"You back with us now Clem?" Winston asked cheerily.

"Yeah, reckon I must be," his brother replied, "What's happened?"

"We don't know yet, still trying to find out, firedamp's gone a right ripper they think."

"Thought it might be, that's why I came out looking for you, knew you was in main road somewhere, put me vest over my mouth, but I fell over a prop or some-ut an dropped it, next thing I knows I'm in here with your ugly mug staring down at me."

Winston told his brother snapping was being provided on site, and Clem, never one to pass up on a free feed if it was on offer together the lads made their way to the smithy. There, they soon found out that there is no such thing as a free feed; Clem's story had to be told over, and over again.

In the manager's office, Joseph Shaw and Arthur Cleaver waited apprehensively for the imminent return to the site of Henry Cotes.

"Did Cotes say what time he would be coming Joseph? Arthur asked.

"Not specifically, no, just said after lunch, what time is it now?"

Arthur checked his watch; the office clock like many other things had not worked for months.

"Five past two, I bet his idea of lunch takes at least a couple of hours, and a bottle or two of a fine wine," Arthur said, imitating the owner's peculiar manner of speech.

This roguish comment relieved the tension slightly, both men grinned, and returned to studying plans of the workings which were still laid out around the room, Arthur, paying particular attention to the 'Rearers' district plans.

"Hold on a minute," he exclaimed, and without further comment left the room, Joseph, surprised by this outburst went over to examine the plan Arthur had been studying. Arthur returned with a rolled up blue print.

"What's that?" asked the bemused Joseph; Arthur's new blue print was laid out next to the 'Rearers' plan.

"If I am right Joseph, and if there are too many roof falls below blocking the main roadways, this could be a back way in to the Rearers."

"How?" Joseph was intrigued.

"By using 'The Old Chonock', look it's here," Arthur indicated something on his blue print.

"The what,—and where?" Joseph, although he was senior to Arthur was still bewildered.

Arthur explained, "When I was a lad, the older men from Bethel Lane used to get their own coal out from a seam they found cropping out close to the surface at Firs Green, it was on common land, nobody bothered about anybody taking it. The entrance is blocked off now, but according to this, part of the main chamber is no more than about twenty or thirty feet from the Rearers. If we sent the best men from the noon shift and an engineer over to check it out, providing they get their direction right, they could have a tunnel driven through to the Rearers in no time."

"Are you sure Arthur, I never heard of 'Old Chonock' before?"

"No Joseph, I'm not absolutely sure, but I think its well worth a shot, and you not knowing about Old Chonock is understandable, you're not local, but I was born and bred up there at Bethel Lane."

"They do pick some daft names round here, and Old Chonock, is as daft as I have ever heard."

"No it's not, look at this drawing, what's it shaped like?—a turnip, hence Chonock, you've been living round here long enough I thought you would have picked up more local slang by now, a chonock is a turnip."

"Well," mused Joseph, "Cotes did say do what you can, if you think it will work I suppose we could try."

The office door opened, Henry Cotes strode in, and Joseph explained their new idea to him.

"Do it," was his immediate instruction, Arthur left the office at once to organise the operation.

Henry Cotes took off his coat, producing from his pocket as he did a bottle of fine single malt whiskey, settled down in a chair, took out his cigar case, took one himself and to Joseph's surprise, offered one to him.

"Any glasses in here?" he asked looking around the office.

Joseph found one for him.

"Do you use this stuff yourself?" Cotes asked.

"I do sir, when I get the chance of it."

"Find another glass then,—now, what is it you wanted to talk about face to face?" the owner asked, obviously hopeful Joseph Shaw had stumbled upon a way to redirect responsibility for the days events away from being laid at his door.

Joseph began, "Well sir, it may not be of any value, but, the regular fan attendant for this shift has not been in most of this week."

"And that helps, how?"

"Let me explain sir, the ventilation fan engine is very old, it's temperamental, sometimes it stalls, and it has been known to start up again in reverse if they don't watch it closely. It seems it did that this morning, ran in reverse, and according to people on the pit bank, for several minutes it was pulling dust and smoke through the fan chimney."

"So?" inquired the owner, not yet grasping the implications, "What is the significance of that?"

"The airflow should be forced downwards, blowing stale air and any gas out of the mine through the return shafts at the far ends of the workings."

"Yes, yes, Joseph, I am aware of that, but what is your point?"

Joseph Shaw was amazed to hear Henry Cotes suddenly begin to use his Christian name, he never had before.

"My point sir is the speed the fan moves air through the tunnels, it displaces sixty thousand cubic feet of air a minute, running in reverse, it may well have pulled methane back into many of the workings instead of blowing it clear. Any small increase in the percentage of methane would have been enough for it to ignite into an explosion if there was a spark, or anything to set it off."

"Well, it's obvious we had an explosion alright, but I still don't see where you are going with this, if, from what you are saying I understand correctly, it's either faulty equipment, or that old engine, which leaves us at fault for poor maintenance or human error responsible. Are you suggesting we shift all the blame onto whoever was in charge in the fan house this morning?"

"None of those sir,—there may be another way out."

"I am listening Joseph,—what have you in mind?"

"I have spoken to the man working in the fan house this morning; he confirmed the fan engine had stalled, and that when it started up again it ran in reverse. I think he was about to say for several minutes, but changed his mind, he maintained it was no more than a few seconds and that would have had little effect below ground."

"You think he has some reason of his own for changing his words,—besides the obvious of course of saving his own neck, saying seconds rather than minutes?"

"I think he may have sir, he gave me the impression he would prefer to work on an estate, as a gamekeeper or something of that sort rather than in a mine."

Henry Cotes smirked, "Ah! Now I see where you are going, but, can he be trusted, if it comes to an official inquiry will he stick with this story?"

Joseph thought a moment before replying.

"Arthur and I are of the opinion he is a very deep young man, we were both surprised by his confident manner, for someone of his background he appears to be quite intelligent. He said he lives with his mother and that his father died before he was born, making him the family breadwinner. We have tried to keep him as isolated as possible away from other people on the pit bank. We thought, if they got to him and heard his explanation of what happened a damaging story might circulate. Just in case, he has been kept out of the way, he is still in the fan house, I told him I thought you may wish to speak to him when you arrived."

Henry Cotes drained the malt from his glass, refilled it, after a brief silence to collect his thoughts and to weigh up this possibility, nodded, and said.

"Very well, I will speak to him; I'll see what I can make of him and if I think he can be trusted, fetch him in."

Joseph turned to leave, it was then Henry realised no name had been mentioned.

"Hold on Joseph, who is he, what is his name?"

"You may possibly know him sir, I believe he used to work on the Highfield Estate and at the Manor House, his name is Zack Morgan." Joseph said turning to continue out through the office doorway.

"Wait!" bellowed Henry Cotes.

Startled, Joseph returned into the office, Henry Cotes was now on his feet putting his topcoat back on; he noted Joseph's alarmed expression.

"It's alright Joseph, I will speak to your young man later, keep him here on site, tell him I wish to speak to him but I have been called away on urgent business, I will be away probably about an hour, it shouldn't take much longer than that providing I can find the person I need to see."

The only response poor amazed Joseph could manage was, "Very well sir, I will do that," as he watched the other man scurry away towards his waiting car.

Arthur Cleaver, having organised, and dispatched a crew to investigate the possibility of driving a road through from Old Chonock into the Rearers, watched as Henry Cotes hurried away, puzzled, he returned to Josephs office.

"I have just seen Cotes storm off at a fair pace Joseph, I take it things did not go well in here?"

"I thought they were Arthur, he was surprisingly sociable at first," replied the still bewildered Joseph, he indicated towards the bottle of malt on the desk, and the cigars in the ashtray.

"He told me to fetch young Zack in, and then all of a sudden he just took off."

Arthur picked up the bottle of whiskey, "It's freezing out there, think he'd notice if we had a nip of this?"

"He gave me one before he left, have a drop if you want, he'll never know." Arthur poured himself a generous nip.

"Strange bloke that Cotes, real oddball isn't he Joseph, so, where do we go from here?"

"I have no idea Arthur, he left instructions to keep Zack here and said he would be about an hour, he would like to speak with Zack when he gets back, best keep the lad as isolated as possible in the fan house for now."

Chapter Five

Oblivious to the inclement weather, Henry Cotes would not be deterred from his objective, although he knew the fresh deepening snow by now would have blocked off the long, steep drive of Highfield Hall to motor vehicles, which meant he would need to leave his car at the top and walk the last four hundred yards to reach his objective.

Within a little over fifteen minutes, he strode along the garden path of Hawthorne Cottage, lifted the doorknocker and rapped it firmly announcing his arrival. The door opened to reveal an extremely handsome woman in her early forties; her long blonde hair caught up in a tight bun, her apparel, selected for its practicality and hard wearing properties was never the less of the finest quality. The cut and style of her clothes complimented her exquisite figure; therefore, her demeanour was far too striking and distinctly out of place for a resident of such a cottage.

"Good afternoon Lydia," greeted a stern faced Henry Cotes, the woman gasped, and startled she took a step backwards.

"Mr Henry," she replied in amazement, "I never thought to ever find you knocking at my door, to what do I owe this honour?"

"I need to speak with you regarding your son," Henry said, and without invitation, pushed past her into the cottage.

"Zack?" her tone now anxious, "I have just heard there has been an accident of some kind down at Tilly Pit, is he alright?"

Henry removed his snow covered top coat and handed it to Lydia while she was still speaking.

"Zack told me a few weeks ago he was not allowed below ground because of his arm, is he alright? Has he been injured?"

"To be perfectly honest Lydia, I have not seen him, but, I am informed that at the present Zack is fine." Henry reassured her.

Somewhat bewildered Lydia continued, "Then I don't understand,—if you are not the bearer of bad news Mr Henry, what brings you here, and what do you mean by 'at the present,' what is going on?"

Henry, was amused, Lydia's reaction to his first ever visit to Hawthorne Cottage was proving to be exactly as he expected, she was courteous, polite but lacking the grovelling mannerisms normally afforded by the lower classes to a man of his standing.

"It has been my intention to call on you for some time Lydia, as indeed I must, but events of today have forced the matter, hence my calling now.—If my information is correct, even though he is an adult you still exert a great deal of control over your son, I am also reliably informed you were always strict with him, and that you have brought him up to be a decent, truthful and honest young man."

Lydia took a slight pause before cautiously asking, "May I ask who has given you that impression Mr Henry?"

"My brother-in-law of course, who else," Henry replied, closely watching for any reaction on Lydia's face, he perceived none.

"Oh yes, of course, I see now, Squire Heath, he always took a great interest in my Zack, he has been very good to us over the years. After the accident when Zack's arm was trapped in that thrashing machine during the harvest before last, the squire found him other work at the pit. I shall,—I mean we shall all miss Squire Heath very much."

"Quite so Lydia, I understand that. You were in the church and at the cemetery the day of his funeral, were you not?"

Lydia dipped her head slightly and smiled in confirmation.

"I was,—yes."

"I could not help noticing you there, keeping well in the background, if I remember correctly you stayed at the graveside long after the family left, did you not?"

Lydia Morgan could not understand why a person of Henry Cotes's rank would make a purpose journey on such a dreadful winter's day, or, for his now being here in her cottage. She studied her visitor closely, he was fishing for something, or, on the other hand, perhaps he already knew something he should not. If her suspicions were correct, and to avoid, if possible what she believed could evolve into a delicate situation, following her natural reaction raised her guard. She forced a gracious smile and changed the subject of conversation to one of conventional politeness.

"Forgive me Mr Henry, your calling took me quite by surprise,—where are my manners, can I offer you a drink and something to eat, tea perhaps, or would you prefer something a little stronger on such a cold day?"

From the limited contact he had previously with Lydia, Henry recalled just how strong this lady could be, "Tea will be fine, thank you," he replied.

Lydia filled the kettle and hung it over the fire, as she did, it gave Henry a brief opportunity to look around the room, it was tastefully decorated, good furniture and fittings, extremely well arranged for an estate cottage, he was impressed.

"You have a nice home here Lydia," he remarked.

"Thank you Mr Henry, I like to think so, we were very fortunate, Squire Heath started a project to upgrade all his estate properties about three years ago, as luck would have it this cottage was the first to be done. But then as you know, the squire's health deteriorated over the past couple of years, and unfortunately he passed away before any others were started,—perhaps young Mr Charles, now he is the new squire will eventually carry on where his father left off with improvements to the rest?"

Henry smiled smugly, "I assure you I fully understand the point you are making Lydia, but as for my nephew continuing any project, I very much doubt it."

A response, which made Lydia even more wary, but skilfully, she allowed no expression or gesture to show it.

Henry and Lydia sat by the fireside opposite each other; Lydia in her usual place, but the chair opposite her, which Henry Cotes now occupied, had always belonged to someone else.

Since the old squire's death, Lydia had been expecting a confrontation of some kind now his son young Mr Charles Heath had become the new squire, was this it. If so, why was it the new squires uncle, Henry Cotes, who now sat in her living room, her courage rose, she needed answers, and she decided she had had enough of this polite pussy footing around.

Lydia adopted a resolute tone, "Mr Henry, you have known of me from the time I first entered into domestic service at the manor years ago. Since then our paths have crossed many times on the frequent occasions I have been called back to help out up at the hall when they were short staffed, and all those times your sister called on me to act as housekeeper when she held her parties and had many guests staying."

Henry smirked and gave a little chuckle, which only made Lydia more resolute.

"When you arrived you said you wanted to speak to me about my son, I know you never do anything without good reason, what has he done. Why are you here, what exactly is it that you want of me?"

"Still have your spirit I see Lydia,—still direct, straight to the point and shortcutting pleasantries,—good, that forth-right manner of yours may be needed."

The kettle boiled, Lydia rose, made the tea, served it in silence taking full advantage of the small distraction as an opportunity to clear her thoughts, she didn't like the idea Henry was making fun of her, nevertheless, before responding to his remark, she settled back into her chair.

"I presume you refer to my reputed frankness Mr Henry, precisely in what way will it be needed?"

Her previous polite servile tone dissipated and her natural confidence now in evidence, to some extent, this pleased her visitor, it placed him on a more familiar business like ground, if Lydia chose to continue to act as his equal; it should be easier for him to anticipate her reactions to what he had to say.

"The accident this morning at Tilly Pit Lydia, you mentioned you have heard about it."

She nodded, "Hawkins called for some eggs about an hour ago, and he told me."

"You mean my sister's footman?" she nodded.

"Well, as I understand it there has been a methane gas explosion below ground, the generally considered opinion is that men have been killed, either by the actual blast or the poisonous gasses it produced, as yet, we do not know how many, but signs indicate a considerable number."

"I am very sorry to hear it,—but how does it concern me? The fact that you have called here to see me implies that in some way it does, but I cannot imagine why. As long as you have know me you have only ever regarded me as a mere servant, so why are you here telling me about this?" this new direction their conversation had taken, though tragic in topic put Lydia more at ease.

Henry, eagle eyed, closely watching for any tell tale reaction, continued.

"There is some talk amongst people around the Pit Bank that the gas was drawn into all the mine because the ventilation fan ran for some time in reverse,—your son, it seems, was in charge of the fan house this morning."

The colour drained from Lydia's face, her expression was one of disbelief, immediately she was on the defensive.

"Are you saying my Zack was responsible for this accident, is that why you are here, to tell me because of my son's actions men's lives have been lost?"

"Not exactly, no! Nevertheless, undoubtedly, there will be some people who will say he was to blame. Undoubtedly, there will be an official inquiry into the whole affair; as it stands at the moment your son is the only one able to give an actual account of a time lapse involved. There is no doubt at all that the fan did run in reverse, a few seconds it seems would have had no effect, but minutes could."

Lydia horrified, shook her head in disbelief, Henry went on.

"Let us say, hypothetically, the fan was running in reverse for several minutes, and Zack knew it, rather than admitting this fact and being held responsible for what has happened, he told everyone it was only seconds, how would you react?"

Henry did not expect any delay in receiving an answer from Lydia; he was not disappointed, her response was immediate.

"This proposition of yours, if I understand correctly, is a 'what if' example only,—right?

Henry nodded answering affirmatively.

"Then I would have to say if men have died because Zack made a mistake of some kind, and he was responsible, regardless of the final outcome, I would do my best to convince him to own up to his mistake, speak the truth and state only the true facts."

"Exactly what I expected you to say, you always were as straight as they come, if you believe you are in the right quite a force to be reckoned with,—that is the reason I am here," Henry confirmed.

It began to dawn upon Lydia, Henry's question was not a 'what if,' and he had said some people would say Zack was to blame. Here in her little cottage, sat a man whose situation in life must be acknowledged to be far above the one she now held, a man of power and influence, who no one from her present class would dare to refuse anything, or challenge his will. She could not help but feel flattered he claimed to regard her as a force to be reckoned with, but she knew his reputation of old. He possessed little or no conscience, his only interest, the pursuit of position and wealth, he used people for his own gain, and far too many of his business dealings were, to say the least, suspect. She knew he would not hesitate bringing about the ruin of anyone who opposed him, and it seemed here he had the perfect scapegoat to blame for the explosion at the pit, her son Zack. On the other hand, if that was his intention, why was he sitting here now?

To be true to her own character and stand by the principles she always held, for her to appose his plans if he did intent Zack as the scapegoat, would certainly mean the loss of everything she possessed. After a moment's reflection of her current situation, she realised that this may well soon happen anyway, as there was now a new squire as her landlord.

She never liked or trusted Henry Cotes, infuriated by what she perceived his intentions to be, Lydia's spirits rose.

"Mr Henry, my son will not lie to save himself or anyone else, his fathe . . . . I will not allow it."

"I am aware of that Lydia, I knew you would never condone such a thing, and neither would his father."

Henry's last remark was completely out of place and unexpected, Lydia felt her face flush from a mixture of anger and embarrassment.

"What do you mean by that Mr Henry, 'his father'? Zack's father died . . . ,"

"Three months ago," interrupted Henry.

An awkward silence briefly fell within the room.

"No, No Mr Henry, you are mistaken, years ago, Zack never knew his father.

"Lydia, don't go all feminine and flustered on me please, if I were to ask you for proof of that fact, and to ask you to show me Zack's birth certificate, would you be able to do so?"

Lydia snapped back, "That piece of paper was lost a long time ago, and no, I don't see why I should give you any proof regarding my private life."

"No matter Lydia, I already know what it says, and more to the point for over a year now I have known precisely why it says it."

Henry Cotes smirked again, fully expecting Lydia's present state of confusion to disappear as fast as it had emerged.

"Yes Lydia, I know all about it, my brother-in-law Charles, shortly after he learned his illness was terminal and that he had, at most, a year to live, confided in me, he gave me precise instructions to be carried out after his death. In addition to which, he made many alterations to his will, and deposited certain sealed documents with his lawyers, call them sort of letters of administration if you like."

These revelations far exceeded Lydia's worst fears, had Henry Cotes, a man she disliked immensely truly been entrusted with a well kept secret, or was this a trap, she studied him more closely, and believed she detected some uncharacteristic warmth in his expression. If as he claimed Charles Heath senior had trusted him enough to disclose their secret to him, she had no alternative but to trust him now, in the knowledge of this, her mood softened.

"I don't understand Mr Henry, we were so careful; Charles must have felt he had good reason to tell you, does anyone else know?"

"Not that I am aware of, accepting of course, Charles's solicitor, nor will they learn of it from me. It was Charles's last wish that your relationship is not to be made public knowledge at this time, but I do know who is named on Zack's birth certificate as his father, what I need to know from you is, does your son Zack know?"

Lydia shook her head.

"No Mr Henry, he does not, he believes the story every one was told, that his father was a labourer on the estate, that we intended to marry but he died of consumption before our marriage took place. He has accepted the fact he was born out of wedlock. But, just in case the local busy bodies suspected this was not actually the case, Charles and I set up an elaborate ruse for the gossips to tittle tattle about, that Jacob Brindley, young Mr Charles's tutor could quite possibly have been Zack's father, and it worked—were you very angry when you learned the truth Mr Henry?"

"What would be the point, No? Not at all, and I think under the circumstances you can drop the 'Mr' now, don't you?"

Lydia smiled in relief, maybe there was a side to Henry's character she never suspected. Evidently, Charles had trusted his brother-in-law with the truth as a safeguard in case he was unable to complete everything he wanted to do before he died, and she nodded in agreement.

The reason for Henry's visit now became clearer, because of Zack's bloodline, this man would be more likely to defend, rather than persecute him.

Henry elaborated further, "I know it was always a great disappointment to Charles that my sister Anne was unable to conceive again after the birth of my nephew, I am sure you know his birth was difficult. Anne was never strong and she has not been well since, very often quite seriously ill. It is a sad state of affairs, but my nephew has proved to be nothing but trouble ever since the day he was born, a disappointment to us all."

Lydia Morgan found great difficulty concealing her amazement that Henry Cotes felt this way about his nephew.

Henry went on, "There are certain things in life Lydia that can be winked at among men. Lord knows most of us have indulged in something of an indiscrete nature at some time or other, but your relationship with Charles seems not to have been a mere fumble below stairs."

Another surprising, unexpected statement from her guest, Lydia, feeling very embarrassed remained silent allowing him to continue.

"Charles went to great lengths to convince me that between you and him, things were very different, there was a genuine mutual attraction, which he assured me grew gradually from a casual friendship, and that over time he found in you, the love and comfort my sister had been unable to provide for many years.

Charles's faith and obsessive sense of honour and duty, 'Those whom God hath joined together,' you know the marriage ceremony words, bound him to my sister for life. In spite of this he confessed to me his love for you became so strong over the years, that had my sister been taken from us, after a respectable period he hoped you would have married and that you would have become mistress of the manor."

Lydia looked at Henry in disbelief.

"That was never mentioned, or even thought of by me Mr . . . . Oh sorry, Henry, this will take some getting used to, perhaps I should stay with the old habit and keep the 'Mr' part."

"As you wish, either way I do not mind, now, before I have to return to the pit, we must discuss this urgent matter of your son's possible involvement in the explosion. I told you that up to now it is only speculation regarding the length of time that the fan ran in reverse. Zack's account of what actually happened will be crucial to any investigation, my main reason for calling on you unannounced is to stop your possible intervention with him to do, or say anything in support of any rumours or gossip you may hear that he was at fault. Different stories are bound to fly round the village, but that one I want killed."

"He was not responsible then?"

"Probably not, I shall be seeing him when I leave here, it had been arranged for me to see him earlier. However, once I learned the name of this mornings fan attendant. I anticipated how you would react to any accusations you heard that he may have been at fault, and I decided it would be better if I spoke with you first. This way you know at first hand how things stand and the best way of handling any awkward situations that may arise."

Lydia looked longingly around her cottage.

"Perhaps it may not be too bad, I expect we will have to leave here soon anyway, I do not pay much rent here at the moment. I have been expecting everything to change when young Mr Charles realises how much I am paying, and I dread to think what will happen if he ever finds out about his father and I, and of course the fact that he has a half brother."

Henry laughed heartily, "I told you Lydia, Charles left me with strict instructions, my nephew cannot change anything, you can decide if you want to stay here when everything is sorted, I have a feeling you may not wish to do so though. I will have to explain all the details at a later date, there is a great deal you must know, unfortunately, Charles's instructions to the lawyers and myself, due to last minute developments will take a long time to implement, nevertheless, be assured you are well provided for, and financially, you should never have any worries again."

"I cannot begin to tell you the relief it is to hear you say that Mr Henry, honestly, the only thing I expected was probable eviction, I rather thought that was why you came here today," Lydia shyly confessed.

"You will understand I have other more pressing concerns now than to spend time attending to Charles's instructions for his estate, don't worry yourself about that nephew of mine. He has no inclination or head for business, his only desire is, as it always was, to live well off the profits made by others, anyway, your concern about eviction, at the moment is academic, he is no longer your landlord, until Charles's final wishes are in place, temporarily, I am."

Henry Cotes took his leave, and in parting reassured Lydia.

"Now Lydia, it is vital you don't listen to any rumours, if people say Zack was at fault this morning, do nothing without my knowledge, and together we will sort all this out. The best interests of yourself, and indeed of Charles's younger son will be taken care of."

Henry Cotes's surprise visit to Hawthorne Cottage, had proved eventful indeed, for Lydia, her well-kept secret, no longer her secret, her son may be facing the wrath of the villager's tongues, and a man she never really liked apparently now in control of her fate.

Charles had always kept a small stock of wines and spirits at Lydia's cottage for their enjoyment; it had remained undisturbed since his last visit there until this moment. Grieving, Lydia had been unable to open the hidden cupboard in the cellar in which they stood. With the reaffirmation of Charles's true feelings for her unwittingly disclosed this afternoon by Henry Cotes, those secret desires her beloved Charles held for them eventually to be together and their love publicly acknowledged. Only now could she find the strength to open this secret cupboard, taking out two glasses, placed one on the table by Charles's chair, the other she set down by her own, poured a little of his favourite brandy into each, settled in her chair and raised her glass.

"To you Charles, wherever you may be, may you and the angels watch over our son."

There, by her fireside, lost in the memories of the happy times she and Charles spent together she remained until total darkness engulfed the room.

Being so close, Henry Cotes made a slight detour before walking back to his car and returning to Tilly Pit, he walked down the short path through the woods to call at the Manor House. He had two reasons; he knew his sister was rarely well enough to be up and about at this time of day in winter. However, Lydia had mentioned the servants at the hall were already talking about the accident, and he doubted his nephew would have returned home after lunch, therefore he felt he should hear from them what facts they knew about the explosion.

Secondly, to leave word at the Hall he would be returning there at lunchtime tomorrow and that he would expect his nephew to be there, and not off carousing around the neighbouring hostelries.

Four thirty in the afternoon, Henry returned to the pit, the crowd outside the gates were milling around in a noisy excited manner; because of this, he had some difficulty passing through the pit gates with his motorcar.

To inquire of the crowd the reason for their exuberance, was, of course beneath him, returning to the manager's office, Joseph Shaw and Arthur Cleaver met him with smiling faces.

"We have some good news Mr Cotes," beamed Joseph.

"The crew we sent up to The Old Chonock have broken through into the Rearers, forty seven men are alive and well in there, they will soon be walking out, we are driving a new crut through from the Chonock chamber, I have sent lorries up there to bring them in."

"Excellent Joseph,—how many will that make that have come out in one piece up to now?"

"Not enough," replied Joseph, his enthusiasm faded at the realisation, "Just sixty so far."

"Still much to be done then," Cotes replied coldly, "Did you keep the fan attendant from this morning on site?"

"Yes Mr Cotes, under the circumstances he was happy to work a double shift when it was offered to him, Arthur and I took the precaution of taking some food over to him ourselves so he didn't need to leave the fan house, is that alright?"

"That is excellent Joseph, I will see him now, have him brought over."

With some relief now their previous arrangements appeared to be back on track, Joseph crossed the yard to the fan house personally to collect Zack Morgan.

"Perhaps you should swill your hands and face Zack before you meet with Mr Cotes," advised Joseph, Zack complied with the suggestion. As they re-entered the office they found Henry Cotes seated behind Joseph's desk, Arthur was sitting nervously on one of two chairs set by the sidewall, another chair had been placed almost central to the room, presumably for Zack.

Joseph attended to the necessary introductions.

"Mr Cotes, sir, this is Zack Morgan, you asked to see him, he ran the Fan Engine this morning," Cotes nodded in acknowledgement, much to the astonishment of Arthur and Joseph, Zack's face beamed with confidence. The two men took the two remaining seats; Henry looked over towards his managers.

"I think I can manage to speak with this young man alone Mr Shaw, I presume, with men expected back here at any moment, you have more urgent things needing your attention."

Joseph and Arthur had no alternative but to take this poignant hint, reluctantly, they left the office.

"Joseph, I don't like the look of that," Arthur said as they reached his own office, "Cotes could be up to something to save his own hide and drop us right in it, he shot off pretty quick earlier, No, I definitely don't like it."

"Hope for the best Arthur," replied Joseph, "We will just have to hope for the best, but for the record, I don't like the look of it either."

In the main office, Zack Morgan studied Henry Cotes, initially, with trepidation, remembering from his youth just how brusque this man could be, no matter, he thought to himself; they would not be here now unless Cotes wanted something from him.

Henry Cotes had observed the confident smile of the young man as they had been introduced, yes, he thought to himself, a chip off the old block, truly his mother's son.

"Well now Zack, I understand you were in charge of the mines ventilation system this morning?"

"That is correct Mr Cotes, I was, I have been left to run the fan engine on quite a number of shifts, I know the job, and I did everything as it should be done," replied Zack warily, still haunted by a suspicion of duplicity and treachery, knowing that he could easily be made the scapegoat for the days happenings.

Henry knew everything hinged on this interview and the young man's responses, he decided to approach the subject from an indirect angle.

"Your face is familiar to me young man, have we met before?"

"Never introduced sir, but I do know who you are, I used to work on Squire Heath's estate in the stables at Highfield Hall when I was a lad, and then on the estate itself, I have seen you and your family up there many times."

"I see, that could account for it," Henry, deciding to appear to probe into Zack's background before any mention of the day's events, continued with pleasantries, "How did it come about that you were employed at Highfield at such an early age? Do you have family up there?"

"Yes Mr Cotes, my mother and I live at Hawthorne Cottage, on a sort of little smallholding, there are only the two of us, my father passed away before I was born, my mother used to be in service at Highfield, and sometimes she still works there as part-time housekeeper when they are busy."

"Your mother works at Highfield, does she really?" teased Henry.

"Yes sir, quite often mother is called back to Highfield for a week or so at a time, and sometimes she works away at other houses if she is needed, but you know that sir, she has worked for you many times over the years,—her name is Lydia."

Zack's face held an expectant expression, he felt sure Henry Cotes would recognise the name and that would work in his favour.

Henry however, was completely baffled, he had seen Lydia Morgan at Highfield on numerous occasions, and to the best of his knowledge, a room containing her uniform, clothes, and personal effects was still allocated for her use whenever she was there, and that no one else was ever permitted to use it.

Lydia however, had never worked at his own estate situated just over the county line in Cheshire, nor had he ever seen or heard of her at any other house in the district.

"I see, yes I believe I do remember to some extent in former years, a Lydia working at Highfield, attractive person, blonde hair."

Zack nodded eagerly adding, "She spent a week at your estate Mr Cotes not six months since."

"Did she?" Henry's retort was too quick, Zack looked puzzled; Henry caught the bewilderment on the lad's face.

"She may have done,—I have been in South Wales quite a lot over the last couple of years, and our housekeeper handles all our domestic arrangements," this answer satisfied Zack.

However still baffled, Henry continued, "This arrangement of your mother working at the Hall, or away, is a recent development then now you are an adult?" the lads puzzled expression returned.

"Why no sir, all my life,—but you must know that, you must have seen my mother there from time to time."

Not wishing to increase the doubts he already perceived in Zack, "Yes! Yes of course I must, but I never take too much notice of servants," Henry replied with mock disdain.

"Just as a matter of interest Zack, if, as you say, there is only your mother and yourself at home, with your mother away from home so much when you were young, how did you manage on your own, did someone come in to look after you?"

Zack could not understand why Henry Cotes persistently asked all these questions about his home and family, he believed he had been called into the office solely to give an account of events at the pit that morning, to Zack these questions seemed irrelevant to that issue.

"No sir, no one came to our cottage to look after me, before I was able to fend for myself, when mother was working, or away, I used to stay at Valley Farm with Mr and Mrs Oldfield, they are tenants of the squire, they were, and still are always good to me. Their daughter Florence and I have an understanding, we have been walking out now for over a year, I am extremely fond of her, and I know she is of me, but I think maybe her situation in life is too far above my own for me to be accepted in that way."

Henry half smiled, it seemed Joseph Shaw had not been mistaken, now it was beginning to come out, this young man would take any opportunity to rise from what he believed to be his lowly status, if only he knew just how wrong he was. Lydia however, should be the one, if anyone to tell him the truth about his heritage; this was neither the time nor place for him to learn of it.

Henry continued to tease the lad, "Oh! Now I begin to see young man, Mr Shaw happened to mention you told him this morning that you hoped for a position in estate work someday, this I take it is to impress the young lady and her family?"

Zack began to regret disclosing that fact to Joseph Shaw, he had been with the mine owner in the office some time now, and yet no mention had been made regarding the explosion. Dreadful thoughts rushed through his head, the fan had run in reverse, maybe Henry Cotes, who he knew to be ruthless and clever, was in some way setting him up to take the blame. He shuffled uneasily in his chair, had he mis-read the signs earlier with Joseph Shaw and Arthur Cleaver, Cotes obviously knew everything that had transpired then. Panic began to set in with him, had he been too bold, tiny beads of sweat formed on his forehead.

Henry Cotes noted the lad's unease, "Now tell me Zack, what actually happened with the ventilation system this morning, the fan engine stalled and started up in reverse, is that correct?"

"Yes Mr Cotes sir, it did," replied Zack, his confidence momentarily having left him.

Henry was not letting this slight advantage go.

"According to Mr Shaw you told him it was for a few seconds only, which of course would not present any great dangers below ground, is that correct?"

Zack realising his answers were once again being led, began to compose himself.

"I changed it back to the proper direction as fast as I could Mr Cotes, but as I told Mr Shaw, I don't have a watch, therefore, I cannot tell you exactly how long it took."

"I see Zack," said Henry, aware the young man was back in control of his emotions, "It seems to have been quite a serious accident this morning, it may be quite some time before this pit is back in production, and no doubt men will have to be laid off until it is."

"I can understand that Mr Cotes," replied Zack, knowing that he would be one of them.

"We shall endeavour to get the mine back into full production as soon as we can, naturally, but I am very busy at the moment, especially as I have recently taken control of a large portion of the Highfield Estate, your young ladies home, Valley Farm included. Tell me, am I right in thinking the two Oldfield boys, are in the army now?"

"Russell and Philip, they were sir, sad to say, they were both killed in the trenches eighteen months ago, at the battle of 'The Somme', Florence is the only one of the three children left now."

"Oh, I am sorry to hear that, I shall need good, loyal men with me to reorganise the parts of Highfield estate now in my possession, if you know of any," baited Henry.

Henry leaned forward pretending to study some papers on the desk, allowing time for Zack to grasp the implied meaning behind his last remark. Once again Zack was at a loss, he knew he had been kept on site especially for this meeting with Cotes, is it, as before when he had realised Joseph Shaw wanted the word 'seconds' rather than 'minutes' to be used.

He weighed up the circumstances carefully, it was true he did not own a watch, the clock in the fan house had not worked for months, therefore, he could not categorically state the exact time lapse before the fan was out of reverse.

Had he just been offered the possibility of a rewarding job on the Highfield Estate, which in the eyes of Florence's father, would make him a far better suitor for Florence than a man labouring as a pit bank's man. Minutes or seconds, either way he would not be telling a lie, there really was, no way he could know, or state a definite time lapse, the thought of his mother's reaction if he wilfully lied, was not something he relished but a guess at the passing of time could not be construed as a lie.

Henry decided, by now Zack had had long enough to register the possibilities.

"Zack," he began, moving his desired outcome towards closure.

"You know, I think, that there will almost certainly be an official investigation of some kind over this affair, however, you may not be aware that your version of what happened with the ventilation will undoubtedly be crucial to it. I strongly suggest, for your own sake, that you think very, very carefully what actually happened, keep clear in your mind your recollection of events, and tell everyone who asks now, and in the future the same story, one changed word at anytime could land you in a lot of trouble."

Zack nodded to indicate he understood.

Henry was now sufficiently confident of the young man's cooperation, enough to risk Zack making an official statement. During their meeting, things were implied, but nothing promised, relying on Zack's obvious ambition and intelligence, he called Joseph and Arthur back into the office.

"Mr Shaw," Henry said as they returned, "I think it would be in everyone's best interests if Zack made a statement as best he can about the ventilation error this morning, now, in front of witnesses. Will you arrange for it to be written down as he dictates so that he can sign it while he still has a clear recollection,—you can read and write, can't you Zack?"

"Yes, I can sir," Zack replied indignantly.

Joseph summoned his clerk into the main office, and there, in the presence of Henry Cotes, Joseph Shaw and Arthur Cleaver, Zack began his short statement.

> *"The fan engine stalled for a short time this morning, I have never known the clock in the 'Fan House' to work, so I cannot tell you the exact time it happened. It only takes a few seconds to start the engine up again, which I did. As the fan slowly started to turn, I noticed it was rotating the wrong way; I stopped the engine again, the direction lever had slipped when it stalled. I moved the control lever back into forward thrust, locked it off and started the engine up again, It has been going at full speed ever since."*

"That should suffice Zack, well done, precise and short enough for you to remember every word," beamed Henry, "Do you agree gentlemen?"

Naturally, they did, regardless of the eventual outcome, to Joseph and Arthur this written statement, which, would be produced in evidence when required, should counteract the undesirable rumours that had been flying around the pit bank all day.

Zack signed and dated the sheet of paper, everyone else present in the office, including the clerk, signed as witnesses to his statement. Satisfied with the outcome and very relieved, Joseph placed the document in the office safe; he intended to ensure that this document would never go astray.

Zack looked around the assembled company; no one was paying much attention to him now, he thought to himself, ah hah that's me done.

"Mr Cleaver," he began, "I presume you gentlemen have finished with me now?"

Arthur looked towards Joseph and Henry Cotes for confirmation.

Joseph answered, "Yes Zack, you may go now."

Zack rose from his chair, "Am I to go back to the fan house, I know I agreed to work a double shift, but . . . ."

"You have been here since six this morning," Henry Cotes finished his sentence.

"Yes Mr Cotes,—I will finish the shift, but I was just thinking, there are four of us in there now, normally it is only a one man job, two at the most, am I really needed in the fan house now, or am I to do something else?"

Zack had been kept on site at Henry Cotes's order, he was not needed at all now the noon shift were in, Joseph sent an inquiring glance towards Henry who immediately understood.

"Is your home far away Zack?" Henry asked, knowing exactly where it was, he had been sitting in it that afternoon.

"On the Highfield Estate Mr Cotes, in 'Bluebell Wood,' it's very isolated, except for the hall itself the nearest neighbours are half a mile or more away, and we rarely see any of them, I was thinking, with this weather, my mother may not have heard about the accident and will be wondering where I am."

Zack was nobody's fool; he knew he had been kept on site only to make his statement.

"Under the circumstances, I think you can go home now Zack," Joseph said.

"Pay him for a double shift anyway Mr Shaw," added Henry.

This came as a surprise to the managers, but Zack smiled, he understood, as far as Henry Cotes was concerned, he had done exactly what was required of him; his statement was worded precisely the way Cotes wanted.

There came loud cheering and shouting from the crowd at the gates, the lorries with the survivors from the Rearers were now entering the pit bank; Zack, unnoticed in the excitement left the office and pit bank to make his way home.

Joseph and Arthur anxious for any new information from the new arrivals also prepared to leave the office.

"Would you like to come with us to speak to the men Mr Cotes?" asked Joseph.

Henry declined, "I think not, but I will stay on site until you have an up-date for me of the prevailing conditions, I will wait in here until you learn how things stand."

Chapter Six

Henry Cotes, alone now and quite at ease in the main office, welcomed an opportunity to reflect upon the day's events, his gaze fell upon the bottle of Single Malt on the desk; he poured a glass and lit a cigar. The approaching evening brought a definite chill to the room, he looked around, which of these chairs could prove the most comfortable, choosing one, he moved it nearer to the stove and settled into it. During his meeting with Zack Morgan, several niggling, unexplainable points had intrigued him. In particular, those references to Zack's mother frequently being absent over the years, and the lads conviction that Lydia had recently been employed as a member of his own household, this had taken him completely by surprise.

Lydia, as far as he was aware, had never even set foot on his estate, why was her son so adamant that she had worked there on many occasions?

As a single parent Lydia excelled, the lad was a credit to her, but how could it be possible such a dutiful mother as she, left her son for long periods at a time in the care of others so often over the years.

From his brother-in laws own lips, Henry knew Lydia had never been without funds, nor would be in the future. Assuming the lad's claims had some credence, that Lydia had found it necessary to find work at his, or other neighbouring estates over the years, and considering the number of social gatherings he was obliged to attend, surely, there was a distinct possibility he would have seen her at one, or other. Such a strikingly handsome woman even if she were only one of the servants, would indeed have been hard to miss.

It was a fact; she frequently occupied her room at Highfield Hall, and so often he had noticed his sister's cheerfulness whenever Lydia was there, although, he never quite understood why Anne, on these occasions entrusted Lydia completely with the running of her household. Previously, he had always attributed this to Anne's poor health.

Many guests there also found it a little strange, and commented on the fact that Highfield Hall was one of the few houses that did not employ a permanent housekeeper, however, with Lydia's competent organisational ability, no one ever disputed every event at Highfield with Lydia in attendance to supervise, always proved a great success.

Why then, had she never been offered the position of housekeeper, when Anne, obviously considered there was an absolute necessity for Lydia to be there on these important social occasions, and would it not have been simpler at those times, instead of the lad being sent to Valley Farm for him to be found somewhere to sleep at the Hall?

Set alone in Bluebell Wood, Hawthorne Cottage, as Zack pointed out was indeed very isolated; whatever possessed Charles to house them there?

He refilled his glass, casually gazing into the amber liquid in a vain hope some inspiration may reach out from there, gradually, a possibility began to dawn upon him.

"Isolated,—of course, isolated," he murmured.

His thoughts strayed to that late summer evening in the Library at Highfield Hall eighteen months ago, when after a good dinner, and over a few cigars and a shared bottle of Malt, Charles confided in him regarding his relationship with Lydia. Could it be their favourite tipple in some way had dulled his hearing or his senses on that evening?

"Charles old lad," he muttered softly to himself, "Either I missed something, or maybe you left a few important details out, now let's see, what was it you said again?"

"Henry," Charles had said, "I know I am to die soon, I need to ask a great favour of you which you must keep secret, there are some things which will need to be done after I am gone. I very much doubt you will approve of the arrangements I have in mind, or even like what I have to ask, but, old friend, you are the only person I can trust to see them through."

"Ask away Charles," had been Henry's jovial reply, "No matter what it is old boy, I give you my word it will be done."

An assurance he gave that evening without knowing how intricate bringing Charles's plans to fruition would prove. Pondering over the whiskey, he spoke quietly, again partly to the spirit in his glass, and partly to the memory of his friend.

"Hmm . . . I really should have found out more about what you had in mind before giving my word old boy, but, no matter, what is past is done; come on now concentrate Henry, think, what exactly did Charles say."

> *"My wife, your sister Anne, as you know never enjoyed the best of health, the birth of our son Charles almost cost her life, the Doctors told me then it was unlikely she would ever conceive again, and they felt it unwise for us to try for another child. They took great pains to stress that in their opinion, if by some mistake or miracle she did become pregnant again, it would be extremely unwise, and it would definitely put her life in great danger."*

Henry recollected he had confirmed that evening, he was aware his sister's health was not good, and that even as a girl she had been of a sickly constitution.

> *"I have never spoken to you or anyone about this before, quite apart from her medical problems Henry, facing, as she did so many difficulties during her confinement over Charles, from then on, she was even more reluctant to indulge in the intimate duties of a wife, an act which was always distasteful to her. Nevertheless, she was my wife and the vows we took bound me to her. I could never force myself upon her, or, for that matter upon any woman in that way, if she was unwilling to respond in a like manner. Perhaps my now telling you this will help you to understand why all the years of our marriage, we have occupied separate rooms in different parts of the house?"*

Henry had confirmed he never gave the matter much thought before, but now, yes, he understood.

> *"I hope you will also appreciate that all men have certain basic needs in regard to their conjugal rights, unfortunately, I have recently discovered to my dismay, some have more than others, in*

> *fact a disturbingly unhealthy appetite, and about which I have done something, nothing which need concern you at present, but something."*

Henry chortled to himself, as he recalled having said.

> *"Yes, we do that; I certainly do anyway, happily, not to an unhealthy degree."*

Henry had replied merrily to Charles in anticipation of some revelation from him, that his brother-in-law was not the dull, stuffed shirt prude everyone always regarded him to be, and had continued by adding.

> *"Not difficult to find for men like us Charles, That little bit of extra marital excitement, it is common place, I quite understand, nothing to worry about at all old man."*

Henry made this remark thinking to reassure his brother-in law that he could understand anyone finding pleasure indulging in coitus away from home. The look of horror and amazement on Charles's face, as he admitted to him his own little indiscretions, would haunt him the rest of his days.

> *"That is the material point Henry, I have always held a strong belief that there must be true affection before indulging in intimacy, casual assignations are, and always have been abhorrent to me. It grieves me to admit, but as I said, Anne, always found intimacy between us distasteful; she seems content that our marriage is now once more, purely one of convenience. No doubt about it, when the medics advised against any further pregnancy after Charles's birth, she took them literally and has never indulged in intimacy with me since then.*
>
> *Bearing this in mind Henry,—I have a confession to make, there is one lady with whom I have formed an attachment, which on reflection, must have evolved from sheer loneliness. For over twenty years, I have found in her the understanding, love, companionship and that necessary physical attention Anne finds so abhorrent. As you know over the past ten years or so Anne's illnesses have come extremely close to taking her from us several times."*

Henry had agreed with this observation.

> *"Don't misunderstand me, I wish her no harm and I am happy she recovered each time. However, if that sad event had actually happened, it has been my intention, after a respectable period, to ask Lydia to become my wife. By making her the mistress of Highfield, it would allow the love we have shared for so long to at last become public knowledge.*
>
> *There are times, I feel I ought to be ashamed of my regard for another woman outside my marriage, but with circumstances, as they are I cannot.*
>
> *I never intentionally sought this extra marital involvement, it came about very slowly, but for many years I have been so deeply in love with Lydia, and for her part, she has fallen in love with a man who belongs to someone else, I understand this is not regarded as an uncommon occurrence. However, in our case it was never just a fleeting affair for the purpose of carnal gratification, the bond, developed between us has held strong and true all these years. Apart from Anne, Lydia has been the only woman in my life, she understood and accepted that our situation was hopeless, but as I have said, we are so deeply in love. Anne is my wife in law, Lydia is my soul mate and wife in all other respects, she never asked for more."*

Henry well remembered his astonishment to learn Charles had happily led a double life for so long, up until that evening he never suspected, although, his wife, who took delight in such matters, on several occasions had remarked she thought there could be marital difficulties between his sister and her husband.

'Husband and wife living in different parts of the house for so long, no sign of any more children, not right at all,' had been her usual grumble.

Several times during this conversation, Charles used the name 'Lydia', but the actual identity of the lady in question never occurred to Henry, innocently he had asked,

> *"Do I know this Lady by any chance Charles?"*

The look of satisfaction and delight on Charles's face as he replied to this innocent question Henry would never forget, beaming happily Charles continued.

> *"You may well do Henry, but humour me a moment, allow me to enlighten you on a little of her background. She was an only child who came to live in this area when she was just a girl of eighteen, her mother died when Lydia was five years old. Her father, an attorney in Shrewsbury, rather foolishly embezzled and lost money belonging to several of his clients. Rather than face prison when his misdemeanour was discovered, he committed suicide in desperation, a heat of the moment act I believe, nevertheless, he left Lydia, a girl in her teens abandoned to fend for herself, without any family or connections. Had she have been a little older, because she had a good education, and many social skills, the role of governess may have been better suited, but with the stigma of her father's actions, all that was open to her was to enter into domestic service."*

The office telephone rang, interrupting Henry's train of thought; Joseph's clerk immerged from his little office next door to answer it.

"It's the main gate Mr Cotes, another rescue team has just arrived, what am I to tell them?"

"Tell the gate keeper to let them in of course and that Mr Shaw and Mr Cleaver will probably be in the First Aid Room, or, perhaps, the Lamp House, they will give them their instructions."

"Very well sir," the clerk replied, "It is getting quite dark now, would you like the light on sir?"

"No, No, leave it off, pleasant enough without it."

Alone again, Henry returned to searching his memory, for anything which may cast light on the possible reasons for Zack's strange claim of his mother's employment at his Cheshire estate.

Yes, Lydia had entered into 'Service' as a teenager at Highfield Hall, he well remembered her at that time, even then, she was an exceptional beauty and all the young men on the estate pursued her, but she would have none of them.

Charles Heath at that time would have been more than fifteen years older than Lydia. The evening Charles told Henry about his double life, he had admitted that at first he regarded her merely as another servant; however, as time went on he became aware she possessed considerably more wit than the average-serving girl, able to engage in lively, intelligent conversation when given the opportunity. Her beauty was undeniable, her bearing always proud but without conceit, her acceptance of the events which reduced her to her present position and of which many would have been resentful, Charles found admirable. Her caring, compassionate nature proved to be endearing to everyone who knew her.

Anne Heath, though it was true never enjoyed the best of health, would, frequently allow her imagination to suggest her illness to be worse than in fact it was. Often she took her meals in her room, or if not, she would retire early after dinner; the task of clearing away generally fell to Lydia. Within a few months Charles found the master to servant simple communication employed when the girl first arrived to work at the manor, gradually progressed, he found himself remaining in the dining room to talk with her as she worked; he came to enjoy their lively conversations. Lydia could converse intelligently on any subject, and her opinions if sought were always valid and logical. Soon, when no other companionship offered, it became a regular occurrence for her and the master to retire to the sitting room and talk well into the night,

Therefore, a platonic bond soon developed between them. Lydia's wide knowledge came mainly from reading, which she loved to do, one evening as she climbed to reach a book from a high shelf she accidentally lost her balance, falling clumsily into Charles's arms. That long, lingering gaze they exchanged after he caught her and helped her to regain her balance could only end one way, with their first tender, bashful kiss.

Stricken by guilt and embarrassment, both immediately went their separate ways, for several days they felt awkward and guilty, avoiding each other as much as possible, until, Charles, not wanting it to appear he had taken unfair advantage of the girl, not to mention his missing her lively company in the evenings, attempted to apologize. To the amazement of both, they realised their pleasant platonic friendship had now developed into one of infatuation and desire; they found each possessed the same feelings towards the other.

Henry's self-annoyance arose; recollection of Charles's overly romantic account of the way his relationship with Lydia began, and their feelings for each other was proving unproductive, giving no reasons for, or any possible answers to Zack's remarks.

"Look at it another way Henry," he said to himself as he replenished his glass, "What else is there?"

Anne Heath rarely, if ever left Highfield Hall, but there was always a steady stream of her female friends visiting, often staying for weeks at a time. An occasional drive in the carriage in summer, a stroll around the garden on a nice day were Anne's limit; any social gathering away from the Manor House, Charles attended alone, Anne always managed to find a reason not to accompany him.

Charles travelled a great deal on business trips for the estate, away weeks at a time; in addition to which, normally, at least twice a year, he would take long holidays alone, Anne, opposed to any change in her routine, preferred to stay at home.

Six years ago, Charles had planned to sail to America on the maiden voyage of the pride of 'The White Star Line,' but once again, Anne's health intervened by taking a turn for the worse and the voyage Charles intended, was cancelled at the last moment because of his wife's indisposition.

"Fortunate for you old man, very few who sailed made it across the Atlantic, that ship was not such a miracle of nautical engineering after all," Henry, observed softly.

He took another sip of his whiskey, on which he nearly choked.

"Damn it, that's it," he muttered venomously, angry with himself for being so slow to realise the obvious. Now his venom turned to a chuckle, speaking very softly, half to himself, and half to his amber spirit companion.

"Henry Cotes, you are getting too slow in your old age, it's true, people are always ready to believe in the invisible, but when something stares you in the face you just can't see it, that's got to be it, all those business trips of Charles's were not only business, and on his lone holidays, he was not alone. Lydia never worked at any neighbouring estate, she is educated, well able to pass as a member of society, they were away together. All these years' people have believed Lydia to be single; and no one ever realised that to all intents and purposes she was married all the time."

Henry raised his glass in a toast, "You lucky old blighter Charles, here's to you, spending time with, and having the love of such a beauty, no wonder you were always happy and content, good on you old lad."

Henry's excursion into memory was brought to a sudden end by the office door bursting open.

"Oh! Mr Cotes, you are still here, with the office being in darkness I thought you must have left," Joseph spluttered; a little startled seeing the owner sitting by the stove.

"No Joseph, I said I would wait until you returned, there was enough light in here from the bank lights, I didn't need the office light on, just trying to relax with my old friend here," he said picking up the bottle of malt.

Joseph noted the amount left and smiled, if he had drank so much he would have been on his back, but the stuff didn't seem to affect Henry.

"Well Joseph, I waited, what is the situation now? Is there anything else you need from me? I shall soon have to be making tracks back into Cheshire if I am to be home in time for dinner."

For the first time, Joseph realised the events of the morning could not possibly be rectified in the space of one working day, a management rota must be set in place, at least one of the senior management should be on site twenty four hours a day until this crisis had passed.

"Yes of course Mr Cotes, I apologize, I should have briefed you when you returned this afternoon, but, you seemed very anxious to see Zack Morgan, and then the men returned from the Rearers, it slipped my mind."

"There were other developments while I was off site then?"

"Yes sir, the remaining men from the afternoon shift, those we had not called in early reported for work, but of course, there was none for them, all of them wanted to help, but of those who volunteered to go down, Arthur selected sixty of the best men.

Some, as you know, we sent over to Chonock to drive a road through into the Rearers, the rest of the men, we have making safe the roadways and ferrying up bodies from those sections of the pit safe enough to enter without Nevito's. We are laying out the bodies as they are brought out in the engineer's workshop; the operation is slow, but on going. I'm afraid I don't know how many have been brought out up to present, but, I have just sent half the men who returned from Bethel Lane down as reinforcements to the crews below ground, the others are in the smithy, to be safe we are working on a two hour, turn, and turn about system."

"How much of the mine do you consider to be safe now?" inquired Henry.

"Not a great deal as yet, little more than the pit bottom and a small proportion of the main haulage roads. We have four rescue teams on site now including our own, they are searching all the workings, but the telephone communications deeper into the pit are still out, we have to rely on some of the men acting as runners for news. The teams report that many of the lower tunnels and workings have been blocked by huge roof falls, they are inaccessible, our men are endeavouring to remove the falls and repair the props as they go.

Henry replied thoughtfully, "I see, but the engineers shop is small; perhaps you should try to find an alternative place as a temporary morgue."

"I wanted to ask your opinion about that sir, the Chapel up the road has offered us the use of their schoolroom for that purpose, do you approve?"

"The Congregational Chapel?" asked Henry.

"No sir, their schoolroom is on the ground floor with the Chapel itself upstairs directly above it, everyone attending services tomorrow would need to pass through the schoolroom, and they would see the bodies. The one offered is higher up the bank, on the left, 'The Primitive,' it has a large separate room at the back which can be closed off."

"Very well if they have agreed to its use, we must see they receive a generous donation for their trouble, I assume you will be able to identify the bodies while they are still here on site."

"I anticipated you would agree, we have begun to send them up, as for identification, we shall try as best we can using the lamp and tag system, but, judging by the ones I have seen, their faces are badly burned. I don't see how in some cases we can be absolutely sure, and to make it more difficult, some of the lamps were carried away from the men they were allocated to by the blast. I don't envy the families who will have to make a final identification when they claim what is left of their men folk."

"No, nor I," Henry replied showing an unusual degree of compassion, "Is there anything else?"

"Well sir, I had wondered if we should bring the ponies out, ten of them were resting in the stables when the explosion happened, of which seven have survived. We have nowhere to stable them on the surface here, but they are of no use below ground until we can draw coal again, I thought we might turn them into the pasture."

Henry pondered a moment, "A good point Joseph, but your Mr Fuller emphasized that the usual heat has greatly increased below ground, if you brought them up now into this cold we would definitely lose them, anyway, the pasture is covered in snow, and it will probably freeze tonight."

"Either way they are likely to perish, if they cannot be moved out of the stables, they will just have to stay tethered in there," Joseph said despondently.

Henry thought a moment, "Leave them until tomorrow, some of Hales Brook now is part of my estate, I will have my steward arrange for them to be stabled at one, or other of my farms, well that help?"

"It will sir, if the farm is not too far away, thank you."

"The place I have in mind is no more than perhaps a ten or twenty minute walk from here, the ponies shouldn't take a chill over that distance if they are covered, now, Joseph, I think it's time I was away, how much longer do you intend to stay tonight?"

"I had expected to be able to leave at my normal time, but unfortunately I will have to stay until we are sure everyone alive down there is out, it may well take all night."

"Joseph," Henry spoke in a sterner tone, "Are you confident with the way you have organised this rescue operation, is everything proceeding according to plan?"

"Yes sir, I am, but there may be the odd thing which will need my attention."

"No Joseph, I don't think so, tired men make mistakes, don't stay here all night, you and your deputy go home, get a decent meal and some sleep, delegate responsibility down to the senior shift men. If, things do go badly wrong, there is always the telephone for them to contact you, go home man; you will both be more use if you are fresh in the morning."

"Very well sir, but I ought to stay another couple of hours at least; and tomorrow I thought I could split the day with Arthur, twelve hours each?"

Henry concurred, "That makes sense, and Arthur seems a very capable man."

Once again, Henry Cotes left his staff at the pit to their own devices; it was pointless for him to remain any longer.

Joseph Shaw's confidence in the ability of his men below ground was well placed; earlier that day, by half past two, Sam Swindon and the repair crew, whilst pressing deeper into the mine making safe the main haulage roadway, had approached the junction to the old workings, where, Clem Turner narrowly escaped his end.

Lijah, conducting an initial examination of conditions in the roadways and the off shooting crut entrances, was slightly ahead of the others, at the junction his lamp's light fell upon the three men still seated there, their snap tins, still open on their laps, he paused a moment, turned back, and returned to the others.

Taking Sam to one side, asked in a hushed tone, "Father, mother told me, our Emily has a half day off work tomorrow afternoon, and you two were thinking of going to see her, is that right?"

"We were lad, but that won't happen now, I reckon we shall be needed down here," Sam replied, affronted that his son would even consider he could forsake the rescue task in hand.

"I think you should still go, come and have a look over here and you will see why," Lijah said, turning and retracing his steps, Sam followed, entering the junction the light from both their lamps fell upon the three men. Sam set down his lamp and kneeled by the men.

"Jim Porter, poor lad, Lijah, this definitely brings things closer to home, our Emily's fiancé gone, how in heavens' name are we to break this news to her?"

"Someone will have to, better I think, if it comes from one of us," Lijah said, and whispering added, "Perhaps it would come best from mother, they were always close."

"Aye lad, perhaps it would at that, but, before she can tell Emily, we will have to break this news to your mother, I for one am not looking forward to that, how about you?"

"Me neither, but, if you like I will help you to tell her," Lijah offered.

The other members of their repair crew joined them, without further discussion about their family problem, Sam, Lijah, and the others carried on with the repair work. They knew men from the noon shift, by now would also be on their way in with more repair materials and would have detailed instructions where it was safe for them to work. None of them, not in their wildest dreams, expected to clear the whole mines miles of tunnels in a few hours. Even with every available man working, days seemed to be far more likely, even stretching to weeks. Every minute that passed narrowed the possibility of finding men alive, but conscience demanded they must try to find their workmates. Orders issued by the owners, that, alive or dead, every man must be brought out to every miner seemed pointless, ordered to or not, they would bring their mates out.

From wherever the telephone system was working again, reports were fed back by the advance teams directing the repair crews to the various safe areas, where no telephones worked, runners were sent back with the safety reports. Men lacking skills to be effective with the repair crews carried out dead men on stretchers or planks.

Arthur Cleaver and Joseph Shaw had planned the whole operation in a precise flowing manner, each of the rescue teams covering a different area, and the repair crews guided to gas free districts by the rescue team captains. Ensuring the work carried on throughout the night, detailed plans had been drawn up for the division of the more experienced men to be selected from the night shift, dividing them into squads with instructions to follow the same system.

Henry Cotes left the pit for the day at six thirty; Joseph Shaw accompanied him to his car. Returning to the offices, he found Arthur and passed on Cotes's instructions, that, providing the operation was running as smoothly as it could, and that everyone knew what to do; they should leave the senior men from the noon and night shifts in charge while they went home for a meal and some rest.

"I suppose there is sense in that Joseph," Arthur conceded, "But before I go, I think I will make a final check on the number of men up."

"Good idea," agreed Joseph, "I will come across with you, are you keeping a list?"

Arthur picked up a notebook from his desk and replied, "Yes, I have it here."

The two managers entered the 'Lamp House,' the only man inside had his back turned towards them, he was busy checking and refuelling the returned lamps, he did not notice them come in.

"How many of those are useless now Len?" asked Arthur.

"Oh, sorry Mr Cleaver, I didn't hear you come in, quite a pile I'm afraid, that lot there for a start," the man said pointing to a box of lamps on the floor.

"We need to know the number checked in so far, and to see the record book Len," Arthur continued.

Len Holding, the head 'Lamp Man' at 'Tilly' produced his ledger, "Here it is," he said handing over the large book.

Joseph glanced at it and asked, "Any chance you can give us a breakdown, where the men up now were working?"

Len came round to the front of the counter, "Yes, I think so, most of them anyway." He thumbed through the last pages, "Here, forty seven from the Rearers, twelve walked out from near pit bottom, and up to now another eight have been carried out injured."

"That makes sixty seven Joseph," Arthur said, "seven more than I knew about," he was glad now he came across to check.

Joseph did not answer, instead he pointed to the lamps in the box, "And those?"

Len's face hardened, "Most of them have legible numbers on them, this batch came in from the Rearers and the other walk outs, the rest have been carried out with the men they were found close to, mostly from the main haulage and the cruts just off it."

Neither Joseph nor Arthur really wanted to speak the words, but they must.

Arthur was the one who voiced the question, "Dead men?"

Len nodded as he opened another ledger, "Afraid so, fifty six up to now, I have started a separate list in here, some of the bodies are unrecognisable. I tied labels onto them as they came out, only wrote the lamp numbers and where they were found though, didn't think it wise to use names, even of the ones I could recognise. Some of it had to be guesswork, because men have been found in groups and their lamps a fair bit away from them, so, we don't know which belonged to whom, and these lamps here; the numbers cannot be made out at all." he said lifting three lamps from the end of the counter.

Arthur noted the lamp numbers of the seven men he did not have, and, Len's comments into his own book.

Joseph concurred, "I think you were right not to try and name them Len, too many women about on the bank, keep to this method and when you leave tell whoever takes over from you to do the same, we will find some way of making definite identification tomorrow."

Len shrugged and said, "Fair enough, the engineers shop is full now, are we still to send the bodies up to the Congregational schoolroom."

"When you have listed and labelled them yes, have them taken to the shop first, make sure they are well covered before they are sent up to the chapel, I am leaving a van on stand-bye all night to take them up there when they are ready," Joseph confirmed before he and Arthur left the lamp house.

"Do you want to check on the First Aid room and Smithy before we leave Joseph?" Arthur ventured to ask, even though his thoughts were now of his home and a meal.

"Don't really see much point in that Arthur, but the cage is coming back up by the looks of it, we'll take a quick look at that before we go."

Riding up on the cage were Seth and all of his original team, every man was exhausted.

Arthur helped to open the cage gates, "How is it going now Seth?" he asked.

"Slow, but we are getting there, better now we are not on our own down there," was the reply, "We all needed a break, something to eat and drink, we'll go back down in an hour."

Joseph looked at the weary men, willing though they were, Henry Cotes was right, tired men might make mistakes, and there was still gas of both poisonous and explosive varieties below ground.

"No!" said Joseph firmly, "You should all call it a day now, go home and get some rest, Arthur and I are just about to do the same."

This order from Joseph met with a chorus of disapproval from the men, so much so, Arthur felt obliged to repeat the instruction.

"I know you want to stay, so do I really, but be practical, we all need some rest, now we have teams from other pits there is a new shift rota made out, I left it in the lamp house. I have made out squad lists for when you and your men will be needed again. Go home lads, turn your Nevito's over to men who are fresh."

Still objecting, the men reluctantly made their way toward the lamp house to turn in their lamps, and as ordered return home.

Sam and Elijah Swindon emerged from the lamp house together.

"What time is it now dad?" Lijah asked.

"Just gone seven by my watch lad."

"Do you think mother will still be in the smithy doing the refreshments?"

"I shouldn't think so, she will have gone home to see to the girls I expect, but we had better go across and check before we leave."

"Aye, we will be in trouble if we don't check, mother will go mad if we leave her here and go home without her," Lijah agreed.

Father and son crossed the pit bank towards the smithy, Sam proved to be correct, Eve had left the site over an hour ago. One or two local women were still there, but now in addition to these, staff from a professional caterers 'Swynsons' had been brought onto the pit bank, the local family's had no need to donate food any longer, the professionals, at the pit owners expense now provided all that was needed.

"Well father, at least it's stopped snowing, we won't get soaked on our way up the bank," Lijah said as they made their way through the pit gates.

Sam's gaze turned towards the heavens, unhindered by cloud every star was visible, he walked to the side of the road, placing his foot on a patch of virgin snow he said.

"Aye lad, but it's crisping over now, we are in for a keen frost I reckon."

The two men made their way homeward up the steep bank, as they neared the Primitive Chapel, a van from the pit overtook them and pulled up outside. The driver climbed out as they drew near.

"Evening Sam, Lijah,—this is a bad business aint it," he said as they approached.

"It is that Joe, what are you doing up here?" enquired Sam.

"I am on this run all night," Joe replied, "The engineer's workshop at the pit is full, too many dead men, when they have been checked in I have to bring them up to the schoolroom here, so as to make room for more as they are brought out. We are laying them out as best we can so their families will be able to identify them; I have four more in the van."

"Not a pleasant job that Joe, especially if you know who they are, who have you got in the van this trip?" asked Lijah.

"Don't know, by the time I get them they are all wrapped up in hessian sacking, with a labels showing lamp numbers tied onto them," Joe replied with disgust in his voice, "My orders are to leave them covered."

"You on your own?" Sam asked.

"I am this trip, thought the caretaker here might give me a hand in with these four."

"We'll give you a hand," Sam offered, "Come on Lijah."

Joe opened the back of his van, took out an oil lamp and lit it.

Lijah asked, "What's in those bags Joe?

"Chlorinated Lime, I have been told to spread it around to try and keep the smell down, coming from that heat below ground, some of these men are beginning to get a bit high. The workshop has an awful smell of death in it, and their lordships don't want to upset the chapel folk too much when they come for services tomorrow, we got to use this stuff."

"Shaw and Cleaver?" asked Sam.

"Yeah, that's them, doing all they bloody well can now it's too late, they should have done something about making Tilly safe before the damn pit blew up," Joe snapped.

"They only work there, same as us Joe," replied Sam, "We all know who really deserves to be blamed for this lot, don't we?"

"Yeah, reckon we do, but the likes of us don't count much too them rich buggers."

Sam and Elijah helped Joe to unload his van, and carry the bundled up men and bags of lime along the narrow entry past the chapel to the schoolroom, and to spread the lime before they continued home.

"Father, have you any idea how we are to tell mother about Jim Porter?" Lijah asked as they left the chapel.

"No lad, I haven't, think it will be best if we get her on her own, no need for the girls to know, what do you think?"

"I think you are probably right, on that rota neither of us are due back in at the pit till Monday, you and mother can still go to see our Emily tomorrow as you arranged."

Sam responded in subdued tone, "Not looking forward to that either lad."

The two weary men gratefully reached their home; Sam opened the back door, and Elijah lifted down the tin bath from its nail, for his trouble, he got the snow off the top of it down the back of his neck. Eve came out of the kitchen to greet them.

"Oh! Thank God you are all right, the boiler is full of hot water ready for you, and there are clean clothes for you both hanging on the rails, Evie washed and dried the things you had on this morning while I was down at the pit."

"Thanks mother," replied Lijah, as he hung the old modesty sheet across the room.

"You won't need that," said Eve, "The girls have gone up the road to see my mother and father; they will have to use the front door if they come back while you're in the tub. Evie decided to go and see them, she says it will be six weeks or so before she is home again, and of course Fanny went with her, but you'd better turn the key in the lock for all that."

"Fanny didn't want to miss out on anything that was going, typical," said Sam as he began to draw off the hot water from the boiler.

"Have you got to go in again tomorrow Sam," his wife asked.

"No," he replied, "They have crews from other pits scheduled on for tomorrow, we aren't needed again till Monday morning."

Eve nodded, and left them to their bath.

"That'll make it easier to tell mother about Jim, if the girls are still out when we have finished," Lijah observed.

"Yes, it will at that, better be as quick as we can then," agreed Sam.

Fifteen minutes later the two men emerged from the back kitchen, clean, and smelling of strong carbolic soap.

"How are things down the road now?" asked Eve, "I left when the Swynsons people arrived, is every one out now?"

"No, fraid not, no where near," Lijah admitted, "A good many men are dead, too many,—as well as the engineers shop they are putting the bodies in the Prim's schoolroom now, must have brought well over fifty out."

"Oh dear! That's dreadful," Eve replied sincerely,—"I'll make you some tea."

"I have put the kettle on mother," said Lijah, stopping his mother from leaving the room.

The two men exchanged awkward glances.

"Sit down a minute lass," instructed Sam, "As Lijah, says, it's very bad this time, there are too many dead, it will take days, or weeks even to clear all the cruts."

"I feel very sorry for the families of those lost men," Eve replied, "I thank God neither of you two were down this morning."

There was another ominous silence, both men dreading having to share their news with Eve, Elijah, endeavouring to assist his father, continued.

"Mother, there are scores dead, and I'm afraid I found someone we know very well indeed."

Again, the silence, Eve waited apprehensively for her son to continue, however, Sam, eventually spoke instead of his son.

"Eve, you made arrangements for us to go over to Bursley to see our Emily tomorrow, well now we have to go, the person Lijah is talking about is Jim Porter, we found him sitting in the entrance to one of the old workings, the choke damp got him."

Eve, aghast, burst into tears, "No,—the poor lad, his poor family, our Emily, Oh no, this will break our girl's heart."

The back door opened, in bustled Fanny closely followed by Evie.

"Any food ready yet, I'm starving," said Fanny taking off her coat.

"Not quite yet, I had to hold it back waiting for your father, it won't be long love, just needs finishing off," her mother replied, swiftly heading into the back kitchen attempting to hide the tears on her face.

Eve, and Evie, set to work preparing their meal, whilst Fanny as usual, disappeared into the front room, swung out the piano's candleholders, lit the candles, picked up a sheet of music, and attacked the instrument with her customary gusto.

Evie, noticing her mother's mood asked, "You seem upset mother, something else the matter I should know about?

"I am upset, yes," Eve, immediately decided Emily should be told the news of her fiancé's death before anyone else in the family, avoided answering the question by saying.

"I am sorry for all those men who lost their lives today, but, very glad your father and brother are home safely."

Evie feeling a little foolish for asking such a silly question, continued to lay the kitchen table. Sam, sitting in his chair by the fire was watching her, he looked at Elijah, who, realising his father's intent, shook his head, Sam nodded and lit his pipe.

"Evie, when do you have to be back at Potterton?" Lijah asked.

"Mrs Hudson, the housekeeper, said if I catch a train on Monday morning, so long as I am back there by lunchtime it will be alright," the girl replied.

Sam looked up again; Lijah caught his eye and smiled.

"Oh, that could be helpful lass," said Sam, removing his pipe from his mouth, "Would you be able to look after Fanny a couple of hours or so tomorrow afternoon? Lijah will be at Sunday school, and your mother and me are going to Bursley to see our Emily."

Out of sight of either man, Evie frowned, she had not come home to baby sit her sister, she had had that job most of today, nevertheless, it was rare for her father to make such a request, and so she could not object.

"Of course I can father, but, will you tell her to behave herself while you are away, she got a bit peevish today."

Sam assured her that he would, it seemed settled, he and Eve could catch the noon train after chapel, and be home again in plenty of time for supper.

Chapter Seven

The next day, Sunday 13th January, dawned clear and bright, but still very cold.

Henry Cotes, at his Cheshire estate arose for breakfast; irritated because despite consuming rather more alcohol than usual the previous evening, sleep had eluded him.

His wealth was considerable, and he had striven many years cultivating influential connections to achieve his driving ambition, much to his annoyance however, he had not, as yet been offered a 'Knighthood.' Nevertheless, his underlying self-obsessive, vain arrogance continued to dictate his optimism; he believed it was just a matter of time before an honour of some kind would be be-stowed upon him.

He now realised, yesterdays events at Tilly Pit could seriously hamper his progress to the upper echelon of society, in truth, the chances of his former partner Charles Heath to receive an honour of that kind far exceeded his own. To those with the power of such things in their gift, Henry Cotes was considered uncouth and dangerous, wealthy enough, but rarely seen at their more elite social gatherings, devoid of social graces, a man to be tolerated, but nothing more.

Henry, alone in his breakfast room consumed his customary large breakfast, there was much to do today, uppermost on his mind was the trivial matter of which type of transport he should use. First he must return to Tilly Pit, and then on to his sisters, where yesterday he left instruction to expect him by lunchtime.

Snow still covered the ground, but compared with the depth of snow he battled through yesterday to reach Hawthorne Cottage, here on his estate there was hardly a skittering, merely enough to hide the green of the grass. Overnight however, there had been a keen frost, which once he crossed the Cheshire border could increase the hazards of travelling.

He had observed this phenomenon before, some historians theorised that the whole of Cheshire was once under the sea, and his destination at Heals End being slightly higher above sea level, was in ancient times the coastline. 'Heals End,' in ancient English dialect, was believed to translate as, 'the hill at the sea's edge.'

It was a fact that large deposits of salt were prevalent in Cheshire, and the soil itself held a high salt content, therefore, whenever snow fell here, this salt in the ground melted away much of it before it could gather, only the heaviest falls blanketed the earth in white. Yesterday's fall had been constant, but relatively slow falling, therefore it would be safe to assume snow had gathered deeper, and would stay longer in neighbouring Staffordshire than here in Cheshire.

It was too cold and the distance far too great for horseback, these days, apart from occasional social gatherings during the hunting season, Henry rarely rode, riding was a pastime he outgrew in both size and inclination. Since the advent of motorized transport, he had not used any of his horse-drawn carriages, the use of a carriage was a possibility but leisurely, not practical when time is of the essence and in winter. His journey home last night, once he crossed the county line had been relatively easy; using a car would be faster and far more comfortable. Yesterday, he succeeded in reaching Highfield Hall, most of the way by car and the last few hundred yards on foot, he reasoned the overnight frost would not make his journey much more difficult today, yes, he would travel by car again, but this time from the selection he owned he would use the largest, heaviest one he drove.

The time, now approaching eleven o'clock, for Henry, who held such a high opinion of his own importance, this was quite early enough for any gentleman of his standing to begin his day, he gave instructions for the car he decided upon to be fuelled and brought around to the front door.

A little after mid-day, Henry drove through the pit gates, although there were still some watchers scattered along the pit boundaries, the vast crowds of yesterday had diminished. Leaving his vehicle near to the offices, he went inside, Arthur Cleaver's office was empty, and so, at the end of the corridor, was that of Joseph Shaw. The manager's clerk, seeing Henry pass his door, followed him into the main office.

"Oh, good day Mr Cotes," he said, "I'm sorry, were you expected today? Mr Shaw is not coming in until later, and Mr Cleaver is below ground with an inspector from the Mining Association."

"I did not specify a time, but I did say I would call in today," Henry replied.

"How are things going with the rescue? Have anymore men come out?"

The clerk, a small, very thin man became flustered, unsure if he was at liberty to divulge any details, even to the mine owner.

"Yes sir, I believe so, a few survivors and quite a few more dead have been brought out, but I cannot tell you how many, if you wish I will have word sent below ground that you are here, and Mr Cleaver will come up to give you full details."

Arthur Cleaver below ground and with a mining inspector, who, would doubtlessly return with Arthur and seize the opportunity to speak to the mine's owner, such a person Henry had no wish to confront today.

"No, that's quite alright, I cannot stay long, I will call back later, what time is Mr Shaw expected here?"

"I believe about four o'clock sir," replied the nervous clerk.

"Very well, thank you I will not detain you, I will call again later after Mr Shaw arrives," mumbled Henry as he hurriedly left the office.

Before reaching his car however, it occurred to him perhaps it may be beneficial, if, during any official enquiry at some future date people would have to give evidence, that on the Sunday following the accident, one of the mine's owners, Mr Henry Cotes was present on the pit bank. This in mind, he wandered around entering many buildings, making sure that as many people as possible saw him. No one acknowledged him, or even challenged his progress, everyone there now knew who he was, and in their minds, he was the enemy.

A few minutes past one o-clock, he left the pit bank and made his way to Highfield Hall to keep the appointment he had arranged the previous day. He very much doubted his errant nephew would be there yet, rather too early for him to find his way home from his previous evening's revelries.

His progress up the bank through Heals End and Augers Bank proved far easier than he anticipated. Almost every resident in house and cottage along the cobbled street, had scattered ashes from there fires onto the snow, which, by traffic and footfall, had now compacted into ice on the road. The skittering of ash and small cinders gave enough traction for his car tyres to traverse the steeper sections with relative ease. At the top of Augers Bank, he turned into the long driveway to Highfield Hall, for about three quarters of a mile this drive was on a level, and then fell sharply downhill to the hall itself. From the top of the hill, it was evident; some wind overnight had carried the snow into drifts across the drive. Not wishing to risk stranding himself or his vehicle at Highfield, he parked his car at the same place he left the smaller one yesterday, and walked the last quarter of a mile or so to his sister's home.

The grandfather clock in the hallway at Highfield struck half past the hour as the maid opened the door to admit him.

"Good afternoon sir," the maid greeted him, "You are expected, the mistress is in the drawing room."

The girl relieved him of his overcoat and hat, Henry gestured to her not to bother announcing his arrival, and made his way to the drawing room.

As he entered, Anne Heath rose from her chair, in comparison with her brother; she was a frail, sickly creature whose plain features and appearance could best be described as 'homely'.

"Henry, my dear brother, it is after one thirty, I was beginning to think this dreadful weather had prevented your journey."

"Not at all Anne, I have made excellent time, all the roads are passable."

"Has your driver been taken below stairs for some food?"

"Driver, what driver?" rebuked Henry with a smile, "I love the challenge of pitting my skills against the winter's elements, I find it most satisfying and enjoyable, I came alone, although, I did take the precaution of leaving the car in your drive at the top of the hill, no point in getting it stuck down here."

His sister smiled, and rang the bell for the maid.

"You must be cold, shall we go into lunch now, or would you like a drink first?" she inquired, even though she already knew the answer to this question.

Henry helped himself to a whiskey, the maid appeared in the doorway; Anne gave instructions for lunch to be served in the dining room as soon as it was ready.

Henry asked sardonically, "Where is Charles?"

"It seems he has not been as fortunate as you brother, the weather stranded him at Castleton last night, he has not returned home since he left to meet with you yesterday, but he did telephone to say he would be staying overnight in town and would be returning later today."

"Hmm, typical, and where is he staying?" grunted Henry.

"At a hostelry, I believe he met an acquaintance in town and is staying there with them," replied his sister.

"Did he happen to mention the name of the gentleman he is with?"

"No, I don't believe he did."

"Hmm—probably another floozy," muttered Henry under his breath, then, in an audible tone continued, "But on the other hand, perhaps it is just as well, I have much to acquaint you with, and the events of yesterday force me to make things known to you earlier than I had planned."

Anne Heath had been expecting Henry as chief executor of her husband's will, to give her some clarification of her position now that she was widowed by Charles's passing, she had assumed he delayed this to allow her, as he thought, time to grieve, a little roguish smirk crossed her face.

"About the mine?" she asked cautiously.

"Yes, in part,—but there is much more besides."

"If it is to do with finance, you know I have little head for things of that kind."

"Yes, yes, I know that Anne, and dear old Charles knew it too, that is why when he realised how ill he was he asked me to attend to such matters on your behalf."

"You,—why you, I would have thought such things would fall to our son, after all he is the heir to this estate, is he not?"

Henry frowned, "Anne, when did my nephew ever take any interest in the running of this estate?"

Anne Heath thought for a moment.

"Well, yes, if you put it like that, he never did, I suppose Charles must have had his reasons for asking you to deal with business matters, I agree you have much more experience," his sister conceded.

The maid entered and announced that lunch was served in the dining room.

"Let us eat first brother; I may be better able to understand after lunch, and, as you wanted Charles to be here, perhaps he will return before we finish."

Anne, knowing her brother's custom of consuming a huge breakfast, had ordered only a light lunch.

The time Henry had come to dread over the past three months was now upon him.

He now faced a delicate situation and an encounter for which he hoped to have had more time to prepare, his normal bullying business tactics would be of no use to him here, this was his recently widowed sister, and he had no wish to course her further grief. How much could he tell Anne about Charles's double life? How much must he conceal from her? How much did she already know?

"Henry, I still don't really understand why Charles burdened you with our estates business, you have quite enough of your own to deal with," Anne remarked, as they ate their lunch.

"Surely the accident at the mine will not be severely detrimental to our finances, or, will it?"

"It will be very detrimental Anne, as far as I can see at present, it is most unlikely we will ever bring Tilly Pit back into full coal production."

"But do we not have other holdings as well?"

"You do, you have the land, the farms, but little else, Charles as a matter of honour committed a great deal of money in payment of my nephew's debts, not to mention funding his extravagant lifestyle. By so doing over the past years, it limited the possibility of his accumulating many other lucrative holdings, there were some, but over the past year, Charles considered it necessary to transfer those and others to my care, in other words, they are no longer part of this estate. Your son, unfortunately, has a talent for spending money which is not his own. Admittedly, I was aware Charles was honouring your son's obligations, and years ago I advised him to set my nephew an allowance which he must not exceed, but for some reason, he did not."

"That may have been my fault brother; our son Charles being the only child, I always indulged him."

"I am aware of that; did you ever consider the possibility of changing that situation by having more children?"

"Oh no Henry, you and father encouraged the match between Charles and I to link our two estates, and you both insisted I accept when Charles proposed marriage, it was my duty as a wife to provide an heir, which I did, after that I never wanted any more children."

"Oh! I see," replied Henry uneasily, his sister noticed his unease, and moved away from the subject.

"How soon will you know the extent of the damage at the pit, surely it is not likely to effect our finances to such an extent my little social gatherings here with my friends will need to be reduced, or cancelled this year, people will be so disappointed if they are."

"I cannot tell you that yet Anne, but don't make any preparations until we are sure."

"If they don't come here to stay, I am not able to see my friends. It is bad enough I will probably have to plan all the arrangements myself this year, I doubt if Lydia will be so eager to do it for me now as she has in the past."

Henry raised his eyebrows at the mention of Lydia's name, "Really, why is that?"

Anne Heath studied her brother, uncertain whether or not to elaborate on her last statement, if he had come to tell her what the future held in store, perhaps he should also know something of the past.

"My dear Henry, I am quite content with my position in life, I ask only a comfortable home, which I have here, but my health, as it has done these twenty years past limits my activities, Charles however, being younger than me, needed more from life than I was able to provide."

"I am sorry Anne, I don't quite follow your meaning," Henry cautiously replied.

"Come, come Henry, I know men talk of such things, you and Charles have been close friends since you met at university, I am sure at some point he must have confided in you."

Henry was embarrassed; his sister's remark implied she knew long before he did of a connection between Charles and Lydia Morgan. Anne noticed her brother's embarrassment and smiled coyly.

Anne continued with delight, "Henry, if indeed you are at a loss, which I cannot believe, let me enlighten you."

Henry nodded, if Anne already knew something of the connection between Charles and Lydia, it would greatly ease his task, and so he encouraged her to carry on.

"From the first day she arrived here, I always liked Lydia, such a pretty, pleasant soul, but when she made that dreadful error of getting herself pregnant by a farmhand, propriety demanded that she be dismissed and left our service, not to put too fine a point on it she was missed a great deal. It was such an unfortunate affair; I believe the result of a moment's madness after one of those servants's party Charles insisted we gave. After her baby was born, I learned that the father of the child had been taken ill and died before they married, and that she was now living in a little cottage, here, on the estate. I discussed it with Charles that perhaps we should allow her to return, he was always very prudish and strict about propriety, I never expected him to agree, but he did."

"It was your idea for her to return then?"

"Yes Henry, it was, and it wasn't long before I noticed how happy Charles became again once she was back here, the cottage she moved into is very close, it is just along a path into Bluebell Wood, she still lives there, but at that time she came in to work as a daily."

"I think I know the one you mean," Henry remarked hypocritically, settling back he was anxious to hear more.

"The other servants did not like the idea of her being allowed back, a fallen woman, and all that nonsense, it was not long before some of them took it upon themselves to point out to me, and not always subtly, she and Charles just as they had been before were becoming very close friends again."

"And you did nothing about it?"

"Of course I did silly, but not what you would probably expect brother, set in the wood panelling opposite Charles's rooms is a concealed doorway, behind which is a very narrow staircase to the floor above, do you know it?"

Henry shook his head; he was not that familiar with the layout of the hall above ground level.

"There is a very nice room at the top of that auxiliary stairway, I took the trouble to have it decorated and fitted out comfortably. When it was finished, I suggested to Charles that perhaps Lydia could stay here at the hall sometimes, to be on hand when I had guests, and we should assign a room for her use whenever she was here. Everyone who visited seemed to like her; she is always so cheerful and very efficient, a great asset. I went on to suggest, that I recognised her abilities and I would like her to take charge of running the household on those occasions. I proposed if he agreed to her taking charge, she should have a room of her own, she would be in charge of the house so it should be away from the other servant's quarters, and not on the same floor, I suggested the room above his own may be suitable."

"And he agreed?"

"Of course he did silly, why wouldn't he, I'm not blind Henry, there had been a closeness between them for years, I noticed it developing a few months after she first came here. The only thing I never understood was how Charles, being the man he was, could ever forgive her indiscretion with that labourer, but he did. Their relationship in no way threatened my marriage; Charles was always very considerate and attentive to me. With Lydia here so often staying in the room above his own, he was much happier and contented, thankfully, Lydia kept him that way, and it was much better for me that she did, her being here relieved me of certain duties expected of a wife. I found myself quite content with the situation."

"One thing puzzles me Anne, if you have known for—"

"Twenty two years," interrupted Anne.

"Charles, was he aware that you knew?" asked Henry, bemused; Charles had not told him Anne knew of his affair with Lydia.

"I never told him, it would have spoiled everything, you know how puritanical Charles could be, his knowing I was aware of his involvement with Lydia would have made him feel guilty, and he may have put an end to it, no, we never spoke of it, and I don't think he ever guessed that I knew either."

Henry felt relief surging through his whole being, the unpleasantness he anticipated arising from telling his sister that Charles, secretly before hand, and also in his will, had made generous provisions for one of their servants, was swiftly becoming none existent. How much more was there she already knew, it was apparent Anne did not know the facts regarding Zack's birth, that point, as he promised Lydia, he could keep to himself.

"Anne, Charles spent quite a lot of time away from home over the past few years—."

His sister raised her hand to stop his further observations.

"Yes, yes, I know, and I confess I encouraged him in that also, when we first married I went with him on one occasion, but, I never enjoyed travel, I much prefer to sit comfortably at home, it became obvious Charles's pleasure would be far greater with Lydia as his travelling companion than me reluctantly accompanying him as his wife."

"Companion?" repeated Henry.

"Oh, very well," Anne scowled, "if you must be pedantic, his surrogate wife."

"Just one point Anne, I presume your son is in ignorance of this matter."

"Yes Henry, he most definitely is and he must remain so, it grieves me to admit that he has a vengeful nature, he would never allow himself to understand the way I feel, he would never allow Lydia near the place again, and then how on earth would I cope with running this house?"

"And you still want Lydia in your home when you have visitors."

"Why yes, of course, I am very fond of her, she has done me many great services over the years. I have my comfortable home, our family estates have been linked by marriage as you and father wanted, for my part, I have enjoyed a marriage of convenience, without any of those bedroom attentions from a man that I find repulsive. Oh yes Henry, I am quite happy and content."

"Anne, you have astonished me, you knew all this time, I only learned some of the things you have told me after Charles became ill, yes, you have astonished me, and that's a fact."

"Yes dear little brother of mine, I thought I might, and I suppose as the executor of Charles's will, you now have to tell me he made some provision for Lydia. But I tell you now, if I ever learn it is not enough for her to continue life as she has come to know it, I shall either ask her to come and live here permanently as my companion, and make sure she is provided for after I am gone."

Brother and sister returned to the drawing room, Henry, his head spinning, still totally aghast at these further revelations from within his family, desperately hoping there would not be more. He always considered himself an expert at intrigue and manipulation, his sister, who everyone believed to be demure, had now proved she could teach him a few things when it came to getting her own way.

Anne Heath, taking great delight in her brother's obvious disillusionment, settled into her chair by the fireside.

"Now Henry," she purred, "It is your turn; my son does not appear to be in any hurry to return home, is there anything you wish to tell me? Or, should we wait until Charles is present?"

Henry, his head still reeling from the disclosure of his sisters scheming over the past decades, found some difficulty in responding.

"Under the circumstances Anne, it may be best if I share with you the details as they stand at present, you must understand that there is still much to do before anything is finalised."

"I will do my best Henry," replied his sister.

"The point is where do I begin?"

"Henry, my dear, begin at the beginning, and end at the end, but do try to keep it simple and brief, I am rather tired, and you know I always take a rest in the afternoon."

Henry decided the best place to start would be with the things Anne seemed to be expecting.

"You are right Anne; Charles has made provision for Lydia Morgan, he has set aside a sum of money, the interest off which should be enough for her to live comfortably for life. The cottage she lives in, and the land on which it stands he left to her.

"I am pleased to hear that, but is there not a chance now he is squire, my son may change that?"

"No, he cannot, the cottage, and several other parts of your estate were placed in trust last year, management of which was transferred to me and the legal bods."

"Other parts, in trust to you, why?" inquired a puzzled Anne.

"As a safeguard, although Charles said that he would like to be, he was not convinced that your son would be able to run the estate efficiently, his fear was it would all be gambled away and your son would not provide for you. In anticipation of that happening, he transferred enough land and other holdings to me to manage temporarily on your behalf, the proceeds from which will ensure your security and comfort during your life."

"During my life, that is an interesting turn of phrase Henry, in my state of health that may not be very long, I have faced my end a number of times already," Anne added pessimistically.

"Yes and every time you have beaten it, as I am sure you will do again, and again," reassured her brother.

"Maybe so brother, but that time will come as it does to us all, what is to happen to the property you hold for me when it does? It will be returned to Charles, right?"

"Providing he settles down, and can prove himself capable as a man of business, marries and produces an heir to the estate, yes. Otherwise, which I trust is unlikely; other arrangements are in place to ensure—the estate survives," Henry had nearly slipped up by saying, 'the bloodline survives'. His sister must not know Charles had, not only temporarily deposited some little moneys in trust for all the illegitimate grandchildren he knew of, and the interest on which was being used for their education and care. There was also the provision that, if her son failed, as he probably would, the remainder of the estate now in Henry's care, after Anne's death, would eventually fall to Lydia's son. As his sons grew up, Charles had ensured Zack's early education was equal to that of the new squire; it may have been different if his eldest son had not been sent down from university for laziness and immoral behaviour, which left the two boys still on a virtual equal academic footing. Charles just prior to his death, charged Henry with the task of guiding both his sons in the ways of business, and, with some reservation, Henry had agreed.

"Henry, my son will not be best pleased when he learns of this," Anne said woefully.

"That is precisely the point Anne, he is not to know, how will he be able to prove his worth and increase his holdings, if he knows there is a considerable sum of money being retained for you, he will not even try to succeed, will he?"

"That is cruel and unkind Henry, but, on reflection, probably true, even now he frequently complains that his father's will is taking too long to be finalised. Are you allowed to tell me how much of the estate passes to him to manage?

"After Charles had provided and set aside what he considered sufficient for you know who, an audit was made of all remaining funds and holdings, your son will get about sixty per cent of the remaining total, and the other forty is to provide for you."

"Was?" Anne queried.

"Unfortunately, of all that was allocated to his share, the item which was producing the highest regular yield, was the coal mine at Heals End."

"And that blew up yesterday," observed his sister dispassionately.

Henry nodded, "Even if the mine never produces coal again, he still has ample to provide for his own and all your needs, and, if he marries well, a woman of substance, you know what I mean."

"Yes, like his father and me."

"Precisely," Henry confirmed, delighted his sister was absorbing this information much better than he expected.

"I am not overjoyed at the possible prospect of relying on you for money Henry; it will be embarrassing to keep asking."

"You will not need to, a number of our holdings are jointly held, and providing he will listen to me, I promised Charles to guide my nephew as best I can on how to make his money work for him. Your forty percent will be administered in a similar manner to the way Charles made good your son's extravagance over the past years, but this time, the lawyers will also be involved, they are to make sure your expenses are met from out of the funds I hold for you, that money cannot be used for anything else."

"I think I understand, if my son finds difficulty funding the running of my home, the money will be released from that which you hold for me, I need do nothing more than I have always done?"

"Now you have it Anne, that's the way dear old Charles left it, any failure on my nephews part you pass on to the lawyers and they will attend to it, you carry on living as you always have."

"But my son is not to know of these arrangements; will I be allowed to—will he be able to use any of my funds for the estate if he does fall into difficulty?"

"No, as I said, not during your lifetime, that will defeat the object, providing he is a success, when you have no further need for them the trust holdings will be returned to this estate. Charles must have given this a great deal of thought; he seems to have provided adequately for everyone."

"When do you intend to tell Lydia she is provided for by Charles's will?"

Henry replied, tongue in cheek, "Very soon, she will know very soon."

"And the rest of the estate, when will my son be able to claim his inheritance, he has just acquired a lovely new motor car and two new hunting horses, but he is waiting for his father's money to come to him to pay for them."

In annoyance, Henry replied. "Anne, I rest my case, he is still spending money he does not have."

"This is all very perplexing Henry; would you think me very rude if I went to take my rest now?"

"Not at all my dear, I quite understand, I have to return to the mine this afternoon anyway, and it does not look as though my nephew is going to return today after all."

Henry took his leave of his sister and began his plod up the steep snow covered hill back to the place where he parked his car.

* * *

Any Sabbath Day was always treated with a degree of reverence in small Mining Communities such as those villages within Broughton Parish, customarily following The Bible's teachings, that, the seventh day should be one of rest. In truth, these villages existed on what, over time, had come to be known in that locality as the three C's, coal, chapel and cricket.

Sunday 13th January in the Swindon household began in the traditional manner, though perhaps a little more sombre than normal. By six thirty, Eve and Evie were up lighting fires, cleaning, dusting and tidying the house before the men folk came down for breakfast. For the majority of village women their lives were simple, what they lacked in materiel things they made up for by taking pride in their home, competition for cleanliness between them was fierce, especially on the Sabbath. In the event a neighbour or friend happened to call on their way to, or from Chapel, any speck of dust, or anything appearing to be out of its place, any visitor might regard the woman of the house to be in neglect of her duties, irreverently tagging her as one who kept a dirty house.

Mother and daughter worked together in almost complete silence, Evie, aware something out of the ordinary troubled her mother, watched her very closely, patiently waiting for a chance to learn the reason.

Their work completed, Eve scrutinised their efforts, it was to her satisfaction, now they could sit at the back kitchen table for their breakfast of tea and toast.

"You are very quiet this morning mother, are you not feeling well?" asked Evie.

"Sorry child, yes, I am well enough, I am just troubled by the events of yesterday, I cannot help feeling sorry for those who lost their loved ones in that explosion."

"Oh yes, I can understand that, lucky for us father and Elijah were not down below when it happened. I haven't heard of anyone we know being hurt or lost, come to think of it, I haven't heard of anyone at all, but I know lots of men were injured, and a good many must have died."

"Yes Evie, they did, but up until the time I left the pit bank yesterday, no names had been released, the families of those men who have not returned home must be beside themselves with worry."

Evie, capable, willing girl though she was, still did not relish the prospect of having to look after her young sister again today, yesterday had proved trying enough, Fanny's laziness tried her patience to the limit.

"Mother," she began tactfully, "Father asked me to look after Fanny this afternoon because you are going to Bursley to see our Emily, surely, Emily won't be expecting you to make the journey in this weather, will she?"

Eve did not reply immediately.

"Are you still planning on going?" the girl persisted.

Eve, somewhat despondently eventually replied, "Yes, we must go."

Evie was quick to notice both her mother's tone and mood.

"Must go?" repeated the girl.

Eve, to mask her feelings, forced her tone of voice to sound more cheerful, "Yes, I think so, the weather is not too bad today, and I wrote to Emily telling her to meet the noon train, yes, we will be going."

Elijah appeared in the kitchen doorway, dressed in his everyday clothes, carrying his Sunday best suit on its hanger, he looked at his mother enquiringly, but before he could speak, Eve rose from the table and answered his unasked question.

"Yes Lijah, we have finished if you want to brush your suit on the table."

A man brushing his Sunday best suit was a custom, which, over time had evolved into an unwritten rule. Best clothes were kept as best, worn only to attend a place of worship on Sunday, or on any other occasion for which services were held. Men rarely undertook any household chores, but, they fastidiously brushed their own best suits before they were worn, and again when removed, before the suit of clothes was put away until the next week.

The suit finished to his satisfaction Lijah returned upstairs to put it on, at the top of the stairway, he met his father carrying his own Sunday best on its hanger.

"Morning father, won't you be cutting it a bit fine, going to morning service and make it down to the station by noon?"

Fanny, inquisitive as ever popped her head around her bedroom door; Sam spotted her before he quietly replied.

"We have done it before lad, but with this snow on the ground you may be right."

Sam joined his wife and daughter in the back kitchen, he gestured to Eve he wanted to speak to her in private, she understood, and nodded.

"Evie dear," she said, "Will you take some kindling, and light a fire in the front room so that Fanny can do her practice when she comes back from Sunday School."

Evie whinged inaudibly under her breath, "Of course, madam lazy bones must have a fire lit for her," she reluctantly complied.

"What is it Sam?" asked Eve when they were alone.

Expecting strong opposition to the idea, Sam ventured, "Lijah just made a very good point, if this morning's preacher is long winded and it is a long service, in this weather we may not catch the train to Bursley."

"Are you suggesting we miss Chapel?" snapped Eve in disbelief.

Sam added cautiously, "I don't want to, but under the circumstances, don't you think catching that train has to be more important than chapel today?"

Eve's tone softened, "Yes, yes, of course, you are right; we must get to Emily before she finds out from somewhere else."

The front room fire lit, Evie reappeared in the back kitchen, Sam his suit now brushed and replaced on its hanger left the room, as he did so, he called back to his daughter.

"Evie, you haven't forgotten you are looking after Fanny this afternoon have you?"

"No father, I hadn't, I will if I have to, but I had thought of coming to chapel with you and mother and then going to see some of my friends this afternoon, it will be a while before I am home again."

"May be not that long Evie," said her mother without realising what she said, "Anyway, with the weather as it is, father and I have decided to give chapel a miss this morning, we don't want to miss the noon train."

Fanny, already dressed in her best and ready for Sunday School, joined her sister in the back kitchen, the youngster learned a long time ago, if she wore her best clothes all day Sunday, no one would ask her to do anything which might get them dirty.

"What's going on Evie, why is everybody talking, whispering and then shutting up when I come into the room?" asked the youngster.

"I don't know Fanny, but they are doing the same to me, and now mother has just told me they are not going to chapel this morning."

"What! But they never miss chapel, something else must be wrong," persisted Fanny.

"I thought that as well, I asked mother earlier, but she said she was just concerned for the families of the men killed at the pit yesterday," replied the older girl.

"Perhaps that's all it is, and then, perhaps there is something they don't want us to know, they were going to take me with them to see Emily you know, but now they say I can't go because of the bad weather."

Evie sarcastically rebuked, "Well Fanny, if you will catch so many colds, what do you expect?"

"Wait a minute, you say you were going with them, and now you're not, mother is concerned about the families of the men lost at the pit, bad weather or not they say they must go to see Emily,—Ah Hah, I wonder?" she said, a snippet of what was said yesterday morning had entered her head. Evie reeled on the younger girl before Fanny had chance to pick up on her train of thought, and immediately changed the subject.

"Do you want some breakfast before Sunday School Fanny?

"Yes please Evie," said Fanny, seating herself at the table waiting for it to appear.

The mantle clock struck nine thirty, Elijah, ready to go, had, as usual to wait for Fanny to ready herself for their walk up to the Sunday school. Fanny was normally the first to appear when things did not concern her, but she was always the last to be ready if she had to go anywhere, often making the family late.

With Fanny's departure the remaining three Swindon's settled in the living room for a welcome hour of piece and quiet, Sam in his chair by the fireside reached for his pipe and pouch, his decision not to attend morning service allowed him time for at least two pipes before he needed to change into his best clothes. Mother and daughter, sat at the table, Evie chattering about things that had happened at work since she was last at home, Eve, her mind on other things, only partially paid attention.

"Evie, hadn't you better be getting ready for chapel?" asked Sam after about three-quarters of an hour.

"I was going to go father, but I can't now, I have to look after Fanny don't I, you know she won't go into chapel if mother isn't there, she will come straight home."

"We had better get ready Sam, no point in missing services is there if we have to rush down the bank after all?" observed Eve.

Sam obediently knocked out his pipe on the hearth and disappeared upstairs to change into his suit, closely followed by his wife.

"Any idea how we can tell Emily when we get there lass?" asked Sam.

"I've racked my brain Sam, but I can think of nothing, no way at all of broaching the subject."

"Same here," confirmed Sam, "But I certainly don't want her to read Jim Porter's name in the Sentinel as being one of those lost, and it's not the kind of thing you can put in a letter."

They returned downstairs to find Evie preparing the vegetables for dinner, she looked up as her parents re-appeared.

"Is it that piece of Brisket on the stillage for dinner mother?" she asked.

"Yes, it is, I had better get it into the oven before we go."

"Don't bother, I can do it, you have your best things on," replied the girl.

"Thank you dear, I really should have done it before I got changed,—"

"But you have other things on your mind this morning," interrupted Evie. "This trip of yours to Bursley, has it anything to do with Jim and Emily?"

"You are brash today young lady," snapped Sam.

To save the girl from a scolding, Eve intervened, "Leave it Sam, she is being helpful, and it's obvious she has guessed why we have to go."

Sam reclaimed his chair, and lit his pipe before he continued.

"Our Lijah knows, but we could lose our jobs if we tell anyone local before the bosses are ready to release details, so tell no one, nevertheless, we thought it's best if Emily hears this news from us."

Evie asked apprehensively, "How badly is he hurt?"

Neither parent answered her, which in itself was answer enough.

"Oh, I see, he's . . ."

"Yes, he is, Lijah found him," interrupted Sam, "The choke damp got him, but judging by how we found him, it would have been quick."

Evie had never been one to show emotion even when she felt it, this was no exception; without further comment, she continued to prepare the mid-day meal.

His pipe of twist finished, Sam pulled aside the curtain hanging from the shelf by his chair, reached underneath it for his own, and Eve's best boots, both pairs were freshly blacked, and shone almost enough for him to see his reflection in them.

"I cleaned those while you were upstairs; I thought you would be wearing them today," Evie said dispassionately, this had always been one of her chores before she left home.

Sam nodded approvingly, "Better get our coats on now Eve, it will probably be slippery under foot walking down to the station, we won't be able to rush today," he said.

Dressed in their best, and wearing their thickest warm winter coats, around his neck, Sam rapped a white silken scarf that he wore more for show than warmth. Eve wearing her favourite bonnet, her handbag looped on her forearm, and her hands tucked into a black woollen muff, stood ready and waiting as Sam flicked a stiff brush around his bowler hat to bring up the nap and remove any dust.

Fanny burst in through the backdoor as her parents were about to leave.

A little breathlessly, she gasped, "Lijah has gone into chapel with his mates from 'The Brotherhood,' and because you weren't there this morning he sent me home. Are you just off now mother? Are you sure I can't come with you, I would like to see Emily."

"Not today Fanny, you stay here with Evie where it's warm," her father replied sternly.

On his way through the door, Sam turned, looking towards Evie, placed his forefinger to his lips. The girl smiled, inclining her head slightly forward to indicate she understood his instruction. If Fanny learned the true reason for her parent's journey, she would be unable to resist chattering to her friends, the news would be all along the street before Sam and Eve reached the railway station.

Chapter Eight

On the platform of Bursley Railway Station, Emily Swindon stood patiently waiting for the noon train from her home village to draw in.

Most young men of her village viewed Emily's departure from Augers Bank to enter into domestic service a monumental loss; many considered it was almost a crime, it was generally acknowledged Emily was by far the prettiest of all the Swindon girls, and quite possibly the most alluring miner's daughter the village had produced in many years.

Emily was not overly tall; she stood about five feet six inches and possessed a classical full figure, her face rounded, her features undeniably exquisite, add to this a flawless complexion, brown shoulder length hair which she preferred to wear loose, and eyes of steel grey that radiated her gentle, caring, compassionate disposition. Unusual for a girl of her size, Emily was extremely physically fit, giving her a deceptive strength equal to many young men of her age; however from her appearance, no one would ever guess her true physical power, nevertheless, Emily was indeed an extremely desirable young woman.

Unlike other people on the station platform, the cold never bothered Emily. With its eventual delayed arrival, she surveyed the three-carriage length train for a door to open and her parents to alight. Emily called and waved as they emerged, hurrying along the platform to greet them, kissed her mother, and rather excitedly exclaimed.

"I wasn't sure you would be able to come after all with all this snow about, it's fairly bad here, but I'll dare bet much worse at home."

Skilfully sidestepping any public display of affection from his daughter, Sam glanced around, "It is a lot worse at home than it seems to be here lass," he agreed.

"Your mother wrote to you telling you to meet this train, so, we decided we had to come anyway in spite of this weather."

"That's thoughtful of you dad, I haven't been on the station long myself, I had to take my time walking down, the roads seem alright but the paths are slippery. I am afraid there are not many places open today; I had thought we could have a nice walk in the park, or something, but with all this snow, perhaps that isn't such a good idea. Shall we have a cup of tea and a plate of cakes in the station buffets first, my treat?"

"If you wish," replied Eve, "But save your money, I will pay."

Sam settled himself at a corner table in the station buffet, while his wife and daughter placed their order with the counter staff. During their short train journey, Eve had strongly advised Sam not to say anything; he was to leave it to her to break their news to their daughter. Sam lacked, as did most men, the tact and discretion needed in such delicate circumstances, but if Emily should ask, Eve thought given the distance from Heals End, it may help to ease the situation if he told their daughter any details of the accident he could.

Apart from the three members of the Swindon family, the buffet bar was empty. As he waited for his tea, Sam could not help but ponder just how Eve would broach the subject, telling the girl of her fiancé's death would not be easy, and ultimately very distressing for them all. From his vantage point, he could see Emily chattering happily to her mother the way she usually did; obviously, rather than immediately blurting out what they had come to tell her, Eve would wait for a suitable opportunity.

Eve brought his tea over to him, and scowled at the sight of his pipe and tobacco pouch on the table, reluctantly, Sam returned them to his pocket.

"Well?" asked Sam.

"Not yet, she has too much to tell me about work and things, be patient," replied his wife.

The family group sat for some time at their table, and indeed, Emily proved to have a great deal to say to her mother. The topics of Emily's rapid conversation Sam considered to be, of that generalised nature he classified as 'woman's talk', he remained silent, wishing Eve had allowed him to light his pipe, sat in his corner uneasily fiddling with the starched collar of his shirt. They had almost finished their refreshments, when, Emily stopped her trivia chatter and addressed her father directly.

"Father, while I was tidying up the drawing room this morning, I saw in the 'stop press' of the master's Sentinel that there was an accident or something at Tilly yesterday, were you below ground when it happened?"

Glancing pensively at his wife, Sam shook his head in a negative response.

Without waiting for a verbal response from her father, the girl continued, "It can't be too serious though, the paper didn't say very much about it at all, just a few lines."

Emily herself had raised the subject of the accident at Tilly, although a public station buffet was less than a convenient place, here, was a possible opportunity to impart their news, but the question was directed towards Sam and not Eve, this made him feel even more uncomfortable. Before he could find any suitable words to answer his daughter, Eve stepped in and parried the question.

"No, he wasn't there when it happened, your father and Elijah were due in on noons but they were fetched into work early, around ten o'clock yesterday morning. Rescue teams had to go down to find out what had happened, but regardless of what it said in the paper Emily, it was a big explosion, but until the owners have officially released details, your father isn't allowed to talk about it."

"Oh! I see," replied the girl, she remembered the same situation arising from the accident of three years ago, "It doesn't matter, I had a letter from Jim on Friday, he is coming over to see me this evening, the letter says he has some good news for me, I will ask him if he knows anything."

Sam's apprehension grew, would Eve take this opportunity, or, would she wait until a place could be found where it was less likely for members of the public to enter at any moment. Perhaps it would be better if somewhere more secluded and private could be found; at present Emily was in a joyful mood, but too long a delay before telling her would be unkind.

"Emily my dear, I think I would like to take that walk around the park, perhaps some people are skating on the lake and we could watch them, your father may be able to tell you a little about yesterday in a more private place," Eve suggested.

Emily smiled approvingly, "I would like that," she said, "And then if you don't want me to walk back down to the station with you when you leave, I shall be three parts the way back to the master's house."

As the three left the buffet, Sam whispered to Eve, "I thought you . . ."

His wife interrupted him, "Yes, yes, I will, but not here, let me choose the time and place."

Emily's cheerful chatter continued as they walked to, and around the park, happily, she related trivial events at her workplace, inquired after her brother and three sisters, but with no further mention of the pit, to her topics of conversation Eve managed to respond in a like manner. Sam, feeling evermore awkward as the time went on proffered very little input, responding only in the briefest polite manner to direct questions.

Emily was well aware her father was a man of very few words, but is was not long before she became aware, today; he was quiet even by his standards. They found a secluded, sheltered seat near the top gate of the park.

"Let us sit here for a while, I need to catch my breath," requested Eve.

Emily sat between her parents; Sam, this time, without intervention from his wife successfully retrieved his beloved pipe from his coat pocket.

Emily laughed, "I was wondering how long it would be before you lit that up father," she said, "Now then, I have given you all my news, and you have told me all about Lijah, Lizzie, Evie and Fanny, what else can we find to talk about?"

Unbeknown to their daughter, Sam and Eve's tension had almost reached breaking point; each taking a long, slow breath, exchanged awkward glances.

"I know mother," Emily cheerfully continued, an idea had occurred to her, "You said father may be able to tell me something about what really happened at the pit yesterday, is this private enough? Or shall I wait to hear about it from Jim when he comes later?"

Eve realised it was now or never, they had come into town today with a purpose, somehow, the girl must now be told.

Eve cautiously inquired, "Emily, in his letter, did Jim say he was coming up to the house, or will you be meeting his train?"

The girl replied, "He didn't say, just that he would be coming on the six o'clock train from Knolsend, I thought I would go down to meet it, if it stays fine that is."

Eve, employing the most sympathetic tone she could muster.

"I'm sorry to be the bearer of this news Emily, but Jim won't be coming tonight, he was on early shift yesterday when the accident happened."

Emily's happy chatter ceased and her face took on a look of bewilderment.

Eve took her daughters hand as she continued, "An awful lot of men were trapped, injured and worse by the explosion."

Realisation of her mother's meaning began to dawn upon her, Emily gasped and the colour drained from her face.

"Are you trying to tell me Jim has been injured? Is he badly hurt? Did you see him at the pit yesterday father?"

Sam quietly and deliberately removed his pipe from his mouth, faced his daughter, and nodded affirmatively in answer to her questions, but, following Eve's implicit instructions to guard his words, he hesitated before speaking.

Emily's gaze reeled from her father, to her mother, and back again, neither parent able to find any immediate appropriate words of succour to offer, or ability to give any answer at all to Emily's panic driven questions. A pregnant silence ensued, which to those present seemed to be an age, but was no more than a second or two at most.

"No!—No, he's not," Emily gasped, sudden realisation of the reason for her father's distant gruff manner today hit her like a steam train, emotion welled up within her, she sat motionless in utter disbelief.

Despite Eve issuing strict instructions to Sam that he must allow her to break the details of their dreadful news to Emily, strong though she was, unable to control her own emotions and choking back her own tears, she was unable to complete her self-appointed task, she could not speak.

Sam, soon realised this odious task had fallen to him after all, he spoke quietly, "I'm sorry lass,—we're sorry, but we didn't want you to learn about Jim from casualty lists in the paper, they will probably start printing them tomorrow, or Tuesday, and this news isn't something that your mother could put in a letter."

Dazed, Emily muttered, "Oh mother, no, no, not my Jim, why Jim, no."

Mother and daughter hugged each other, tearfully trying to console one another; Sam could do nothing except look on and wait for any opportunity where he might offer what comfort he could to his daughter. Sitting on a park bench next to two weeping women he felt self-conscious and embarrassed, furtively, he looked around, not a single soul in sight or sound of where they sat, Eve, at least had chosen a place of seclusion well.

Once her initial shock had passed, Emily still sandwiched between her mother and father on that park bench, gradually began to accept the news brought by her parents. Every woman knew if their men worked below ground, in conditions hazardous, and often very dangerous, accidents of this kind were an inevitable, if unpleasant fact that they must accept. After about five or six minutes, mother and daughter had calmed enough to release each other, reaching her handkerchief from her bag, Emily, dried her eyes and turned to face her father.

"You saw him, you are quite sure?" she asked.

Sam nodded affirmatively, and once again removed his beloved pipe from his mouth, but before she allowed her father to speak, Emily continued.

"Was he,—was he badly mutilated by the explosion?"

Sam shook his head, offered a comforting smile and gently replied.

"No lass, there was hardly a mark on him, it was Lijah who found him and fetched me over, as far as we could make out, the explosion happened at snap time down deep in one of the far workings. Jim was sitting with two other men in an offshoot junction not far from pit bottom eating his snapping. The rush of choke damp must have been sudden and very strong to take them before they could move; because we found them just sitting there with their snap tins open on their laps I think it must have been very quick,."

Emily, after a slight pause for thought, sighed, and steeling herself to the facts, said with resolution.

"If he felt no pain, I suppose that must be a blessing, if losing ones life can ever be thought of as a blessing."

All her hopes of happiness and all her plans for the future now cruelly dashed away from her.

The sky darkened, small, light flakes of snow began to fall gently and danced around carried on the slight breeze. Three members of the Swindon family watched the dancing snowflakes in silence, for some reason the beauty of the scene seemed to offer them a little comfort, eventually, Emily realising old mother nature was about to take control and was threatening a heavy storm, stood up.

"This began as such a pleasant afternoon," she said, "Will you walk with me back to the master's house please Father, I need to ask permission, but I am coming home with you."

"If you wish," replied her father, "If that is what you really want but there will be very little you will be able to do. Jim is one of many, all the men brought out are being laid in the Prim's schoolroom, and as far as I know, no families have been informed yet who they are, it may be quite a while before anything can be done. We only know because Lijah and I recognised Jim, and as I said; we didn't want you to find out from the paper. Jim's parents probably still hope he is alive, just trapped somewhere below ground."

"Your father is right my dear," Eve added, "While I was helping out on the pit bank yesterday, survivors were coming up in penny numbers all day."

Emily wheeled on her mother, "You were there, did you see—."

"No, she didn't," Sam answered swiftly, "Elijah and I told your mother what we found when we got back home, but nobody else."

Eve grasped Sam's arm, "Sam, you didn't tell anyone, but, remember, Evie has guessed why we insisted on coming here today."

Emily gave a little sigh, and with just a hint of a smile, "Always was just a little bit too sharp that one, that's my sister, misses nothing and tells you nowt."

Three thirty, with daylight now fast fading away, the three members of the Swindon family approached the servant's entrance to a huge house situated well away from the smoke and soot of the pot bank chimneys on the outskirts of Bursley; this had been Emily's place of work since she was eighteen years old.

It was a truth universally acknowledged; unless in an absolute emergency, family members of those engaged 'in service,' should be discouraged from calling upon their relatives at their place of work. Eve was not comfortable, the reason for their being at Emily's work place did not yet constitute an emergency, although in the very near future it would, whilst for Sam, just being in such close proximity to people of wealth and importance made him very nervous.

As they neared the servant's entrance to the great house, Eve paused, grasped her daughter's arm to halt her step.

"Emily, what do you intend to say, remember, nothing has been released yet about yesterday's accident, don't get your father and brother in any trouble, it's a slim chance I know, but who's to say your master doesn't know the owners of the pit, please be guarded in what you say."

"Don't worry mother, I have thought of that, I will be careful." replied the girl, who, after her initial shock seemed to have gained in strength and composure from the exercise of their silent walk up the hill to this house.

Emily ushered her parents into a passage that led to the kitchen, she asked them to wait while she went further into the house in search of the housekeeper. Within a few moments, she returned, accompanied by the person she sought, Mrs Quint, the housekeeper, a sturdy woman, whose general appearance indicated she was a woman of an uncertain temper.

Addressing Sam and Eve in a gruff manner, "Mister and Misses Swindon," began the housekeeper, "Emily informs me, due to some family crisis she is obliged to request urgent 'leave of absence,' this is not convenient at present, we are expecting a large party of house guests to arrive tomorrow and I shall need all my staff on duty."

Sam was both taken aback and incensed by this pretentious attitude of the housekeeper; Emily had undergone enough distress today without this woman adding to it. After all, she was also a mere servant; just whom did she think she was to speak to them in such a manner. The housekeeper's attitude also annoyed Eve, but having been in service herself, she had encountered this air of self-importance before in servants who had risen to the position Mrs Quint held. Sensing rising anger in Sam, Eve intervened before he said something very inappropriate.

"If you please Ma'am, we do have a genuinely serious problem at home; my daughter does not make her request lightly."

After a slight hesitation, Mrs Quint's attitude seemed to change somewhat, and with just a hint of satisfaction in her voice said.

"Oh, very well, I will consult with the Mistress to see if Emily can be spared."

She instructed Emily to show her parents into a small room which the servants used as a rest room. Returning to the kitchen Mrs Quint was in time to stop the 'tweeny', who today was deputising for Emily from taking the tea tray up to the drawing room.

"I will serve the tea today Sarah," she snapped, dismissing the tweeny.

In the drawing room, Victor Wickersby was seated at a small mahogany desk writing a letter, his wife Charlotte sat embroidering by the fireside as Mrs Quint entered the room.

While she served the tea Mrs Quint, speaking in a far more amiable tone than she used when addressing Sam and Eve said.

"Excuse me ma'am, I need to ask you about a slight staffing problem which has occurred for next week."

Charlotte Wickersby looked up from her embroidery, "Oh, what might that be Quint?" she asked.

"Well Ma'am, you are aware that Emily is to leave us later this year to be married."

"I am, what of it?" Charlotte inquired in anticipation.

"You may recall Ma'am; I mentioned to you some time ago, I have a cousin who has a daughter seeking a placement in service."

"Yes, I have some recollection of that, what has that to do with next week or with Emily for that matter?"

"Today is Emily's afternoon off, she has returned and is downstairs with her parents, there seems to be some sort of crisis involving her family at her home in Augers Bank, and she is requesting leave of absence, am I to allow it?"

"I suppose you must, but it is very vexing, you know I have guests arriving tomorrow, you will have to cope as best you can."

"It will be difficult Ma'am, but it occurred to me, if you gave your consent, it would be an ideal opportunity to give my cousin's girl a trial, and I thought the tweeny could take over Emily's duties."

"Very well Quint, arrange things as you see fit."

"Thank you Ma'am," replied the housekeeper smugly.

As she turned to leave, Victor Wickersby, who had been paying particular attention to the conversation suddenly intervened.

"Wait a moment Quint," he ordered, "You say Emily, and her parents are downstairs?"

"Yes sir," replied the startled housekeeper.

"Ask them to come up," he instructed.

"Here sir, to the drawing room?" blustered Quint.

"Yes Quint, here," reaffirmed the master.

In answer to Charlotte's puzzled expression as the housekeeper left the room, Victor smiled and explained.

"Far be it for me to interfere with your running of the house my dear, but as you know, last night I dined at the 'Castle Hotel' in Castleton with friends from my club. That young Charles Heath fellow was there, not a member of our party of course, but he was there, cruising around the lounge in his irritating manner and making a complete nuisance of himself."

"Charles Heath?" Charlotte repeated the name, trying to recall.

"Yes, you must remember him, tall chap, reddish hair; he was at the Bursley Christmas Ball, paid a lot of attention to our Alexandra, and every other eligible young woman he could latch onto within our social circle."

Recalling the occasion Charlotte replied, "Oh, that oily character, he is handsome enough I suppose, but Alexandra did not like him at all."

"I am very pleased to hear that, by the way, where is Alex?"

"Gone to Potterton to visit the Coleridge sisters, you gave her permission at breakfast for Jenkins to take her in the car, your memory really is getting shocking these days," Charlotte mockingly rebuked.

"So I did, anyway, I was telling you about last night," continued Victor, "That young Heath chap, he was drinking heavily in the lounge bar, and complaining bitterly to anyone who would listen that he owned a coal mine at Heals End, which due to the workers negligence had just been blown up."

"I am afraid I still do not understand," Charlotte persisted.

"Don't you see? Heals End, and Augers Bank are virtually the same place, I am curious, these people may know something about it, if it is the 'Tilly Pit' at Heals End that has gone, that mine has been supplying a large quantity of our fuel to the pottery for years. I will need to find somewhere else able to supply such top grade fuel to replace them, and preferably before our competitors get wind of it."

"Oh, it's business, now I understand," Charlotte replied, and coyly scolding added, "Now Victor my dear, you won't frighten Emily's poor parents, will you?"

"I will do my best not to my dear, and if I am allowed to voice an opinion on another matter, I was not impressed by the way Quint tried to pre-empt the possible absence of Emily to sneak one of her relations into this house, one of her is quite enough thank you."

"Oh Victor, I think you exaggerate."

"Perhaps I do, I know Quint came here with you, and that you have a tendency to rely on her. I have always found her a little too surly and fierce for my liking, and what's more she has got a lot worse since her husband took off with that barmaid from 'The Bull's Head', although I can't say I blame him for that, might have done the same in his place."

"Victor, really, was that called for," scolded Charlotte.

Below stairs, a grumpy, red-faced Mrs Quint re-entered the servant's rest room, Emily recognised that face, and knew only too well, in such a mood, she should not be crossed.

With extreme caution Emily asked, "May I go home Mrs Quint?"

The housekeeper glared at her and snorted in disgust.

"I do not know, the mistress had agreed, but then the master for some reason intervened, he wishes to speak with you, you are to go to the drawing room," growled Quint.

"I will change as fast as I can Mrs Quint," replied a very bemused Emily.

"No time for that, you will not need your uniform, you are to go up at once and you are to take your parents with you," Quint snapped, her annoyance at this development becoming extremely evident.

Both Sam and Eve, very hesitant to comply looked wide-eyed at each other; this was entirely unexpected.

Sam muttered under his breath to Eve, "Oh my Lord, whatever does he want us for?"

"No idea; doesn't look good though does it?" she replied.

"Go! Go now, don't keep the master waiting," Quint snarled angrily, "You may leave your top coats in here; Emily will show you the way," that said, she left them alone in the room.

Before Mrs Quint had taken many steps along the servant's passageway, she had second thoughts and waited for them. Emily was a good worker but she had never been one of her favourites, Emily was far too pretty, and Mrs Quint did not intend to pass up any opportunity of replacing her, by accompanying them to the drawing room she would not need to ask later of the outcome.

Climbing the main stairway, Eve whispered to her daughter.

"I hope our being here has not made things awkward for you my dear, what is your master like?"

In bewilderment, Emily replied, "Normally, very polite and gentlemanly, but I can't think why he has sent for you as well."

Reaching the drawing room door, Mrs Quint tapped upon it, opened it and entered, instructing Sam, Eve and Emily to follow.

"Emily and her parent's ma'am, sir," she announced to the room, Sam awkwardly attempted a respectful bow of his head, but Eve had not forgotten the art of the bob curtsy, whilst Emily's actions were autonomic.

To the surprise of the four entrants to the room, Victor Wickersby acknowledged the housekeeper's announcement.

"Thank you Quint, you may leave us."

Household staffing matters normally fell to the mistress of the house, who, on this occasion merely smiled acknowledgement of their entrance, and continued with her embroidery.

Quint looked towards her mistress in anticipation of a contradiction to the master's dismissal; however, none was forthcoming.

"Thank you Quint," Victor repeated in a sterner tone, she bobbed, scowled and left the room.

"Emily, we are given to understand there is some difficulty at home and that you have requested leave," Victor began, as he arose from his chair and crossed the room.

Emily bobbed again, "Yes sir, my parent's have brought news of a distressing nature from—," but before she could finish, Victor had crossed the drawing room and extended his hand to Sam.

"Mr Swindon, delighted to meet you," he said, Sam shook the unexpected offered hand, which was then offered to Eve, in embarrassment she took it and bobbed once more, Victor continued as he indicated in the direction of a settee, "Mrs Swindon, delighted, please be seated."

Sam and Eve, though baffled by this reception followed the instruction. Charlotte in despair shot a side-glance to her husband, he was attempting to comply with her request not to frighten their unexpected visitors, but he was overdoing it, treating them as, and expecting them to behave in the way members of their own class would, he was most probably terrifying them. Emily, looked on in disbelief, and remained standing; Victor Wickersby turned and spoke to her.

"Emily," he said, indicating she was to sit with her parents, astounded by this instruction, she could not move, Victor indicated again, Emily looked to her mistress for confirmation, to which Charlotte smiled warmly motioning to her to sit as invited.

Charlotte covering her mouth coughed as if to clear her throat, an action intended for the sole purpose of catching her husband's eye, as their eyes met, her familiar 'the look' indicating her disapproval Victor took as a warning that perhaps he was going a little too far, as usual it had the desired effect and he restrained his gusto.

Victor spoke in a friendly, subdued tone, "Emily, I can see that you are distressed, may I enquire the nature of the problem which calls you home?"

Sam and Eve, ill at ease with their current environment, worried in case their daughter let slip some snippet of information not yet in the public domain, and which, by rights, she should not know.

"Begging your pardon sir," Emily answered confidently, with complete trust in her master.

"My parents have brought news of an accident at the coal mine at home, it was mentioned in the 'stop press' of last evening's newspaper sir, my fiancé was working on the early shift when it happened, and he has been—," Emily paused, choked by emotion and trying not to show it. Taking heed of her mothers warning not to give away too much information, she began again.

"I meant to say sir, my father and brother were part of a rescue team which were sent down to investigate, but, my fiancé has not yet returned to the surface."

"I see," replied their host, turning to Sam, "Some men have been trapped in the mine, is that the case?"

Sam taken off guard by a question put directly to him, replied without thought, "Aye sir, and much more besides."

Victor began to quiz Sam, "You have been below ground since the explosion Mr Swindon?"

"As Emily said sir, my son and I were part of a rescue squad, but Emily never said anything about an explosion," this time, Sam replied more carefully.

Victor smiled, "I am aware of that Mr Swindon, but others have, I take it the outcome is of a serious nature, many men trapped, injured, dead even?"

Emily could restrain her tears no longer, as she buried herself in Eve's comforting embrace.

Charlotte, closely observing events as they transpired, intervened.

"Victor," she beckoned him to her, and speaking softly to avoid the visitors overhearing, pointed out to her husband those little nuances a man would not notice but a woman would, meanwhile, Sam and Eve tried to console their daughter.

"Mr Swindon, a word in private if you please," Victor requested, taking Sam to the far side of the drawing room.

"I have an impression I have not been given the full facts on this matter, my good lady suggests, the reasons Emily gave are rather short of the truth, you have brought her news which she has not, or, cannot relay to us at this time?"

"Cannot sir," Sam replied, expecting wrath and retribution from the master of the house.

"Am I to take it the actual meaning of Emily's words 'has not yet returned', means in fact he will never return, and that you are in possession of these facts because you were there at the time, but are not permitted to divulge?"

Sam inhaled slowly and lowered his head in silence.

"I see," acknowledge Victor, nodding towards his wife to confirm her suspicions were correct, "I heard someone say the explosion was due to the negligence of the men.

Sam stiffened, "Certainly not, no man working below ground can be negligent, all our lives depend on each other, if there was negligence, and I am not saying there was, it was not on the part of the miners."

"I thought that may be the case Mr Swindon but you know how rumours fly; will the mine ever reach full production again?"

"For my part sir, I would very much doubt it," Sam replied, now a little more at his ease in the company of this illustrious personage.

Charlotte, her suspicions confirmed and knowing by now her husband would have the information he wanted, took control of the situation.

"Emily, you may, of course, take the leave you requested if you wish, but, if you returned with your parents today, will you be able to do anything to ease the situation? You are aware we have many guests arriving this week, perhaps, under the circumstances, it may be for the best if you keep yourself occupied here, you may, of course, return home the moment you have any more definite detailed news."

To allow a little privacy for their visitors, Charlotte and Victor discreetly moved to the far side of their drawing room.

Eve whispered to her distraught daughter, "That is a very kind offer from your mistress Emily, she is right, there is absolutely nothing you can do at home, what do you think Sam?"

"I think it's up to Emily, but it will be quite a while before any burial arrangements can be made, there will be inquiries, inquests and all that, yesterday we concentrated on looking for, and bringing out survivors, nothing more."

Emily seeing the logic in her parent's remarks, dried her eyes, stood up and addressed her employers.

"If you please ma'am, I believe you are right, it may be better for me to stay here and keep busy, for the time being at least."

Charlotte whispered something to her husband who went over to his desk, whilst she crossed the room towards Emily.

"I think you are right my dear, but, if you feel distressed at any time and wish to be alone, you may go to your room, or go out for a while, I will inform Mrs Quint you have my permission to do either at any time you wish."

Victor came over; and thrust a sheet of paper towards Sam.

"Mr Swindon, these are the private telephone numbers of my factory, and of this house, if you need to get word to Emily urgently, use them, ask for me personally, or my good lady here if need be, and we will make sure Emily is home immediately she is needed."

"That is very generous of you sir," Eve graciously exclaimed.

Sam took the sheet of paper and bowed as best he could; folding and placing the paper in his inside pocket, he took out his watch from his waistcoat.

Noting Sam's obvious concern, Charlotte asked, "You have a train to catch Mr Swindon? "Yes Ma'am, there is one at twenty five to six, but I doubt if we will be able to make it to the station in time, the one after that is something past seven I think," Sam replied.

The drawing room door opened, admitting a very attractive young woman, Alexandra, Charlotte's daughter, followed by a middle-aged man carrying some packages.

"Jenkins, is the car out front?" Victor inquired of the man.

"Yes sir," the servant replied.

"Take Mr and Mrs Swindon to the railway station to catch their train home will you, and if the train has gone, see to it that they get home."

Sam and Eve took their leave of their daughter's employers, and followed the chauffeur to the main hall while Emily scurried off to collect their coats from the servant's quarters, Mrs Quint glared at her as she entered, but before she could question the girl the bell rang summoning Mrs Quint to the drawing room.

Emily escorted her parents through the front door, kissed her mother goodbye and gave her father a big hug.

Eve, naturally concerned for her daughter asked, "Are you sure you will be alright Emily staying here?"

With as much composure as she could muster under the circumstances, Emily assured her, "Yes mother, I think so, like the mistress says, best if I keep myself occupied, you will write and keep me up to date, won't you."

"Write child," her father contested, "I've just been told to use the telephone, it's faster."

Sam looked at the huge shiny black automobile standing in the driveway, the door of which Jenkins now held open for them.

"Never rode in anything like this before," he whispered softly to his wife, "It's a bit different than the tram or a charabanc."

"No, nor I," replied Eve, "Never thought I would either."

"Me neither mother," agreed Emily, "I'll bet there is somebody at home who will turn green with envy when you tell them."

Sam and Eve laughing replied in unison, "Fanny."

Chapter Nine

Thanks to Victor Wickersby's unexpected generosity providing them with transport to the railway station, and by the grace of God, snow and ice on the tracks delaying the train making it five minutes late, Sam and Eve were able to catch the five thirty five train home.

During the Swindon's visit to Bursley, Victor Wickersby's curiosity prohibited them catching their choice of train home, the four o'clock, which enabled them to be home in plenty of time to attend evening service at Chapel. Their walk home from Heals End station took Sam and Eve passed both the Congregational, and the Primitive Chapels; evening services were taking place in each. Eve lingered outside the Primitive, turning to her husband, she said.

"It can't be easy for them to hold services in there Sam, if, as you say most of the dead men have been laid in the schoolroom."

"No, I expect not, but when Lijah and I called in yesterday to give Joe Harris a hand, the corpses were shut away in the back. I expect the doors will have been locked to keep out anyone who shouldn't be in there, it's not a pretty sight you know, but for a while at least the death odour will be masked by that lime we put down."

"I wonder how many poor souls are laid in there now," Eve added as they began to continue their way up the bank, but Eve took only a few steps before she turned, and looking back, asked.

"Do you think young Jim is in there?"

"Quite probably, they are sure to have moved the men from near the pit bottom, but as for how many more have been brought out I shudder to think," was her husbands earnest reply.

A little before seven o'clock Sam and his wife were climbing the steps to their house, from which someone, most probably Evie had the foresight to remove the snow and skitter salt on them. The sound of hymn tunes being played on the piano could clearly be heard as they walked around to the back door. Evie sat at the back kitchen table reading, she rose as her parents entered the house.

"Oh, your back, I thought you were coming home in time for chapel, how did our Emily take the news?" she inquired.

Eve removing her top coat answered, "How do you think child, very badly."

"Yes," added Sam, "But after a while, she seemed to come to terms with it much better than I expected, I have to confess, I was rather proud of her."

Evie continued, "I expected her to come home with you, why hasn't she come?"

Sam sighed as he answered, "What could she do here if she did? Coming home was her immediate reaction, but, nothing as far as I know has been released yet and no one is supposed to know exactly who has been lost. Her mistress suggested, under the circumstances she should stay on there and keep herself busy, try to keep her mind occupied rather than moping about at home, eventually Emily saw some sense in that."

Realising, the sound of the piano had ceased in the front room, Evie lowered her voice to a whisper, before continuing.

"Her mistress's suggestion, she told her then?"

Everyone's eyes drifted towards the back kitchen door, expecting Fanny to appear in the doorway, she did not, instead, a piano arrangement of Handel's 'Largo,' Fanny's set lesson piece for this week could be heard, they all breathed a sigh of relief.

"Emily had to tell them something, she had to give them some reason for asking permission to come home," Eve added in a whisper.

"And Emily came back outside to you and said they talked her out of coming home," Evie persisted.

Sam smirked as he set the girl right, "No lass, we were there with her when she asked."

In amazement, Evie forgetting to keep her voice down retorted.

"What! Mrs Wickersby invited you into their home, never, I don't believe it."

Eve looked anxiously towards the front room door before replying.

"Shh! Keep your voice down, Fanny will think she is missing something and be out here in a shot, yes, Emily took us into that servants passageway at the back of the house, you know the one?"

Evie nodded, she had been there several times to call for her elder sister on their days off.

"The housekeeper, a Mrs Quint, dreadful woman, went to ask their mistress if Emily could come home, next thing we knew, we were all being ushered upstairs to the drawing room."

Evie's jaw dropped in utter amazement, "No way!" she gasped.

"Yes, it's true, and of course, being invited upstairs by Mr and Mrs Wickersby scared your father to death; he's not used to talking to people of that quality."

Sam frowned, and in embarrassment, protested, "I wasn't that bad,—was I?"

"Yes you were, you kept fiddling with your collar, no wonder I have a job getting them clean," Eve replied with a titter.

"But as it turned out they are very nice people, very caring, they even had their chauffeur drive us back to the station."

"Well I'll be damned," exclaimed Evie, "No wonder it's snowing, the sky will turn pink or something in a minute, upper crust people socializing with the likes of us."

With a smirk, Sam corrected his daughter, "Language Evie."

Fanny heard her parent's voices, and as predicted emerged from the front room.

"You're back then; did you have a nice time? Apart from Evie walking down to the pit with me, I've been so bored here; I still say you could have taken me with you to see Emily."

"It was too cold for you to be out long Fanny, we were outdoors most of the time, but it was pleasant to see Emily," Eve responded swiftly changing the subject.

"Outdoors, most of the time," Fanny began suspecting she had in fact missed something.

Sam interceded, "We had a cup of tea in the station buffet when we got there."

"Oh, is that all," Fanny whined and returned to the front room in disappointment.

"Phew! That was close," Evie murmured, "I have kept your dinners for you, I didn't know if you would have anything while you were out, I'll pop them in the oven to warm up."

Up until then, it had not occurred to either Sam or Eve that they were hungry, apart from the cakes in the station buffet; they had eaten nothing since breakfast.

Evie reached out two plates from the pantry stillage, both covered with a tin plate, which when removed revealed what began as an excellent meal, but now rather a sorry looking sight; Sam examined the plates.

"Hmm! I don't know about you Eve my dear, but I fancy something with a bit more taste in it than this warmed up again," he said.

For both mother and daughter, it was easy to anticipate his next remark, Evie smiled and disappeared back into the pantry, and re-emerged with a slab of lard hidden behind her back.

Eve, straight faced asked, "And what might that be Sam?"

Evie, by now had sneaked past them and reached the range, quietly, out of sight of her father she picked up the frying pan.

Sam, fumbled in his pocket for his pipe before continuing, "Well, I was just thinking a—."

Evie turned grinning at her father, the slab of lard in one hand, and the frying pan in the other.

"Good girl, you guessed it, fry it up, and make sure you catch it a bit, give it a bit more flavour," Sam settled into his chair in the kitchen and filled his pipe.

"Elijah gone to chapel Evie?" asked her mother.

"Yes, I was going to go with him, but he said seeing as you weren't back, best if I stayed in with Fanny, he guessed Emily was taking your news badly and he didn't know what time you would get back."

"You and Fanny went for a walk down to the pit bank then?" Eve queried.

"Oh yes," Evie replied, extremely willing to furnish details of her rather trying day with her young sister, "You know how nosey she can be; she insisted on it, she said she was the only one in the house not to have been down there since the explosion."

"Were there as many people down there as yesterday?"

"No mother, very few, there was an awful lot of activity around the reading room though, not the little one by the ironmongers, the one behind the Congregational Chapel. The reporters, ambulance men and such seem to have set up a base there, they probably decided it was too cold for them to stand about outdoors, and there is a telephone in the reading room for them to use I think."

"If by reading room you mean the 'Miners Welfare,' there is a phone in there now; I don't think many people ever use it though because you have to pay."

"Did you manage to find anything out while you were down there?"

"No, nothing we didn't already know, and Fanny soon got bored with there not being much to see, we weren't out all that long. When we got back Fanny disappeared into her hidey-hole in a sulk; she has been in there ever since, apart from when I fetched her out for her tea."

Eve cut some thick slices of bread, and warmed up what was left of the gravy Evie had saved from their lunch for her daughter to add to the frying pan. A distinct combination of aromas filled the kitchen, from the meat and vegetables of the saved meals now mashed together, bubbling and squeaking merrily in the frying pan mingling with that of the 'Twist Tobacco from Sam's pipe.

"Is this done enough for you mother?" Evie asked as she added a little more salt and pepper to the frying pan.

Eve replied chuckling, "Yes that's plenty done enough for me, take half out and keep the rest going a bit longer for your father; you know how he likes it burned a bit at the edges, he moans if he can't see black crusty bits on it."

Sam and Eve sat at the kitchen table enjoying their simple supper, Evie sat with them, as a little treat her supper was some toast with lashings of best butter and her mother's blackberry and apple jam, when the kettle boiled on the stove Evie rose to make a pot of tea.

"Will I see you in the morning father? I have to be back at work by mid-day, what shift are you on?" Evie asked, replacing the kettle on the hearth.

Her father replied, "You'll have to be up early to do that lass, Lijah and I are on early shift tomorrow, no knowing what time we will get back again."

Their suppers finished, Sam settled back into his chair while the womenfolk attended to the dishes, Fanny appeared from the front room carrying a coal bucket.

"My coal has all gone, and the fire is getting low, can I have some more?" she bleated, even though she expected to be refused.

Sam took his watch from his pocket, checked the time and frowned.

"Not at this time of night young lady, it's pushing nine o'clock and well past time you weren't burning gas in there, high time you were in bed."

The youngster scowled, dropped the bucket on the floor where she stood, and with her customary impish swish of her skirt, turned and returned to the front room.

"Another ten minutes then," she said as she slammed the door behind her.

Before he could react to this peevish behaviour, Eve snapped at him, "Sam, leave her, I will deal with her later."

"She's been like that all day, had a right strop on, I nearly slapped her more than once," Evie complained.

"She is getting to be a handful," observed Sam disgruntled, "If you don't take her in hand soon Eve, I will."

"I know," conceded his wife, "But we will have enough to contend with now with our Emily, I will take Fanny in hand soon."

Eve had her back towards her daughter, who, unseen by her mother, silently mouthed across the room to her father, 'She always says that.'

Sam sighed, and nodded slightly to his daughter confirming that, although they could not be heard, he knew exactly the words that fell from her mouth.

* * *

Monday arrived, cold, dry and clear, every star in the sky twinkled cheerfully, and the moon, shimmered a silvery light illuminating the early shift's way through Heals End, Sam and Elijah arrived at the pit bank by a quarter to six.

"Well lad, we're back again, I wonder what we shall find today," Sam said as they passed through the pit gates.

"No idea dad, can't be as bad as Saturday though, and with luck the damps will have cleared, make it a bit safer down there."

In the lamp house, Seth Fuller was selecting his teams from the men as they arrived; he smiled at Sam and Lijah as they walked in.

"You two want to stay together today?" he asked.

"We usually do," Sam confirmed, "What are we on this morning?"

"There are still a lot of cruts blocked off deep down; the visiting crew's equipment is better than ours so they will be attempting to break through, or dig out fresh cruts until every man is found. Our lads are to concentrate on repairs, seems there lordships want the mine back in production pretty quick," Seth said with a devilish hint of sarcasm.

Sam, joining Seth in sarcastic comment replied with a chortle, "They believe in miracles then do they Seth? They expect dead men to draw coal from a dead pit. From what I saw on Saturday, old Tilly will never produce in quantity again."

"I know that, and you know it Sam, but it doesn't seem to matter to them, as for us, we have to follow the tradition of the working man through the ages, obey the orders of those who pay the wages, however foolish they may be."

"Aye Seth, I suppose we do, foolish they are and mean with it as well, the old girl wouldn't have blown if those rich blighters had spent a bit more making her safe. They are only spending now because they are worried about what is going to happen, they've lost their income from the pit, and what's more, I'll bet we shall all be out of a job before long."

Seth frowned, "I hope you are wrong on that one Sam, but then with an inquiry in the offing you may well be right."

During the next hour the various crews, visiting and home, caged down to pit bottom each with their own scheduled tasks. George Sanders and his team from Larchwood, renowned for their superior rescue equipment and experience had not yet landed, when they arrived, they were scheduled to undertake the dubious task of breaking into the Dips and exploring the seven-foot seam, where it was presumed the explosion had occurred. The teams from the various pits had pooled their Nevito Breathing Units at Tilly Pit's stores where they were checked over after each use and made ready for the next. Those men, who were to venture into locations where there was still a possibility of damps being present collected charged units from this stored pool.

Seth and the home crews from Tilly, continued where they left off on Saturday with repairs to the haulage tracks replacing metal rails in the main tunnels for the tubs to run on, steel ropes and chains onto which the tubs could again be hooked and drawn out. Wooden slides in the offshoot tunnels, along these the ponies would drag smaller tubs out to the junction chambers, the coal could then be transferred by haulage hands onto the main haulage. In addition, as they progressed deeper, every airflow door was checked, repaired, or renewed in order to re-instate a proper ventilation system, to replace the high-speed erratic blast of air still being produced by the fans working at maximum.

Wooden planks were installed along the tunnels near to the roof, later; onto these, inert stone dust would be piled. The theory being that in the event of an explosion, this dust would be shaken loose into the airflow, mix with the coal dust flying with the moving air, and, being of a none combustible material would reduce the intensity of any future fires. A crude safety precaution, which, had it been in place throughout the whole mine prior to the explosion, may have reduced the devastation of the previous Saturday.

With reluctance, the men installed these planks, they knew the owners and management were only taking this precaution now for the benefit of the local mine inspectors, who, since the explosion had been frequent visitors, the owners would no doubt claim that these were replacements, when, in fact they had never existed before. Few, if any, of the workers would dare contradict such a claim if it were made by the mines management during an inquiry.

Almost all of the coal seams in the areas the Tilly Pit repair crews had laboured to make safe were now practically worked out, leaving only low-grade coal still to be harvested; precious little profit would be made from extracting the remaining coal left there. Deeper within the pit it may be a different matter, especially in the locations known as The Dips. If it proved feasible to re-open the original tunnels the initial rescue teams found blocked off, impassable due to major roof falls and caved in walls, there was a high probability men had been, and were still trapped in these sections. However, finding anyone still alive behind the tons of fallen rock seemed unlikely; nevertheless, these workings had to be explored. To this end, there had been rumours in the lamp house that an exploratory squad was to be formed; consisting of the most experienced and best-equipped men of the rescue team from Larchwood, and a few men from Tilly, who, having worked in those sections would be more familiar with the underground layout.

Yesterday, being the Sabbath no repair work had been undertaken, the only miners to descend the pit were the men of the rescue squads and relay teams recovering bodies. Seth and his gang, continuing from the place they left off on Saturday had advanced in total about two miles along the main haulage roadways; everything behind them, every airflow door, every offshoot crut, track and signalling system now safe and in working order.

The gang entered a four-lane end junction chamber.

Seth said to his men, "We are not on regular meal break times today lads, I recon we should check on the signal bells here, put in one of these new phones and then take a break."

No one raised their voice in descent, they had worked hard to reach this spot and a break would be welcomed. The men sat down and took out their snap tins, and their water bottles from their belts, while, Seth removed the old charred phone and replaced it with a new one from the pit tubs containing their tools and other gear. Seth first tested the signal line with the pre-arranged code, the bell he had just fitted above his head rang to signal the test acknowledged.

"Fine," he said as he whirled the handle on the side of the telephone to ring the surface. A voice in the earpiece said.

"Test acknowledged Seth, what is your present location?"

"That you Bernie lad?" Seth answered, "We are at four lane ends, and just having a bit of snap."

"Yes, it's me," replied the voice, "Cleaver has been after you, said I was to tell him as soon as you reported in."

"Better tell him then," Seth answered.

"Can't connect this phone through to his office yet, I'll shall have to send somebody to find him and bring him here."

"We shall be here about half an hour or so before the lads and I move on, or, on second thoughts, we will wait until we hear from you lot."

A remark, which brought a unanimous thumbs up sign and laughter from the men eating their snapping, even though they new they would not get much more than their usual half hour break.

A period of twenty minutes passed before the phone rang, Seth went over to answer it, he was speaking for about four or five minutes with the surface to which his men paid no attention. As he rejoined his crew they could see even in the dim lamplight, Seth was stern faced.

"Better take those few bits of our stuff out of these tubs lads; they are calling them back to the cage," he said.

Lijah asked, "You requested more stuff then Seth?"

"No, they have authorised a bloody ride down for the Larchwood team now it's safe, well, as far as here anyway."

"Ride down?" Chorused the men, they themselves would often cadge a lift in the tubs, but it was never officially sanctioned and most definitely frowned upon.

"Aye, so they aren't tired out carrying all their tools and stuff when they get here, bringing quite a bit by all accounts, too much to carry in one load and we have the only linked tubs so they need them back up. They're bringing a couple of consultant engineers with them, what's more, when they get here they want a few of you to go with them, they are bringing spare Nevito's in," Seth's tone conveyed both his concern and disgust.

"Go where?" Sam asked.

"They are going to try and break through the rock falls into the dips, seems no one has been in there yet."

"But I thought you said you made it that far in on Saturday," Sam queried.

"We did," Seth replied, "But we hadn't got the kit with us to break through, and if you remember Shaw and Cleaver wouldn't let us come back down again, they sent us home."

"True, they did," Sam said indignantly, "But I thought they would have sent somebody else in by now, men are most likely still trapped in there."

"I know Sam, but they haven't, they are going in now."

"Bloody typical!" exclaimed Albert Beech, "They aren't bothered about us men, never were, anybody left in there they'll all be dead by now and that's for sure, but of course, there lordships will want that top grade coal coming out again, the bastards are only interested in profit for themselves."

"Yeah, yeah, chorused the crew."

"That Albert is a lot we have to bear," Seth cautioned, "Mine owners here are not aristocratic by birth, they just have heaps of money and power, we don't, now then, how many of you have worked in the dips?"

Seven of his men at some time had worked in the dips, all of whom volunteered to go, taking account of their experience and skills Seth selected the three he considered the best able, included in his selection was Elijah Swindon. The tubs emptied Seth signalled the surface, the freshly laid ropes and chains he had left coupled on a direct line to the cage for his own teams use whirred into action, and the tubs slowly disappeared into the darkness back up the main haulage road.

The thirty men in his squad, Seth divided into three teams of ten, carrying what was left of their repair materials; ten men to each they began to advance from four lane ends into the three tunnels. Progress was slow; there was much to do making safe the crut entrances, so it was that each team remained in sight of the junction chamber.

Half an hour after the tubs left on there return to the pit bottom, every man of Seth's crew, attracted by the rumbling of iron wheels on iron rails, wondered back to the junction chamber. A faint glimmer from advancing lamps now became visible up the main haulage, four tubs left, and six returned, they came to a halt in the chamber. The leading three tubs were loaded with tools and other equipment, and the remaining, each carried six men.

A huge man climbed out of the last tub and called out, "Seth, where the blazes are you?"

Emerging from the centre crut, "Over here," came the reply.

The leader of these new arrivals, George Sanders, known because of his size and strength to his mates as 'Bull,' made his way over to Seth.

"We could only muster twenty Nevito's Seth that are ready for use, so I will only be needing two of your chaps".

Seth examining the Nevitos queried, "Are these all yours George, from Larchwood?"

"Some are, some aren't, hard to tell down here, drew them from the stores pool, they said these are all that are ready for use," replied George, oblivious to the fact Seth may have some ulterior reason behind his query.

All Seth's men, looked on in amazement, the men of George's team hopped out of the tubs, excluding two, whom the onlookers presumed to be the engineers Seth had mentioned earlier, these strangers, to say the least were looking rather pensive. Eventually, even these, began to struggle to climb out of the tub; each was wearing what appeared to be some type of leggings, and a kind of smock coat tied around their waists with a length of stout string, the type of garment normally worn in the past by farmers.

Seth indicating towards these oddities asked George, "What's this you've brought with you?"

George smirked," You might well ask, never clapped eyes on either of them until this morning, they are what held us up, they arrived on the bank just after we did and we had to wait while somebody showed them how a Nevito works. My orders are to take them to the Dips, and they are to make a report on how soon coal can be drawn from there again."

Seth, like his men studied the pair; both wore spectacles, not a good idea down a pit, one stood about five feet eight inches, being of a medium build and possessing a head of curly hair and huge bushy sideburns, he looked to be in his mid to late forties. His facial expression was twisted in a sour, supercilious manner giving him a look of a posturing braggart. The other, possibly in his mid twenties, could be no more than five feet two inches in height and small of build. He was virtually bald, but wore on his chin a badly trimmed goatee beard; his small round spectacles emphasized his little piggy eyes.

Seth griped softly to George, "I thought better of Joe Shaw and Arthur Cleaver than to pull a stunt like this, I take it; it's because of them you rode in."

"Why of course," responded George, still amused by the situation, "but I got the impression it wasn't your manager's idea, seems to have come from higher up."

Seth, still rather baffled, questioned his counterpart on the Larchwood team, "Who the hell are they? Where are they from? What are their names?"

"Don't know Seth, nobody introduce them, and I'm not bloody asking, we've been referring to them as sideburn and goatee."

"To their faces?"

George shook his head, "No, they haven't said much to us at all, big one hasn't spoken, but goatee was mouthy enough topside, flirting about, giving Cleaver and your lamp man a real hard time of it."

"Oh, did he, serves Arthur right for fetching them in," Seth tittered.

"When I say mouthy, that is to say until the cage started to drop, haven't heard a squeak out of him since then," George added.

"Bit quick for them was it?"

Sardonically, George replied, "Probably."

None of the miners made an obvious point of showing it, but everyone watched the strangers with a mixture of disbelief and amusement, Seth still could not believe his own eyes, these two men would be a distinct liability, he spoke quietly to George.

"They'll cook down here in that get up."

Again, George grinned, "Oh, I do hope so; I have high hopes that telling the tale of today's excursion will keep me in free ale for months to come."

George's men set about unloading the tubs and placing everything against the wall of the tunnel leading to the Dips.

George asked, "Which of your lads are to come with us Seth?"

"Cleaver asked for three George, although, seven of this lot know the workings in the dips, we had decided on Albert here, who you already know, Frank Willis and young Lijah Swindon, but if you don't need all of them, it's your choice who you leave with me."

The three miners hearing their names mentioned joined the team leaders.

"Albert, you old dog, still with us then?" George said cheerily as he greeted the eldest of the three.

Albert returned the banter, "Aye, still here George you great overgrown Ox."

George smiled, there were few who could get away with making a remark like that to his face, but George and Albert's paths had crossed on many occasions. As a fresh faced lad, George had worked with Albert. There had not been many calls for rescue teams locally over the last twenty years of which Albert Beech was not a part, George, as did many others respected Albert's knowledge. Surveying the volunteers before him, George made his choice.

"Albert, it's a bit more serious than that bit of a pop you had this time three years ago, if you're still up to it? You're coming."

"Course I'm still up to it you daft bugger," Albert rebuked as he turned towards the tunnel to collect the tools and equipment needed for the task.

George lingered over choosing a second man.

"Well?" Seth interceded, "Do you need another man?"

"With that old git along, probably not, but I like the look of this one, he looks handy and he's damn near as big as I am, what's your name son?"

"Elijah,—Elijah Swindon, Mr—"

"George, call me George, or Bull, if you're as good as your size says you might be, I take it you've used breathing apparatus before?"

"I have had training with it, yes," Lijah replied and followed Albert.

While Lijah collected his tools from the wall, Sam went over to him and grasped his arm.

"Lijah lad," he said quietly, "There's not much old Bull doesn't no about mining, but have a care down in that hell hole, don't take any unnecessary risks and come out safe."

"I will father," Lijah re-assured him, strapping the Nevito to his chest.

"Albert, Lijah, there are full lamps here for you clip your identity discs onto them then we can make a start," George ordered, his previous light-hearted jovial tone now completely disappeared.

The two engineers deep in conversation and still standing by the tubs realised the team was about to set off.

"Just a moment if you please my man," goatee chirped up, "We shall need two men to carry these Nevy things."

The Bull stopped in his tracks, he turned slowly and towering over little goatee, replied calmly.

"Oh, I'm sorry, how dreadfully remiss of me," the little man indicated towards a Nevito still on the floor.

"Let me enlighten you sonny," his voice stern, almost a roar, "I will take you along to the dips as ordered, but down here everyman carries his own kit, and as far as you are concerned, until we get there, I am God, got that, now pick up that bloody Nevito and follow us."

The little man rose to the rebuke, "How dare you speak to me like that?" he squeaked.

Bull roared back at him, "Shut it you little squirt, I don't want you here, having to wet nurse you puts us all at risk, now either pick up your kit and follow us or piss off back out of my world."

After an hours steady walking, the Larchwood team and its augments approached the dips. They should have found entrances to two tunnels, one swinging away to their left, and a little further along, a second one running virtually parallel to the first. The first one appeared to be blocked apart from what seemed to be a six to eight inch gap at the top, after a quick look, the team went on to the second crut in the hope this one was passable, it was not, completely blocked of by tons of fallen coal and rock.

Intrigued, the miners watched as the two engineers took large blueprints out of the satchel they carried, laid them on the ground attempting to read them by the light from their lamps, their actions greatly amused the watchers, but as these engineers, technically, were senior to them, they restricted their amusement to a quiet titter.

"Albert! Where the hell are you?" George called out.

"What," snapped a voice from the darkness.

George traced the sound of the voice, and found Albert hiding around a slight bend in the roadway, sitting on a pile of fallen coal grasping his stomach.

"What's the matter?" George asked with concern.

Albert raised his head, by the light of his lamp George could distinguish two lines of clean flesh beginning at Albert's eyes, and running down his cheeks, a result of the older man's tears washing the coal dust away from his face, he was doubled over with silent laughter.

George asked softly," What's so funny?"

"That pair of toffee nosed pillocks with their maps and fancy overalls, I've been watching them ever since you brought them in, they're shitting themselves, and they haven't got a clue why they are here," Albert chortled.

Smirking, understanding the old miner's amusement, George asked, "You got any ideas?"

"Yes, if we open it up, about twenty yards in, the first tunnel doglegs to the right for about five yards, there is only about a six foot thick standing column of coal between the first and second tunnels, we could cut through that quick enough, be faster than shifting that rock fall at the entrance of number two crut."

"I knew I was right to bring you along old man, we'll try it, Oh, and before you come back; rub some muck on your face, your tears have left it a bit streaky."

Albert raised his hand in acknowledgment, George made his way back to the tunnels, passing the engineers, he asked sarcastically.

"Any ideas gentlemen?"

"It's very hard to read in this light, we will let you know when we find an answer," little goatee replied, sideburns nodded his agreement.

George totally disregarded their comment and rejoined his men.

"Right lads that bit of a hole at the top of this fall, see if you can make it big enough for us to climb through."

His men set about cutting a way through; eventually a crawl way stretching around fifteen feet was opened up, George led the way through and half his men followed. On the other side, the air was rank and sour, from the blast of the ventilation fans they left behind in the main roadway only a gentle breeze reached them, common sense told them all the return shafts in this tunnel must be blocked off, the air could not circulate. Tests for damp proved negative, but the lamp flames went low; George decided it was time for precautions, for his men at least.

"Get your Nevito's on lads, and watch those flames, just up here there should be a bend to the right, we're going to cut through into the other crut."

George himself preferred to rely on his nose at this stage; therefore, he did not use his own Nevito. A fast examination of the stand of coal determined that it was looser from about waist height to the roof, blasting was definitely out of the question, but the short bladed, short handled miner's picks would soon be through. George and Lijah were the first to crawl through and drop down into the tunnel. The rest of the team joined them, and passed through the tools and props, very cautiously, the engineers brought up the rear, they had never used the heavy Nevito units before and little goatee tripped over something falling very heavily; sideburns helped him up to his feet.

"What was that I fell over?" he asked his companion.

Bending over, they both used the little light from their two lamps to examine the floor.

"Oh shit! It's somebody's leg," exclaimed little goatee.

Sideburns waved his lamp around, "Whe, Whe, Where's the rest of him?" he stuttered.

Albert Beech, still watching the pair saw everything, he could not help himself and this was too good an opportunity to miss.

"Have a good close look around gentlemen, you will probably find bits of him on the roof, on the wall, on your boots even."

Hesitantly, they held their lamps out, looking around, a few feet away lay a human hand, which clinched it, both men parted company with their breakfast against the sidewall.

"Gentlemen," Albert continued, "I think you would be better off the other side of the roof fall, you don't need respirators there."

Neither man lost any time following his suggestion and scampered off to relative safety.

Sweat poured out of the miners as they worked, but soon a crawl way around four feet in diameter was cut through to the second dips main tunnel, and temporary props fitted. George looked at his men; they were exhausted.

"All right lads, take a bit of a break," he ordered, turning to John Tomkins, his second in command, "John, you and young Lijah follow me into the crut; I'll go ahead and check the tunnel out and call you if it's safe."

Nevito's at the ready, he led the way through the new crut, John following, and with Lijah standing ready to enter when John climbed out the other side. Dropping out of the crawl way George proceeded warily into the tunnel, he had gone no more than twenty feet when John, waiting in the crawl way heard him curse loudly, George began to stagger, his lamp fell to the floor, John shouted at the top of is voice back to the rest of the team.

"Bull's down, quick, get him out."

Like a flash John was out of the tunnel, swiftly followed by Lijah, wearing the bulky Nevito's it was not easy, when the two men reached George he was thrashing about on the floor, they tried to restrain him, but, he was not called Bull for nothing, and his strength seemed to have increased as he struggled to breathe. One by one other members of his crew dropped out of the narrow crut, until there were enough of them to restrain the big man and drag him back to the cruts opening, Albert was just about to start through as they pulled George back, he took one look at his friend, and yelled back to the others.

"His Nevito's a duff; get a good one fast off those bloody engineers."

George lay still as his men passed him back along the narrow crut and out the other side; they ripped the breathing unit off him, and replaced it with a fresh one. No one dared remove his own unit; the collapse of their leader could only mean one thing, a high concentration of chokedamp in the second tunnel, which would now probably be seeping through into this one. As fast as conditions would allow, George was carried back, fed over the rock fall through into the main roadway and laid on a stretcher. John and Albert knelt by him trying to find any sign of life, he did not appear to be breathing and they could find no sign of a pulse.

In shock, Lijah asked, "What do we do now?"

"The only thing we can do," Albert replied, "Carry him back to the surface, and take those bloody idiots with you, we can't baby sit them, we're in here looking for men, not the owner's bloody profits."

"I agree," said John, "It's not very likely anyone survived in that second tunnel, if we close off the hole, and as we've come this far I recon the rest of us should take a look along this first one, you never know, OK with you Albert?"

"Good idea, pick two of your men to carry old Bull out, and make sure to tell them to make our fancy friends take a turn carrying the stretcher."

Once the stretcher party had started back, the rest of the men re-entered the workings, quickly fastened a sheet of tarred canvas over the new hole they had made, and in single file, John leading, stumbling over debris, squeezing through narrow openings, made their way deeper inside.

They covered about three quarters of a mile, almost to the end of the working, bodies and dismembered body parts littered the entire way, within sight of yet another major fall that completely blocked the tunnel, Albert called out.

"Hold on a minute John."

John Tomkins stopped and walked back to Albert, "What is it?" he asked.

Albert held his lamp just above his head, "Here, in the roof," John looked where Albert indicated, "Here John, this is a return shaft, it seems to be blocked, but if we can get it cleared from above, chances are that the air would blow clear and we could get these bodies out of here safely."

"You're right," agreed John, "It might even blow that second working clear at the same time."

"Not much more we can do now though," Albert said looking at his watch, "Best be making our way back, if your lads are making them take a turn carrying the stretcher we might even catch up with those fancy boys."

"That we may Albert, you know, I doubt if those two have ever done a proper days work, the book learned buggers, did you see their hands, softer than my six year old lass's, they'll get a few nice blisters from those stretcher poles."

Albert and the rest of the team burst into laughter, and Albert replied.

"Oh yes John boy, I clocked their pretty little mitts, shame isn't it, but great though."

The whole team laughed at the prospect of delicate hands acquiring the trappings of hard work, as they made their way out, the thought of discomfort for members of the upper classes helped to lift their spirits, even though after the loss of their leader everyone had cause to grieve.

Chapter Ten

Henry Cotes left his home and was about his business considerably earlier than his usual time, the Sabbath over, and with the rebirth of a new working week there was much to do, many people to see, a great deal to arrange, and if his fears proved justified even more he would need to conceal. Henry considered the possible advantages of involving his nephew in all that had to transpire; he may never have a better opportunity to honour his brother in law's request to instruct his wayward nephew in the ways of commerce. On reflection, he decided against it, the probability his nephew had been out carousing around some town or other the previous evening was highly likely. Henry learned from bitter experience, his nephew tended to imbibe liberally most evenings, and at this hour would be in no state to leave his bed. The young man rarely emerged much before mid-day, and it would be some time after that before he exhibited any semblance of intelligence. In fact, Charles Heath Junior had acted out of character by returning home quite early in the evening and spent last night at Highfield Hall.

Henry arrived at Tilly Pit at eleven fifteen, with some relief, he noted the number of people milling around outside had greatly reduced on the previous two days. Along the lane from the main gates, a few vans and ambulances still stood in the roadway at the ready, a clear indication that all the men from the Saturday early shift had not yet been located. He was perturbed; the possibility of survivors being discovered after more than forty-eight hours was slim indeed. From the offset, he feared the loss of life may be considerable, but up until now, no one had offered confirmation of the actual numbers of those lost or injured.

Henry entered the office block, strode along the corridor and into Joseph Shaw's office, Joseph sat behind his desk engrossed in a blueprint laid out before him, startled, he looked up as Henry walked in unannounced.

Joseph greeted his visitor, "Good day Mr Cotes, I had thought you would be calling yesterday afternoon, my clerk informed me you called before I arrived and that you would be coming back."

"Yes," Henry replied, "That was my intention, but as time went on I found family business took longer than I expected, and by the time it was concluded I needed to go straight home because we were expecting guests for dinner,"

"I quite understand sir, after all it was the weekend," Joseph acknowledged.

Henry removed his top coat and sat down.

Anticipating grim news, he asked, "I thought perhaps by now you would have a better idea how things actually stand?"

"We do have some figures now sir, I assume you mean regarding losses and survivors?"

Henry nodded affirmatively, "Yes Joseph, you can start with the bad news."

Joseph searched among the papers under his blueprint, "Ah! Here it is," he said retrieving several sheets of notepaper, "As you are aware Mr Cotes, at the time of the explosion, two hundred and forty eight men were below ground. Of those, so far seventy-nine are now confirmed deceased and their bodies have been recovered, but we are having trouble identifying some because they are unrecognisable, and we have not been able to locate their discs."

Henry frowned; the confirmed loss of life was heavy up to now, and likely to increase.

Joseph continued, "This last report is an hour old, but up to that point, ninety two men have either walked out of the mine, or been carried out injured but alive, and seventy seven men are still unaccounted for."

After a moment's hesitation Henry replied, "The loss of manpower is as expected, high, but what of the men still unaccounted for, what has been done to recover them?"

"Many of the workings are still inaccessible, especially in the Dips, there have been a great many major cave-ins in that district, but your consultant engineers are down there now with the Larchwood team."

"Consultant engineers, what consultant engineers?" Henry was baffled.

Joseph, astonished, set down his papers and looked at the mine owner, he was somewhat alarmed by the bewildered expression on Henry's face.

"The ones who arrived here this morning sir, Arthur Cleaver sent them down as instructed."

"Instructed by whom, I gave no such instruction," Henry retorted in annoyance, "What were you thinking man, letting outsiders down the pit?"

Panic began to surge in Joseph Shaw's stomach; this reaction from Henry was unexpected, trying to justify the actions that caused his superior's annoyance, Joseph went on to explain.

"But sir, your nephew, Mr Heath, called here last evening, my clerk had informed me you would be returning, and when Mr Heath arrived I presumed he had come in your stead."

Henry grimaced at the mention of his nephew, inhaled slowly, but restrained himself allowing the pit's manager, who was now becoming very pensive, to continue.

"Mr Heath told me that engineers from a consulting establishment would be arriving this morning, and that they had been engaged to compile a report for you regarding how soon the mine could be in full production again. I tried to explain to Mr Heath that there are still many roof falls and dangers below ground, but he would have none of it, he insisted that we give the engineers our full co-operation, and that they were to start their report in those areas where the best coal comes from."

Henry remained silent; gritting his teeth, he breathed deeply trying to remain calm.

Joseph, realising Henry Cotes knew nothing about this, swiftly added, "I believe one of the engineers is known personally to Mr Heath sir, your nephew made a remark about his friend soon sorting this bit of a problem out, and getting the coal flowing again."

Henry rose from his chair, thumped his fist on the desk and exclaimed, "Stupid boy!" he paced the room trying to calm his temper.

"They are down there now?" he bellowed.

"Yes sir, they have gone to the dips, but we had to instruct them on how to use the Nevito's before they left, and then they demanded transport be provided below ground for them as far as the repaired tracks would allow.

Henry snapped in response, "Did they by Jove, they are not what you would class as mining engineers then?" A possibility occurred to him; these visitors even if they were below ground would probably have no idea what to look for, he began to calm down.

"I do not know sir, I have never seen either of them before, or heard of the establishment they claim to represent, but we were ordered to give them every co-operation."

"I understand Joseph, it seems I will have to have words with my nephew, perhaps no serious harm has been done."

"I confess sir, I did think it rather strange, but it was not my place to question Mr Heath's orders, however, I did telephone your home last night for confirmation when Mr Heath left, but I was told you had not yet returned."

Henry, calmer now returned to his chair, and to the business of the day.

"What has been done in regard to notifying the next of kin of the men you are sure lost their lives?"

"We have a list ready, of those we were able to identify sixty seven names in all, and twelve we cannot, I have notified the 'coroner's office' and am waiting for confirmation that the bodies may be returned to their families, merely a courtesy you understand requesting the coroner's permission, but under the circumstances I thought it best."

"Quite right Joseph, an excellent idea, I take it no details or names have been released yet?"

"No sir, not yet, but I expect some names will have leaked, the rescue teams are bound to have recognised some of their mates as they were carried out."

"Yes, of course, may I see the list?"

Joseph handed the papers to him, Henry studied them for a moment, they detailed lamp numbers, names, and the location and time the bodies were found.

"There is too much here," observed Henry, "Have this done again, instead of locations and times, only show lamp numbers, names and where they are now, that way as soon as you are cleared to release the bodies, their families will know where to claim them. I see no reason why the revised list should not be posted when it is completed, there did not seem to be many members of the press outside this morning."

"There is one reporter on duty outside Mr Cotes, the rest of them have retreated up the village and congregated in the Reading Room waiting for news."

"Oh, have they, when you post the original on the board I suppose you had better do another copy and send it up to them."

"Offer a little and keep them at bay?"

"Precisely Joseph, prepare a statement for them at the same time, but, make sure you only state the obvious."

Seeking guidance Joseph asked, "What am I to do about the bodies we cannot identify?"

Henry pondered a moment before replying, "That is going to be a problem, if we cannot identify them, we will have to hope their families can."

"Those were my thoughts sir, but I needed your authorisation before I acted upon them."

"Make it so Joseph, I rather suspect the only people to profit out of this tragedy will be the local undertakers, it's always sickened me, they have chosen a dying trade but I have yet to find one who is, as they say, financially embarrassed," Henry remarked with an air of disdain.

Joseph ventured a smile at Henry's cynicism.

"I will see to it sir, do you have any other instructions?" Joseph asked, attempting to steer Henry Cotes towards another subject, hoping for some indication of his superior's actions and intentions following on from Saturday's events in this office, Henry paused to think, ran his hand over his bald head, hesitated again, shook his head and replied.

"No, I don't think so, you seem to have everything in hand, and I have places to be today, unless, there is anything you can think of that I have missed?"

"The engineers perhaps?" Joseph added cautiously.

Henry snapped back, "Good God yes, I forgot about those, when they come back to the surface, get shut of them pretty damn quick and don't let them back on the site again, if my nephew challenges you over this, tell him to speak to me," and then under his breath barely audible, added, "If the young idiot dares."

"If you don't mind me asking Mr Cotes, are you planning on returning here today? If not, how may I contact you if I need a decision from you on anything which may arise and require your attention?"

"That will be difficult Joseph, as I said; I have many places to be today, I am afraid I have been rather remiss over other things, for one, I have put off touring the farms which have passed to my control since my brother-in law's demise. My being in this area because of the explosion offers an ideal opportunity for me to catch up on the things I have neglected. By the way, did my steward arrange suitable stabling for those ponies you wanted to bring back to the surface? I told him to see to it when I returned home on Saturday evening."

"Yes sir, he did, we brought them out yesterday afternoon, they are in a barn on a farm at the top of this lane, I think Arthur called it Valley Farm, I am not familiar with many of the local farmers myself but Arthur being a local man knows most of them."

"Oh yes, the Oldfield farm, that is one of the places I intend to call, I may as well do that one first, if you need me send a runner along with a message, I may remain there a couple of hours or so."

Henry left the mine and turned his car along Tilly Lane towards the farm at its far end. Light rain over night, and traffic along the lane had virtually cleared away the snow from it. Henry found the first few hundred yards of the lane easy, tons of hardcore had been used to provide a good solid surface to accommodate traffic to, and from, the mine. Nearing the farm itself however, the surface turned to one of mud and slush, ruts and potholes appeared as pools of water, this presented a welcome challenge to Henry, a chance to exercise his driving prowess, excitedly he wrestled with his vehicle as it slipped and skidded at a pace along the track.

Swinging his car through the open gateway, Henry felt relieved to find the farmyard itself was surfaced with hardcore stone; at least he would keep his boots and trouser bottoms clear of mud. The sound of his vehicle entering the yard lured two men out of a cow shed, one quite elderly and the other young, as Henry climbed out of the car and stretched his back the young man touched the beck of his cap in acknowledgement. Touching of the forelock by the lower classes was a gesture expected by the likes of Henry Cotes, rarely, if ever did he acknowledge it, the younger man spoke to his companion, who in turn apprehensively approached Henry, the young man returned into the shed from whence they came. Only now did the younger man's identity register with Henry, by the blaze of red hair visible beneath his cap, there could be no doubt.

Henry thought to himself, Hmm, young Zack Morgan, what do you do here?

"Good day sir," greeted the old man, "I am George Oldfield, and I believe you are Mr Henry Cotes."

"That I am," Henry replied, no hand of friendship was offered, or expected, "I was in the area, so I took the opportunity to call and take a brief look around this farm now you are my tenant."

George Oldfield staggered backwards with surprise, "I beg your pardon sir, you are mistaken, we are tenants of the Highfield Estate."

"You were, Mr Oldfield you were indeed, but following the death, and in accordance with the terms of the late Squire Heath's will, this, and other farms within its vicinity now form part of my estate."

George Oldfield was rendered speechless at this news. He had always enjoyed an excellent working relationship with the late squire, George surmised, if the man now standing in his yard, whom he knew only by reputation as being hard and ruthless was in fact now his landlord, he could expect many adverse changes in the conditions of his tenure, and a substantial increase in his annual rent. Protocol dictated, contrary to George's nature, to be hospitable with everyone with whom he did business, to this man however, he took an immediate dislike, but if his tenancy was to survive on anything near to the terms that already existed, he must not show it.

"Is that a fact—," George started to say, but then thought better of it, "I am not implying I disbelieve you sir, but you have chosen a poor time of year to view the farm."

"I have no intention of inspecting the whole farm Mr Oldfield, it is more a matter of introducing myself to you, and informing you of the current situation regarding your tenure, now, did you say your Christian name is George?" Henry asked beaming an unexpected smile.

"I did sir," George suspiciously confirmed.

"Then, in that case, I presume you will have no objection to my calling you by that name."

George Oldfield had not expected any such familiarity from a man of Henry Cotes's standing, but he knew better than to attempt to call his visitor by his given name.

"Why no sir, none at all," George began to suspect this man may not be quite as bad as his reputation would have people believe, "We are about to take lunch in a few minutes sir, it is simple country fare, but if you haven't already eaten, would you care to join us?"

George, in no way expected his visitor to be as amiable as the old squire, to his utter amazement Henry smiled as he replied.

"I would be delighted to take lunch with you and your family George, if it will not be putting your good lady out in any way."

"That it will not sir, she always prepares enough for a small army, never quite got used to the lads not being here," George answered exhibiting a degree of sadness.

"The lads?" Henry repeated bemused, and then he remembered, "Oh, you mean your sons, yes I heard about that, Battle of the Somme wasn't it? That is one of the things I wish to speak to you about."

George looked in amazement, how this person from the next county knew about the loss of his two sons he could not imagine. Crossing the yard to the farmhouse, the sound of several ponies could be heard from inside a small wooden barn.

"You keep horses do you George?" Henry asked, hoping for an appropriate lead into the true reason for his visit.

For a moment George Oldfield was visibly uncomfortable, they were not his animals, and they should not really be on his farm, he needed to think quickly to avoid immediately falling out of favour with the man who claimed to be his new landlord.

"I am sorry Mr Cotes, but they do not belong to me, a man called here yesterday morning, he said his name was Herbert Carver and that he was the new steward of the estate. He asked if I could stable some ponies here from Tilly Pit, I agreed because I thought I was doing a service for the new squire, I know the pit belongs to him, I will have them moved off your land as soon as I can."

"No need for that," Henry replied, "Carver is my steward, I am joint owner of that particular coal mine, and he was acting on my instructions."

George felt a sudden surge of relief, "Oh, my daughter will be pleased about that sir, they are in terrible condition and she has taken quite a shine to them, she has taken it upon herself to look after them."

The daughter, the young woman Zack had mentioned on Saturday, the girl he was sweet on, Henry was rather keen to make her acquaintance; after all, she might one day be a member of an unofficial branch of his family.

On one side of the yard was a large, long garden in which the farmhouse stood, a raven-haired girl appeared at the doorway, without looking in any direction she called out, "Father, Zack, dinner is nearly ready," and then disappeared back into the house.

George lingered a moment, "Begging your pardon sir, I hope you will not mind, but there is a young man, a childhood friend of my daughter here this morning, he works as a labourer at your mine, but from time to time he helps out around the farm, will it be alright if he eats with us?"

"Quite alright George, he has more right to be here than I do, especially if he is to wed your daughter."

George's brow furrowed, it was obvious and a well-known fact in this village the two of them were keeping company, but this man from the next county knowing seemed a little odd, nevertheless, Henry had hit upon a sore subject.

"There has been no mention of that as yet Mr Cotes, he is a good lad and did a lot of his growing up here, but I think Florence can do better than a labourer at the pit. I would prefer someone who will be better able to provide for her than a lad like him with no prospects."

Henry chuckled softly, "Perhaps he will surprise you George, he may be better suited than you think."

The two men entered the house, George introduced the visitor to his wife and daughter, both women were embarrassed by Henry's presence in their humble home, such men did not normally visit tenant farmers in person unless things were very wrong, and never socially. The door opened, and in walked Zack Morgan.

George felt uneasy as he began to introduce him, "This is—,"

"Good afternoon Mr Cotes," Zack greeted the visitor, his face beaming.

"Afternoon Zack," Henry replied cheerfully.

The Oldfield family looked on in amazement; obviously, these two men were acquainted, but how could it be that Zack seemed so at ease in the company of a man of Henry Cotes's social standing. Pleasantries concluded parents and guests sat at the kitchen table whilst Florence served their lunch. Simple fair it was, vastly different from his normal diet, but from its aroma, Henry relished the thought of it. He was surprised what the girl had managed to concoct out of a joint of old mutton, potatoes, turnips and greens, the freshly baked bread that accompanied the meal added to his expected enjoyment of it.

Despite everyone's efforts to appear relaxed by nervously exchanging small talk, the ambiance within the room embraced tension, George; his wife Edith, seated either end of the oblong kitchen table, Zack and Florence together on one side, with Henry, directly opposite the girl. Only when she had satisfied herself everyone at the table had been served and was comfortable did she take her own place. Henry's eyes, like those of any other red-blooded male coming into contact with such a creature meticulously followed her every movement, from his position Henry was able to, and indeed did, pay a great deal of attention to this vibrant young lady. Florence, he estimated to be around five feet eight inches in height, her figure a perfect example of symmetry in the female form, her raven hair, she wore loosely falling about her shoulders exquisitely framing her face. Her skin shone like the finest of porcelains, a hint of rose in her cheeks extenuated the warmth of her expression, and her eyes, the most strikingly exquisite Henry ever beheld, were of a pale azure with just a hint of luminescent silver, they seemed to sparkle with permanent laughter. The smile, which rarely left her face Henry thought could well light up the heavens, who could blame him, or anyone else for taking notice of her. Who that is, except for Edith Oldfield, she had not failed to notice and be concerned by the amount of Henrys' attention focussed upon her daughter, her maternal protective instincts aroused, unobtrusively she kept a careful eye on this influential stranger. To any mother, had he been thirty years younger and in want of a wife, Edith would have been delighted by his attention towards her daughter, as he was not, she could only assume his intentions were less than honourable.

Zack also noticed the attention Henry paid to Florence, but he knew her nature far too well for it to give him any course for alarm. She was paying no more attention to this visitor than she would to anyone else; Florence always exhibited the same caring cheerful disposition. His meeting with Henry two days ago convinced Zack, Henry Cotes could be generous if something pleased him, or he was in need of a service of some kind from his host. Perhaps Henry's interest in Florence could be turned to their advantage; after all, he must have an ulterior motive for lowering his social status and taking lunch with a tenant farmer.

Gradually, as the meal progressed everyone at the table became oblivious to the fact there were people from three distinct social classes eating together.

Their meal concluded, George said, "You wished to see around the farm Mr Cotes, I'm afraid this is not the best time of year to be on the land, and this blanket of snow will not help."

"I am aware of that George, perhaps just a look around the yard itself, and anything which can be seen from there, I well remember riding over this land with my brother-in-law some years ago, it is my intention to bring to fruition some ideas he had at that time."

The two men left the house, inspected the buildings and viewed the fields from any vantage point, the old farmer still at a loss why this new owner took the trouble to tour the yard. Hesitantly George put into words a niggling point that had troubled him since the arrival of his guest.

"I had an excellent working relationship with Squire Heath sir; I confess I am surprised he parted with this farm, even if it was posthumously, I was always under the impression it is one of the more valuable farms on the Highfield estate."

Henry laughed, "It is, or at least it was one of the more prosperous farms on the estate George, and its transfer to me is intended as a temporary measure only, one day it will be returned to the Highfield heirs."

Henry's use of the plural in reference to Highfield heirs completely escaped the notice of George Oldfield; he was more concerned by possible changes this new owner had in mind. True, since his sons joined the army, he had struggled and the farm had not reached its full potential of productivity, but under the circumstances, he had done the best he could.

Henry continued, "You have some fine shades and woods here George, quite a surfeit of woodland in fact, do you not?"

George dreaded the next comment, expecting an instruction to clear them and provide land that is more arable.

"Yes sir, I do," he replied.

"The distance between this farm and my main estate may not have reduced, but the advances made with the internal combustion engine and motorised transport now puts it within easy travelling distance, I have decided to turn these woodlands into a private shooting ground. Come this spring I want you to rear game birds for me, and, as I am very fond of venison, if possible, attract a few deer to take up residence."

George was aware, and immensely disapproved of the obsession the rich had for shooting, killing purely for pleasure. Providing food for the family table by taking a few rabbits and the odd bird or two he could understand. However, to rear birds in cages and release them solely for rich yahoos to shoot at he did not like. As far as he was concerned, the only redeeming feature this pastime held was, by the time the upper classes got out into the field; they were usually so well lubricated by wines and spirits that they invariably missed their quarry, leaving the birds to fly free.

Henry noticed the silence from his host and asked, "Is there a problem with that George?"

"Begging your pardon sir, we have seen a few deer from time to time and there are birds already on the land, but to follow those instructions will mean I will have to neglect the rest of the farm. I am struggling to cope now since the boys left, I don't see how the time can be found to rear game birds, and I would not know where to start on how to attract more deer here."

Henry smiled, that was just the reaction he hoped for, "Then perhaps you should employ more men," he suggested.

"Yes, that would be one answer, but I can't afford permanent hands, and casuals always need too much watching, I find it quicker to do the job myself," insisted George.

"But George, I am not suggesting you attend to rearing game personally, we none of us are getting any younger, and you really must take on more men if this farm is to pay, there will undoubtedly be many looking for work very soon."

Reference to his age suggested to George that the new owner might consider looking for a new tenant, he dared not flatly refuse the order, if he did, he and his family may be homeless, he decided to try avoiding the owner's idea another way.

"But sir," he entreated, "I know the farms return has been down for the past couple of years, and yes with more men it will produce more, but it will take time, as things stand I cannot afford to pay wages, I just don't have the money."

Henry was delighted; the elderly farmer seemed to be falling just where he wanted him.

"Very well George, you follow my orders and I will see to the funding."

George did not believe his own ears, lingering thoughtfully in disbelief on the new owners last words, surely he must have misheard him; why would such an offer be made by such a man, he ventured to request confirmation.

"Am I to understand you are prepared to pay for the necessary labour sir, if so, for how long?"

"Until I am satisfied this farm is financially viable again and running well enough to stand the cost itself, providing, of course I get my sport."

Henry had primed the old farmer well, now he was confused and taken off his guard by the offer of financial support, he was ready, time for Henry to lay down his real conditions.

"The lad who ate with us, I believe you said he spent much of his youth here and that he helps out from time to time."

"Zack Morgan," George queried cautiously remembering the two seemed to be acquainted, "Yes he did, and does, he's a decent enough youth but there is some question regarding his parentage. It's well known his mother was never married and people do talk so, no one is sure who the lads father is, but according to the tales there are quite a few in the frame as possibilities, they say there were many, from farm hand to scholar."

"Oh no, I know that is an exaggeration George, you shouldn't pay attention to gossipy old women, but tell me, is that why you frown on his obvious attachment to your daughter?"

"I know I shouldn't, but yes, those stories are at the back of my mind, Florence can do far better for herself."

Henry's face darkened, George noticed, and wisely softened his own tone before continuing.

"He is a local village lad sir; lives about a mile and a bit away over the fields, may I ask how you come to know him?"

"You may ask George, his mother Lydia quite often works for my sister Anne at Highfield, and my sister relies on her a great deal, she is very fond of her. In addition, I remember Zack as a lad; he used to do odd jobs at the hall, sometimes he looked after the horses. I know he is educated far above his class, if he knows this farm I would have thought he could be well worth your consideration as a possible assistant in a couple of months."

"But the lad's a cripple, he's only got full use in one arm," George parried, not wishing to bring Zack and his daughter any closer together by having him at the farm even more often than he already seemed to be.

Henry recognised the old man's dilemma, a similar situation had recently occurred regarding his own daughter and an unacceptable gold digging suitor.

"George, the lad has a good brain, and he comes from good stock," realising his slight slip of the tongue, Henry quickly added, "On his mother's side that is, I think he would be fine in a supervisory role, and that injured arm didn't seem to hamper him much at lunch. Whatever the cause of that injury he seems to be recovering, think it over a few days George, Zack knows many of the men at Tilly Pit who will be out of work soon, and you won't want anyone here who is work-shy. I suggest you ask his advice, after all, it is my estate which will be paying the wages of whoever comes to work here, I think he will be an invaluable asset, but the final decision of course is yours."

Both men now knew, although Henry graciously implied the choice would be George's, Zack Morgan would be offered a permanent position at Valley Farm in the near future, he may not like it, but George had no choice but to concur.

Henry felt satisfied his business here was concluded, and turned towards his vehicle. The daylight now beginning to fade and the evening air taking a chill, at the other end of the yard Florence could be seen entering the wooden barn close to the house.

"I don't think we looked in there George," Henry said, indicating towards the barn, "Let us check it out now."

George had purposely left this building out of their tour, the pit ponies were in there, they were not his beasts and their condition would not impress anyone.

There was only one small window high on one wall above a loft, lighting oil lamps around the barn, Florence gently moved between the ponies, she smiled as the two men entered and came over carrying a lamp for them.

"Have you come to see my ailing charges?" she asked, "They are in need of feeding up, some grooming, and a lot of love and tenderness."

"Do you like horses Florence?" Henry asked.

"I do sir, very much, but these poor things are in a sorry state, I think some of them may be blind, or very nearly."

"Do you ride?" Henry asked innocently.

Both father and daughter looked shocked at the question, "Ride, why no sir, girls don't ride, but we did have a pony when I was young, my brothers rode him but I was never allowed to, sometimes they would take me out in the trap though," the girl replied.

It was Henry's turn to exhibit his own shock at the reply, "Of course girls ride nowadays Florence," he corrected, "My daughter has several horses, I bought her another grey mare only last year, but she hardly ever rides it, seems it's far too steady for her liking, my daughter prefers a horse with spirit."

"I have often thought I would like to ride my own horse Mr Cotes, but dear papa won't buy me one, will you?" she aimed the last remark towards her father.

George rebuked his daughter, “No child, I cannot, ladies of high society may ride, but you are a farmer’s daughter, not your place, anyway the cost would be too great.”

Despite Henry Cotes’s hard heart and the fact of late he rarely rode himself, he did love horses, the sight of the ponies before him, their bones showing through their flesh, they were little more than walking skeletons, even he was moved to compassion.

Henry walked around the barn with Florence as she tenderly petted and comforted the beasts, after a few minutes he returned to George and quietly asked.

“Is it just the cost which prevents you finding a horse for Florence?”

The old man was ashamed to admit it, but nodded that it was.

Henry turned on his heel and spoke in an agitated tone, “Florence, you have taken it upon yourself to care for these ponies have you not?”

The girl was startled, afraid she had done something to displease the man who was now her father’s landlord.

“Yes sir,” she admitted, and unsure of the consequences of her actions added, “Am I not to?”

“On the contrary, do what you can to make them comfortable, I was not aware ponies used below ground were allowed to get in such a terrible state,” Henry reassured her.

“Do a good job, as I am sure you will, and Indy, the grey mare my daughter has told me to sell, plus all the tack you will need shall be yours.”

“But sir,” Florence began, “My father has just said we cannot afford a saddle horse for me.”

Henry laughed, “I know he did, I heard him, Indy will be a gift to you for taking care of these poor creatures, and in addition, I will send someone over to teach you to ride, you can wait a month or two until the weather improves I hope.”

The hint of rose in the girls cheeks flushed all over her face, embarrassment faltered her response, “Sir I don’t know what to say, I cannot accept such a gift from you.”

“Of course you can and say nothing of it, just make sure you have a stable ready, say, by the end of February, beginning of March, or preferably sooner,” Henry turned to George, “You can arrange that, along with the other things we discussed can’t you?”

George inhaled slowly, he understood the meaning of Henry's gesture, do as you are told, and I can be generous, cross me and look to your future.

George conceded, "I fully understand your meaning Mr Cotes, Florence shall have her stable, it will be ready, and your other instructions will be followed."

Florence rushed across the barn, threw her arms around her father's neck and kissed him on the cheek, "Thank you, thank you father," she exclaimed in excitement.

George was embarrassed by this display of affection in company, "Yes, Yes, well well," he muttered incoherently, "But it is Mr Cotes you should be thanking my dear, but perhaps a little less passionately."

The girl turned to Henry, curtsied perfectly, "Thank you sir, I will look after your ponies, you will not be disappointed."

"I am sure of that young lady, if you need anything do not hesitate to ask, send word to my steward," Henry replied with a rather smug smile. This young lady when groomed and introduced to society, a task he intended passing to his daughter, would be a welcome addition to his family, even if it was only to the clandestine branch he had recently discovered.

Driving back along Tilly Lane Henry had the opportunity to reflect on the afternoons events at Valley Farm.

As he comfortably navigated the car down the slight incline of the lane, he decided, yes, overall, a most satisfactory outcome, a profitable afternoon, several loose ends tied up at very little expense.

Two days ago, Zack Morgan had provided a very useful written statement, which would go a long way towards exonerating Tilly Pit's owners and management of the responsibility for the explosion and its subsequent aftermath.

This young illegitimate son of his late partner had done so under the impression that by so doing, his status in life would be improved and a suitable position would be his in return for his co-operation. Henry had, this very afternoon set wheels in motion to this end, the lad would believe Henry had kept his side of the implied bargain, and Zack should keep his in return. Little did Zack Morgan know his father, the late squire of Highfield had left Valley Farm to him regardless of how his elder legitimate son fared in running the estate. The title deeds were to pass to the younger son following the demise of the squire's invalid wife. A further condition of the will existed regarding all other holdings transferred on a temporary basis to Henry. He was to manage these and provide the old squire's widow with a comfortable income. In the event of Charles Heath junior proving to be, as everyone expected, completely useless when it came to managing his business affairs, and he squandered or lost his share of the estate, following the death of Anne Heath, all of the temporary holdings under Henry's administration would also fall to the younger son.

The onus would fall upon Lydia to produce the lads' birth certificate in proof of his heritage and entitlement to the legacy.

Henry tittered to himself as he swung the car to the right out of the end of Tilly Lane, heading towards Highfield, he thought to himself, Nice move Charles old boy, even I wouldn't have thought of that one, you crafty old devil, but maybe there are a few holes in your well laid out plan?

Henry was prepared for the time being to execute the will as it stood and to provide an income for his sister, unfortunately, he was not alone in these proceedings, family lawyers were also involved, he was relying that in time they would not be watching as closely as they were at present. Being the man he was, Henry fully intended, once his sister had departed this earth to keep a fair proportion of the temporary holdings for himself. As he turned left at the top of the hill into Highfield Hall's long driveway, an annoying thought occurred to him. Lydia Morgan denied all knowledge regarding the contents of Charles's will, she was however very clever, and she knew how to keep a secret, if Charles had ever discussed with her the bequests he intended, she may prove troublesome if he tried keeping anything for himself.

"Don't underestimate that woman Henry, be on your guard," he muttered to himself, a habit of his, which, he found not only helped to clear his mind, but also helped him to remember something important without risking committing it to paper. Even he, at times found it difficult keeping so many dodgy balls in the air at the same time, writing anything down could be dangerous if it fell into the wrong hands, he was under stress now, he had Charles's will to sort out, and, responsibility for an explosion causing loss of life to avoid.

Henry Cotes brought his car to a standstill at the same point he had used on the previous two days, the wide verge at the top of the steep hill in the drive, took out his hipflask and took a large nip of malt. He lingered there in the car a few moments to clear his mind, he had a choice, Lydia's son was still at Valley Farm and would probably be there with the alluring Florence until quite late. Should he call again on Lydia and try to ascertain, if she in fact did have any knowledge of the conditions in Charles's will. Without asking her directly it would be difficult, Lydia was clever and astute, a match for any man. His other choice would be to go directly to the hall. He took a cigar from his case and put a match flame to its end, as he did so, he remembered Joseph Shaw's confusion brought on by the arrival of two engineers at the pit that morning. Henry's decision was made for him, he was now beginning to feel a little tired, and the lesser of the two evils appealed to him, he would not have to think quickly with someone he just had to bully. Right Charles, you young idiot, time to sort you out, resolutely he climbed out of his vehicle and strode off down the hill towards Highfield Hall.

Chapter Eleven

A little after one o'clock and the men of the Larchwood rescue team steadily returned along the main roadways towards cage bottom. The teams captain George Sanders having fallen as a casualty to the choke damp, the deputy captain John Tomkins now led this column of men. Diffusion of the light cast from their combined lamps prevented all but the leader's eyes from penetrating the blackness ahead, in the distance, John could just make out the glimmer of four stationary lights ahead, finding this and its probable implication amusing, he shouted back.

"Aye up Albert."

"What's up now?" Albert grunted in response.

"Nowt really, just that it looks like you were right, there's a light up yonder and it's too far in for Seth and the rest of your lads to have landed yet, reckon like you said, we've caught up with them toffs, them so called engineers."

"You got to be joking; I was taking the piss when I said that, they should have been out of here long since, better get a move on and see what's up."

Weaving around the collapsed pit props and roof falls in their path, the men picked up their pace as best they could, as they closed the distance, one flickering lamp ahead appeared to rise from the floor and float back along the crut towards them.

The ghostly lamplight approached the column, rejoining the rescue team the bearer of which was immediately recognised.

John greeted him, "Why are you still down here Ernie? What's going on? You should have reached the cage long since and be out by now."

"John, I know that, but you saddled us with looking after that pair of fancy buggers, they might have brains an be clever like, but no brawn, they've had it, they've collapsed, and two of us can't carry three men out, so we decided to wait for you lot to come back and give us a hand."

"Collapsed, why, did you run into a patch of damp?"

"No, nowt like that, the air is clean enough, think the heat's got to them, seems they're still wearing all their fancy topside clothes under them overall things they've both got on, we told them lose some layers and to strip off like we do, but they won't have any of it. They've drank all their own water and most of ours, they slowed us down all the way and we finished up only covering about twenty yards at a stretch, then half an hour ago they gave up and insisted on resting. Little goatee says they shouldn't have to walk carrying breathing apparatus and the like, not to mention a dead man the size of Old Bull as well, he says that's what servants are for."

With the men huddled into a tight group, Albert complained, "I still can't figure out what they are doing down here in the first place, it's obvious they know nowt about the workings of a pit, they're down here as spies, nowt but the bloody owners puppets, and I for one ain't going to carry them back out again."

"Someone will have to Albert; there was no way the two of us could manage them," Ernie insisted.

"They can bloody well walk out, or wait where they are until the rails are fixed and next wagon train comes this far in," the old man added with his customary contempt for the upper classes.

John, well aware of the older man's dislike of the gentry, and his vicious distrust of their motives, countermanded his cynicism.

"Don't be like that Albert, have a heart man, we can't just leave them in here, it will be days before the haulage rails get repaired this far in, but I have to agree with you, this is no place for soft, weak, toffee nosed sods like them. How about we chuck their Nevito's and packs on one of these stretchers, the rest of you lads can take turns keeping the pair of them on their feet, at least until we get back to wherever the crews have reached repairing the track for the haulage tubs. Then we load them in one of the tubs and send the pair of them on their merry way."

"I'll still bet them sissies will want carrying out," Albert insisted scornfully.

John snorted a response, "If they demand that, we tell them only dead, or badly injured men who can't walk are carried out,—Albert, any idea how far it is to where the haulage rails are back down?"

"Wouldn't like to guess on that, it's been a while since I worked this far in, you got any idea Lijah?"

Elijah pondered before offering his opinion, "Reckon about a third to half a mile up the crut, maybe a bit more."

Albert chirped up, "Oh! In that case John, we tell those bastards it's only a couple of hundred yards or less, make the buggers walk. Old Bull wasn't taking any of their crap; he knew that unlike the rest of us they only come down here looking for money not men. Make them find out the hard way what it's like down here everyday for the likes of us."

Most of the other men had developed a distinct dislike for the comical pair; they were all in agreement with the old hands roguish suggestion. George Sanders had been right, even a tragedy such as this should have its lighter side, tales of the mornings exploits of Sideburn and Goatee may well provide the villagers with an amusing anecdote to lighten their spirits for some time to come.

Therefore, it was in this way those who went into the mines deeper districts that morning made their way out, George's body reverently carried on a stretcher by his loyal men at the rear of the column, whilst the visiting engineers, supported between two miners staggered laboured step by laboured step at the columns centre. None of the party could be certain if it was heat exhaustion, or just sheer terror that robbed these visitors of the use of their legs, nevertheless, within half an hour, the sounds of Seth's repair crew working up ahead could be heard.

"Are the phones working this far in Seth?" Albert asked as the two groups joined.

"Yep, just tested this last one," Seth replied looking around expectantly, "Where's Bull? Is he bringing up the rear for a change?"

After the briefest pause, which, to the Larchwood squad seemed an interminable age, the last men of their column carrying two stretchers entered the pool of light cast by the hung lamps; John Tomkins laid down his pack and quietly answered.

"He is Seth, but not by choice."

Seth again looked expectantly back down the tunnel, suddenly he realised one of the stretchers was not loaded with equipment.

"Oh no!" he exclaimed, "What the hell happened down there?"

Exhausted, the Larchwood men all deposited their loads at the side of the tunnel and sat to rest a while, Albert and Lijah came over to Seth to report the morning's events that led to his counterparts' body now lying on the stretcher. They explained how they found a narrow way into the first of the dips, and the entrance to the second completely blocked off. How they had cut a way through the stand of coal at the dogleg section from dip number one into the second dip's tunnel, and that George, being team leader, had crawled through first to check it out before they all entered.

"We had to crawl through on our hands and knees, I was third in line waiting for George to signal us through," Lijah said.

John came across and took over the story, "He had gone about four or five yards in when we heard him cursing, and then, he just collapsed. It turned out the crut is full of choke damp and his Nevito wasn't working right, by the time we got him out it was too late, he was a goner."

News of the loss of the visiting team leader came as another sickening blow for Seth and the men of Tilly. Seth's face indicated he suspected this loss might have been avoided; his mind was racing, he had never liked the idea, and certainly did not agree with the management's decision to pool every team's equipment for anyone to use. Now a visiting volunteer leader had been lost because of a faulty breathing unit, by rights, they should have been thoroughly checked before being issued, had a faulty one accidently been missed and found its way into the ready pool.

Seth asked, "Which is the Nevito George used?"

John rummaged through all the units dumped in a pile at the side of the tracks.

"Pretty sure it was this one," he held aloft a unit with its harness damaged by the Larchwood men ripping it off their leader, preserving equipment had been the last thing on their minds.

Seth asked apprehensively, "Is it one you brought with you from Larchwood?"

John replied angrily chucking the offending unit back onto the pile, "Might be, there's no way of knowing for sure none of ours were marked, not numbered or anything, they are the same type you chaps use here, why do you ask?"

"Oh, no reason, just wondered," Seth tried to sound nonchalant, but inwardly he seethed with fury, he remembered when the Larchwood team joined up with the Tilly crew that morning in the tunnel, George told him they had been delayed, and had drawn their equipment from those units which remained left over in the apparatus pool. This may have been one of Tilly Pits own units, and Seth knew very well, at Tilly, equipment was not well maintained or replaced if faulty, this was a suspicion he must keep to himself, to mention it now without proof, and a man dead on a stretcher would help no one.

Any fault on the unit, could well have been compounded by John Tomkins launching the offending breathing unit back onto the pile at the side of the tunnel, as he did; he only narrowly missed hitting the dishevelled visitors who the men had dropped in a heap along with their other equipment. Seth indicated in their direction, and making sure everyman heard him, changed the subject.

"I hope your trip down wasn't a total loss John, were your guests here able to compile their report?"

The visiting engineers, as he intended heard him, both looked up, neither man spoke but Sideburn limply waved his hand gesturing they could not comment.

John Tomkins sank his elbow into Seth's side and whispered in his ear, "Shut up, tell you later when we've got rid of them."

Six tubs stood fifteen yards up the haulage road, the day shift now nearing its end most of the contents of these had been used, they were almost empty. Seth picked up the receiver of the nearest telephone, cranked the handle, relayed a brief report of the repairs and of the mishap in the dips. He ordered Bernie in the engine room either to put his call through to the office, or to get authorisation for men to ride up.

While they waited for an authorisation from the surface, Seth's men transferred all of their remaining materials onto the last two tubs, and unhooked them from the other four.

Of the remaining four still hitched, George's stretcher was laid across the top of the lead tub, and the Nevito's loaded into the end tubs, filling one and half filling the other. After five minutes the phone rang, it was Arthur Cleaver.

"Bad news this Seth, we aren't drawing coal, so the men can ride out at their own risk. Cotes has been in this morning, seems he knew nothing about those visitors you have with you, don't say too much now if they are in earshot, come into the office when you get back up and make a full report. Signal Bernie when the tubs are ready, and make sure those engineer bods are in them."

"Understood," Seth replaced the receiver.

"Well?" John asked.

"Yes, a ride up, pick as many of your lads as you think should go," Seth replied, turning to the engineers he said in a sarcastic tone, "Right Gentlemen, your carriages await."

Sideburn and Goatee, sweat still pouring from them staggered towards the waiting train. The tubs were iron and high-sided, hours ago when they arrived on a similar train, these men had been cocky and arrogant, at that time they were relatively fresh, but even then they struggled to climb out of the tub, now neither man could muster enough strength to climb into one.

As they struggled, Seth, John and the men watched in disbelief and amusement, shaking their heads and muttering, until John finally lost his patience.

"Oh for God's sake lads, lift them into that second tub," he shouted.

Goatee glared at him but said nothing; neither he, nor his silent companion had the strength left to argue after their excursion descending into the bowels of the earth. Two men climbed into the lead tub, one either side of the stretcher to hold it steady on the way back to the cage, the engineers plus three miners rode in the second, and another two men squeezed into the little remaining space with the Nevito's in the third. The train ready, Seth signalled Bernie, within seconds there was the clanking of tightening chains, slowly, they took the strain and the tubs departed at less than half their normal speed.

The rumble of the departing train faded into the distance, during the ensuing silence the remaining men relaxed, the absence of the strangers, allegedly engaged by the mine owners meant they could now speak freely of the morning's events.

Albert Beech was the first to comment, "Glad to see the back of those two idiots, honest to God, I have never seen their like in a pit before, what the hell they were doing down here I have no idea."

"No Albert," John added, "Neither have I, they didn't seem to do anything except make our job a lot harder, they were like a pair of spoilt kids wanting to be waited on all the time, if any of my kids behaved like that they would get a clout round the ear."

Sam Swindon intervened, "Oh come on Lads, they must have had a good reason for coming down, surely they did something, what did the rest of you make of them? Lijah, did you form a different opinion of them than these two?"

"No father, I have to agree with Albert, all I saw them do when we got to the dips was to get blueprints out of those bags they carried, lay them on the floor and pretend to read them by lamp-light, they were a burden to us and held us back something shocking."

"Aye, that's right lad," chorused the men.

Sam persisted, "Are you telling us that not a single one of you knows why they were down here?"

All the men who returned from the dips, in confirmation, shrugged and muttered amongst themselves expressing their utter confusion regarding the stranger's actual purpose.

"Well Sam, I for one can believe that," Seth announced.

Everyone's eyes turned attentively towards him, he went on to explain his reason.

"Just now when the surface rang me back about a ride up, it was Arthur Cleaver on the phone. Seems that Henry Cotes bloke, you know, the bigger one of the two owners, he has been on the pit bank this morning, and he knew nothing about them being here either, or even who they are, and according to Cleaver, he was not best pleased they had been allowed down here."

General murmurs of amazement at Seth's revelation ended in boisterous laughter, if the pit's deputy manager didn't know who the visitors were, and the owner didn't know either, just who the blazes were they. The end of their shift approaching, Albert, Lijah and the Larchwood team spent time narrating incidents of their mission into the dips, both comical and tragic.

Their shift ended, the men began to prepare for their long hike back to pit bottom, the phone rang and Seth answered it, when he rejoined them, most of the men looked toward him expectantly, half-expecting more problems or new instructions.

"The noon shift is riding down," he said, "Bernie says if we hang on here until they get down and unload the gear they have with them, the tubs will be going back for the rest of it so if we want to we can ride back up in the empty tubs."

"That's jolly nice of them," Albert scoffed with his unmistakable air of sarcasm, "All of a sudden we are important, still I suppose after a long shift it's better than walking."

Waiting on the surface by the cage gate for the morning shift and remaining members of Larchwood's rescue team to return above ground, stood Arthur Cleaver.

"Everything alright with you lads is it?" he asked, more in hope than expectation.

"Aye, right enough, apart from what you already know about," Seth replied sombrely, "You'll be wanting that full report I take it."

"Yes, but under the circumstances, we mainly need to know what happened in the dips from John here, and our own men who went down there with him. Mr Shaw wants it filed in writing as soon as possible; his clerk is waiting to take notes from you men and type it out for you to sign, it may take some time so Mr Shaw suggests you all have something to eat and a hot drink before we start."

Everyone was surprised at the offer of a free meal, however, those men not required for the report, declined, preferring the hot meal they expected at home than sandwiches.

Seth asked in surprise, "Have those engineer bods made a report already?"

"No, not exactly," Arthur replied with a broad grin across his face, and to answerer the inquiring looks of the other men, he continued.

"When they finally arrived back up here, they went across to the first aid room for the medics to check them over, then they got cleaned up a bit, got straight back into their little motor and scampered off, back, from whence they came."

Albert Beech could not resist asking, "They said nothing then?"

"The little mouthy one with the beard did, I accidentally on purpose overheard him tell Mr Shaw, that no matter how big a fee he was offered, he wouldn't go back down there again, I seem to remember the phrase, 'not for a kingdom,' being used."

All the men burst into fits of laughter.

"Oh dear, what a shame," John said in mock sympathy, "The poor buggers have had a little taste of our lifestyle and toddled off back to their comfortable offices no doubt."

"Shot off to change their bloody trousers I reckon," Albert added gleefully, "I'm sure I detected a distinct, delicate odour from the pair of them when we lifted them into that tub and sent them on their merry way back to pit bottom."

"Albert, you mischievous old bugger, sometimes you have an eloquent turn of phrase," laughed Seth.

"Well, what do you expect," muttered the old hand, "Useless pair of toffee nosed pillocks, treating us like dirt and lording it over us like they did, the likes of them have no business being here at times like these."

By the time John Tomkins, Albert Beech and Elijah Swindon, made their way towards the office block to begin to compile a report on the incidents of the day, the majority of the early shift miners had long since left for their homes. Their report would definitely be needed at the inquest on George Sanders, and probably again at an official inquiry into the explosion itself. They all knew it would have to be as accurate as possible, and the contents agreed by all of them. On their way along the corridor to the manager's office, they met Seth Fuller on his way out, his own report on the repair work already made.

"Be careful how you phrase things lads," he said quietly, "That Joseph Shaw can be slippery; he may try to lay the blame off on you if you let him, and I know it was no fault of yours Old Bull met his end down there, be very careful."

Albert grunted, "Oh, that's his game is it, he's got no bloody chance."

Seth raised his hand to silence the old hand, "Just be careful, Eh, just be careful," he said, his voice fading to an almost inaudible whisper, when, out of the corner of his eye, he caught sight of Joseph Shaw appearing at his office doorway.

"This way men," Joseph called along the corridor, "I trust you have had some refreshment after your shift, I won't keep you long, well, I hope not anyway, but we need to get all the details of this sad affair down on paper, you understand don't you?"

The three men confirmed they understood the necessity of a written report, and disappeared into the office.

* * *

Daylight fading fast as Henry Cotes passed through the wrought iron gates of Highfield Hall; he checked his watch, a few minutes before four o'clock, if his nephew spent the night at home even he should be out of his bed by now.

Henry coveted this Georgian style grey stone building, standing as it did three stories high and having attics and servant's quarters in the apex roofs of all four wings, at its centre, topped by turrets a higher ornate square tower, above each of the four wings, chimneystacks rose cleverly disguised to give the appearance of yet more turrets. The large, lavish windows adorning the front of the hall were bayed on all three stories. Every window around the hall, including those in the tower had been decorated with leaded glass, and tipping at the roof, ivy climbed ornately up the walls. Courtyard, outbuildings, and stables at the rear were of similar design, lawns and gardens, due, largely to his sister's obsession with them kept immaculate, even now, in the middle of winter they were a remarkable sight.

By comparison, Henry's manner house in Cheshire, 'Kirkleston' was a plain, tall, narrow building of red brick, externally nowhere near as aesthetically appealing to the eye, but inside, lavishly furnished as any home belonging to other men of wealth and influence.

Henry breathed a sigh of relief to see his nephew's new motorcar parked in the front drive; for once, he had managed to catch the errant young man at home. However, he was less pleased, when, as he drew closer to the vehicle he noticed the front bumper bar and nearside mudguard badly bent out of shape, obviously, Charles had collided against something with a great deal of force, only yesterday Anne had told him payment for this car was still outstanding. Henry was just about to ring the doorbell when a sickening thought struck him; he turned and looked again at the badly damaged car on the drive.

Perhaps Charles has just left this here and taken one of his father's cars instead, in which case, I have had another wasted journey.

Desperately hoping he was wrong, Henry rang the bell.

Highfield Hall employed neither butler nor permanent housekeeper; eventually the door was opened by the footman, Hawkins, a middle-aged man resplendent in his blue and gold livery.

"Is your master at home?" Henry asked as he passed through the vestibule.

"I believe the squire is in the billiard room sir," replied the footman, relieving Henry of his hat and overcoat.

Without response, Henry strode purposefully to the billiard room.

Charles Heath Jnr laid down the cue with which he had been amusing himself by potting snooker balls.

"Good afternoon uncle, I am pleased to see you, mother said you called yesterday afternoon, unfortunately however I was delayed in town, but now you are here there are quite a few things I wish to discuss."

Henry smiled, highly amused by Charles's arrogant attitude, as a boy his parents always indulged his whims, the result of this only contributed to turning him into a rather obnoxious character. Charles now pompously played the role of master of the house, in doing so making himself look even more ridiculous.

"Do you?" replied his uncle, heading straight for the whisky decanter, "I am very pleased to hear it, I have one or two points I need to discuss with you also." Sarcasm had always been one of Henry's favourite tools; he relished the chance to tease the lad before taking him down a peg or two.

"Quite so uncle, mother is encouraging me to take an interest in business matters," Charles continued in what he believed to be a business like manner, "I have been looking through some of the ledgers and papers father left in his study, you, as executer to his will were present at its reading. True, I wasn't at my best that day, but I remember something being said about a few paltry bequests expected to be made to servants, and there being some kind of special conditions which would take time to arrange, that was weeks ago, I need to know how much longer before my father's estate is released to me?"

"Have you discussed these matters with your mother Charles?"

The younger man leered, "With a woman? Certainly not, she knows nothing about business matters; now the estate is mine I intend to make a great many changes, and I need everything including all available capital released to me as soon as possible. Since my father died all I have received from the estate is a token allowance, a situation that I do not believe is right, or fair. The whole estate is mine by succession; therefore all holdings and money should be in my control, not still lodged with some firm of lawyers."

Henry raised his glass to his lips; and smirking behind it, he took a sip of malt.

"I was not aware you had ever taken an interest in the running of this estate or any other business matters Charles, after all, you were rarely here; tell me, have your recent studies enlightened you as to the extent of your late father's holdings?"

"Everything he owned you mean, no I never bothered to look into that, I presumed I would be told at some date in the near future, I know he owned, and now I own, everything for miles around, thousands of acres of land and all the properties on it, is that not correct uncle?"

Henry frowned, "No Charles I'm afraid not, your father was successful building the family estates in his younger days. He vastly increased its value and accumulated a sound business portfolio from that which he inherited from your grandfather; but covering your debts reduced it a vast amount. You as the new squire now have the responsibility to work the estate and other holdings to re-establish any of its lost value."

Charles Heaths' eyes widened and his jaw dropped, Henry had used a word totally alien to his nephew, clearly, he was not amused.

"Work uncle? Surely running an estate is just a matter of occasional supervision, does not wealth increase on its own. What is the point of being rich if you are still expected to work; we have people to do the work for us, do we not?"

Henry Cotes had spent that afternoon in enjoyable convivial company. Now he was torn, if he was to achieve his prime intention this evening to reprimand his nephew severely for his ill-timed interference at the mine, and also honour the promise he made to the lad's father to guide him in the ways of commerce, he would need to temper the rage he felt. Reluctantly he chose to remain patient.

"Charles, there is manual work which many do for a pittance of a wage, which we do not, instead we have to plan ahead, negotiate deals which makes our money work for us, you are under a misapprehension if you think money multiplies of its own accord. Did it never occur to you to seek guidance from your father in readiness for the time when you became squire?"

Charles lapsed into thoughtful silence for a few seconds, "There was a time uncle after I decided not to attend university, for a couple of months father tried to persuade me to take an interest, but I found it boring, no fun in it, I just couldn't be bothered. However, I can remember some scratchy details from that time about the land he owned here, and I am pretty sure he had properties and business interests in Wales and Shropshire."

Henry now began to understand why Charles Heath senior made such detailed provision for the future of the family and estate when his cancer was diagnosed, and in view of his nephews naivety, now in many ways respected that decision.

"You have a great deal to learn Charles, it will not be as easy as you seem to think, but, as you are taking an interest now, perhaps you would like to discuss with me the things you have in mind, and the changes you wish to make."

Charles Heath, with the vanity of youth, seriously believed he had the upper hand over his uncle; he poured himself a drink, settled himself in the chair by the fire opposite Henry, and confidently continued.

"For a start uncle, a good many of the workers and tenant farmers will have to be replaced, I am not impressed with the lazy way they are working my land, and the estates income from them is by no means enough. Receipt of rents for the houses on the estate is erratic, some of the ones I now know of I can find no record of any rent being paid for years. As far as I can make out from the few documents I found, the only thing which yields a regular high return is the coal mine, and even that is not producing at present, but, I have done something to remedy that."

"Really, what have you done?"

Henry knew the answer, after all, it had been the deciding factor of his two possible destinations this evening, but the opportunity to aggravate his nephew and possibly teach him a lesson was far too good to miss.

"I had some good fortune uncle, the bad weather stranded me in Castleton on Saturday evening, and I had to stay over night at the Castle Hotel."

"Had to stay, or preferred to because of the company you were in?" Henry scoffed.

A lecherous grin covered Charles's face as he admitted, "I did have a young lady with me, not from our social circle of course, but very pretty, so I suppose preferred to is nearer the mark, but that is beside the point."

Henry frowning, shook his head in disgust, to which his nephew grinned in satisfaction, this old man, his uncle, what he would know about the delights to be had with a young woman he could not imagine, delighted, he continued with his story.

"We were in the lounge bar after dinner, and by chance, an acquaintance of mine, Geoffrey Webster was there, he is a first class engineer, always takes delight in talking about how clever he is and his degree, anyway, he said he has worked on tunnels quite a lot."

"Tunnels,—what kind of tunnels?" Henry inquired fast becoming bored with his nephew's conceit.

"Railway tunnels, canals, that sort of thing, I told him about the trouble we had at the coal mine and that coal production had stopped because of it, and as a result, considerable income for me. He said it was not a major problem, and that he could have it producing again in no time at all, even more than it has ever yielded before, so I engaged him to compile a report for us, he should be there now. I called at the mine yesterday and told that stupid manager to give him all the assistance he needed when he arrived; we will have money flowing from the mine again very soon."

Henry had tolerated his nephew's attitude long enough, slowly and deliberately he set his glass down on the small table by his side, leaned forward in his chair, fixed Charles with a stern gaze and said in a quiet, forceful tone.

"Just what kind of bloody fool are you, you young idiot, you call the pit manager stupid, incredible, Charles, to me you are the living example which gives credence to the theory of reincarnation, no one could possibly be as stupid as you in one lifetime."

His nephew was stunned by the rebuke, his face turned crimson; opening his mouth tried to respond but could not speak his mind a complete blank, Henry continued in the same tone.

"Quite apart from there being a world of difference between a permanent brick built railway tunnel and a mine's crut propped up on posts, you have sent strangers into our mine, men who could well be called to give evidence when the inquiry into Saturday's accident convenes. Money flow from the mine, it is more likely it will never operate again. I told you on Saturday you could lose everything, including your estate if things go badly and negligence is proved against us. I also suggested you find a wife with the financial means to support you, and what did you do instead; go cavorting around town with some young tart."

But, but . . ." Charles began.

"Shut up and listen to me," Henry snapped, his voice no longer quiet, nearing instead high pitched rage, "You will not go near that mine unless I am with you, you will not discuss anything regarding it with anyone, and you most certainly will not issue any more orders to Joseph Shaw or anyone else, is that understood?"

Charles cowered in his chair; no one had ever chastised him in this way, he liked to exude the impression of being bold and debonair, however, his upbringing had done little towards building character, instead it left him cowardly. Slowly Charles regained his composure, events had taken a turn he had not anticipated, his uncle, obviously furious, may not be inclined to cooperate and hasten the release of his legacy. Now, he realised if anything could be salvaged after this error of judgement that so infuriated his uncle, he must appear humble and submissive.

"Uncle Henry, if my actions have displeased you I am truly sorry, the mine producing coal again was my only thought, I will contact Geoffrey and cancel my instruction."

"Too late for that, the mine was the first place I called this morning, and two men from some engineering establishment were down below ground then, you made me look stupid, Shaw thought I sent them, and of course I knew nothing at all about it. We can only hope that from the description you have given of this person you engaged, like you he is all blether, and neither he nor his companion will have any ideas regarding the significance of anything they might see."

Charles sheepishly asked, "You do not want me to contact Geoffrey and tell him his services are not required then?"

Henry's temper mellowed slightly, "In fairness, perhaps you should, they will not be allowed onto the site again, I left strict instructions with Joseph Shaw to that effect this morning."

"I really am sorry uncle; I thought you would be pleased, not angry."

Henry, with a little help from his glass of malt had mellowed completely, "Very well, but in future, do as you are told,"

"Now, the other matter you mentioned, your father's will."

Charles immediately cheered up at the mention of the will and paid attention.

Henry noted this and continued, "I know lawyers are renowned for working at one speed if they are not continually chased, that speed being almost stopped, the longer they take, the more they believe they can charge for their services. However, the last time I saw them to discuss the matter they were in the process of proportioning which of your father's properties is to pass to you."

"Proportioning uncle, proportioning, I don't understand, as his only son and heir it should all come to me."

Henry inhaled slowly, "I knew you weren't listening when your father's will was read, you started celebrating becoming squire too early, before he was buried in fact. If you had been sober and paid more attention, you would know a large proportion of the estate is to be held in trust. It was your father's wish you prove you are capable of managing an estate, rather than loosing everything by some rash action."

Charles leapt up, stamped his feet in anger, "That's not fair," he screamed, "Why shouldn't it all come to me now."

"There is more to being a squire than an honouree title Charles, there are many responsibilities, people to look after, to my knowledge, and I'm sad to say your father's, you have never thought of anyone but yourself."

Charles stormed, "People to look after, whom for instance?"

"Your mother, the servants, employees and tenants of the estate to name but a few," Henry replied calmly.

"Oh, that's marvellous, father didn't trust me at all, is that what you are saying?"

Henry could not help feeling a little sorry for the lad; clearly, he was hurt by this revelation.

"He wanted to trust you Charles, but your wild ways did not inspire confidence, and your father being the man he was decided not to leave anything to chance, I know it was a very difficult decision for him to make. However, eventually he decided to leave in trust a sum of money and some properties."

Charles began to panic; he had made many rash commitments and issued promissory notes on the strength of his expected inheritance, he had incurred many bills since his father's death. Before, when this familiar problem arose he only needed to complain to his mother of being short of funds, she in turn would speak to his father and the problems disappeared, for over a year this had not happened, he had complained but his father had not settled his debts. His visions of great wealth and renewed pleasures seemed to be slipping from his grasp.

"The part of the estate in trust, what happens to it, who is to look after it, does it revert to me once I succeed and prove you all wrong?"

The question hit Henry with a jolt, rational, logical reasoning from his nephew was the last thing he expected, if this continued he would need to be cautious, some of the lands held in trust would compliment his own estate very nicely, and he intended to have them.

"Your father believed you have much to learn, he has arranged for the administration of the trust to be undertaken by the family solicitors Carpenter, Chaddock & Carr and myself, and yes, regardless of your success or failure the estate remains in the family."

"How much of his fortune, excluding the trust is left in my control?"

Henry lied, "I do not know exactly, but I imagine quite a considerable proportion. A few moments ago, you mentioned Wales and Shrewsbury,

I know something of the predicament your father found himself in near the end, and I mean his business, not health. Any holdings outside this immediate area, for some reason, quite possibly your spending habits, your father found it necessary to dispose of. All that is left now is the Highfield estate itself, and even some of that has now gone, but as you said, the coal mine did provide the most regular income, and that may now have gone for ever."

Charles remained silent for some time, refilled his glass to the brim, "So uncle, my position seems to be, I only have part of father's estate, to continue living as I do I have to expand, but how?"

Once again, the logic from his nephew astounded Henry, but he knew this would soon pass, his nephew was holding a full glass of malt whisky.

"I have already made a suggestion as to how Charles, a good marriage is always a sure way to increase ones wealth."

Charles smirked, "True uncle, you have, and someone comes to mind, a young lady by the name of Alexandra, she is an exquisite creature and her father is extremely rich, owns about half of Bursley, I met her at the Christmas Ball there last year."

Henry burst into a fit of laughter, "You mean Alexandra Wickersby I take it, forget it my boy, no way on God's earth would her father allow a rake like you within a hundred yards of her. You would be better employed passing the beauties over, look instead amongst the wallflowers, the plain girls to whom nobody pays particular attention; there are a few very wealthy ones amongst those who their families are desperate to marry off."

"You would have me marry a hag uncle, no way, that I definitely refuse."

Once again, Henry took a sterner tone, "No Charles, I would not have you marry a hag as you so charmingly put it, if you and this estate are to survive, I would have you marry for wealth and property. No matter whom you take as a wife, I am sure your carousing, wanton ways will not change, find a rich wife able to support you, and if you can provide a legitimate heir to this estate, so much the better."

"Uncle, you ask too much of me. Seek a prospective bride irrespective of their appearance from amongst those who have long been rejected by other men, no matter how hideous they may be, or even someone much older purely because she has money, and then produce an heir. How can you possibly expect me to breed with someone like that, even I need some stimulation in that department, I am not a machine you know."

Henry smiled, and shaking his head quietly replied, "Charles dear boy, how little you know, how much you have to learn. Young women of good social standing, unlike the ones you cavort with, more than likely will have been told by their mothers that in order to perform their marital duties in the bedroom, it is often better to close their eyes, lie back and think of England. Although, it is a fact, some do eventually develop an appetite for the conjugal rights. If your wife does not excite you in that way, make sure the necessary activity takes place in the dark; sometimes it is necessary to ensure the family line continues with a legitimate heir. You will not be the first man to perform his marital bedroom duties in the dark with his imagination running wild. As for your other conquests, I care not whether they infect you, or you infect them, contracting a malady is common for those who choose your favoured lifestyle, assuming that is, it is not already with you."

"I take exception to that last remark uncle, and what do you mean by continual reference to a legitimate heir."

"Charles, Charles, don't give me that, how many illegitimate offspring's do you have up to now, or have you lost count?"

Charles Heath scowled and sank the remaining malt in his glass, "Damn it," he growled, "I forgot you and father knew about that, are those floozies getting money which is rightfully mine, and is it left to them in fathers' will?"

Henry could not help but smile at the outburst, "No Charles, they already have settlements arranged long ago and managed by your father personally, just remember, an illegitimate child could have a claim on the estate if you fail to produce a legitimate heir, and having said that once, I shall not say it again."

Charles showed a spark of bewilderment at his uncle's last point, but the half bottle of whisky he consumed rather quickly was now taking effect, dulling his wits, and he failed to query the last remark.

As far as Henry was concerned, his nephew had now been warned of the consequences of failing to succeed in business and produce an heir to the estate, not quite in the way his brother-in-law had suggested Henry should tell him. The main secret still safe, no mention had been made of the fact Charles actually had a half brother, a young man who in Henry's eyes seemed twice the man Charles Heath Junior could ever be.

There was a gentle tap at the door and the maid entered, "Excuse me sirs," she said, "But the mistress is asking if Mr Henry will be staying for dinner."

"Thank you Hannah, but I think not," Henry replied.

The maid curtsied and smiled, "If you declined Mr Henry, I am to tell you it is venison sir."

Both men smiled at the girl's embarrassment, Henry realised Anne, expecting her brother to call today had ordered the dinner especially.

"In that case," Henry chuckled, "Inform your mistress I would be delighted to stay for dinner, and, dependant on the travelling conditions outside, possibly the night."

Chapter Twelve

Tuesday, 15th January 1918, dawned damp, drizzly, with a hanging mist shrouding the countryside in an eerie ghostly cloak, however, the early morning promised the distinct possibility air temperature would climb higher than it managed to reach over the previous few days. Three days of intermittent rain showers had almost cleared away the grounds blanket of white, only the dirtied, dismal remains of snowdrifts where they had formed in dips and gullies were still visible.

Henry Cotes had spent the night at Highfield Hall, and today he breakfasted earlier than normal. The previous evening he had voiced his intention of visiting Tilly Pit again this morning, and mischievously suggested his nephew accompany him, much to Henry's surprise, he had just taken his place at the breakfast table as Charles joined him in the room.

"Good morning uncle," greeted Charles as he entered, and seeing Henry's full plate added, "Oh good, I have plenty of time for breakfast, but I will be ready to leave as soon as you are."

Henry grunted in amazement, "Wonders will never cease Charles, you, out of your bed and it is not yet ten o'clock, but I have to say you look rather the worse for wear, you had too much to drink last night. Still, if you are intent on coming with me this morning, do remember my advice, no more interference, keep your mouth shut, watch, listen and above all, learn."

"Very well uncle, I concede I was in error engaging consultants without discussing it with you first, and as you so adequately put it last night, there may not be any serious repercussions resulting from my error of judgement."

Henry smiled; despite the amount of alcohol Charles consumed last night, he appeared to have remembered the events of the evening clear enough.

"Perhaps not Charles, on that point at leased let us hope I am proved right."

Chatting about trivial things the two men ate breakfast, until suddenly Charles remembered something he found whilst rummaging around in his father's place of solace and favourite lair, the tower study. Charles Heath senior often used to retreat to this room, it was the highest in the hall and overlooked one of the prettiest spots on the estate, the Bluebell Wood; everyone, including the servants knew the squire was never to be disturbed there. Following his demise, out of curiosity, his son entered this room to try to understand his father's attachment to such an insignificant place, and while going through some of the personal possessions left there by his father, he came across something of an oddity, innocently he remarked to his uncle.

"Uncle Henry, I have been meaning to mention something to you; I found something amongst father's belongings which I think you may like as a keep-sake."

"Oh, really, what was that?"

"Well I told you I had been looking through some of father's papers and things."

"You did,—what of it?"

"As you know, he never could tolerate inane female chatter, whenever mother had her friends staying here he used to escape to that room of his in the tower, you know the one. Anyway, there is an old chest up there; inside I found many old textbooks, his cap and gown from university and a small case with some silly things in it.

"Silly things,—what kind of silly things Charles?"

"I can't remember everything exactly, or what they could be used for. I didn't stay at university long enough, but from the short time I was there, I know students have all sorts of clubs and things to occupy their free time. You and father were at university together and I thought the contents of the case might be connected with something he joined then, and perhaps you had been a member or something. It occurred to me, as father saved those things all these years and I have no use for them, I thought you could have them, that is if you want them."

Charles's simple enough comment immediately caught Henry's undivided attention, "Can you remember anything of the contents Charles?"

"Yes, didn't make much sense to me though. There is a pair of white silk gloves, some sort of coloured sash, a notebook with gibberish in it, a fancy looking knife, no; it is double edged, so it's more of a dagger, and a beautifully embroidered big silly bib thing, blue with golden tassels, be about the size of a cushion cover. They must have cost him a small fortune in those days. Not the kind of thing I would have spent my allowance on, I can think of better things much more entertaining. There were other things as well, but I can't for the life of me remember, do they mean anything to you?"

Henry inhaled slowly and deeply, trying to steady the palpitations that suddenly afflicted him, after the death of his brother-in-law; he had, at every opportunity discretely searched Highfield for the items his nephew now described. Over a number of visits, he looked everywhere he could think of, the library, Charles's bedroom, his study, cupboards, chests of drawers, but it never occurred to him to look in the small tower room. For Charles to have kept something of value so close to the servant's quarters seemed to him to have been incredibly foolish.

The memory flashed through Henry's mind of the time he and Charles had been accompanied on that dark journey, not, as his nephew surmised at university, but some years later after they established themselves to be men of influence. The ceremonial oaths they had taken, *'on consequence of having their throats severed, their tongues rent from their mouths, and of being denounced as an intentionally perjured liar,'* still held true for him.

Charles's steadfast nature had been instrumental in his progression higher up the ranks of the brethren than Henry could ever hope to achieve. Henry always regarded as it is with politics, duplicity and lying to be an essential method of business, any solemn oath, or loyalty meant little to him if it hampered his own advancement, consequently, he had no hesitation in lying to his nephew now.

"It is true, there were student organisations with interests in many things, I can't say the items you describe mean an awful lot to me, but in memory of your father, I would be delighted to have them as a keep-sake."

Charles beamed, "I will make sure to fetch them down for you uncle before we leave, in fact, if you wish I could fetch them now."

Agitated, Henry replied, "No, no Charles, if your father kept them safely hidden all these years, leave them where they are for now, better than carrying them around in the car, I will collect them later."

Membership of that illustrious body of men had proved most useful in the past; and Henry was relying on this in his present dilemma to be beneficial now. The brethren, men of influence and power, many of whom also owned, or had financial interests in various collieries, even though his former partner Charles as a high-ranking member was now deceased, if the cause of Saturday's explosion were found to be largely the fault of the mine's owners they would almost certainly unite in his support. Similarly, should any subsequent inquiries findings of malpractice threatened his position and social standing, none of them would risk anything similar which could incriminate them at their own establishments, therefore, he surmised they would come to his aid.

Despite recent meddling by those Henry, and many other owners classed as 'do-gooders,' and the introduction of new legislation the majority of coalmines still employed similar working practices to those at Tilly, although, Henry would be the first to admit, working conditions in most other mines including others of his own, were better and safer than at Tilly Pit. If, by chance he was compromised by Saturday's explosion, and found to be lacking by not providing adequate safety precautions, other owners would also, therefore, Henry felt confident the brethren would unite in order to assuage any possible accusations of neglect on their part.

Breakfast finished, the two men left the hall.

"Are we using one car uncle or two?" Charles asked as they stepped into the driveway.

"We will use mine Charles, your new toy seems to have had some kind of serious mishap, I noticed the damage you have inflicted on it yesterday when I arrived."

Charles hesitated in the doorway, "Where is your car uncle, I can't see it, did you take it round the back of the house?"

"No, the bank on the drive looked too slippery to bring the car down yesterday; I left it in a gateway at the top of the hill."

Charles turned to re-enter the house, "Where are you going now?" asked his uncle in dismay.

"To fetch Hawkins and tell him to bring one of fathers' cars around."

"You really are the limit Charles, by the time Hawkins brings a car round we could have been there and back twice, you have younger legs than me, if I am not afraid of the walk neither should you be, now get a move on."

Remembering last nights outburst from his uncle, Charles was not prepared to aggravate him again this morning; reluctantly, he fell into step behind Henry.

The owners arrived at Tilly Pit a little before eleven thirty and made their way straight to Joseph Shaw's office.

"Good morning gentlemen," Joseph greeted them as they entered.

"Is it Joseph? I do hope so," Henry gruffly acknowledged, "I presume you have more idea as to the extent of the damage by now."

Henry indicated to a chair in the corner of the office, Charles, obediently complied and settled into the corner, Joseph noted this with some surprise, however, looking towards Henry, he soon realised the young man must have been severely reprimanded for bringing outsiders onto the site.

"I wish I could say I have good news sir, but I cannot, and I'm afraid I can only give you a brief outline of things as they seem to be at present."

"Have . . . ." Charles began to ask, but a swift glare from his uncle cut him off before a second word could be uttered, he cowered back into his corner.

Joseph began in desperation, "Mr Cotes, Mr Heath, the damage is extensive, we have some of the smaller seams virtually ready to be re-opened and they could be in production again by tomorrow. However, from the reports I have received it will be a long time before the main seams of coal, the seven foot and others in that district can be opened again, if at all. The Rearers section can be back in production tomorrow, or Thursday, but at best we can only expect around twenty percent, or thereabouts of last week's tonnage in the near future, and for some considerable time to come."

Charles shuffled in his corner; as he moved both men glanced in his direction; an unmistakable look of bitter disappointment covered his face.

"The men, who were down on Saturday, are they all out now?" continued Henry, more in hope than expectation.

Joseph sighed and shook his head slowly, "No, I'm afraid not, and something else happened yesterday which we could have done without, alas, we have to assume that it is highly improbable anyone else will be found alive after four days, so at least we can now anticipate the exact number of lives lost."

"Something else?" Henry reiterated, and in annoyance added, "What now?"

"A mishap occurred on yesterdays morning shift, the leader of one of the visiting rescue squads ran into dense carbon dioxide, unfortunately, the breathing unit he carried was faulty, and by the time the other men were able to reach him he was dead.

Henry, his elbows resting on the arms of his chair, thoughtfully caressed his lower lip with his thumb and forefinger as he said.

"That is most definitely news I could have done without, I presume you have complied a written report?"

Joseph opened his desk drawer, took out several sheets of type written pages and handed them to Henry, he read them in silence, and passed them to his nephew.

"That reads as though it was a genuine, if possibly avoidable accident, it is unfortunate, or fortunate depending on how one looks at it, that the offending article, the Nevito unit he used was severely damaged by the men before they came back out. They admit there they completely destroyed it in their haste and have no idea where it originally came from, here, or from another mine."

Joseph nodded agreement, at the time the report was made he had realised the possible implications, therefore he had carefully steered the wording used in order to lessen their responsibility for the incident. If indeed, a faulty piece of equipment had been issued to the team, all the men had agreed to the sequence of events and to their reports validity.

Charles Heath rose from his chair, handed the report back to Joseph Shaw and returned to his corner. He began to realise why his uncle had been so resolute ordering him to be quiet, to watch and learn. The subtle sparring between his uncle and the pit's manager, the innuendoes, the implications not spoken, even he could see them, the subtext of their conversation having far greater importance than the words used, his uncle had been right he did have much to learn. He could not decide whether he was a spectator to a verbal game of Chess, or was it Poker. Either way, both men appeared highly skilled in the art, he regretted his own blundering efforts by involving one of his drinking companions and arranging for him to descend the pit, now he realised how dangerous involving outsiders could prove.

Henry continued, "Joseph, you have some numbers for me, regarding lives lost."

Joseph took up a book from a shelf behind his desk.

"By using the lamp and tag system, yes, we have compiled a list, although it has to be said, many men are still below ground and quite possibly buried beneath tons of coal and rock, as I said, most unlikely any of the missing men are still alive."

Henry grew impatient, "How many?"

"Sorry, I thought I said," Joseph blustered, "Of our own workers, we believe, one hundred and fifty five, plus the man from Larchwood lost yesterday, making a total of one hundred and fifty six souls in all, and fifty eight of those have not yet been found."

"My God," muttered Charles, "So many."

Under the circumstances of Joseph's revelation, Henry disregarded his nephew's remark, although he could not distinguish if it were made from concern for loss of life, or, from the fear of the loss of income, the second option Henry considered to be more likely.

"Uncle," Charles whispered while Joseph's back was turned replacing the book, "What happened with Geoffrey?"

Henry raised his hand slightly indicating to his nephew he had not forgotten.

"Joseph," Henry tried to appear nonchalant, "Yesterday when I called, you said a couple of engineers were down with one of the rescue teams inspecting the tunnels, did they make any report to you before they left."

The pit manager became anxious and ill at ease, it was Charles Heath who had issued the order to allow the visiting engineers to descend the pit, and for him to cooperate fully with them. The same Charles Heath now sat in the corner of this office listening to every word that passed between Henry Cotes and himself. Joseph's apprehensive gaze alternated several times between the two owners, Charles clasped his hands together over his lap and lowered his head in embarrassment.

Apprehensively, Joseph ventured a reply, "No sir, they did not, I was under the impression they were to report directly to you, at least, that is what the smaller gentleman told me when they arrived here yesterday, have you not yet received their report?"

"No Joseph, I have not," snapped Henry, "Anything you can tell me regarding their visit, anything you may have overheard will be useful, they will not be allowed back on site, and their commission will be cancelled today."

"But I understood they were friends of Mr . . ."

"Be that as it may Joseph," interrupted Henry, "I will not tolerate outside meddlers, unless they are sent here by government agencies on official business, those, unfortunately we cannot avoid."

Joseph realised some major disagreement had taken place between the owners over this issue, which, could account for the younger man's unusual submissive behaviour; he relaxed a little before replying.

"There is not much I can tell you sir, they went into 'The Dips' with the Larchwood team and two of our own men, if you wish I could speak to our men who accompanied them, they may know something."

"Larchwood team, the team which lost its leader yesterday?" there was a trace of aggravation in Henry's voice.

"Yes Mr Cotes, I'm afraid so, losing a man from that particular team and in a section of the pit so severely damaged, from all the reports up to now, the dips is by far the worst affected and the most dangerous, it may well have put the visitors off."

"Meaning?" Henry asked attentively.

"Well sir, as I understand it, the visitors struggled quite considerably below ground, the men of the rescue team had to virtually carry them back along the main roadway tunnel, it was the only way to get them out again. They were carried to where our men have reached with the haulage track repairs, and from there they rode up in one of the tubs.

"They said nothing to you at all?" Charles could not resist asking, and received a glare from his uncle for his pains.

Joseph observed the silent reprimand, and with a hint of a smirk on his face, continued to address Henry Cotes.

"All I know is that once we had them back on the surface, we sent them over to the first aid station, there, the medics examined them, they were exhausted and shaken up but otherwise alright. After about half an hour in the first aid room, when our people had cleaned them up a bit, the pair of them just made their way to there car and left."

Henry persisted, "And they said nothing to you at all?"

"No sir, but, Arthur Cleaver told me he heard one of them mutter something about 'not for a king's ransom' or words to that effect."

"Oh, I see," replied Henry as he caught the meaning of Joseph's slight smirk, and joined in the jesting, "One expedition below ground, they have to be carried back up, washed like babies, and then, they climb into their sticky little motor and scamper off back to the safety of the city. Absolutely bloody marvellous, they were made of stern stuff then, had true British grit, bloody good job they aren't fighting in this war, if they were, we would probably be speaking German by now." A little smile of relief and amusement crossed Henrys' face. Charles, in fear of causing further annoyance with his uncle, decided not to intervene on his friend's behalf and to speak only when spoken to, he kept his head bowed and never even lifted his gaze.

Hard man though he was, Henry Cotes felt a little compassion for his nephew skulking in the corner, perhaps, he had been humiliated long enough, the danger of outside interference initiated by him now seemed unlikely, if the lad was ever to learn, he should include him in the discussions.

With a stern look to his nephew as a warning to think before he spoke, Henry said.

"Charles, you have been unusually quiet this morning, is there anything you wish to ask Mr Shaw before we leave?"

Charles in amazement, lifted his head, he had wanted to join the discussions for some time but thought it wiser to heed his uncle's instructions and remain silent.

"Yes uncle, there are two things really I would like to know about, firstly Mr Shaw, you mentioned that fifty eight men are still unaccounted for, can you explain why that is?"

"It is difficult to explain to anyone who has never been below ground Mr Heath, but if you would care to come over to the table with the plans and blueprints on I will try."

"Very well, I suppose I do fall into the category of a surface dweller, I certainly have never been below ground, have you uncle?"

"Some years ago Charles, yes, your father and I went down this mine, your father persuaded me, he felt as the new owners we should at least acquaint ourselves with the conditions down there. Admittedly, we did not spend long down below and we did not go far from the place where the cage stops, we went as far as the stables and came back again, even so we were paddling in dust up to our ankles that was enough for me."

Joseph, surprised at this admission by Henry, "That must have been before my time here Mr Cotes; I have no recollection of you going down the pit shaft."

"Yes it was, and if memory serves, the ponies at that time were in much better condition than the ones you brought out and sent to Valley Farm the other day."

Joseph Shaw had not suspected Henry could be a horse lover, but then, the English are renowned for caring more for their animals than people, he decided it would be wiser not to labour this point, and quickly changed the subject.

"Mr Heath, the plans on the table are in no particular order I'm afraid, if you come over, I will try to clarify your queries."

Henry was also curious, all three went to the table, "Here, Mr Heath are the sections which have been repaired," Joseph indicated on the print the area's nearest to pit bottom, and the small cruts off the main roadway.

"We can draw some low quality coal from here anytime now, and these," Joseph produced the plans of The Rearers, "This area can also be producing again as soon as this last stretch of haulage track is replaced."

"Some good news at last Mr Shaw," Charles said in delight.

"But here . . . . ," Joseph laid sheet after sheet on the table as he continued, "Here, where the best quality fuel has always been drawn from, there are combinations of roof falls blocking off many of the tunnels and dense pockets of carbon dioxide, especially here in the dips. The falls need to be cleared away where possible, and the tunnels made safe to prevent any further falls, and then the tracks need to be replaced, unfortunately, we do not know where the missing men are, they may be buried under the falls, or trapped in those sections that are completely sealed off. Where it is not safe to follow the route of the original tunnels, new ones will have to be cut towards the most profitable coal seams."

Joseph produce the plan of the dips, "The report of the Larchwood team made yesterday on their findings is quite comprehensive, we know there are a good many men, or should I say corpses here, they also reported finding a considerable number of dismembered body parts, but the whole working is full of choke-damp. We will need to cut a new return shaft through to draw the gas out before our men can safely retrieve the dead from these areas, or work those seams again. The men who undertake the retrieval work will need to be highly skilled, and at the beginning, all of them will have to use breathing apparatus, naturally, using those units will slow down their progress."

Henry half-expected Charles's second point, especially as he was currently short of funds, he was not disappointed.

"Are you able to estimate how long it will take to bring these sections back into production?"

"No Mr Heath, I'm afraid I can't give you a definite time, working as we are, with every man on repairs, it could take weeks, months, a year perhaps?"

Henry, suitably impressed decided to allow Charles to continue until he showed signs of being foolish or insensitive.

"Mr Shaw, that is an awfully long time, and the men will expect to be paid as normal while they are undertaking these repairs, would it not be better to use fewer men on repair work, use some to draw coal from the workable sections you indicated to offset the cost of the wage bill?"

Henry had planned to issue this instruction, but to his amazement, his nephew had thought of it, there was hope for the boy yet.

Joseph studied the blueprints; his only thought up until now had been to get all the men out, which had been Henry Cotes's parting order on Saturday, after consideration, he agreed.

"Yes Mr Heath, that is possible, no one left down there will be alive, I suppose we have too many men searching, but the number of leading hands we have capable of doing those repairs is limited. Loaders, labourers and the like will have to be dismissed and let go to bring numbers down to match the workings we have brought back into operation up to now."

Charles looked imploringly at Henry; Henry nodded slightly giving Charles permission to continue.

"In that case Mr Shaw," Charles ordered with pride, "That is what you must do, see to it as soon as possible," it seemed at last, in his uncle's eyes, he had done something right.

Joseph hesitated, if he was destined to lose unskilled men, by rights they would have to include the protégée of the late owner. He looked nervously at Henry.

"Mr Cotes, disposing of unskilled labour may include the young—,"

Henry, seeing Joseph's troubled expression caught his drift immediately, and rather than allow Charles into the dubious, clandestine arrangements regarding the precious document in the office safe, quickly interceded.

"Yes, yes, of course, all that need to go Joseph, everyone, we cannot continue with the same numbers if the mine is only in partial production, and we certainly cannot retain any who are only partially fit."

Joseph breathed a sigh of relief, he understood and welcomed this order; the crippled odd job man must go, once off the pit bank, he would be well away from any prying inspectors the Mining Federation may send in. Joseph, not being privy to Henry's arrangements with Zack, if any, the lad being off the site reduced the chances of slip-ups.

"I shall have to divide the skilled men between repair work and production, it will be difficult, we lost too many skilled men on Saturday there may not be enough."

Henry pondered, after a while he offered a possible solution.

"If that proves to be the case Joseph, I have other mines in South Wales, I could offer attractive propositions to some of the skilled men, some of them I'm sure can be tempted to transfer and relocate here for as long as we need them. If a specialist team can be formed, with no one related or emotionally connected to the deceased, they will be valuable; some may even wish to move to this area permanently in the future."

Since he arrived at Tilly Joseph had proved to be a good manager, production had been steadily rising, sales were good, and since the explosion, stockpiles had been adequate to meet the orders, but these were now almost exhausted. However, in order to carry out the owner's latest orders successfully, he must delegate division of the workforce to a local man, and now was the time to seek authorisation.

"Mr Cotes, Arthur Cleaver knows the men and their capabilities much better than I do; he is a local man as you know. I think he is better suited to rearrange the shift patterns and to allocate men to the various repair and production groups, especially the senior hands, once that is in place we shall know if we need more men bringing in, and how many."

Henry's confidence in this manager's ability to follow orders given directly, and those by implied subtexts, grew daily.

"That will be fine Joseph, whatever it takes, have there been any developments regarding the inquest, or an inquiry into the accident?"

"Nothing concrete yet, but there have been several visits by inspectors from the local 'Mining Federation,' with the gasses and lack of air throughout the tunnels we limit them to seeing only the areas which are repaired and safety measures have been installed,—I mean reinstalled." Joseph shot a glance towards Charles Heath, there was no indication he noticed the slip of the tongue.

Henry merely smiled, nodded and continued, "Anything else?"

"Well again it is only rumour, but we have heard via the federation the 'Home Office' is to appoint an acting inspector of mines to conduct an inquiry into the causes and circumstances of the explosion."

"That is to be expected considering the severity and the number of lives lost."

Joseph Shaw, and indeed, Charles Heath were amazed at Henry's composure at this news, Joseph and Arthur had been worried ever since the rumour surfaced, Charles, although he knew little, had learned enough for him to be very apprehensive at the mention of the 'Home Office.'

"Now Joseph, this is what you must do, approach any contacts you may have, discretely try to find out before hand when the appointment is to be made, someone is bound to let it slip if you press them. More importantly, the name and location of whoever is to be appointed, but, and this is vital, tell only me, the earlier you have the information, the better."

The manager was confused, and his face showed it; nevertheless, this was a direct order from his superior, whether he understood the reason behind it or not, it must be obeyed.

"Very good sir, if that information should come my way I will notify you immediately, perhaps, as you say, one of the inspectors from the Federation may have some advance knowledge of who is to be appointed, one in particular has a tendency to be indiscreet."

The telephone rang, Joseph lingered a moment before answering it, he did not wish to offend either of his visitors by giving any impression he was ignoring them, but, he had been expecting the arrival of the local doctor for some time.

"Gentlemen," Joseph began as he replaced the receiver, "I wonder if you could excuse me for a few moments, Dr Thomas has just arrived, since his last visit there have been a few more men brought out, we need him to certify death, and to issue the necessary certificates."

"Certainly Joseph," consented Henry, "I noticed you have marked those plans in pencil where obstructions have been located, I would like a closer look through them, take as much time as you need."

Joseph left the owners in his office, when the manager was well clear and out of earshot, Charles felt secure enough to speak freely.

"Did I overstep the mark uncle by asking those questions, I know you told me to say nothing, but I felt rather silly just sitting in that corner, Shaw was looking at me rather quizzically and I didn't like it, nobody likes to think people regard them as a fool do they?"

Henry smiled reassuringly, "No Charles, you didn't, in fact most of the points you raised were valid, they showed me you can think in a logical manner, and in fact you beat me to the little matter regarding offsetting the wage bill. I think your father would have been proud to see signs of maturity in you."

Both men began to shuffle through and study the plans of the underground workings, Henry paying more attention to detail than his nephew.

"These things are all gibberish to me uncle, do you understand them?"

"Not fully Charles, no, but over the years I have acquired a reasonable idea of how to read them."

"Is it as bad as you thought uncle, all these pencilled in sections?"

"No Charles, not as bad as I thought, if anything, far, far worse, it will cost a fortune to bring this mine back into production, not to mention finding and bringing out those men who are still missing, that is going to be a huge drain on our resources. We should seriously consider cutting our losses and closing the whole thing down completely. Our problems are bad enough without that rumour of Home Office involvement, appointing and sending an independent inspector here, it is all very disconcerting."

"I didn't understand your reaction to that piece of news uncle, I confess, it scared me, but you seemed to remain calm enough. I noticed Shaw looked puzzled when you told him to try to find out who it is to be; surely, your contacts are more likely to have that kind of information long before a man like this Joseph Shaw can learn of it?"

Henry smiled, "Quite possibly, but strategy demands I am not seen to make inquiries along those lines, all I need is a name, and better it comes from elsewhere without my involvement being noticed."

Charles pondered a moment over his uncle's motive before admitting defeat.

"But uncle, I still cannot see how knowing the identity of this person will be of any use at all."

"Charles, Charles, you have too much to learn, it may not be to our advantage, but if there is any chance it may then I want to know about it."

Henry had no wish to explain in detail, but the vacant look on his nephews' face, coupled with his ability for indiscretion, Henry decided it would be better to reinforce the point.

"Let us say for instance Charles, there are people throughout the world with the ability to get away with practically anything, people so powerful it is too dangerous to make any kind of accusation against them, because any accusation you make will never stick, and they are extremely unforgiving, in short Charles, people you don't cross."

Charles's vacant expression remained, "Oh, I think I see uncle, some kind of government thing hence this inspector fellow that may be coming, and you want to deal with him in case I put my foot in it again."

Charles had mistakenly adopted a simple viewpoint, Henry found difficulty in restraining himself; he turned his face from his nephew's view to hide the broad smirk he carried.

"Yes, that sort of thing Charles, perhaps when you are older and more experienced in the ways of business you may encounter such people, but for now leave it to me, say nothing of this to anyone, understood?"

Without the slightest comprehension to whom his uncle made reference, Charles Heath gladly replied conceding any such dealings to Henry.

Henry Cotes continued to study the plans of the underground workings, his nephew however soon became bored looking at drawings he did not understand, and instead amused himself by wandering around the office and being generally nosey.

"Whey hey!" Charles exclaimed, "Look at this uncle, this Joseph Shaw fellow has expensive tastes, ruddy well mean with it."

Henry turned to see the cause of his nephew's outburst, smiled, and returned to his studies.

"A bottle of father's favourite malt uncle, just sitting here three parts empty and that Shaw fellow never offered us any, I've a good mind to help myself, never had much time for people who are mean with their liquor, can't trust them you know."

"On the contrary my boy, the fact that it is still there is a sign that Joseph Shaw is indeed trustworthy. I brought that bottle in the other day, it is mine, but if you are still in need of the hair of the dog after last night, help yourself, you'll find some glasses in that little cupboard on the wall over there to your left."

Charles did not hesitate, no matter the time of day; he never passed over any chance to take a drink.

Joseph Shaw re-entered the office, Henry turned, "Everything alright Joseph, the doctor supplied what you needed?"

"He is just finishing off now Mr Cotes, I mentioned to him that you were on site and I needed to get back to you, he said he would be coming over to the office because he would like to speak to you. Is that alright?"

"Yes, quite alright Joseph, did you say his name was Thomas, I don't recall the name."

"I understand he is new to this area sir, Arthur Cleaver told me he took over the practice last November when the old doctor retired."

"I've never heard of him either," chirped a now more courageous Charles.

There came a gentle tap at the office door, and in walked Dr Thomas, a man possibly in his mid to late thirties, for a local doctor he was immaculately dressed, tall, slim and sporting a well-trimmed reddish brown beard, and a mass of curly hair.

Joseph ushered him further into the office, "Dr Thomas, may I introduce the owners of this mine, Mr Charles Heath."

They shook hands uttering the conventional greetings.

Henry left off his study of the plans and joined them.

Joseph continued his introductions, "And this doctor is his partner Mr Henry Cotes."

Stone-faced the two men shook hands, each recognised the other's handshake, and both returned the response. Henry shot a glare towards his nephew, and then slid his eyes in the direction of the chair in the corner; dutifully, Charles casually made his way back to his chair taking the remains of the malt with him.

"Doctor," Henry began, "Mr Shaw tells us you wish to speak to us, how may we be of assistance?"

"Mr Cotes, I am very concerned regarding the number, and the condition of the remains of all those men who lost their lives on Saturday. I rather hoped you could spare the time to accompany me up to the schoolroom where they are laid out; I think you will understand better at first hand, rather than me trying to explain the problem which has arisen."

Neither Henry nor Charles had any wish to make such a visit, but Henry new he would need allies in the near future, and this doctor may partially fill that need.

"Of course doctor, how remiss of me not to have looked into that before, but my home is quite some distance away and there is much needing my attention, did you wish to go up to the schoolroom now?"

The doctor nodded affirmatively, "If you can spare the time, yes, but let me warn you, it is not a pretty sight."

"I expect not," Henry concurred, "Charles, get your coat, Joseph, perhaps you should come with us."

The four men left the pit bank, Joseph rode with the doctor, Henry, and Charles followed in Henrys' car. As they walked along the narrow entry to The Primitive schoolroom, Charles held back.

"Uncle, do we have to go along here, it smells worse than a piggery."

Overhearing Charles's remark Dr Thomas agreed, "Not a pleasant aroma Mr Heath, but in my profession you eventually learn to get used to it, and that is the main reason I asked you to come here. That is no piggery you can smell, that is the putrefaction that spreads after death, and with so many dead here, it could well prove to be a public health hazard unless something can be done, and soon."

The two men on duty at the door acknowledged Dr Thomas and unlocked the door letting them pass. With the opening of the door, a waft of even fouler air drifted out, Joseph and Charles reeled backwards reaching for their handkerchiefs to cover their faces, Henry being a little stronger stomached, lit a cigar to combat the smell.

"You see my problem Mr Cotes," Dr Thomas indicated the rows of bodies. "I have never known deterioration this fast, the lime you supplied has helped a little to reduce the smell, but the sacking they are wrapped in is not enough. The local undertakers have done their best to temporarily stop the escape of bodily fluids; but these bodies really need to be more securely sealed to prevent any spread of disease."

"I agree, what have you in mind?" asked Henry.

"The problem is a race against time, some families have already claimed their kinfolk, and those have been removed to various undertakers' premises prior to burial, but, there again is another problem. Many families are too poor and cannot afford a funeral, bearing in mind, in some cases more than one ceremony will be required, besides which the undertaker's stocks of caskets have run out and it takes time for them to make more. If we cannot clear all these bodies out of here, and we cannot because there are only so many funerals the clergy can cope with in one day, and I might add, some of those will be held in this chapel."

"I have seen enough," spluttered Henry, he too was beginning to be overcome by the stench, "Let us go where the air is a little sweeter."

Nobody argued with Henry, he continued, "I suggest we should go up to that small hotel at the top of the bank, I need to wash this stench out of my throat, and perhaps we can get something for lunch, Joseph you will join us?"

Dr Thomas chuckled, "If you are referring to the 'Boars Head Hotel' Mr Cotes, I can only assume you have never set foot inside it."

"No I haven't—, why?"

Dr Thomas explained, "It's a misrepresentation of the word, it says hotel on the board over the door, but there are no facilities for overnight guests or anything like that. It's a pleasant enough place I suppose, and the fact they call it a hotel is nothing but an excuse to charge more for their wares than your average local Ale Parlour. They only provide hot meals if they know in advance you are coming, but if you are lucky you may get a cold meal of sorts, ploughman's and the like, cold meats and pies."

"If they can provide a private room doctor, a cold lunch will be better than no lunch at all, what say you Charles, Joseph?"

Charles disrespectfully chirped, "It will suit me uncle, just get us away from this awful stink." A comment, which met with a scowl from the two men at the schoolroom door, and three distraught women just arriving to try to identify their men muttered angrily at the young squire's ill-timed remark.

Dr Thomas having previously visited the establishment, took it upon himself to inquire of the proprietor of The Boars Head if lunch in a private room could be provided, at first the landlord declined, until the identity of the doctor's companions was revealed, suddenly, nothing was too much trouble. The man made a comfortable living as proprietor of the hotel, but the Highfield estate owned it. A cosy room at the top of the back stairs was soon made available with a table set for four people to take lunch, and a young serving girl detailed to attend to their needs. Conversation between the four men, intentionally limited to trivia until lunch was served.

Charles's eyes however, much to the displeasure of his uncle followed the girls every movement as she set the food, a jug of ale and a bottle of wine on the table, before retiring to the side of the room to await further instructions.

Henry wanted complete privacy, "Thank you young lady, we will call you again if we need anything further," he said, dismissing her from the room, she curtsied, and withdrew.

"Now gentlemen, to business, Dr Thomas, you brought things to our attention, which I admit had not occurred to me, what exactly do you have in mind?"

"You have seen for yourself Mr Cotes the problem facing this community, so many lives lost that it will take weeks for individual funeral services to take place, the first ones begin tomorrow, two at Broughton and one at Fursgreen. Permission has been given for these to take place before any inquest is convened, and under the circumstances, bearing in mind the principle cause of death was of course the explosion, whether it was the blast itself or the ensuing poison gasses, only one inquest is being scheduled for all the deaths later this year."

Charles paid little attention, he had food and drink on the table to occupy him, he did not intend being involved with any details regarding the final disposal of the deceased miners; he considered such trivia beneath him.

Henry and Joseph on the other hand, were keen for any input the doctor could provide, he, obviously possessed details of arrangements made by those officials in the district not directly connected to the management of the mine.

Henry's mind, ever working for his own ends, began to see a possibility of a long-term solution, a way of saving a great deal of money for a little outlay now, it was worth a try.

"Dr Thomas, while we were at that make shift morgue, you mentioned your concern that many families would find it difficult to pay burial fees, and also that the unfortunate men should not remain in that public building wrapped in cloth."

Dr Thomas paused before answering, "I did Mr Cotes, since the news broke, there have been many offers from various organisations, miners federations, chapels, theatres and the like to help raise funds to assist with the expenses the families of the deceased now face, some of whom, having lost more than one man, will have multiple arrangements to make. Broughton Urban District Council has set up a sub-committee to oversee the distribution of any available funds. My main concern is that there just aren't enough caskets, the decomposition of those men already brought to the surface is advancing at an expeditious rate, and I dread to think what the condition is of those not yet found and still below ground."

"I am no carpenter doctor," Henry said, "But I would imagine the shaping of timber is a long process, it is not so long ago that people were buried in a plain oblong box, much faster to produce, would that not be better now?"

"From my point of view Mr Cotes, most definitely, but I have found the locals here to be a poor, but very proud people, if they are to spend money which they don't have to spare to pay for a funeral, they will insist on having only the best for their loved ones."

Henry pondered a moment, "Yes, I can understand the way they would feel, but what if they didn't have to pay for a burial casket?"

Dr Thomas smiled, it seemed Henry was about to voluntarily propose something along the lines he intended to suggest.

"Don't have to pay for a casket?" the doctor reiterated Henry's words.

Joseph listened intently, he knew Henry Cotes well enough to know he gave nothing unless he would benefit from it. Charles happily consumed the cold lunch provided, liberally washing it down with a half decent wine, the only other thing on his mind was the pretty serving girl his uncle sent away, this talk of dead mine workers was boring. However, the serving girl he found very pleasing, somehow, he would find the girl again later, and while he ate, he fantasized on the possible pleasures to be had with her.

"It occurs to me doctor, I have a sawmill and timber yard in Castleton, if such a simple casket as was used in the past would be acceptable to the families of the deceased, I could order all other work postponed and my entire staff set to making them. Would that not be a healthier way of retaining the bodies until the clergy and local undertakers can perform the last rites. If as you say many organisations are busy raising funds to assist, I will happily donate the required caskets and perhaps a monetary contribution as well. Charles, I presume you will also contribute?"

Charles awoke from his fantasies, "Pardon uncle, my mind was elsewhere."

"I know, and I can guess where," snapped Henry, "I was just assuring our good doctor here that we will contribute to the relief fund being set up for the benefit of the widows and orphans left by Saturday's accident."

Charles replied, as usual, without thinking, "Not before father's will is settled I won't."

Dr Thomas dumfounded by this reaction studied the younger man, under the circumstances, quite a remarkable sight, a chicken leg in one hand and a goblet of ale in the other, gorging himself without a care in the world. Since the doctor first arrived in the parish he had heard stories of the young squire's excesses, none of them seemed to have been exaggerated, obviously, Henry Cotes was the man to deal with, not his nephew.

"That will be of great help Mr Cotes, but they will need to be reasonably air tight when closed, how soon could you arrange for them to begin work?

"Telephone the yard after lunch if you wish, will six and a half by two and a half by one and a half feet internally, be big enough?"

"That is the average size; I don't expect anything larger will be required. I presume you know it is the custom for the families to have the coffin open in the home for a few days before burial, would it be possible for them to be cloth lined, linen or the like, silk would be far to expensive.

"Yes of course, I wasn't thinking on the lines of a packing case doctor, the dead are entitled to some respect, just something quicker to produce if you are concerned about the public health issue. The only thing that troubles me is if the decomposition is happening more rapidly than normal, and you predict it will take weeks before all those already recovered can be buried. Those funerals which due to the volume fall well down the list and the bodies have to be stored; will it be wise for the coffins to be opened again to stand for days in their own homes?"

"I know that will present a problem Mr Cotes, and I am well aware of it, if a death is the result of a contagious disease of some kind, an epidemic for instance, regardless of the tradition the coffins would not be allowed to be opened. I'm afraid as time progresses, regardless how much the relatives object, I shall be obliged on public health grounds to disallow that custom, no knowing what disease could spread throughout the neighbourhood if I don't."

Joseph Shaw, conscious of his lower social status, listened intently to the conversations without interruption, he was impressed by Henry Cotes's affability and generosity, it surprised and bewildered him, perhaps there was a side to the man he had not expected. Suddenly it struck him; Henry Cotes was making provision for a possible future saving, even if it was morally wrong, it may prove necessary.

"Mr Cotes," Joseph began, "I was wondering if your people are to make coffins for the workers, would it be possible for them to construct one or two basic ones for use at the pit?"

Henry smiled in satisfaction, "What do you mean Joseph, I don't understand?" "Well Mr Cotes, you read the report from the Larchwood team this morning, if you remember they reported finding a number of bodies that are no longer intact, I believe it would be more respectful if they could eventually be brought out in a kind of simple sealable casket, instead of piled onto a stretcher. I am sure the men who have to carry them out would find it less distressing."

"That Joseph is an excellent observation," interceded Dr Thomas, "Less chance of spreading any infection."

By now, Charles was well on his way to being very merry, he had drunk and ate more than the other three put together.

"I don't see the point uncle," he said.

Warily, his uncle asked, "What point Charles?"

"Well, as I see it, they are already buried, what's the point of bringing the bodies up at our expense, only to bury them again."

His three companions glared at him in utter disbelief at this remark.

"Charles," snapped Henry, "Don't be obtuse, have some respect for the dead, their grieving families must have something to bury, they have to say farewell to their men folk in the customary manner, even the poor have feelings, and probably more than you."

Henry and Dr Thomas exchanged a long, knowing look, and both nodded to each other.

Chapter Thirteen

Henry Cotes found their lunch at the Boars Head highly advantageous, not only had his hunger been satisfied, but, although part of Dr Thomas's face was shrouded with a beard, Henry believed he read something of the man in the doctor's eyes when Charles made his indiscrete comment regarding returning all the deceased men to the surface again. Here, he hoped was a man who, if the worst came to the worst may be prevailed upon to allow practicality to override any forthcoming ethically challenged situation.

With lunch coming to an end, Henry suggested, "Perhaps gentlemen, we should continue our discussion in the absolute privacy of the office at the pit bank, with establishments such as these, I usually find walls have a tendency to sprout ears."

"That, Mr Cotes sounds like an excellent idea," agreed the doctor, "The fire in here is getting rather low and this room is developing a chill. Fortunately, I do not have anything else pressing this afternoon, at least until evening surgery, and there are one or two other things I would like to know, details of which I suspect are kept at your offices.

Charles Heath took on a look of dismay, up until now he had found the days events very boring indeed, except for the slight diversion brought about by the serving girl's presence.

All this business talk about coalmines and dead men he had had enough, something more enjoyable for him seemed to be in the offing, he began to devise a scheme whereby he could turn this present situation to his advantage, cautiously Charles began to set it in motion.

"Uncle Henry, I don't see any reason for me to come back to the pit with you, I won't be of any help, you all know far more about this affair than I do. I think I will stay here a while longer, if they have a telephone

I will call to Highfield and have Hawkins bring a car for me in time for dinner."

Henry's observations of his nephew's behaviour earlier left him in no doubt as to his motive for remaining at the hotel.

"I am sure we will be able to cope adequately without you Charles, and from the amount of wine and ale you have just consumed, no doubt by now your brain will be fuddled. The gatehouse to Highfield Drive is right outside the front door of this hotel, it cannot be more than a mile, why on earth do you need a car, the walk home would help to clear your head."

Charles grinned broadly, shrugged his shoulders and nonchalantly tilted his head to the side; Henry now convinced of Charles's motive, allowed a slight smirk to grace his own face, this did not go unnoticed by the doctor.

"Well gentlemen," Henry said, "If you will remain here a moment, I will locate the proprietor and settle our account."

Henry left the room, as instructed; the serving girl had dutifully remained hovering within earshot the whole time in case she was required again.

Henry asked, "Where will I find your master young lady?"

Curtsying, the girl replied, "This way sir," she led Henry to the lounge bar where Stan Smith, the Boars Head proprietor was preparing for the evening's trade, he ceased his work when Henry entered the room.

"Was everything to your satisfaction sir?" he inquired.

"Quite, thank you, tell me, do you have a telephone here?"

"No sir, I'm sorry, we do not."

"Oh that's a pity," Henry remarked impishly, "Never mind, what do I owe you for the meal?" Stan Smith made out the bill and presented it to Henry.

"The girl who served us, is she your daughter?"

"Ruth, no sir, I have no children now, the war took my only son, did the girl displease you in some way?"

"No, quite the contrary, does she live-in here?"

"No sir, her family live about a quarter of a mile away, in Libsley Road."

Stan Smith was curious, why would a man like Henry Cotes make inquiries about a mere serving girl.

Henry continued to be quizzical, "She will be on duty the rest of the day I presume?"

"She will sir, but since the accident at the pit last Saturday, trade has been very slow."

"You imply that you can do without her services this evening?"

"I could yes, but if she does not work she does not get paid, I shall keep her and the rest of the staff until the end of this week. If business does not begin to pickup again, she is only a casual worker and the last one I took on, so she will be the first to go."

"Oh, now that will be a shame, I was very impressed with her attitude. Let me make you an offer that may go some way to compensate you for lack of trade. I have a few local errands which need attending too urgently, and I have not the time to do them myself, if I gave you an extra five pounds in addition to the cost of our lunch, could I borrow that girl for the rest of the day?"

Five pounds was far more than Stan Smith would be likely to take in several nights over the bar, he had no hesitation in accepting.

"I wonder landlord; could I trouble you for a sheet or two of paper, and a couple of envelopes?"

Stan Smith scuttled off and returned as requested with writing paper, "I will send Ruth to you in here sir," he said, disappearing again.

Henry swiftly scribbled a note.

Anne,

At his request, I have left Charles at 'The Boars Head'. If he has not returned home in time for dinner, send a car to collect him.

Henry.

Tentatively the door opened, and Ruth, ashen faced and very nervous entered the bar.

"If you please sir, Mr Smith says he does not need me here for the rest of today.

Henry interrupted before she could say more, "I know . . . . Ruth isn't it?" the girl nodded, still ashen faced and obviously terrified.

"He also said you want me to do something for you, I am to come to see you before I leave."

With some dismay, Henry realised the reason for the girl's apprehension.

"Yes, that is right, you are a local girl I understand," Ruth, still fearful, curtsied clumsily in acknowledgement.

"You will know where Highfield Hall is then?"

"Yes sir, it is about a mile down the drive," she pointed out of the window to the closed gates across the driveway opposite.

"I want you to take this letter to Mrs Heath the mistress of Highfield, and here is a little something for your trouble."

Henry handed over the letter, and a few silver coins that totalled over a guinea, Ruth's eyes widened, and her jaw dropped at the sight of the coins in her hand.

"Excuse me sir, all this for a miles walk, I don't earn this for a full weeks work, have you made a mistake?"

With a smile on his face and an impish sparkle in his eye, Henry replied. "Don't you ever get tips here my dear?"

"Well yes sir, sometimes, but it's always in copper, and never this much."

"Well Ruth, consider that payment for delivering my letter, and a tip for serving our lunch, but, there is one condition I must impose."

The girls face darkened, she had heard stories of the way young girls like her were often compromised by men of the upper classes. This man was obviously rich, but that made no difference to her resolve, should the condition or proposition be of an intimate nature she had no intention of complying.

She stiffened slightly as she nervously asked, "What would that be sir?"

Henry laughed seeing the girls discomfort, "Very simple Ruth, you are not to come anywhere near here again for the rest of the day, go home or visit your friends, but keep well away from here, go now, off you go."

In utter disbelief, Ruth dropped the coins into her apron pocket, curtsied once more and disappeared.

Henry smiling, returned to the hotel's back staircase to rejoin the others in the small parlour, as he went he chuckled, "Costly Charles, but that is one young lass you won't get your grubby mitts on today."

"Whatever took you so long uncle?" Charles asked as his uncle re-entered the room, "I was beginning to think you had gone off and left me to settle the bill myself."

"No Charles, I would not do that, you are all here at my invitation and so naturally it is my place to settle the account, which I have done, you may get up to tricks like that, and what is more, I am reliably informed you often do, but, if I offer someone a meal I will pay the bill."

Clambering back into his huge winter coat, Henry continued, "If you gentlemen are ready, perhaps we should return to the office at the pit," Charles, not impressed by the prospect of returning to the coalmine, was happy he had made alternative arrangements for the rest of the day.

"Oh by the way Charles, I have sent word to Highfield you will be staying here at the hotel, I took the liberty of suggesting that a car be sent for you in time for dinner, I believe that is what you intended, was it not?"

Charles Heath's face beamed, partly from the amount of alcohol inside him, and partly at the prospect of beginning his seduction of the pretty serving girl.

"Thank you uncle, I am sure you gentlemen will be able to conclude your business much faster without me, although, it is getting rather cold here in this parlour, I think I will go downstairs to the lounge bar."

Joseph Shaw and the doctor exchanged a disapproving look; they had both noticed the younger man's lecherous interest in the young girl as she served their lunch. Henry smiled and winked at them, the doctors face darkened behind his beard, he assumed Henry was assisting his nephew's pursuit of the girl.

As they returned towards their cars, the doctor whispered to Henry, "If you don't mind me mentioning Mr. Cotes, your nephew seemed to take a great deal of interest in that servant girl, I rather think that she maybe his reason for remaining here.".

Henry laughed, "I am quite sure your observations are correct doctor, however my nephew is in for a disappointment, I am well aware of his nature, that is why I took the liberty of engaging that serving girl to run some errands for me, she will not be returning to the hotel today."

Joseph Shaw had left the pit bank with Dr Thomas, observing a matter of politeness he elected to return with the doctor. Henry Cotes lost no time to begin his return journey; the doctor however hesitated, making pretence of searching his pockets for his car keys.

"Joseph, this man Henry Cotes, what kind of a man is he?" the doctor asked.

"I'm afraid I can't say Patrick, prior to the explosion I doubt if I met him more than a half a dozen times, most of our dealings were with the old squire Cotes's partner and brother-in-law, young Mr. Charles's father. I believe our Mr. Cotes has a rather large estate in the neighbouring county, Cheshire, and, from comments he has made recently, considerable assets in Wales."

The doctor persisted, "Have you been able to form an opinion from your recent dealings with him?"

"I had heard he was a shrewd, ruthless man, and from our recent dealings I would suspect that is no exaggeration, but thankfully he has more about him than the old squire's son."

"Ah, I think I know what you mean, that young man struck me as having a hedonistic nature, but, what of Cotes, is he a man that can be trusted? Will he do the right thing with regard to the families left grieving by Saturday's explosion?"

Joseph thought for a moment before responding to the doctor's query.

"From his actions over the past few days, I tend to think he will do his best, he lost no time authorising unlimited resources to bring the injured and trapped men out, and you yourself heard his offer to provide the necessary caskets for anyone who requires them."

"You are prepared to put your trust in our Mr. Cotes then Joseph?"

"Yes Patrick I think we must, although, having said that, I think our Mr. Cotes's main problem will be his nephew."

"The least involvement we have from that young man the better, I was a little concerned back there for a moment, but Henry Cotes played a nice hand by sending that young girl away, I will have to give him credit for that. Your young squire will be sitting in that hotel expecting to get his little jollies, and Cotes has removed young Ruth from the scene, devious, sneaky, but quite, quite admirable."

"I very much doubt if the young squire will see it that way Patrick, I thought that class of people always stuck together and helped each other, and I have to admit, I thought the young girl was being set up as fair game for the young squire," Joseph added with a slight titter. "Quite a surprising twist when we learned the true reason for Cotes taking so long paying the bill."

The doctor mused, "Perhaps Joseph, our Mr. Henry Cotes possesses a streak of compassion and generosity he prefers to keep hidden from his competitors lest it be seen as a sign of weakness. On the other hand, I suspect he possesses some expertise in the use of the old adage, those who want, give."

"Now you have lost me Patrick, I have no idea what you mean by that."

"Never mind Joseph, as time goes on we shall see what we shall see."

The doctor and the pits manager entered the office at Tilly Pit to find Henry Cotes had already made himself comfortable, and, true to his word, was speaking on the telephone to the manager at his sawmill arranging for his workmen there to begin constructing caskets.

* * *

Eleven o'clock on Tuesday morning, 15 January, brought a surprise but not wholly unexpected visitor to the Swindon household.

Eve Swindon answered the gentle knock on the front door.

"Mrs. Porter," Eve exclaimed as she opened the door.

These two women had met only once before, and at that very briefly, therefore, the atmosphere between them, was, to say the least, uneasy. Both women in their youth had been 'in service,' being comparative strangers to one another, both made a clumsy attempt to emulate the characteristic etiquette mannerisms of the upper classes, which they believed to be the correct form when entertaining guests.

"I believe I know the reason for your visit, please do come in out of the cold, may I offer you my sincere condolences at this time," Eve continued in an uncustomary starchy manner.

"Thank you Mrs. Swindon, I presume you are aware from the lists of names of those men lost on Saturday which have now been posted, my son Jim is amongst them."

Gladys Porter, before leaving home that morning had resolved to appear strong to anyone she met, but, for a mother who had just lost her only son, not letting her grief show proved impossible, her voice began to crack and a lonely tear trickled down her face. Eve, could empathize with her visitor, and tried, as best she could to offer consolation.

She took her visitors coat and bonnet, settled her in Sam's chair by the fire and hung the kettle above the range.

"I'll make us some tea,—I have not seen any casualty lists posted, I did not learn of Jim's loss from them, but we are aware of it. Sam and Lijah were amongst those who found your son, we are all very grieved indeed, I know that can be of little comfort, no one would have expected such a dreadful thing to happen."

"No Mrs. Swindon, if everything was fair we wouldn't, but, from some of the things I have been hearing about the conditions down that pit, some say that safety precautions were nonexistent."

"Do they really? I helped out with the refreshments there on Saturday before they brought in professional caterers. I admit I did hear some similar stories, but then, there are always rumours, people always try to lay the blame on someone else. Everyone knows working in a coal mine has always had its drawbacks, but then, how else can our men earn a living?"

Gladys Porter nodded, "That is true, but when something like this happens to you and you lose someone, the knowledge that every time they went down into that black hole they were putting their lives in danger is of little comfort. I saw you arrive at the pit on Saturday, and I tried to reach you then, but you were escorted through the gates before I could get near to you."

"You were there, outside in all that snow, how terrible for you, you must have been freezing standing at the fence."

"I was, we all were, but I have always loved the snow, I always think it's like a magical blanket, hiding what is ugly and making everything seem so beautiful."

Eve could not help feeling both guilty and relieved, her men folk were alive, they had not been at work on that fateful morning. Eve assumed the reason for Gladys Porter's visit could only be because of Jim's engagement to Emily, and to inform them of the arrangements made for his funeral, however, she did not wish to raise this topic herself, preferring instead to allow her visitor time to approach this delicate subject.

"Mrs. Swindon," the visitor began in a purposeful tone of voice.

Eve, with a reassuring smile attempted to remove the apprehension between them. "Oh, Eve, please, not Mrs. Swindon, don't let us try to be formal any longer, I am sure we are making a complete hash of it, after all it's not our way."

Gladys Porter smiled in return, this comforted and relaxed her a little, "And I am Gladys, after all, we were to become related by marriage next summer."

Eve smiled graciously, dispensing with borrowed formalities instantly reduced the tension, which, in turn, allowed Gladys to approach the true reason for her visit far easier.

"Eve, I believe you mentioned that your husband and son were amongst those who found my Jim, have you been able to get word to your Emily what has happened?"

Eve now knew she must be wary, and adopted an air of caution; it was highly likely because Lijah had been the one who found Jim, Emily knew the bad news before his parents had been informed.

"Yes Gladys, we went over to see her the other day, naturally, she is heartbroken."

"I thought she would have,—she didn't return with you?"

"She wanted to, that was her immediate intention, but her employers could not spare her. Sam and I got the distinct impression, that if she had have come home with us the housekeeper would've made sure she would have no job to go back to."

Gladys retorted with the familiar venom of the working classes towards their social superiors.

"Now isn't that just typical, those people of wealth have little regard for us dead or alive, we don't count. I take it then she'll not be able to attend Jim's funeral?"

Eve hastily corrected her visitor, "On the contrary Gladys, we found Emily's employers to be very caring people; they were kindness itself towards us."

"You actually met them—and they received you?" Gladys was utterly amazed by this revelation.

"We were surprised ourselves, they were expecting many guests, and as it would leave them short staffed they were reluctant to allow our Emily to come home. But as her mistress pointed out, what would Emily be able to do here. They gave Sam and me every assurance that as soon as we knew any details she would be sent home, the master of the house gave Sam a telephone number and told us to call him at any time."

"Really! Well, well I am all astonishment, I never thought I would hear of people of that class actually showing any consideration for the likes of us," Gladys retorted, momentarily forgetting her grief.

"They are not all bad Gladys," Eve said, again with her reassuring smile, "I will make sure our Emily is kept informed, you mentioned a funeral, have you been able to make the arrangements?"

"Yes, unlike a lot of the other poor souls, Jim won't have to wait long to be laid to rest, it is to be at 11:30 on Friday morning at our chapel, Jim's father and I would be pleased if you, your husband, and, of course any other members of your family who wish to, would attend."

Eve nodded and refilled the teacups, "I understand the chapel at Heals End has been used as a temporary morgue, sorry, I have to ask, is Jim still there?"

Gladys Porter shook her head, "No thank God, he is at Mr. Oliver's chapel of rest, you know, the undertaker in Broughton."

Eve's face took on a look of slight bewilderment, "I'm sorry, and I don't understand why you thank God, I have lost children myself, but I certainly didn't thank God for it Gladys."

"No, nor I, I thank God because we have been able to move him, Eve, have you been in that schoolroom?"

"No, I haven't, but Sam and Elijah did soon after they started to use it, just for a few moments anyway."

"I didn't think so, if you had have been you would understand what I mean."

Eve did not wish to dwell upon, or to press her guest further on this subject, however, Gladys in order to clear Eve's misunderstanding went on to explain the reason for her odd remark.

"As soon as we knew Jim was lying in the chapel schoolroom we went to identify and claim him; I suppose we should think ourselves lucky, we had no trouble in finding our son, or in recognizing him. All the bodies were wrapped in a sort of sack cloth and had labels tied to them, some with their names and lamp numbers, some just their lamp numbers, but a good many were marked, unknown."

"Unknown!" Eve interrupted hardly able to believe her ears.

"Yes, unknown, the smell in there was absolutely dreadful, I suppose they had done the best they could to lessen it, they had spread lime all around, on the floor not on the bodies naturally, we ended up covered in the stuff. As I said, we were lucky in some respects, when we got there, the man sitting in that first little porch as you go in asked us who we were looking for, checked the list he had with him, and showed us where our Jim lay.

People were coming all the time we were there, if the name of those they were looking for was not on the list, they had to search amongst the ones whose labels did not give definite identification. Some people had to try to find and claim their men folk identifying them by their general build, and what little was left of their delph clothes. Eve, I have never witnessed anything like it, or would want to ever again, to see so many heartbroken people searching amongst mutilated bodies trying to find their husbands, fathers or sons. I for one would not be surprised if mistakes are made, and that was early on, I have heard most of the bodies that have been brought out since are in far worse condition."

Eve's face paled as she silently listened to Gladys's disturbing tale, she knew things were bad, but it had not occurred to her that the task of identifying the lost men could be as dire as this.

Eventually Eve said softly, "Now I think I understand why you said thank God Gladys, at the very least you know that you have your son back again."

Gladys Porter nodded, happier in the knowledge Eve now understood the meaning of her earlier peculiar comment.

"Aye, we have him back, but it will be a hard task to meet the expense of laying him to rest."

Eve opened her mouth to speak, but Gladys Porter's hand was immediately raised to stop her, "If you are going to offer to help Eve, please don't, my husband would never hear of it, we have bought the coffin, paid a deposit on the funeral, and hopefully the burial club will take care of the rest."

"If you are sure Gladys, we would help if we could you know."

"Oh yes, quite sure, that schoolroom is full of dead men, so we paid for Jim's coffin in advance because it was the last one Mr. Oliver had in stock. No way of knowing how long it will take him to make more, enough that is, for every man lost to this catastrophe."

"Now Gladys that is something which never occurred to me, undertakers running out of coffins, under normal circumstances they make them as required don't they?"

"That they do, and charge the earth for them, I won't be uncharitable and say undertakers are happy this has happened, but, rest assured, they will all be a lot richer when it's all over."

"Gladys, even if it's true, that is unkind," scolded Eve, "I feel really sorry for those families who have lost more than one, we buried three of our children in one day, and it took years to pay for it."

Gladys's mouth dropped in astonishment, "I did not—."

Preventing further discussion Eve raised her hand, nodded adding, "Tuberculosis outbreak, thirteen years ago."

Gladys Porter and Eve Swindon passed another hour engaged in what Sam always termed as 'woman's talk,' a great deal being said but of very little significance, fashions, recipes, who had said this or that, and to whom, for both women a very pleasant hour.

The kitchen mantle clock struck half past the hour of one, Eve rose to her feet.

"If you will excuse me a few moments Gladys, I must top up the boiler for Sam and Elijah's bath, their shift finishes at two."

"I quite understand Eve, when the men are due back from the pit it's not a time for visitors; I will take my leave of you now. You will be sure to let Emily know about the funeral arrangements won't you?"

"Rest assured Gladys, I will see to it that Sam telephones her place of work as soon as he is clean, Mr. Wickersby said he could ring at any time," and with an impish grin, Eve added, "I don't think Sam has ever used a telephone before, except those things down the pit, it will do him good."

Sam and Elijah arrived home around a quarter to three; Eve greeted them with the news of the morning's visitor. Sam, as Eve expected made a great fuss about telephoning the news to Emily, making the excuse he did not know where there was a telephone he could use. His reluctance proved a source of great amusement for his wife and son.

"Now father," Lijah rebuked, "You know very well there is a phone that the public can use in the 'Miner's Welfare', I will come with you and see you get through to the Wickersby's, but as Mr. Wickersby told you to ring, you will have to speak to him yourself."

Reluctantly, Sam agreed.

When they were bathed, as they ate their meal Eve related Gladys Porter's account of the conditions she found at the Primitive Schoolroom when she and her husband went to identify Jim. Husband and son listened without interruption, Eve's story concluded, Lijah thought for a moment.

"You know father," he said, "I believe Mrs. Porter has a point, mistakes could be made."

Eve was in the back kitchen washing the dishes, so Sam answered very softly, "Aye lad, wouldn't be the first time either boxes of bricks have been buried instead of bodies."

"What was that Sam?" Eve screamed from the back kitchen, Sam's hearing may have been dulled, but his wife's was keen.

Elijah's face took on a look of disbelief, his mother came storming from the back kitchen.

"What was that you just said Samuel Swindon?"

Sam, sheepishly moved to his chair, and reached for his pipe and twist, Elijah made himself scarce by disappearing into the front room. Whenever his mother used their full names, they knew they were in trouble.

Glaring at Sam she roared, "I ask again, what was that you just said?"

Lighting his pipe, Sam's mind was racing on how to get out of this, shaking out the lighted spill, Sam took his pipe from his mouth, if he could get away with it, he had an answer.

"Don't take on so love, I have heard tell, if someone is killed by an explosion, and parts of them cannot be found, to save their families more grief the weight of the coffin is made up with rocks. Can't say if it's true or not, but that is what I have heard."

"Oh! To save the families grief, and it's only a rumour then, don't say things like that if you're not sure, it's not nice," she turned and went down the yard to the privy.

Elijah heard his father's reply from the doorway, he sniggered, "That was close father, good, quick thinking, but which one is true?"

"First one lad, there's more than one body still in those old bricked up workings, and yes it was too bloody close, I had forgotten how keen your mother's ears are."

Lijah frowned, "Are you thinking that might happen again father?"

"Who's to know, if our own men are the only ones on recovery it won't, but if they bring in strangers it might, depends I reckon on how much damp is still down there."

Eve returned, and the subject was dropped immediately.

"Right, now Sam, when you have finished your pipe you must go and let Emily know about Jim's funeral, best be gone before Fanny gets in from school, she is calling at my mother's for her tea."

Eve remembered her husband's discomfort in the company of Emily's employers, just in case he got flustered, either by having to use a telephone for the first time, or by having to speak to a member of the gentry, she wrote down all the details Sam was to pass on. She also wrote a brief note to Lizzie and Evie, informing them of the arrangements for Friday, which as the men would pass the post box she handed to Lijah to post on his way.

Once Eve had satisfied herself nothing could go wrong and all the details would be passed onto her daughters, father and son set off back down the bank to the 'Miner's Welfare.'

It was a little before five o'clock as Sam and Lijah entered the Welfare building situated behind the Congregational Chapel in Heals End, fortunately, not many people were in. His father, still objecting profusely, Elijah took responsibility for the task; he took the sheet of paper Victor Wickersby had given to Sam before they left on Sunday. First, he tried the number marked work, a female voice answered, rather than handing the phone to his father, Lijah asked.

"Could I speak with Mr. Victor Wickersby please?"

"I am sorry sir," the voice replied, "Mr. Wickersby left for the day at four o'clock, can I take a message." Lijah declined, and instead tried the number marked, home, this time a gruff voice answered.

"Wickersby residence, Mrs. Quint speaking,"

Lijah repeated his request, but this time, asking for either the master, or the lady of the house.

The sly old Quint realised from the tone of Lijah's request that the call was not from anyone of the class of people who normally rang.

"The master and mistress are not to be disturbed, who are you, and what do you want?"

Lijah was not in any way fazed by this; he had heard much of this Mrs. Quint from his sister.

"My name is Swindon, and I was given this number by Mr. Wickersby, and instructed to ring anytime in an emergency, this is such an emergency, your master will wish to speak to me, kindly fetch him to the telephone."

"One moment," there was a clatter as the receiver was laid down, Lijah, from the corner of his eye noticed his father, red faced and fiddling with his collar, he smiled as he handed the receiver to Sam.

"He's coming Dad."

Sam held the receiver to his ear, and after a moment a cheery voice said, "Victor Wickersby here, I take it you have some news Mr. Swindon."

Sam relayed the details from the note Eve had written for him.

"That is awkward Mr. Swindon; we have a large party planned for Thursday evening, we really need all our staff here, but leave it with me, I will see that Emily is home in good time for the services, they are not in your village you say."

"No sir, a good three quarter of an hour's walk from our house," Sam replied.

"I understand, she will be there, leave it with me, just don't leave your home without her."

Puzzled, Sam agreed, said goodbye and handed the receiver back to Lijah.

"Problem?" asked Lijah.

"Don't know lad, he said they need all their staff for a party on Thursday, but we are not to leave home until Emily gets here, I guess that'll mean she will be coming on Friday morning."

"Just so long as she gets here father that is the main thing, perhaps the less time she has to work herself up into a state will be a good thing, strange thing to tell you not to leave home without Emily though isn't it, as if we would."

Sam shrugged, "That Victor Wickersby is a very surprising bloke, I find it hard to say this lad, but I trust him."

They arrived home to the familiar sound of Fanny hammering away on the piano.

"Oh botheration," grumbled Lijah as they climbed the steps, "I wanted to do some practice tonight; I shall need a stick of dynamite to shift madam off that stool."

Sam laughed, "It's your own fault, you let her get away with far too much."

Eve, patiently waiting in the kitchen to hear the outcome of her husband's mission, but when told, she also thought Victor Wickersby's remark not to leave home without Emily rather a strange thing for him to say.

Chapter Fourteen

Henry Cotes spent most of Tuesday afternoon with Joseph on the pit bank, having one of the owners there able to authorise any additional finances necessary to recover men from below ground, was a God Send for Joseph. Not only would this save a great deal of valuable time, but Henry's presence would also give a certain amount of reassurance to the workers and their families, every effort to recover the missing men was being made. It was highly unusual for a man like Henry to involve himself in the general day-to-day running of the pit, or indeed, any of his other business ventures, he employed staff for that, but in this instance, he did. The dilemma as he saw it was simple, for this little village community to survive, the mine must be brought back into production to some degree. His only alternative would be to cut his losses and write off his investment completely, the financial loss, consequences, and other repercussions from this drastic action was not a prospect he relished, closure was definitely not his first choice.

With indispensable assistance from Arthur Cleaver, who, drawing upon his extensive knowledge of the conditions below ground, and by furnishing details as to the capabilities of the remaining workforce, the three men formulated what they hoped would be workable plans to draw the maximum possible coal again from Tilly, beginning, not later than Thursday morning's shift.

Either resulting from their own caution, or being in receipt of leaked information, some customers had already cancelled their orders; taking into account the quality of coal likely to be produced in the weeks to come, and the future projected output, all other existing contracts would need to be re-negotiated.

Most of the richest coal seams would be inaccessible for some considerable time, some forever. New, safe cruts would need to be dug out in an attempt to reach as many rich seams as possible, but it was blatantly obvious to the three men the best seams would never produce again. In addition to this future production planning and the execution thereof, there was the pressing rescue task currently underway. Since the incident four days ago, skilled men were now in short supply, certainly not enough to run the normal three shifts and a rescue operation.

Tilly's full complement of underground workers had been four hundred and five men, last Saturday morning two hundred and forty eight had been below ground at the time of the explosion, of these, so far only ninety-two had returned alive to the surface, the rest were either confirmed dead or still missing.

After much debate and discussion, although, no one actually admitted the rather dubious underlying reason for the proposal, the three men agreed it would be beneficial for Henry Cotes to bring in a skilled, trusted team from his coalmines in Wales, recruited to concentrate on the rescue operation. They convinced themselves that by so doing, local men with their knowledge of Tilly could then be freed to return to drawing coal again from the safe areas within the pit, and to dig out new cruts towards the richer seams.

Following Saturday's explosion, it was an obvious fact to all, management and workers alike men would be laid off; the question on everyone's mind was, how many? If Tilly could somehow be brought back into production again, fewer men than it seemed likely at present would need to lose their jobs and their family's livelihood.

By five thirty, plans were in place to begin drawing coal again, and as much other business as possible completed; Henry Cotes, unable to contribute further took leave of his managers. Leaving the building and walking towards his car, Henry noticed a now familiar figure also apparently leaving the pit bank; it was Zack Morgan making his way towards the pit entrance gates. Henry paused and watched Zack, who took the opposite direction to the one Henry had expected him to go, he was heading up the lane leading away from the village towards Valley Farm.

Henry had arranged to spend another night with his sister at Highfield Hall; tomorrow he would now have to travel into Wales for a few days to recruit a team of trustworthy men who were willing, for the right price, to undertake the rescue operation here at Tilly. Henry believed, and had proved times without number that every man has his price, and as a result, anything can be achieved; there was no reason for him to suspect anything different now.

Zack heading towards Valley Farm and his beloved Florence prompted Henry to reconsider his immediate plans, he sat in his car, took out his cigar case, only two left, he scowled and replaced the case in his pocket, he hoped that his sister Anne still kept a supply at the hall from which he could refill his case. The likelihood of the shops here in this primitive backwater, stocking any tobacco other than Twist or Woodbine cigarettes, he regarded as most unlikely.

As he watched the young man leave, Henry smiled muttering to himself, “Yes Zack lad, if I were single and nearer your brother’s age, no matter what her heritage, I would be very tempted to give you some competition for that prize waiting for you up at that farm. But for now, I have done as much as I can to make you acceptable in her families eyes without revealing who you actually are.”

The probability Lydia would be alone at her cottage was a chance he could not pass over; at his first visit, time had been pressing and he was only able to give her some sketchy information; it was her right to know all arrangements made on her behalf. His promise to Charles made it his duty to fill in the blanks for her as soon as possible, and quite apart from anything else, her cooperation in the weeks to come would be indispensable.

Henry swung his car to the right at the end of the lane heading up through Heals End and Augers Bank towards Highfield Hall, as he drove he deliberated his best course of action, and the best place to leave his vehicle. He needed to see Lydia, but did not want it common knowledge that he had called on her. He eventually decided that her cottage was so isolated and it was dark enough now, he would drive straight up to Hawthorne Cottage, anyone poaching in the woods may see his car, but it was very doubtful they would say anything and have to explain why they were there themselves.

The cottage door opened as he walked along the garden path, Lydia had heard the car and stood waiting in the doorway, her long blonde hair hanging free and shimmering in the light from the hallway.

“Good evening Lydia,” Henry greeted her as he neared the door, “I hope this is not an inconvenient time for me to call?” and then in an undertone, “Are you alone?”

Lydia's face beamed with mischievous delight at Henry's implied need for secrecy, and his obvious embarrassment calling upon a woman at home alone.

Jovially, she replied, "Quite alone Mr Henry, I was wondering when you would return, do come in, you left me in a bit of a quandary the last time I saw you, I trust you have come with a better explanation and to clarify things for me,"

"I have indeed, well that is to say, as best I can without divulging anything too complicated which you have no need to bother about at present."

Lydia rebuked him, "Be as complicated as you wish Mr Henry, I will be attentive, not all my sex are incapable of understanding the intricate dealings you men seem to thrive upon."

Henry laughed, "I know now that you are not, but you misunderstand me, I meant no offence but there is still a great deal I have to attend to, the results of which I am unable to confirm until they come to fruition, for now, you will have to be satisfied with some knowledge of the progress made to date."

Henry hung his top coat and hat on a peg, Lydia indicated he should take the same chair by the fireside, this he did and as before found it most comfortable.

Lydia adopted the role of hostess, "Have you eaten Mr Henry? Would you like a cup of tea, or perhaps something stronger?"

"No I haven't eaten, but Anne is expecting me for dinner, tea will be fine, unless—."

Lydia interrupted, "Cup of tea, with something stronger while the kettle boils, just like Charles, brandy or malt?"

"Oh! Malt if you have it, thank you."

Lydia hung the kettle over the range and disappeared down the cellar, she returned carrying a bottle of ten-year-old malt whisky and two cut crystal glasses, which she placed on the table.

"Help yourself Mr Henry; I'll get some cake for you to have with your tea."

Henry poured a generous glass of malt, sat down again, inadvertently taking out his cigar case from which he took the top, shook his head despondently and replaced it.

Lydia emerging from the pantry with her cake tin smiled as she watched him.

"I have missed the smell of cigars Mr Henry, do smoke if you wish."

"I can't, that's the second time Lydia I have done that in less than half an hour, I have only two left and as I shall not be returning home tonight I'm afraid I shall have to save them, unless of course, Anne still has some at the hall, these will have to last."

Lydia held out her hand, "May I see?" she asked.

Henry handed his case to her; Lydia took out a cigar and examined the band, placed them on the kitchen table, and lit a candle.

"Excuse me a moment Mr Henry," she said and disappeared upstairs, she returned carrying a wooden cigar box which would originally have contained fifty cigars.

"You smoke the same brand Charles did, I don't see why you shouldn't have some, or all of these, Charles won't smoke them now."

Henry noticed a slight tremor in her voice as she spoke of his late brother-in-law.

"You have a great many unexpected items here Lydia, fine cigars and malt whiskey are not the things one would expect to find in a cottage such as this."

To his amazement, Lydia blushed, "Charles spent a great deal of time here Mr Henry, why shouldn't he be able to indulge in those things to which he was accustomed, he made sure many of his little luxuries were stored here for his enjoyment, the only problem we had was hiding them from Zack. Charles had a few secret hiding places built into the cottage for that very purpose."

"Quite so my dear, a man should have his comforts, and the fact that some of Charles's are left here serve as a reminder to you, and you take comfort from them."

Lydia Nodded, affirmatively.

"In that case, I thank you for the offer of his remaining cigars, but I will take only enough to last until I get home tomorrow, if that is alright with you."

"As you wish Mr Henry, but as I said, you are welcome to them, I would never smoke myself, but I enjoy the aroma of a cigar, and yes, it would remind me of Charles."

"Perhaps Lydia, one day your son will develop a taste for them."

Lydia threw back her head and laughed at this seemingly ridiculous suggestion.

"Now Mr Henry, that is hardly likely, a labourer at a coal mine smoking something which costs more than his whole week's wages, I don't think so."

"That is the point Lydia; Zack will not always be a mere labourer. As Charles's friend and former business partner, I have an obligation to oversee the implementation of certain things Charles set in motion before his demise, one of which is an inheritance for your son. However, it was Charles's wish that if Zack ever learns who he really is, or should I say who his father was, it must come from you and you alone; I am not permitted to disclose that fact to him.

"An inheritance?" repeated Lydia with surprise.

Henry nodded, "Yes, Zack will be quite a wealthy young man very soon, and with more to come, but the bulk of the inheritance is to be staggered over a period of time. It will be difficult, though not entirely impossible to arrange the first part with Zack still in ignorance of his true parentage, but you must find a way to tell him quite soon."

Totally bemused, Lydia echoed, "First part?"

Henry continued, "The farm, at which you and Charles arranged for him to stay as a child while you were away on your many trips is to be his. Hopefully, even if he is still in ignorance of his father's identity, he will be able to take it over when the current tenant retires; I have already started negotiations to that end."

Lydia replied somewhat amazed, "Valley Farm, that is the biggest on the estate, the tenancy is to be Zacks when it becomes vacant?"

"Tenancy to begin with, and then later the freehold, lock stock and barrel, everything. A few other smaller holdings, land, property and the like are guaranteed eventually to pass to him, furthermore, there is a distinct possibility other holdings left in trust from his father's estate could also be his by default, in addition to which, as your only child, everything Charles left to you will eventually fall to him."

Henry allowed Lydia time to absorb this information, silently she rose and made the tea, allowing it to brew a moment or two, she regained her seat, Henry waited, expecting some kind of reaction from her.

"I confess I am surprised Charles told you about our travelling, he always insisted we kept it secret, I don't understand why he would confide in you and not tell me that you knew."

Henry replied smugly, "He didn't, well not exactly; he gave me very few details of your life together, I worked that particular snippet out myself from a remark your son made the other day, thanks for the confirmation."

The expression on Lydia's face left no doubt in Henry's mind that her nimble brain darted from past to present, searching for possible answers, why had Charles seen fit to act as he had and give her no inclination.

"I will have to tell Zack won't I, and then, after all these years the truth will come out, your sister Anne and young master Charles will find out, not to mention every other gossip in the neighbourhood, they already regard me as a loose woman of ill repute, it will be dreadful."

"Not necessarily Lydia, as for my sister, from a recent conversation with her I believe she has been aware of your romantic involvement with Charles for many years, and has been quite grateful for it, encouraged it in fact. On the other hand, she has no idea that Charles is the father of your son. Like Zack and many others, she is of the impression that Zack's father died of a serious illness before you could marry, which if you think about it is now actually a fact."

Lydia, in a remorseful tone replied, "Oh no, that is terribly distressing to hear, I am really very fond of your sister, neither Charles or I ever wanted to course her grief, we were very careful and tried to be discreet, but we couldn't help it, we just fell in love."

Waiting for Lydia to work out the relevance of his last statement, Henry sat glass and cigar in hand, his face bearing a cheeky grin and a twinkle in his eye, Gradually Lydia began to see the light.

The realisation dawned upon Lydia, "Hey, hold on a minute," she said, "That remark of yours regarding your sister could explain an awful lot that has niggled me for years. The room they gave me at the hall when I went back was far too good for a servant, that convenient little staircase down to Charles's rooms, the way we were never caught out all those years, I was always troubled that it was too easy to conceal that Charles and I, as they say, were an item."

After a moment's reflection her mood changed to one of mild anger, "I am not sure I like this, how could Charles deceive me so, his wife knew about us all the time and he kept it to himself."

"Steady now Lydia," Henry reassured, "Anne knew that you could make Charles happy in ways she could not, and from our conversation the other day, she assures me that Charles never knew she had guessed correctly about your feelings for each other, it seems it suited her purpose for things to continue the way they were."

Lydia took a moment to calm down again, her keen mind always working.

"Henry, I believe you said some things could be arranged without revealing to Zack who his father was, just how exactly?"

Henry smiled; Lydia realising she was to be a woman of independent means, the courteous 'Mr' had now at last disappeared.

"Charles thought of that, very soon your son will more than likely inform you he is thinking of giving up his job at the pit, and that he will be going to work full time at Valley Farm. This is something planned by Charles and which I have arranged, and you will need to encourage it. When this happens, if nature takes its course Zack's union with the delightful Florence Oldfield will soon follow, and, as she is the only remaining child of that family, management of the farm passing to her husband will cause little or no speculation. However, possible later events may, but you will have time to prepare for those."

"Later events?" queried Lydia.

"Yes, and this is the part regarding his possible inheritance which is highly confidential, therefore I must insist on your secrecy."

In mocking tone, Lydia teased, "Very well Henry, I am rather good at keeping secrets you know."

Henry smiled and nodded, "I know you are,—before he died Charles divided all his assets at that time into three almost equal parts. Everything out of this area, his properties in Shrewsbury and Wales, plus stocks and bonds, and the trust funds I believe you were instrumental in his setting aside to help the girls who fell foul of my nephew's passions into one. The remainder of the estate he split into approximate halves, with the most profitable holdings, which includes Valley Farm being placed in trust, for the present this trust is under the management of Charles's solicitors, my people, and me. The income from the trust is to provide an annuity during Anne's lifetime ensuring my sister is able to enjoy the lifestyle to which she is accustomed. In the event of Anne's demise, Valley Farm becomes Zacks, and if my nephew is not married and there is no legitimate male heir to the estate, all the additional holdings within the trust also pass to your son. I hope by then you will have told Zack the truth regarding his parentage, and whose son he really is.

Your cottage here, which Charles told me you loved, and the smallholding on which it stands are, as you already know, is now yours from a bequest in Charles's will, this was announced at the reading, so it is no secret. Charles felt that a smallish bequest such as this to a servant is very rarely challenged by anyone. In addition to this, not mentioned in the will because it was all arranged before he passed away, some considerable property and funds are set aside for you. To be precise, the third of his assets which are away from this locality, the only local item included is the trust fund for his illegitimate grandchildren which you already knew about."

Lydia interrupted, "Yes, we did discuss that matter, and yes I did encourage Charles to help those girls financially, our son was born out of wedlock, in some ways I can empathize, it must be hard for them, but I thought he had just given them money, he said nothing about a trust fund."

Henry shook his head, "Lydia, come on now, Charles was sharper than that, if he handed over a lump sum, how much do you imagine would have gone to those children, I am not saying the girls are dishonest, but I know, and Charles knew the dangers, someone would have relieved them of the money. Instead, a regular amount is theirs for the asking, the money comes from the earnings and interest on the trusts assets, which are now, or very soon will be yours to do with as you wish. I would suggest because everything is to remain secret, for the time being, and to avoid unnecessary speculation, you take only a nominal amount of money from your assets."

"And what of young Mr Charles," queried Lydia.

"He is to receive the other remaining portion of his father's estate, which as far as he will be concerned is all that remains of the family fortune. Sadly, my brother-in-law eventually came to share my view and recognised my nephew as an utter wastrel with no head for business. However, Charles, being Charles has made provision for his only publicly recognised heir in the hope he is able to redeem himself by successfully managing and expanding the remaining estate, if he does, which I doubt, it will prove the general opinion of him wrong. As his illness worsened, Charles found great comfort in the fact that as the new squire, should my nephew remain true to his nature and lose the portion he has in his control, most of the family estate would remain safely with his family."

"Do you think that likely Henry; your nephew's share of the estate will be lost?"

"Most definitely, the lad is incompetent, pretentious and obnoxious; he thinks only with his crotch and spends money as if it is going out of fashion with little concern for replacing it."

Lydia shied at this outburst; Henry noticed and was swift to retract.

"I am sorry Lydia, I didn't mean to offend you, but the lad makes my blood boil."

"Oh I am not offended Henry, just surprised you as his uncle would feel that way, I and many others have shared that view for sometime. Maybe under the circumstances I should not tell you this, but it always amused me when I heard it."

"Oh, please do," said Henry.

Lydia mischievously smirked, "I overheard your sister voice an opinion several times to her friends when the children were younger, that first cousins could marry and she had high hopes in that regard, her son and your—."

"Over my dead body!" laughed Henry, "No way on God's earth will that ever happen, I presume you are referring to my eldest girl Antoinette, I know she dislikes Charles immensely, can't stand to be near him, and who can blame her, let him stick with his little skivvies who are easier to impress."

"But Henry, if the name and the estate are to continue, he should marry, perhaps now he is squire it may attract the right partner for him."

"Yes, yes, he should marry; in fact I have spoken to him recently on this very subject, but to little or no avail. Whosoever it is that takes him on will need to be strong willed, rich and very tolerant. A young woman from a new money family looking for social advancement perhaps, people who would regard a union with our family as such. My nephew's brain power being situated rather lower in his body than everyone else, I'm afraid he has other ideas, in fact the young lady he mentioned to me the other day as a possibility, with her he is definitely setting his sights far too high."

"I rather think Zack has done something like that, set his sights too high, not the other thing, it is obvious to anyone who sees them together that he and Florence adore each other, but her father is very much against the match."

"I am well aware he was Lydia, but I think not any longer, as I said earlier, let nature take its course. George Oldfield has been made an offer it will be stupid of him to refuse. For a smooth transition and Charles's plan to work with little or no antagonism, we need that marriage to take place, and soon."

Lydia was waiting for Henry to divulge a snippet of information vital for her peace of mind, but it had not yet been forthcoming, she could wait no longer.

"Henry, your sister and the new squire, are they aware of the arrangements Charles made prior to his passing, as well as the contents of his will? He never intimated to me he planned to do anything like this, leaving things the way he has."

"They are aware of those things which have a direct bearing upon them, but not in as much detail as I have entrusted to you. Anne is quite happy with the prospect that as far as she is concerned, nothing needs to change. My nephew on the other hand is outraged that he cannot get his hands on his father's entire fortune, unlike you, he does not grieve Charles's passing, merely sees it as a way to indulge his hedonistic pleasures. He has been told the estate is now much smaller than he imagined, and I very much doubt he will ever manage to ascertain the true size of Charles's estate prior to its division. If he does and queries the missing assets, it will be relatively easy to convince him that his father was in financial difficulties, and as such, was recently forced to sell a considerable portion of his holdings, Valley Farm for instance; I assure you it is highly unlikely he will ever trace Charles's out of the area properties.

There is no necessity for him to know of the arrangements for you and Zack, with luck he will not find out. My nephew is a vindictive sod at the best of times; even his mother admits that, which is why Charles completed most of the title transfers before he died. I understand that just over a year ago Charles asked you to sign some documents for him which you were not to read, did he not."

"Yes I do seem to recall something of that, why?"

"Charles told me he made light of it to you at the time, but they were important. I am not well enough versed in legal matters to understand exactly how it works, but it seems Charles's lawyers found some legal contrivance to guarantee you receive your share of his assets after his demise. The legal bods assure me no one, and I do mean no one can take it from you. Charles believed that if special arrangements of this magnitude were made simply as bequests in a will it would prove problematic. He convinced himself that although my nephew does not possess the nous himself, someone would convince him to challenge his father's bequests.

There are just a few loose ends still to tie up, but the legal boffins have nearly completed all the intended transfers, they will be inviting you to their office very soon to receive your share, I could take you in the car if you wish."

"That's very kind of you Henry, but Charles insisted I learned to drive a car some time ago, I may be able to acquire one of my own now."

"Not you as well, I thought that daughter of mine was the only female rebel in these parts who drives a motor car."

"Did you say there as been a formal family reading of Charles's will already?"

"Oh yes, I didn't see how we could avoid that tradition, fortunately at the time my nephew was suffering the ill effects of his previous evenings celebration and paid little attention, and Anne never bothers herself with such matters, but you know that, you ran her household often enough. My nephew grows more impatient by the day, expecting to be handed a pile of cash to finance his extravagant lifestyle, unfortunately, he is in for a rude awakening and I anticipate a great deal of pleasure watching how he copes in the real world."

"Oh! Come now Henry, that is a little too unkind, to derive pleasure from another's misfortune, surely you would do better to help and encourage him to succeed."

"I know, I know, you are right of course, and I did promise Charles that I would do all I could to help the lad, but unfortunately he is a victim of his own imbecility."

Lydia shook her head compassionately, "You really don't like your nephew very much, do you?"

Henry shrugged, "I find it very difficult, Anne is my sister, but as a mother she was so excessively possessive that she became more of a smother than mother, gave in to his every whim and completely ruined the boy."

"He was a very difficult child I agree; he always treats all the servants like dirt, and I know Charles never agreed with your sister allowing him to do so. But once a parent rationalises the first miss-step it is easy for a child to fall into a pattern of behaviour, I believe, we are all reflections of the way in which we were brought up."

Henry helped himself to another glass of malt, studied Lydia for a moment, smiled and nodded in affirmation.

"Now I begin to see why Charles first became attracted to you on those long evenings at the hall when you kept him company after Anne had retired, that is where your relationship began is it not?"

Lydia blushed, but made no answer.

"In addition to your delightful physical attributes, under those golden locks of yours there is a mind capable of logic and reason, quite a rarity in members of your sex, I have never met a woman before capable of anything more than inane chatter."

"That is a severe comment upon my sex Henry; surely there are many women able to hold a man in conversation?"

"None that I have met, although, come to think of it, my own sister Anne amazed me only last Sunday by revealing she possesses a manipulative prowess which I never suspected, and now I begin to wonder if she has ever used it on me without my knowing."

Lydia allowed herself a wry smile, "Henry, for all your wealth and power, you are such a typical man. Has it never occurred to you that a woman's wiles and arts, taught by mother to daughter for centuries are her greatest weapons, and from things I have seen over the years, your daughter Antoinette has you wrapped around her little finger."

"No, of course not, that is plain daft, my father always told me, women are so inapt at thinking because they rarely do it, so when they do it is pointless trying to understand them.

"If that's what you choose to believe Henry, carry on, but one day it might pay you to be a little more open minded on the matter."

"I think not, there is a danger with being open minded ones brains might fall out," he smirked, having tried to make what he believed to be a joke.

"As I said Henry, a typical man, but it would seem with a little more compassion than the young squire, nevertheless, I still think if you promised Charles, you should do all you can to help your nephew find his way in the world."

"I must say I am surprised, considering your own son would benefit if he does not, I would have thought it was in your best interest for my nephew to fail. Not to mention you also now have the means to acquire directly, or through mediators, anything he is forced to part with by bad management and thereby increasing your own wealth."

"No Henry, true, I never enjoyed the security granted by a good marriage, but I have had a good life with the man I loved, even if I did have to share him, and now it seems I have the means to continue to live in comfort. There is no point in my being greedy, I shall be quite content as I am, and Zack's future is to be much better than I could ever have dreamed. I accepted my life with Charles for what it was, I never sort anything more."

"So Charles told me, I didn't understand then and I don't now. You are still a young, and if I may say a very attractive woman, would you not consider marrying if the right man came along, surely a woman like you would have no shortage of suitors, if you did, it will make no difference to your legacy."

"No, no one could ever replace Charles, there were many young men who would have liked the chance and sort my favour when I was younger, but Charles was the only man I ever loved, or ever will."

Henry laughed, "I can understand that Lydia, no one ever forgets their first love, I certainly haven't, but for pities sake don't ever tell my wife."

Lydia joined the laughter, "That is highly unlikely Henry, we move in very different social circles."

"For the moment maybe, but now you are a woman of independent means as they say, things may change, I rather think Anne is planning to—," he stopped short.

"Planning what?" Lydia asked intrigued.

Henry was flustered, "Not my place to speculate, it was just something I thought she was hinting at, you will have to wait and see, but then again I could be wrong, forget I mentioned anything."

"Hmm, more secrets and disingenuousness, will I ever be able to relax around people, when will all this end so that I can enjoy a carefree peaceful life."

"Never Lydia, when you have money, as you will soon find out, there is always someone who would take it from you, and even I on occasions have envied the uncomplicated lives of the working classes. A few coppers in their pockets, a roof over their heads and a simple meal to fill their stomachs, they own nothing and they seem to achieve more happiness than we ever do, wealth can provide life's comforts but are we truly happy?"

"They also have a faith in God which helps them through life Henry, but I would never have considered you as someone with philosophical tendencies, you have a reputation as a rather ruthless businessman you know, I think you had better be careful the cracks are showing."

"Philosophical, me, no heaven forbid, it's just a temporary mood, most likely due to a combination of the ill timed extra anxiety with that blasted pit over the past few days, and this rather excellent malt."

Lydia smiled knowingly, and offered to refill his glass as the grandfather clock in the corner struck half past the hour; Henry declined the offer of another drink and took his own watch from his pocket.

"I had best be going, it's half past seven and as I said, Anne is expecting me for dinner, and tomorrow I have to go into South Wales."

"Wales," Lydia echoed, "Not the best time of year for travelling any distance Henry."

"I am aware of that, but we need more skilled men to work the mine here, and there is a surfeit of men at my welsh mines, it is my intention to bring a dozen or so back with me."

* * *

Zack Morgan arrived at Valley Farm at six o'clock, Edith Oldfield, catching sight of him as he came through the farm gates called to him.

"Florence is in with the ponies Zack."

Zack waved in acknowledgement and turned towards the barn.

Since they arrived at Valley Farm, due to Florence's care and attention the dishevelled pit ponies had been transformed into much healthier and happier looking beasts, they stood munching on the grain and hay in the troughs before them, Florence was tenderly grooming one as it ate.

"I will give you a hand with those," Zack said as he entered the stalls.

Florence, casting a wary glance in his direction answered, "Father was asking earlier if you would be coming tonight Zack, he wants to speak to you about something important."

Zack sighed, "Really, can't say I am surprised, I have been half expecting some adverse reaction from your father ever since the weekend, he doesn't think a pit bank labourer is good enough for you, and one about to lose his job because the pit blew up definitely won't be."

"Don't be so hard on yourself Zack he has known you since we were children, I doubt if father could be that cruel."

"There is something important I would like to say to him, but we both know how he would react and what he would say if I did."

"I know my dear, but I think if we wait long enough someday he will soften his resolve, mother is on our side, she knows how we feel about each other and has accepted it, even father will have to come around eventually."

"Maybe, did he give you any clues as to what he wanted me for?"

"No, not exactly, but I think it has something to do with the gentleman who called the other day, you know, that Mr Cotes."

"Crikey," gasped Zack in astonishment and adding under his breath, "That didn't take long."

"You have some idea what it is then?"

"Well—err, no but—."

"Zack," George Oldfield called from the doorway, "I need a word with you, come and give me a hand with the milking."

The two men, both apprehensive, made their way to the main milking parlour.

Valley Farm was always a favourite of the old squires, and as such with his financial backing had been maintained to a very high standard, therefore, it now possessed all the most up to date equipment and labour saving devices.

For a few moments both men worked in silence, neither feeling entirely comfortable, George was unsure how to begin, whilst Zack waited patiently expecting the worst, was the old man whom he knew disliked their friendship finally going to ban him from keeping company with Florence?

"Well lad," George finally broke the silence, "This job of yours at the pit, how long do you expect to keep it after Saturday's fiasco?"

Zack thought, here we go, "Not very long I expect, if the old squire was still alive I might have stood a chance of keeping it, but not now, a lot of us are bound to be laid off, but I have high hopes of acquiring a much better position, one which comes with a house and everything."

George stood up from behind the beast he was milking.

"Hope, or has an offer been made to you?"

Zack felt his spirits begin to wane, any minute now he would be told he was no longer welcome at Valley Farm, and to stay away from Florence. By its very nature, he could not divulge how, or from whom he expected an elevation in life, if he did, he would definitely lose it.

"At the moment Mr. Oldfield, it is a very tentative hope only," Zack confessed.

"Right then young Zack my lad, you were here the other day when our new landlord paid us a visit."

Zack's ears pricked at this, and he nodded in affirmation.

"Well," George continued, "Mr Cotes has decided to make part of our woodlands into a game shooting ground for himself and his rich friends, not that I hold with that sort of thing you understand, but orders from the landowner are orders."

Zack's heart leapt in anticipation of what was to come next, could it be Henry Cotes had already kept his part of an implied bargain.

"Why are you telling me—," Zack began to inquire.

The old farmer stopped him, "Let me finish lad, this is hard enough without interruptions, if I am to have shooting grounds up and running here by October or thereabouts, when those who kill for sport usually start their antics, I will need a lot of extra help. Cotes suggested, as men are to be laid off from Tilly and that as you work there, you may know of suitable people who could be approached to do the work."

Zack felt his spirits dip again; perhaps he expected too much too soon of Henry Cotes, after a slight pause he said despondently, "Yes I can think of one or two."

"Good, any chance you can sound them out and see if they would be interested in working here, over the summer at least?"

Zack's despair continued to grow, "I will do that for you Mr. Oldfield if you wish."

"Try to find two or three or as many as you think fit, they need to be willing to start as soon as the weather clears a bit, men, who you can trust, preferably single and not afraid of work."

"As I think fit? Surely that is your decision, not mine."

"It should be, but I got the distinct impression that Cotes is of the opinion you are the right person to supervise the whole thing, so there you have it."

Zack was confused; he pondered a moment before seeking clarification.

"Mr. Oldfield, are you suggesting that once I have found the men that I leave the pit and come and work for you here?"

"Yes, isn't that what I said?"

"Not clearly, no, when Florence told me you wanted to speak to me, I thought you were going to stop me coming here to see her, not to offer me a job."

"Oh, little madam got in first did she, I was forgetting just how close you two have become."

Zack was quick to realise that this, although small, was the first positive sign that George Oldfield may be beginning to accept the fact that he and Florence were very much in love, he decided to risk pushing the subject.

"Mr Oldfield, it is obvious you are aware of how Florence and I feel about each other, and we are aware that you do not look kindly upon me as a possible husband for her, which is the reason I have not asked you for her hand in marriage. Dare I hope that your offer of employment here is a sign that one day you may change your opinion, and there may be a chance of your consent?"

George Oldfield stopped what he was doing, sat on a feed trough, reached for his pipe and lit it.

"I wondered when you would finally get around to asking that Zack, you are right, I always thought Florence could make a better match for herself than with you."

Zack failed to notice the old farmer spoke in the past tense and his face darkened with disappointment. George, aware of a slight noise and draught glanced towards the now slightly open door; he caught a glimpse of Florence peeping in and listening, he grinned broadly, relit his pipe and continued.

"Zack, this is a conversation normally conducted in the parlour of a house not a milking parlour. I am well aware old Squire Heath thought a great deal of you, and somehow you have managed to make a favourable impression on Henry Cotes our new landlord, who incidentally, to my amazement spoke very highly of you. Perhaps there is something about you those influential men can see that I cannot, that being the case, I have recently come to the decision, if you are the one Florence wants I am prepared to agree to your engagement."

Zack's mouth opened in utter amazement, but he was unable to speak.

The door to the milking parlour was swung open and in rushed Florence, she flung her arms around her father and kissed him, blurting through her tears of joy.

"Yes father, yes, I do love Zack so very dearly, he is the only man I could ever love and we would like to marry as soon as possible."

Embarrassed by this display of affection, George could only manage to mutter, "Yes, yes, well, well, if it is Zack you want you have my consent, get along with you now, get back to your ponies and give your old father a bit of space."

Chapter Fifteen

At seven thirty on Wednesday morning 16th January 1918, Lydia Morgan was awakened by the distinctive aroma of frying bacon wafting up the stairs of her cottage, and to the sound of her son Zack, cheerfully whistling as he pottered about downstairs. She dressed quickly choosing to leave her long hair hanging loose, a style she preferred when at home, and made her way down to the kitchen.

Hearing her footsteps on the stairs Zack called to her, "Morning mother."

"Good morning Zack, what's all this, you up before the lark and making about as much noise," she replied with surprise, "You were very late home last night; I waited for you until after ten, until the fire was nearly out anyway, what time did you land home?"

A broad grin almost split Zack's face in two, "Getting on for midnight I reckon."

"You stayed at the farm that late?" his mother scolded disapprovingly.

"Yep," Zack's grin got even broader.

Lydia scowled at him, "I don't think that was very clever Zack, whatever will Florence's parents think, just what do you think you are playing at?"

No amount of scolding or disapproval from his mother could dampen Zack's cheerful mood today, "Well mother, at the moment, I'm cooking breakfast, I have done us bacon, sausage, eggs and fried bread, it's nearly ready and the kettle is on in the other room, can you make a pot of tea when it boils?"

"I thought we were nearly out of bacon, I hope you haven't used it all Zack."

"Nope, I brought half a side from the farm last night, and some fresh sausages, but the eggs are from your own birds."

"You paid for the bacon and sausage I hope?"

"Not exactly, no, I did most of the butchering on the beast, so they gave me the sausage and bacon as payment for my labour."

Lydia studied her son; his grin and flippant attitude now beginning to irritate her, it was far too early for him to be in such a mood.

"Why are you so chirpy this morning, have you no work to go to?" she rebuked.

"I am due at Tilly for a few hours relief work in the fan-house, but that isn't until this afternoon, come and have your breakfast, there is something I want to tell,—err,—I mean ask you."

Taking her usual place at the table, Lydia humoured him, "Well then, out with it?" "Mother, what would you think if I told you Florence and I want to get married?"

"I'd say you are taking me for a fool, anyone who sees you together can be in no doubt as to the way the pair of you feels about each other."

Beaming all over his face Zack continued excitedly, "Florence and me decided last night that after a short engagement we are going to get married this Easter, isn't it wonderful."

Unable to take her son too seriously, Lydia added, "It might be if you hadn't overlooked one minor detail, like George Oldfield."

"That is the point mother; George Oldfield gave his permission last night, both he and Mrs Oldfield agree Florence and I can marry this Easter, and what is more, they want me to work at the farm when men are laid off at the pit. I haven't been there long and I only do odd jobs, I reckon it's a sure thing I will be one of those who have to go."

Lydia's knife and fork slipped from her grasp, her jaw dropped in amazement.

"Blimey, that was quick," she unintentionally muttered.

"No it isn't mother; Florence and I have been friends ever since we were children, although I never really thought this could ever happen. Everyone said with me just being a labourer Florence is way above me; neither of us thought her parents would ever allow us to marry. You have always told me that you and father were very much in love, now Florence and I are, and it seems we still have friends in high places able to put in a good word."

"What do you mean by that Zack?"

"Come on mother, it was obvious even to me that the old squire was sort of fond of you, and me to some degree, after all, he did find me the job at the pit after my accident?"

Lydia suspected to whom her son referred, as a friend in high places; nevertheless, she needed more clarification.

"But he is no longer with us, so who are your friends in high places now."

"Well, Mr Oldfield dropped it last night that Mr Henry put in a good word for me, gave me a reference like."

"You mean Henry Cotes?"

"Yes, that's the fellow, the squires brother-in-law, he's the new landlord of Valley Farm, seems before he died the old squire sold it to him."

"You were fond of the old squire, weren't you Zack?"

This out of the blue, unexpected question stumped the lad for a moment, "Well, yes, he always treated me well, sort of loved me in a way I think, and with me not having a father around I suppose I looked on him as a substitute."

"I see."

Henry Cotes had told Lydia yesterday things would run smoother if Zack knew who his father really was; she deliberated whether this morning was developing into the right moment to follow this advice, and tell him.

Zack's train of thought continued, "You always loved my father didn't you mother, and no one else, that's what you always told me."

Weighing up the situation, cautiously, Lydia replied, "I did, and still do, always will."

"You know mum, sometimes I have regretted that you remained true to him for so long after he died, it denied me the possibility of a living father, even if it was only a step father."

Lydia, aghast at this remark reeled back in her chair, "You never gave me any inclination you felt that way, why bring it up now?"

"Sorry mother, I didn't mean anything bad by it, but sometimes, you know?"

Lydia remained silent and deep in thought for a few moments, her face took on a troubled expression, Zack began to worry, he knew better than to offend his mother, and from her silence he thought he was in for it.

"Zack, you know because your father and I never married it makes you a—."

"Bastard, yes, I am used to people referring to me as one, it used to bother me but not anymore. Doesn't matter anyway because you and father loved each other and that's what matters, I know slip ups can happen, that's why Florence and I have never—."

Lydia hastily interrupted, "I am very glad to hear that."

Zack's countenance changed shade to match his red hair, he was embarrassed, his admission slipped out before he realised what he had said.

"Yes Zack, you are right, I did, and still do love your father very much. Now then, changing the subject, what have I always taught you about telling lies?"

Although confused by his mother's deviation from the current conversation topic, Zack answered.

"That I am never to tell lies, unless, a little white lie is absolutely unavoidable to protect someone, or something I love, why?"

Lydia took a deep breath, "I hoped I would never have to tell you this, but things have happened very recently which make it imperative you now know something, which, until now has remained secret."

"Know what, what secret?" Zack queried, confusion detracting from his previous euphoric state.

Again, Lydia paused taking a few deep breaths before continuing, "For your own protection something has been kept from you, and I am sorry, but it was done for the best,—your father didn't die before you were born as you always believed, he passed away very recently."

It was Zack's turn to be silent, gathering his wits again after such a shocking revelation, he asked in confusion.

"Then why didn't you and he marry? Why did I never know him?—Or was it one of those cases where the man does a runner and leaves the girl in the lurch, or something like that?"

Lydia snapped back at him, "No, certainly not, as I always told you, your father is, was, one of the best men that ever lived, and we couldn't marry because he was already married."

Zack's astonishment was obvious, "A married man, mother, how could you?"

"I assure you Zack, it was not in any way sordid, it just happened, we fell in love, and I mean really in love. If you and Florence have as much happiness together as your father and I did you will be blessed indeed. It is a universally acknowledged fact of life that we cannot help who we fall in love with you know, you said yourself, you never believed you stood any chance with Florence, I, for different reasons was in the same boat."

Irate, and indignant Zack went into a fit of pique, "But mother, if he only died recently, why didn't I get to know him, it isn't fair, all these years I had to make do with a sort of substitute father in the old squire. You have not been fair to me at all, not to mention not being truthful; I had the right to know my own father didn't I?"

Lydia pursed her lips, and continued calmly and deliberately, "You did know him Zack, very well in fact, and one of the reasons his true identity has been kept from you until now is that you also have an older half brother, and he may not take kindly to your existence."

Zack's fit of pique began to show signs of turning into pure rage.

"Half brother, something else kept secret, wonderful, now you have me completely fogged, if I am not, as I always believed the son of a farm labourer, who the hell am I?"

"Zack, Zack, calm down, I have told you times without number losing your cool stops your brain working, you have the intelligence, use your reasoning."

Zack, being one who rarely lost his temper, poured himself another cup of tea, as he did he assimilated his mother's cryptic revelations and his anger began to cool down again. Silently he began to work it out, he had a half brother, he did know his father but not as his father, suddenly a possibility hit him.

"No, No way, no way, it can't be him, is it—."

Lydia read the sudden realisation on her son's face, smiled and nodded.

"Yes Zack, Charles Heath is your father, and unpleasant though he may be the new squire is your brother, now can you see why you were not told."

Mother and son sat at the table, neither knowing quite how to continue, eventually, Zack broke the awkward silence.

"How many people actually know about this bombshell you have just dropped on me?"

Hesitantly Lydia answered, "To the best of my knowledge you are only the third who definitely knows who you are, and there is one other whom I believe has guessed about your father and me, but not that you are his son. Fortunately for us almost everyone believes as you did, that I was indiscreet, played the part of a wife before the marriage vows were taken, and that your father passed away before we could marry."

"Three, then that will be you, me, but who else mother?"

"Before your father passed away, he confided in someone he believed he could trust, although I have to admit I am not entirely convinced about the reliability of his choice, Henry Cotes is the third."

"Henry Cotes, why Henry Cotes?"

Zack, you must understand your father and I were together long before you were born. Henry Cotes has been appointed as the chief executor of your father's will. I learned some weeks ago your father, the old squire, left this cottage and the smallholding to me, and I recently learned a little money as well. Your father decided, to be sure his bequest of leaving me this cottage could not be challenged, it would be necessary for Henry to know the truth about us."

"Let me get this straight mother, this cottage, the land we work for ourselves is now yours, and therefore may one day come to me?"

"Of course it will."

Lydia was about to tell her son of the other arrangements made for him, but Henry's insistence on secrecy had not authorised her to share that information with him, or anyone else for that matter, quite the contrary in fact, Zack had learned enough for the time being.

Zack pondered, "And these then are the things you spoke of, which, have happened recently to make it imperative I know now who my father was, and you have decided to tell me this so that I don't ask any questions later about you owning this house and land, and more importantly, how you came to own them?"

Lydia hesitantly nodded, "Yes, sort of."

"Well mother, all I can say is you certainly know how to make my own news pale into insignificance. On the other hand, Henry Cotes knowing who my father was may have had some bearing on bringing about my engagement to Florence. Do you think he will have told Mr Oldfield, and it was that which changed his opinion of me?"

"Definitely not, he is sworn to keep the secret, now that you know, what do you intend to do, your father and I kept your identity secret for a very good reason; Henry seems to think if the new squire finds out about our legacy, he may try to take it from us."

"Young Master Charles, yes I can see that, if anyone should carry the label of bastard it's him not me, but you would need to add the word arrogant in front of it, I never liked that man."

Lydia was unable to stifle her smile ensuing from her son's cynicism.

"No mother, I see no point in anyone else knowing what you have just told me, I have existed all these years without knowing, and now I am to marry the girl I love, oh no, we will tell no one else."

"Not even Florence if the marriage goes ahead?"

"Someday, perhaps, but for the time being I cannot see any benefit in her knowing, it may put her off me if she thinks I am descended from such an old, aristocratic family, she's not overly fond of the toffs is my Florence."

Lydia laughed, "Wealthy maybe, an old family and well established in society yes, but I wouldn't term the Heaths as aristocratic, even if there are still a few Knighthoods and such amongst their more distant relations."

"You are probably right mother, but I still think Henry Cotes has let something slip, which has had something to do with Florence's father suddenly changing his mind about accepting me as a prospective son-in-law, and offering me a job at the farm to boot. I am not complaining, but it is all very perplexing indeed."

"No Zack, I am sure you are wrong, Henry is a strange, unscrupulous man but I cannot believe he would willingly betray the secret of your heritage, anyway, it is in his own interests not to. There must be some other more practical reason why George Oldfield has offered you a job; after all, he has no children of his own now except Florence, it must be sheer coincidence."

Lydia hoped her face did not betray the fact she knew this was no coincidence at all; the old farmer's change of mind had been engineered. She had revealed too much already today, and in so doing had robbed her son of much of his thunder, in many respects she had diminished his own exciting news, she must now consider damage limitation and allow the subject of his forthcoming engagement to take precedence.

"Have you any idea how you will tackle the work at the farm Zack, has Mr Oldfield given you any indication what you are expected to do?"

"Sort of, yes, and that's what makes me think Henry Cotes may have had a hand in it."

Eager to play along Lydia asked, "How's that?"

She knew Henry Cotes was responsible for these recent events, not by choice but she was now obliged to put her trust in him. She knew him of old and she was convinced there must still be something being kept from her, something on which perhaps her son may now shed some light.

Zack's elbow rested on the kitchen table, his chin cradled in his hand and he began to stroke his top lip with his forefinger as he went on to explain.

"It was on Saturday, after the explosion at the mine, I was called into the office to see Henry Cotes and give a report on what happened with the ventilation fan. He asked me all sorts of questions, most of which had nothing to do with the mine, and I happened to mention that I would prefer a job on the land, Gamekeeper or something like that. Next thing I know, low and behold the woods at Valley Farm are to be turned into a sporting ground for Cotes and his posh mates to shoot game, I have to organise the rearing of pheasants and the like for them to shoot, and he is even talking about having deer on there."

Lydia smiled, "Zack, that does not surprise me, it is not a new idea, your father talked about doing just that, he even started to plan it out, I am sure there are still some of his books and notes here at the cottage. He left them here because it seems Anne Heath does not hold with that sort of thing, hunting, shooting, hypocritical really considering how fond she is of venison and game birds on her table."

Zack's jaw dropped in amazement, "Mother, you are not telling me that amongst everything else you know something about rearing game birds?"

Lydia laughed, "A little yes, but I am no expert. If I remember correctly your father intended to pen-rear pheasants from June onwards, buying an initial batch of chicks sometime in July, some to retain for breeding and the bulk to be released for shooting."

"That sounds risky, turning them loose, no knowing where they will end up, they can fly you know."

"Of course they can fly Zack, isn't shooting them on the wing the point of the silly sport. You will always lose a few, but I understand if you keep feeding them grain most of them won't stray far; it's normally around October when current year birds are fat enough for the table and the men go after them with their guns."

Zack's surprise at his mother's knowledge was evident, "OK, OK," he said, "If you're that clever, now tell me how to attract deer, I've only ever seem a couple of Roe's all the times I've been down the farm."

Lydia responded playfully, "Don't be so cheeky or I'll box your ears, you're not too big you know."

Zack muttered, "Sorry."

"Your father didn't hold out much hope in that direction, but I do remember once while we were visiting friends in Shropshire, a keeper from one of the big estates told us they planted small patches of turnips in clearings and along the rides, he said deer can't resist them. Deer can travel a fair distance and I have seen herds of Fallow and Roe deer myself not more than eight or ten miles from Valley Farm, it might be worth doing a bit of planting and enticing them in with a free offering or two, like the birds, feed them and they will stay."

His mother's remark registered immediately with Zack and he was quick to query it, "You visited friends in Shropshire, as a couple?"

Lydia regretted her slip, now she would have more to explain, after a pause, she smiled, and the lad should now be told of her life with his father.

"When there was enough distance between home and wherever we happened to be, people new us as man and wife, yes, it seemed the only logical thing to do; our only regret was that you always had to stay behind. It was painful for your father that he could not acknowledge you as his son, he was very proud of you. I learned from Henry this week, it was your father's intention that if Anne's illnesses had taken her first, after a suitable period for mourning, we would have married, it came as a bit of a shock to me because your father never told me his thoughts lay in that direction. For my part, I never asked for more than we had."

Zack shook his head, "Ah, now I begin to see, all those times I thought you were working at some fine house or other, you and the squire were travelling around the country as husband and wife, no wonder Henry Cotes was puzzled when I said you had been working at his house last summer."

Lydia replied in a remorseful tone, "I know, I'm sorry, but the deceit was not intended for you but for everyone else, your father and I had to grasp every stolen moment we could to be together."

"I can't complain, I was never happier than when I was living at the farm with lads of my own age, nearest thing I had to brothers and a sister, but now you tell me I actually have a half brother." Zack's face darkened and he shook his head.

Concerned by her son's change of mood, Lydia asked, "Does it bother you that much Zack, knowing the new squire is your brother?"

"Not in the least, I was just thinking, those I regarded as brothers, Russell and Philip Oldfield and many more besides got themselves killed in this senseless war, not to mention the good men who lost their lives last Saturday down Tilly, and that posing popinjay still lives, can't think what God is playing at."

"Zack!" snapped his mother, "That is quite enough of that sort of talk; don't tempt providence by questioning the will of the almighty."

Zack grinned broadly signifying he was only teasing, and replied, "You can talk."

Lydia smiled and gave him a playful scuff on his left ear.

"But seriously mother, if I could have chosen a brother it would have been Russ or Phil, not Charles Heath."

"I know, I know, but as the saying goes, God gives us our relations, but thank God you can choose your friends."

* * *

True to his word and in accordance with his instruction, by ten o'clock on Wednesday morning two Lorries arrived in Heals End from Henry Cotes's sawmill, one destined for Tilly Pit, and one for the Primitive Chapel. Both lorries were laden with coffins, linen lined plain oblong boxes made in haste and lacking the customary embellishments of stain or varnish, but a far more effective method of storing the remains of the ill-fated mine workers than sackcloth until the clergy could administer their burial rites.

This being the fifth day following the explosion, the turmoil had virtually subsided, Joseph Shaw and Arthur Cleaver had returned to their normal working pattern at Tilly, both starting at eight o'clock.

Arthur had completed a short inspection below ground and was making his way from the headstock to the office as the lorry carrying the coffins pulled onto the pit bank; Arthur examined the load and gave instructions for the lorry to be unloaded at the Smithy.

Arthur entered the office to find Joseph Shaw on the telephone, desperately trying to reassure a customer that the pit would be in a position to fulfil their coal order from stocks, and that production would be underway again well before stockpiles ran out.

"Seems Cotes was as good as his word Joseph," Arthur said as soon as Joseph replaced the receiver, "Think you'd best come and take a look at this."

"Look at what?"

"Cotes has sent a load of coffins, they're rough, but they will do the job."

The last two boxes were being carried into the Smithy as Joseph and Arthur arrived.

"Why two separate stacks Joe?" asked Arthur.

"Well, I was guessing you would want me to take these up to the Chapel in the van," Joe replied indicating the stack nearest the door, "This other pile here, they aren't finished off, no lining in them, and then there are these things here, don't know what the hell these are for."

Joe held up one of four lengths of three by two inch timber, about nine feet in length, at the ends the last six inches had been rounded off to a diameter of one and a half inches. Each length had two, inch and a half by one quarter strip iron 'J' hooks secured to them about two feet six inches from each end.

Joseph Shaw studied the weird contrivance, "No, nor I, you any ideas Arthur?"

Arthur took the length of timber from the van driver, and went over to the unlined boxes. "Yep, must be like stretcher poles, look, these hooks marry into these handles here on the boxes."

"Well spotted, that must be what they are for," Joseph said as he examined one of the lids, "Look Arthur, these have been drilled and counter sunk, and like the boxes numbered in chalk so you can tell which lid belongs to which box,—hold on, what's this?"

Joseph removed a small brown paper bag, which had been pinned to the inside of the box.

Joe Harris chirped up, "They've all got those inside boss, eight holes in each lid, and ten size twelve two inch screws in those bags, whoever made these thought of everything, it's a bugger when you drop a screw, but they put spares in, pity they didn't finish all the coffins off with a lining though."

"Perhaps they ran out of cloth and thought it best to send what they had Joe, they knew the job was urgent," Arthur suggested.

"Maybe, anyway if you don't want these moving again I have things to do."

"No Joe, leave them here, we understand a batch has already been delivered to the Chapel," Joseph said as he dismissed the driver, "Actually Arthur," Joseph added, "I did ask Cotes for something to use here in place of stretchers to bring the men out, but I thought two, not ten, which is what we seem to have here."

As soon as the van driver was clear of the Smithy and out of earshot, Joseph turned and spoke quietly to Arthur, "You don't really think they ran out of cloth do you?" Arthur shook his head,

"So," Joseph continued, "You're thinking exactly what I am thinking?"

Arthur nodded, "I think you had best phone the doctor Joseph, he needs to come and check on this lot, if need be, it will be his place to ban the opening of these coffins on public health grounds when they come back out of the pit with more bodies inside."

"I intended to do just that, I think it's a fairly safe bet no one will have survived down there until now, judging from the remarks the good doctor made yesterday, the remaining bodies will come out named and sealed in those coffins, and they will stay sealed."

Arthur sighed, "Difficult, true identification will be almost impossible, all we have to work on is the location the remaining men were supposed to be in at the time of the explosion, of those we have brought out, too many were found where they should not have been."

"I know," Joseph agreed, "And in addition to which, the lamp and tag system has proved unreliable, the blast carried some lamps away from the bodies, and mutilated the men so they are unrecognisable."

Arthur shook his head, "These are very close communities Joseph, I cannot see our men going along with just bringing out a body and putting a label on the box, many of them are related."

"That is the main reason Henry Cotes is going to Wales to bring in outsiders to do that job, not knowing our men and having no connection with their families, they will get on with searching where they are told and not ask too many questions, hopefully they will find those they seek."

"I figured that, and what is more you can bet whoever he gets won't be on a standard rate of pay, and he will make sure they shuffle off back to Wales as soon as the job's done. Having said that, you have to give Cotes some credit, he must have had his joiner's working day and night since he agreed to make these boxes, and those dropped off at the Chapel."

"Arthur, we cannot afford to show any signs of doubt about the expected location of the men still below ground. When the Welshmen arrive, our confidence in the identification system will need to be plethoric, our attitude so positive that no one, visiting workers or local families will question the identity of whom, or what is in each box. If we say, our system says it is Fred Blogs in that coffin, then Fred Blogs it must be, death and burial certificates can be issued without medical examination and verification in a situation like this."

"Yes I can appreciate that Joseph, but you heard the rescue team leader's reports, there are a lot of men down below scattered about in pieces, and that is only in the districts they have been able to enter, whose to know what will be found when we regain entry to the rest?"

"Arthur, confidence and positive attitude, Fred Blogs is Fred Blogs, regardless of the contents of each Coffin; you can be assured that is precisely why Cotes has sent so many plain boxes to carry men out. He expects us to know how many men remain lost below, and where they will be found, and that is eventually the number that will be brought out for Christian burial."

"I can't say I like it Joseph, but it won't be the first time it has been done that way."

"Precisely, we shall have to practice the methods of the upper classes and politicians, in other words Arthur, maintain a convincing air, a smile on our faces, and tell bare faced lies."

With morning surgery taking place Joseph Shaw was obliged to wait a few minutes for Dr. Thomas to finish a consultation before responding to his telephone call.

"Good morning Mr Shaw," after some time the doctor's voice on the phone acknowledged his call, "My receptionist tells me you have some news for me."

"I do indeed Doctor, it is in response to your request yesterday, for us to implement a more efficient and decent method to lay out our deceased men instead of sackcloth and lime until burials can take place. I have no idea how he has managed it so quickly, but we have received a delivery of basic coffins from Mr Cotes's sawmills, we have enough to accommodate the dead still here in the smithy, and with one or two spares."

"You have, really, I'm impressed, I thought it would be a few days at least before any arrived."

"So did we, and I understand another batch have been delivered to the chapel. The thing is, before we do anything with them, and as you raised the point about public health, would it be possible for you to come and inspect them, I don't want to disturb the bodies too much, that is to say, lay them in these boxes and have to move them again if the coffins don't meet your requirements."

"Quite right, with the condition of most of those bodies the less you move them the better, I will call up after lunch before I start my house calls, shall we say, one thirty, two o'clock, or thereabouts."

"Thank you Doctor that will be a big help, I will expect you this afternoon."

Joseph was in the process of replacing the receiver, when Dr Thomas's voice stopped him, "Just for clarification Joseph, I am right in thinking no charge is being made for these coffins to those families who choose to accept them?"

"We were both there when Henry Cotes made the offer Doctor, by now I would expect most of the residents living in these villages are aware they will be available and free. We made it known here yesterday afternoon by posting notices, and also informing our senior men, these little village communities can spread news and gossip extremely fast."

Doctor Thomas laughed, "That is true enough, I only hope Cotes's offer is not misconstrued, from my experience there is little love lost between workers, their families and owners, and in your case, one of those owners is, to say the least rather indiscrete."

Dr. Patrick Thomas arrived at Tilly Pit just before two o'clock; Joseph and Arthur had been watching for him to arrive; they walked across the pit bank to meet him as he parked his car outside the engineer's shop.

As they approached the Doctor asked, "Well gentlemen, where are these boxes you want me to check? Are they in the smithy?

"Yes," Joseph replied, "Seemed the obvious place to store them until you arrived."

"I was surprised by your call earlier, and I confess to having some reservations about there suitability with them getting here so fast," continued the Doctor.

"We were surprised when they were delivered," Arthur added, "But they look pretty good to me, I thought they were well made, but of course the final decision is yours to make."

In the Smithy, Joseph and Arthur erected a trestle table not yet returned to Hales Brook Chapel, and lifted one of the lined coffins onto it.

"Right, lets have a good look at it," Dr. Thomas half muttered to himself as he removed his hat and gloves.

Joseph and Arthur frowned, expecting the Doctor was going to reject them at first sight.

"Straight planking," said the doctor as he examined the coffin, "Screwed to external struts, I would have preferred them to be air tight, I suppose I should have mentioned that to Henry Cotes. Oh! I see how they have done it, the planks have been edge glued as well, that should seal it well enough. Serviceable handles fixed to the struts, Hmm,—struts continue underneath to reinforce the base and to allow any lowering ropes to be withdrawn, and they are lined with white linen."

Joseph and Arthur rather pensively awaited the Doctor's verdict.

"You said another batch of these has been delivered to the Prims as well?"

"That is what the driver said when he dropped these off, he said another lorry was unloading at the chapel," Arthur confirmed.

Dr. Thomas let out a low whistle, "Good grief, Cotes must have had his entire workforce making these, they are very basic but well thought out, and yes, I would have no objection if they buried me in one of these, you were right Arthur, they are fine."

Joseph interrupted, "There are two types,—Arthur, we need one of the others."

The two managers removed the lined coffin and replaced it with one of the plain boxes; a quick evaluation by the Doctor was all he needed.

"Identical apart from the white lining, they're OK, no point in taking white linen into the filth down a coal mine. Actually, I was going to speak to you about that, I have consulted with my colleagues and it has been decided, when you eventually locate the remaining men below ground, no matter how much their family object, the coffins will not be re-opened once the identity of the occupant is proved. The rate of decay is such that they will probably be unrecognisable anyway, better the coffins remain sealed, both from a public health point of view and to minimise their family's distress."

The Doctor purposefully watched for a reaction from the two men, it was very slight, but he caught it.

"I take it you were expecting me to say that?"

Joseph and Arthur were uneasy at this remark.

Dr Thomas smiled, "Obviously the lost men must have a Christian burial, but I fear in some respects that the young squire may have a valid point, I hope I am wrong, only time will tell."

"Do you have time for a cup of tea, or something stronger before you leave Doctor?" Joseph asked.

"I will make time, there is something else I feel I should tell you, and your office may not have as many ears as this building," Dr. Thomas indicated towards several surface labourers, obtrusively hovering about outside the open door.

Returning to the offices, Joseph instructed his clerk in the outer office that they were not to be disturbed.

"Cup of tea Doctor?" Joseph asked as he put the kettle on the stove, "Or I think there is still some of Cotes's whiskey left, young Mr Heath didn't quite manage to finish it off."

"Tea is fine Joseph; I have a lot of patients to see this afternoon, wouldn't do to be smelling of alcohol."

Arthur Cleaver wasn't sure he should remain with the manager and doctor; he stayed near the office door expecting to be asked to leave if the 'something else' was of a confidential nature.

"Cotes has gone to South Wales today then Joseph," Dr. Thomas began, "Looking for skilled miners to bring out the rest of your men."

"He has, but I don't think he is looking as such, I got the impression before he left he knew exactly who he would be bringing back from his mines down there."

The doctor's expression became pensive, "So technically, the young squire is in charge in his absence."

Joseph and Arthur smiled, "Technically yes, I suppose he is, but Henry Cotes's instructions are not to involve him, and if he comes here to tell him as little as possible. Also, if he gives us anymore instructions like he did over those engineer fellows he sent in, to use our discretion about carrying them out," Joseph reiterated his orders, which gave some relief to the doctor.

Arthur, still uneasy, decided it was time he knew if he should stay or leave, "Doctor, the information you have, am I to stay to hear it, or would you prefer me to leave?"

"It will concern you Arthur, but it isn't exactly information, more of a rumour regarding the actions taken by the Home Office in London."

Both Joseph and Arthur stiffened at the mention of the Home Office.

"Last night I had a phone call from an old friend of mine who holds a fairly senior position there; he visited me a few weeks ago and stayed just over a fortnight, when he came across a report about the explosion here, he put two and two together and guessed I would be professionally involved after the accident. Don't let this go any further than Henry Cotes until you have official confirmation, but as you probably expected, the Home Office are to appoint an inspector to conduct an inquiry into the affair. Up until yesterday, nobody had accepted the position, but it seems they have approached someone named George Walklate CBE to undertake it, or to be more precise, he is pushing for the appointment. My friend has a sarcastic turn of phrase; he says if Walklate accepts, he moves so fast with these things the inquiry will most likely begin around Christmas next year."

Arthur and Joseph looked at each other in amazement, "But that is two years away," Joseph spluttered, "Peoples memories will either be clouded or exaggerated by then."

"I know, very risky on their part, in more ways than one," Dr Thomas agreed with a smirk, "That is why I for one am making sure all my notes and observations are recorded in great detail, if my friend is correct, with that timescale I don't even expect the inquest to start until about three months before the inquiry. On the other hand, if a certain body of 'gentlemen' have become involved, which I would expect, it could prove useful to Cotes. Nevertheless, whoever is appointed by the Home Office will be expected to visit this mine, and possibly go below ground within the next few months, but only where it is safe to do so."

Joseph smirked, but Arthur was obviously puzzled and repeated, "Body of gentlemen, I don't understand."

Dr. Thomas cut him short, "Speak no more of it, just watch your own backs."

"That is something we have every intention of doing Doctor," Joseph assured him, "I rather think I am with your implication, and if I may say, had half expected something of the sort."

Realisation dawned on Arthur, "Oh! The—," he started to say.

"Leave it Arthur," Joseph snapped, to which Arthur with a knowing nod dutifully complied.

Joseph asked, "Are we to pass on this information to Mr Cotes if he telephones?"

Dr Thomas smiled, "Why else do you imagine I have told you, forewarned is to be forearmed, anyway, it is time I was leaving, patients to see and all that you know."

Dr. Thomas took his leave of the pits senior managers and went on his way. When they were alone in the office, Joseph turned to Arthur.

"Well Arthur, what do you make of that?"

After a moments reflection Arthur replied, "Joseph, I am a simple man, never been far from these villages, but I reckon, the Doctor, his mate at the Home Office and Henry Cotes are all members of the little pinny brigade."

"I agree, or something very similar, and if we are right, no harm will come to them, they get away with practically everything because it is too messy to prove the things they do and make it stick, we should follow the Doctors advice, and make sure the blame for the accident doesn't fall on us."

"You figured that out days ago Joseph, and it seems you were right, I certainly don't fancy being made a scapegoat."

Chapter Sixteen

It is a well-established concept that good animal husbandry centres largely upon routine, her chicken's morning feed finished, Lydia Morgan stood at the kitchen sink and with a cloth dampened in warm water, she carefully wiped the collected eggs. Her task was interrupted by a gentle tap at the front door, in response she made her way through the living room drying her hands on a small kitchen towel as she went.

Lydia opened the door to be greeted by the ruddy complexion and beaming features of Hannah Wilkins, a parlour maid from Highfield Hall.

"Good morning Miss Lydia, and how are we this fine Thursday morning?" asked the cheery melodic voiced girl.

"Fine Hannah, and yourself? To what do I owe the pleasure of seeing you here on my doorstep this morning?"

"If you please Miss Lydia, the mistress has sent me round with this note," Hannah handed over a small, delicately perfumed envelope, "I am to wait for a reply."

Lydia invited the girl into her living room indicating she should take a seat, Lydia sat in her favourite chair before opening the envelope.

"Your kettle is boiling Miss Lydia; shall I do the honours while you read your letter?"

"Please Hannah; the tea is in the pot, fill it to just over half full, you know where the mugs are kept."

My Dearest Lydia,

I find myself quite alone today as Charles has gone away on business for a few days.

Would you do me the honour of having lunch with me today at the Hall? There is a little matter I wish to discuss with you which could be to your, and indeed my own advantage.

Do please come, around midday, or as near to that time as you can.

In anticipation,
Your friend
Anne.

Lydia turned her attention to her young visitor, "The Squire is away on business then is he Hannah?"

Hannah's face took on a roguish grin, "He is, yes, and knowing him we can guess what kind of business took him away."

Lydia smiled, indicating she understood the girls implied mischievous meaning, "Do you or the other girls get pestered by him in that way Hannah?"

"Sometimes, usually when he has had too much to drink, not that I, or any of the other girls at the hall would want him anywhere near us, you can never tell where he has been, or who with. Fortunately for us he dare not let his mother find out just what he tries to get up to, we figured that out ages ago, all we need to do when he starts his antics is threaten to tell the mistress, and he usually goes away in a huff."

"True, true, he is such a man, but Hannah, I would advise you and the others to be more cautious now that he is Squire, it won't be long before he realises whatever else he inherits as part of his father's legacy, he has power now."

"I know that Miss Lydia, we are more wary of him these days, he is becoming quite unpredictable, the sooner he takes a wife the better for us all, there must be someone in his own class daft enough to take him on."

"Daft enough to take him on, now that is a peculiar expression Hannah for you to use, he is not bad looking, and he has this estate now which should rank highly in his favour, would you not agree?"

"Maybe so Miss Lydia, but his reputation will precede him where ever he goes, everyone knows him to be a rake, he may chase us but he definitely wouldn't dream of considering the likes of me, or any of my friends as a prospective bride now would he?"

Lydia smiled shrewdly, "No, probably not, he will be too afraid to marry below his class, he will seek a bride with money, the way he spends it, dowry will be important to him, but sometimes, on a rare occasion love and commitment can happen between differing classes, it's not absolutely impossible."

Hannah shook her head, "No, it is impossible; people from our class could never learn to mix in high society that is something you're born with, or you never possess, definitely impossible."

Lydia laughed, "Pour the tea Hannah, while I write a reply for your Mistress, Oh, and there is some cake in the pantry if you would like some."

The girls face glowed in delight, "Parkin?"

"Yes, there is a slab of Parkin, in the tin with Roses on the lid."

Lydia scribbled a note of acceptance and handed it to the girl.

"Have you found yourself a young man yet Hannah?"

"No such luck Miss Lydia, young men have not been a natural asset round here these four years or more, what with the war and all, and now that explosion at the Pit has killed even more of them. Mr Charles may have inherited a lot from the old squire, what did you call it, a legacy?"

Lydia nodded.

"Ah well, as I see it, after that fire damp explosion at squire's coal mine, the only legacy we have from him is a flaming damp legacy, this parish of ours has turned into nowt but Villages of Women."

Lydia paused, she studied her guest in silence, "I had not thought of that, but you are right, and that description will probably stick for some time to come, a damp legacy leaving a village of women."

Lydia Morgan had inadvertently brought to the fore a subject Hannah had been struggling to raise; coyly she broached the question playing on her mind.

"How is your Zack Miss Lydia? I haven't seen him for a while."

Lydia realised the clandestine motive behind this seemingly innocent question, smiling she asked.

"Still got a soft spot for him have you Hannah?"

The girl's face turned crimson with embarrassment.

"How do you know that Miss Lydia I never told a soul I liked him, I am not the only one who does either, but he never notices anyone except Florence Oldfield the lucky little madam."

"As you say Hannah, sadly, there is a definite shortage of eligible young men around these parts, I am sorry to be the one to reveal this news to you, but I expect it will be common knowledge soon enough, Zack and Florence are engaged and are to be married this coming Easter."

Hannah's jaw dropped, "Really, I can scarce believe that Miss Lydia."

Lydia's face took on a look of bewilderment, she was about to query the girls meaning, but Hannah read Lydia's expression and continued before she had chance to speak.

"Don't misunderstand me Miss Lydia, I don't doubt your word, it's just that Flo and I have been close friends ever since we started school together. The last time we spoke, only last week in fact, that subject came up and she said she had little hope of her father ever agreeing to a marriage between her and Zack. Everyone knows how they feel about each other, and I admit it, I am a little jealous, but if her father has consented, I'm pleased for them nevertheless."

Lydia smiled and nodded, "I can understand that Hannah, I never thought George Oldfield would give his permission either, but it seems things have taken a little turn for the better, Florence's father has given his consent and they are to marry at Easter."

"Is that what you meant by it could happen on rare occasions, a match between different classes?"

Lydia chuckled, "No, not exactly, class wise Florence and Zack are not that far apart you know, the Oldfield family are nothing more than successful tenant farmers, maybe a bit better off money wise than the average, but it doesn't put them higher on the social standings."

By her continued blushes, Hannah's embarrassment was evident, Lydia, aware of the girl's discomfort smiled, offering Hannah another slice of her favourite cake.

"Don't upset yourself, you have not given offence child; I know exactly what you mean, now if I remember correctly, wasn't there some talk of you and Philip Oldfield becoming rather friendly?"

"There was, and yes we were walking out, it's not so bad when you are the second son, Mr Oldfield didn't seem to mind about Phil and me, but the damn Germans put an end to all that, not much hope left for any of us girls finding a chap now."

"Oh Hannah you exaggerate, if you think about it, when Tilly Pit is up and running at full strength again men will be needed to work it, and you said yourself there are none around here, so, they will probably have to bring workmen from elsewhere. I can't see any men who are already settled with families wanting to move here, so my guess would be if they do bring men in, there may well be plenty of young eligible bachelors amongst them."

"Maybe, but I've heard talk the pit is more likely to close than ever work again, unless Zack has said something to you making you think more men will be brought here?"

"No, he hasn't, but it's pretty obvious don't you think? While they are not at full strength Zack and maybe one or two others will be leaving the pit to work on the land instead."

"For the squire?"

"I don't know about anyone else, but Zack is definitely going to work at the Oldfield farm."

Hannah's cheery face was momentarily bewildered, and then she began to laugh, "Why the crafty old devil, that's why George Oldfield has given in about Flo and Zack getting married."

"How do you mean?"

"He's getting too old to run the farm on his own, Russ and Phil were taken by the war, and the farm's tenancy can't pass to a woman, Flo I mean, she's the only one left, if the Oldfield's are to keep that farm, old George needs a son-in-law who knows the land, I'll bet I'm right you know."

"Perhaps you are, but I wouldn't spread that about too much if I were you."

Lydia smiled; she knew only too well the girl would not be able to resist talking about her imagined intrigue, which, once it spread on the gossip grapevine, would in turn, do everyone, especially Henry Cotes and her Zack a great service by diverting people's attention.

The mantle clock made a slight metallic clunk as the mechanism cocked ready to chime, Hannah's eyes followed the sound.

"Good Lord, look at the time," she exclaimed, "I shall be in for it taking this long to bring you your letter, I'd best be making tracks, thanks for the tea and cake Miss Lydia."

The girl rose to leave, Lydia accompanied her to the door, however, before setting foot on the garden path Hannah hesitated.

"Miss Lydia, have I your permission to tell the girls at the hall about Flo and Zack's engagement?"

Lydia laughed, "Of course you have my dear, it is no secret, as I said everyone will know soon enough."

Alone again in her kitchen, Lydia picked up the note from Anne Heath, she read it again. There was no indication of malice that she could detect in the words, but she could not think what Anne could mean by advantage to them both, although, she recalled Henry hinting at something his sister had mentioned to him. Her only option was to wait and see, with everything else going on around her; another couple of hours spent with Anne Heath wouldn't hurt.

It had been Lydia's intention, if the weather held fine today to take a walk down to Valley Farm; because of the double life she had led with Charles, Lydia had always been wary of forming any close friendships with the local people. She had many friends outside the locality where she was known as Mrs Charles Heath. Amongst her local acquaintances however, she considered Edith Oldfield to be the closest. Whenever Zack stayed with them, invariably it had been Charles who made the necessary arrangements, nevertheless, over the years, she and Edith had grown to understand each other to some extent, even though her husband considered Lydia to be a fallen woman of ill repute, Edith had never given any indication that she shared his views.

Zack's surprise announcement that after all this time George and Edith had consented to his engagement to Florence definitely unsettled her a little. Not that she really believed Henry Cotes would have betrayed any confidence entrusted to him, but Zack's doubts niggled her, if she could speak to Edith, or even to George, it would go a long way towards putting her mind at rest. Anne Heath's invitation to lunch, for today at least had put an end to that idea, now it would have to wait. Besides which, it was increasingly apparent to Lydia, Anne Heath knew more about her relationship with Charles than she had ever disclosed, and an invitation to take lunch with her was, quite possibly the last thing Lydia expected, nevertheless, Lydia resolved during lunch to learn just how much Anne knew about her intimate association and life with Charles.

Lydia was startled by the realisation, that at the prospect of lunch at the hall, she was experiencing a similar rush of excitement to the one of years ago, when she and Charles had laid their plans for the concealment of their love. That web of intrigue however now appeared to have developed a few minor tares, and these needed some urgent repair.

She pottered about her cottage doing little more than killing time before she needed to get ready, and wrestled with the age-old problem of what she should wear. Her wardrobe was extensive; packed away in travelling trunks she had dresses and gowns of the finest quality with all the necessary accessories, which, up until now had only been worn when she was playing the role of Mrs Charles Heath away from these villages. Perhaps now was the time to bring some of them out, eventually she decided against it for today, settling instead on what she called her 'home best.' However, she did augment this with a few of the simpler items of her jewellery. She had become very used to, and now preferred wearing her long hair loose and free, but under these circumstances, she thought it more fitting to gather it once more at the back of her head into a formal tight bun.

Fifteen minutes before midday, Lydia left her cottage and took the short walk through Bluebell Wood towards Highfield Hall, passing through the wrought iron gates for the first time since her beloved Charles had passed away, out of habit, she turned and took the path towards the rear entrance, however, after only a few steps, she stopped.

"No Lydia," she muttered to herself, "You have been invited as a guest today, you're not here as a servant, the front door for you my girl."

Lydia's ring of the doorbell was answered by Hannah, "My, my you look very nice Miss Lydia; the mistress is in the drawing room, she is expecting you, had I better announce you do you think?"

"Don't be silly Hannah; I know it's a bit different me being invited to take lunch with the mistress, but in this house, like you I am regarded as a servant. I have a sneaky feeling that is what the mistress still has in mind, am I right in thinking there have been no guests here since Mr Charles senior passed away, it is getting to the time of year when visitors generally arrive."

Hannah smiled, "Yes, I told Hawkins and cook about Zack, and that's what we thought; it will be nice if you came back, when you aren't here and in charge everything that can always seems to go wrong."

"Not as bad as that, is it Hannah?"

"Seems to have got a lot worse since young Mr Charles started spending more time here, nobody really knows what they are supposed to be doing, he says one thing one minute and before you know it he has changed his mind, and we have to do things over again. We have had to manage as best we can, but if there were the usual guests here; Lord knows how we would cope."

"Doesn't the mistress take charge and keep things in line?"

"She tries I suppose, but as long as I've been here she never bothered with such things, it was always the old squire who ran the house, or you, when you were here."

"Hmm, perhaps my guess was right then, but I'm afraid she will be disappointed, she's in the drawing room you said?"

Lydia entered the drawing room and found Anne Heath seated by the fire occupied with a piece of embroidery.

"You wanted to see me mistress?"

"My dear Lydia, yes I do, punctual as always, and you can cut that guff out for a start."

Lydia's hackles rose slightly, Anne's acknowledgement of her arrival seemed double-edged and out of place.

"I'm sorry mistress I don't understand—."

Anne interrupted her, "That 'mistress' guff, that has been obsolete for more years than I care to remember, although it was considerate of you to continue to use it all these years, and I appreciate the fact. I have asked you here today as an equal, a guest, and hopefully a friend, I expect you to call me Anne as I'm sure you always did when you and my late husband spoke of me, come, sit with me."

Henry Cotes had been correct, Anne Heath had known about her and Charles for a very long time, Lydia's adrenaline surged, she was ready for any outcome, her wits were keen, but up to now she could not see the direction this confrontation would take, Anne's smiling face indicated no malice.

Anne studied her guest closely, "Very elegant Lydia, you look very elegant and smart indeed, but I suspect you have dressed down from the way you can look when you play me."

"Play you," Lydia began to speak but Anne once again interrupted her.

"Yes my dear, after all it could be said we are now both widows, I think it's high time that the two people known in different quarters as Mrs Charles Heath were honest with each other, don't you? For my part, I acquired the prefix of Mrs, which, incidentally I never wanted, thrust upon me purely to consolidate the union of two neighbouring estates, my father pushed me into this marriage, you see, unlike most of our sex, I never desired to marry. It is unfortunate that when Charles eventually found the love of his life, due to an arranged marriage of convenience I was in the way. Charles and I, although we got on well together, our relationship was always more of friendship than one of passion, however, for some reason I never understood, to him it was important that to the outside world we appeared to be happily married. He was, as you know years younger than me, after we married, I soon realized he was lonely, and he deserved more from me than I was able to give, and then one-day destiny strikes. Into this house as a servant comes an extremely beautiful, intelligent, highly educated young woman from good family who had fallen upon hard times. When you first arrived here you were a mere slip of a girl, but your looks and proud bearing made it impossible for you not to be noticed whenever you entered a room. Charles was always amiable with all the servants, but you Lydia were cut from a different cloth, and I could see Charles paid more attention to you than the rest, it was not long before I realised the way you felt about each other, probably before the pair of you did."

Lydia elected to remain silent, taking everything in until she was sure of her ground, this was a very different Anne Heath to the naïve woman the world saw, and she could not help but admire the way Anne had fooled everyone for so long, suddenly she remembered Henry's remark that his sister had recently surprised him with her savvy.

Judging by the way she continued, Anne was obviously enjoying herself; "Now my dear, to business, I have missed your presence here, I know Charles left you your cottage and smallholding in his will."

Lydia remained frozen, not even the slightest blink to betray her feelings.

"Ah, I see you know about that, has my brother been to see you recently?"

Lydia nodded.

"But such a bequest will not give you the lifestyles to which by now you have become accustomed; I don't think you received enough. I would like you to consider coming to live here at the hall as my companion; in my opinion you have as much right to live here in comfort as I do. I have some money and property of my own which is not connected with this estate, and when I am gone, I intend my personal fortune shall be yours in recognition of the service you have done me all these years. I asked you here today with the intention of suggesting you come to live here as my companion, I admit, I had reservations whether or not you would accept, but when young chatterbox Hannah brought your reply, she also told me your son is soon to be married. When he leaves home you will be alone like me, that news gave me some hope that you may possibly consider my offer favourably."

There came a gentle tap at the door, and in walked Hannah, "If you please ma'am, lunch is ready in the dining room."

"Thank you Hannah," Anne acknowledged, "I hope you are hungry Lydia, I told cook to make a special effort today."

Hannah Wilkins eyes never strayed from Lydia's face, and as she walked passed the girl, Lydia smiled and gently shook her head; Hannah's expectant expression became downcast.

As soon as the first course had been served, Anne dismissed the servants from the room.

"Have you nothing to say Lydia, I realise my proposal may have come as a surprise which you may need time to consider, but we must have some conversation."

"Indeed we must," Lydia, conceded, "When I think of all the trouble Charles and I went to in order to conceal our relationship, not to mention saving your feelings, how long have you known the truth?"

Anne laughed, "As I said, probably long before either of you did, you were a young innocent, and Charles was such a stuffed shirt he wouldn't have realised how he felt until it leapt up and hit him in the face, is that how your devotion to each other began in the first place?"

"Well, sort of, yes, in the beginning it was innocent enough, until one evening I fell off a chair and he caught me, after that things began to get more complicated, but I find it hard to believe you knew all the time and you weren't bothered that your husband had become involved in that way with another woman, why?"

Anne sat in quiet reflection for a while before she answered.

"Difficult to find a way of expressing this, I know you are able to keep confidences. I said I never wanted to be married, because I am not inclined towards the physical attentions of the male, flesh can be tempted according to natural instincts, and for some, instincts most unnatural, I prefer the gentler convivial company of the female of the species. I had fulfilled my duty as a wife and provided a male heir for the estate, the whole process I found repugnant, and once was more than enough thank you, when Charles realised how he felt towards you it made my life much easier."

"Is that what you referred to as the service I have done you over the years?"

"It is, our marriage was nothing more than a business arrangement, nevertheless, over the years I became fond of Charles. On the other hand, you made him very happy and content. All I ever wanted in life was a comfortable home, nothing more, had Charles not been so obsessed with duty and honour, if he had asked to end our marriage I would have gladly agreed, but then, he would have regarded divorce as some kind of failure on his part."

"I still don't understand how you could have lived with the knowledge for so long, true, Charles did have old fashioned, unshakable beliefs over such things, I presume you made him aware you knew about us?"

"What would be the point of that, I found myself quite content with the situation, and even with there being two Mrs Heaths, however, there was just one time I did worry things might change, fortunately, they did not. You asked how long I have known, about your feeling for each other, as I said, before you did, but about you masquerading as his wife, well that came later."

Lydia's expression was inquiring, and Anne happily continued.

"It must be a good twenty years ago; I received a letter from a distant cousin, sadly, she passed away shortly after sending it, she had been at Bath taking the waters for her health. There she learned that Squire Heath from Highfield Hall in Staffordshire, and his young wife had left the hotel the day before she arrived, she wrote to say she was sorry to have missed seeing me; however, she had been surprised to learn I had been there because she knew I loathed travelling. You were not here at the time, I knew you would be with Charles again, and not on another bogus 'loaned out to another household' jaunt, others may have fell for it, but I did not. It was then I realised you must be known as Mrs Heath when Charles was away from home, and you were 'loaned out'. Charles told me then and did on many subsequent occasions that a business acquaintance of his was short staffed and would like to borrow an experienced maid, I always agreed, sometimes I would be a little naughty and suggest you by name."

Lydia was aware of the irony of this, she smiled, "How would that give you alarm that things might change?"

"I am coming to that; I never thought Charles, who as you know was overly obsessed with decorum, would ever forgive you or allow you to remain after the birth of your child. When your condition became an obvious fact and you began to show, it placed me as mistress of this house in a very difficult, and I might say undesirable predicament, propriety demanded that an unmarried pregnant servant should be dismissed immediately.

I do not want to know any details; there are so many stories about how it came about you found yourself in that condition, some say someone forced himself upon you against your will. Some say you got yourself involved with a worker off the estate and matters got out of hand, some say Jacob Brindley was responsible, anyway it doesn't matter, men are such pigs.

The fact is, when I had to let you go because of the child, Charles did forgive you, he let you have that rundown cottage in Bluebell Wood, I know you had a son, but I doubt I would recognise him if I saw him."

Lydia felt more at ease now, Anne seemed to have taken the contrived stories at face value, unless, which seemed more likely, she was denying the obvious by choice, either way they would not pursue that subject.

"I confess I am surprised by your request Anne, and I can see your reasoning in making it, but are you not forgetting one rather important minor detail?"

Anne Heath was pleased Lydia had at last chosen to use her name, speaking as an equal, but now it was her turn to hold an inquiring expression, Lydia continued before Anne asked her meaning.

"Your son, The Squire, he will not want me here, especially not as your companion, have you discussed this idea with him?"

"No, there is no need; he has made it very clear he has no intention of living here at the hall, the country is too quiet and boring for him, he says when he marries he will find a house in town. He is in Bursley now in pursuit of a young lady who will make him an excellent wife."

"Really, do you know the young lady in question?"

"I have not had that pleasure, no, but I have heard much of her family, they are very high in the social ranking. I always hoped for a union between my son and his cousin Antoinette, but she spent so much time away at boarding school, and then she was away at a finishing school abroad, after which she stayed so long with our cousin in Surrey that she and Charles have had little or no contact. Henry wanted her to become a real lady you know, well, to marry a title at least; I have only seen her once since she came home. She has changed a great deal, and for the better I might add, nevertheless, I believe she still has that wild streak, but now, she has developed into a real beauty, a rival for you my dear. She reminds me a great deal of you when you were her age, every young man she meets must be pursuing her, but she won't have any of them, if she settles down she will choose the man not the other way round, and she won't be pushed into marriage as I was. I rather think poor Henry will have his hands full with her now."

As a young girl, Antoinette Cotes had always been able to charm and manipulate her father with great success, if she had returned home skilled in the adult feminine persuasive arts and allurements, Henry Cotes would not know what hit him until it was too late, Lydia found the prospect of this highly amusing.

"Anne, I cannot give you the answer you hope for, not at present anyway, due to a recent bereavement my circumstances have changed considerably. A few days ago I heard I am to inherit some property around Shrewsbury; I have not received all the details as yet, perhaps there is a house or something included, I am given to understand the inheritance is quite substantial, nevertheless, I promise I will give some consideration to your offer."

Anne responded in a slight pique, "Shrewsbury, is that not where you came from, someone in your family has finally remembered you exist have they?"

Lydia was tempted to respond aggressively to this unkind remark, but she realised Anne made it out of pure disappointment.

Anne's tone softened, "Let me assure you Lydia, as long as I live, you will always have a home here if you want it, especially when—."

Lydia interrupted, "When you have people here to stay."

Anne blushed.

"As I was about to say Anne, I cannot give you the answer you hope for right away. However, if I am able, I am prepared to come back for a while to help out when you have your guests here this spring, if that is what you really want, but until I am certain of my future circumstances, it cannot be on a permanent basis."

"I would like that Lydia, but not as a servant, come as my friend and equal. If you wish to organise everything in your usual way I would not object, but wear no uniform, give orders, don't take them and do no work yourself, let the people around here see you as the person you were when you were away with Charles."

Their luncheon engagement came to its end, and when Lydia returned to her cottage, mistress of the manor house, and her former servant now better understood each other's former roles in life.

Anne Heath hoped her revelations and confession might lead to a strong, lasting and closer friendship with the person to whom she believed she owed so much. However, if this was not to be, at least, Lydia had tentatively agreed to return for this years early social gatherings at the hall, thereby ensuring there success. Anne had decided after her brother's recent visit, that this year, her gatherings should be extra special, future finances unsure and her own health being in fast decline, the possibilities these could well be her last was uppermost on her mind.

Zack was in the kitchen brushing his best suit when Lydia returned home.

"Oh there you are mother, I was wondering where you had shot off to, I checked in all the sheds but you were missing."

"Anne Heath sent a note round this morning inviting me to lunch."

"You're kidding, right?"

Lydia shook her head, "No, that's where I have been, quite enlightening actually."

"In what way, were you right about her knowing things about my father and you?"

"Knowing things, knowing things," Lydia replied sarcastically, "Apart from her choosing not to see the possibility of her husband being your father that crafty old vixen has known all about us since before it began, or so she claims, seems to have been to her advantage, I rather think she is a woman's woman."

"What on earth is one of those when it's at home?"

"Never mind," Lydia snapped, "What's with the suit, it's not Sunday, are you going to a funeral or something?"

"Oh no you don't mother, you're not changing the subject, I want to know what is going on, the likes of us don't get invited to lunch by the gentry, or is it different for you, has it happened before, do you often have lunch at the big house with the lady of the manor?"

"No, never, I admit I was wary, and I still don't believe the reason she gave for inviting me, she has heard about you getting married and has asked me if I would like to move into the hall as her companion when you leave, now, the suit?"

Zack knew well that granite like expression on his mother's face and knew not to pursue the subject, if, and when she was ready, she would tell him.

"Not a funeral mother, Florence and I are engaged but she has nothing to show for it, so tomorrow we are going into town to choose a ring."

Lydia picked up her sons jacket and examined it, "Can you afford a decent ring? And you had better get yourself a new suit, you're not getting married in this thing, I have the address of a local tailor your father used sometimes, I'll fetch it for you, get yourself measured properly and have one made."

Lydia disappeared upstairs, Zack's spirits dropped, he had some modest savings, and he wanted to buy the best ring he could for his special girl, if he had to go to the expense of buying even a cheap suit of clothes it would severely dent his finances.

His mother came back and laid a business card on the table in front of him, "Your father was always pleased with the clothes he had from these people, get a good quality suit, but not any shade of green, if you get married in green it's bad luck and your marriage will be doomed, if you're superstitious that is."

Zack's spirits fell even lower, a made to measure suit, and one of quality cloth would more than likely take all the money he had and more besides, he began to object.

"Mother—."

Before he had the chance to continue Lydia laid next to the business card, some rolled paper tied with white ribbon.

"Put that towards the cost, I'll not have you looking shabby on your wedding day, or looking a cheapskate in the Oldfield's eyes by giving their daughter an engagement ring that looks like you won it at some fairground."

"What is it?"

"Open it and find out," Lydia said smiling broadly.

Zack untied the ribbon, and counted fifty, five-pound notes, speechless, he dropped onto the chair by the table.

"You know who you are now, your father always made sure I never went short, and you're not the only one who can save, if you need any more for the new suit, just ask."

"Mother, I can't accept this, I can't take your savings, Florence and I talked about this, she will be happy with whatever I can afford."

"Florence is a lovely natured girl and I'm sure she would be, but I will not, there should be enough there to get her something decent without causing too much speculation, and it isn't actually all my savings, the money you have there your father and I put to one side for this event if ever it came to fruition. Your position in life has now changed from what you have been accustomed to, get used to it, no arguments, understood?"

* * *

The skeletal noon shift Arthur Cleaver had selected from amongst the men who turned up at the pit hoping for a days work, made their way across the yard from the lamp house to the cage, the remaining men were allowed home again. Arthur had no choice in the matter; only the best men could be used at present, nevertheless, he felt a little guilty; those who were not chosen would receive no pay.

Joseph Shaw had just made a pot of tea as Arthur joined him in the main office.

"I've got a bit of news for you Joseph, and I'm not too sure whether it's good or bad, so I'm leaving it up to you to decide."

"What now? Joseph asked, "I can do without more bad news."

"Young Zack Morgan came to find me at the end of his shift, well part shift; he only did a few hours relief this morning, anyway he found me to ask if he is needed tomorrow, I told him he isn't. Anyway, it seems he has just got himself engaged to a local farmer's daughter, and he wants to finish here as soon as possible to go and work on her father's farm. I know he is on the list to go, but considering his involvement on Saturday, I told him I would need to ask you to set a finishing date for him, he is calling in tomorrow morning about eight o'clock for an answer."

"As far as I am concerned Arthur, he can go right now, the sooner he is off this pit bank and away from the other men the better."

"I guessed you would say that, but just in case I thought I'd better check."

The telephone rang and Joseph answered it to hear the familiar voice of Henry Cotes.

"Shaw, Henry Cotes here, I have an urgent job which needs attending to immediately, I have been trying to contact that nephew of mine for him to sort it, but he's gone missing again, you or Cleaver will have to do it."

Joseph mouthed across the room to Arthur, 'It's Cotes.'

"We will if we can Mr. Cotes, I'm glad you telephoned, we have some news for you, if you can tell me what you need first."

"What I need Joseph is for you to arrange lodgings for twelve men who will be making their way from here to you over the weekend. There is just one very slight problem, preferably, they will all need to lodge together, or at least in two batches of six because only two of them speak English, do the best you can for them regardless of expense."

"I doubt if we will find anywhere that will house a dozen, especially as they will leave here still in their pit dirt."

"I am aware of that, which is why I was after my nephew, I thought if we hired local women to look after their cooking and cleaning, there may be an empty cottage or two on his estate they could use. It has been explained to all of them that they may be crowded and have to rough it for a bit. They have been given directions from the railway station to the mine; most of them will be arriving on Saturday. Gethin Jones, their leading hand can be trusted, he is fluent in English, and so is his deputy, but the rest only speak their mother tongue with the odd English word or two, regardless of cost, find them somewhere they can keep to themselves, if you follow my drift?"

Joseph smiled, a rescue squad who, if they said anything incriminating would not be understood by the local residents.

"If cost is not an issue, Arthur and I will find somewhere for them Mr. Cotes, even if we have to bring some beds and things into one of the buildings on site, would that be acceptable?"

"Anything Joseph, do what you can. Have you dismissed the men yet that we decided are no longer needed?"

"I'm afraid we haven't yet Mr. Cotes, everyone is still turning up here when their normal shift is due, Arthur picks out the men he wants and sends the rest home again, many of them have not worked since before the accident."

Henry Cotes was pensively silent for a moment, eventually he said, "That can't go on, we have to face facts here, those you know you will never need again, pay them up to the end of this week at rate and a half, and explain that they are no longer needed. You can sweeten the bad news if you like and promise to re-employ them if,—no say when the pit is in full production again, on second thoughts, we hadn't better make any distinction between those we can't use, and the ones that were lost on Saturday, pay the same amount to the families of those who were killed."

"Mr Cotes, that is a huge wage bill considering we have very limited revenue coming in, I don't think we will be able to meet it."

"I see,—have the figures worked out anyway, I am coming home tonight and I will arrange for any shortfall of funds to be made available first thing in the morning, is there anything else?"

"Just one thing Mr. Cotes, you told me to try and find out the name of the person the Home Office appoints, Dr. Thomas has heard the name George Walklate as the man probably heading the inquiry, he has also learned the procedures will possibly begin sometime around Christmas next year."

"Walklate, I am not familiar with that name, did Dr. Thomas give you any indication as to where the man is from."

"No, I'm sorry he did not, but he heard it from an old friend who now holds a post in another department at the Home Office, he made a point of telling me to pass the information to you, Oh and I seem to remember he said Mr Walklate holds the C.B.E."

"Does he indeed, well it's nice to know at least some people get rewarded for services to the old boy's network, thank you Joseph, it's a start at least. You have my home telephone numbers there do you not, when you have the shortfall figure inform my steward Herbert Carver, don't tell him too much, just the amount, or better still, send it over by hand and tell Carver that I shall need the information as soon as I arrive home."

Henry Cotes rang off; Joseph spent the next few minutes filling in the details that he could not hear for Arthur of Henry Cotes's other half of the telephone conversation.

"Not asking much is he Joseph," Arthur said very sarcastically, "Finding lodgings for a dozen Welshmen by tomorrow, I heard you say about bringing beds here on site, not very practical that you know."

"I had to say something he caught me off guard, have you got any ideas?"

"No, nothing springs to mind, but you promised, so we shall have to—hey, wait a minute, he did say regardless of expense right?"

"Come on Arthur, let's hear it, you've had a brain-wave haven't you."

"It's slim, but it might be worth a shot, the main problem is their pit dirt and delph clothes, right?"

"One of them, yes, unless we arrange for them to change here, what have you in mind?"

"My wife's sister's eldest girl sometimes works as a cleaner at 'The Bell', that fairly large ramshackle place near the top of Augers Bank on the left; I remember her saying once that the cellars there are vast, but the interesting part is, I'm pretty sure she said there were quite a few washing boilers down there."

"So, what's your point?"

"My point is it's a big place, and my niece told me there are rooms upstairs that have been shut off and under raps for years, it seems the only parts in use nowadays are the family rooms and the bars downstairs. Think about it, they have unused rooms, if we provided bath tubs, and as my niece says they do have boilers in the cellars to heat enough water for the men to wash, the Welsh bods could possibly stay there all together."

"Taking in guests is one thing Arthur, but to have a dozen filthy miners trailing through everyday is another matter, I can't see anyone agreeing to that."

"No, nor me, but you're missing the point, the boilers are supposed to be in the cellars, there is bound to be a back entrance into those, and the men could go in the back way after their shift, get washed, change and leave their delph clothes and pit dirt in the cellars until the next day."

"But didn't you say the rooms there haven't been used for years, whoever runs the place won't be geared to cope with a dozen men moving in, do you know the people who run it?"

"No, never met them, but I do know people's nature, nobody is going to be daft enough to turn down the sort of money Cotes is prepared to spend to save his own skin."

"It's worth a try as you say, but if it works it's too easy, anyway, you go and find Joe Harris, we will go up in the van as soon as I've been to the wages office and started them working out the rate and a half figure for the men we have to sack. Oh, and grab the petty cash tin, we'll take it with us just in case."

Within twenty minutes, Joseph and Arthur were knocking at the front door of 'The Bell,' to their dismay, there was no reply.

"Looks like a wasted journey Arthur, we will have to try later on," Joseph said as he turned back towards the van parked on the cobble-stoned forecourt.

Joe Harris was leaning on the bonnet of the van laughing, "They are in boss, saw the curtains move," he said, "It'll be them suits you're wearing, old Jonah probably thinks you're after money, shall I have a try?"

"If you think you will have any better luck, by all means," Joseph concurred, not expecting any different response.

Joe lumbered up the path and hammered three times on the door, paused and knocked twice more. Joseph and Arthur not expecting any different outcome from Joe's efforts climbed back into the van, both of them could see the door open slightly and Joe speak to someone inside, the door closed again. Joe waited until the hinges creaked as the huge door began to open again before he beckoned to Joseph and Arthur to join him.

Joseph vacated the front seat of the van and moved around to open the rear door and let Arthur out again; as he did so, he heard a girl's voice shout, 'It is him Mr. Baldwin.'

Tilly pits two managers and Joe Harris who was now heading back to the van crossed on the steps up from the forecourt level, waiting in the doorway stood a girl in her early twenties, she was quite attractive in a homely sort of a way, and beaming all over her face. Joseph acknowledged her, but she paid him little attention, instead she was looking straight past him at Arthur who followed a few paces behind.

"What brings you up here Uncle Arthur?" the girl asked.

"A bit of business with your boss Isabel if he's about, and what's all this skulduggery business with not answering the door to us?"

Isabel Green shot a wary glance in Joseph's direction and whispered to her uncle, "We have been told not to let anybody in who looks a bit on the smart side, the boss hasn't paid for the last three loads of ale we had from the brewery yet, and I haven't been paid for a fortnight."

"Really, is that a fact," Arthur laughed; he smiled and winked at Joseph.

A corridor stretched from the front door dividing the ground floor of The Bell into equal sections, at the far end an elderly, grey haired man appeared carrying a bucket of coal; Isabel disappeared into one of the side rooms.

"This way gentleman," the old man called.

Joseph started down the corridor but Arthur gently grasped his arm, pulled him back and went in front, as he moved passed Joseph he said softly, "Milk it, Issy has just told me he's short of cash."

Joseph and Arthur declined the drink Jonah Baldwin offered, straight away, they got down to business, the old man sat and listened attentively as Joseph outlined the reason for their visit. Joseph played on the fact that men were still missing below ground and that it was absolutely vital that a crew of miners highly trained in rescue work would be needed to be brought in from South Wales; the reason being because so many local men able to do that kind of work had been lost on Saturday.

Arthur joined in, elaborating his idea of using the disused cellar as a bathhouse if accommodation for the Welshmen could be made here at The Bell, still not a word from old Jonah, the way his eyes looked through them made both Joseph and Arthur feel uncomfortable. When neither manager could think of anything else to say, after a moment's silence, at last, Jonah Baldwin responded, looking straight through Arthur he said.

"I suppose Young Issy told you all about what there is here?"

"It was ages ago Mr. Baldwin, just after she started to work for you, I put it down to youthful excitement nothing more," Arthur quickly parried any retribution which could be levied at his niece.

"Can't help you gentlemen, sorry," Jonah said.

"We have been wrongly informed about your premises have we, so sorry to have disturbed you Mr. Baldwin," Joseph said as he rose to his feet, "We shall have to find somewhere else then, my orders are to find somewhere for the men to lodge by Saturday,—regardless of cost, which the mine will be meeting."

Joseph cast his bait, and Jonah took it, the old man's eyes lit up at the words 'regardless of cost'.

"No Mr Shaw, you have not been misinformed, there are six double rooms and one single on this side of the building that have not been in use for years, those rooms could sleep the twelve men you spoke of, and yes there are wash boilers in the back cellar."

"Are you saying there is a possibility you would be able to house the men here?" Arthur asked.

"Space isn't a problem if they shared the rooms, and I could live with the bathhouse idea, I just don't have the staff to cope with so many, there's only me, the missus and her sister, and none of us are getting any younger, oh and yon girl Issy three days a week. Twelve men coming to lodge in less than forty-eight hours, rooms to get ready and air, not to mention all the extra food we would need to get in, and I've been to Broughton and banked the takings for the week only this morning, no sorry, don't see how it can be done. If it were the old squire instead of that son of his I might be able to chance it, Squire Heath always paid his bills and would help anyone he could, but there is talk about his son owing loads of money everywhere."

Joseph interrupted quickly, "Mr. Baldwin, we take our orders from the senior partner," Joseph had noticed the old man's resolve beginning to weaken at the prospect of more income, "My orders came from the new squire's uncle, Mr Henry Cotes, he gave us the instructions to find lodgings, not Mr Heath."

"Cotes you say, Hmm, I've heard about him from Stan Smith up the road, still can't be done in the time; there's no way my missus could get the rooms ready, and trudge about getting food in, even after I went and fetched enough money from the bank."

"If you reconsider, perhaps we can help with that, our instructions were very clear, and Mr. Cotes is proving to be very generous to those people who help with the current difficulties caused by the accident at the mine."

Joseph realised, this was the time to go in for the kill, "I can't help with your staff shortage, but would motorised transport be a help with the grocery situation?"

"It would, yes, carrying is a problem," Jonah said, "Paying for it when my money is in the bank is another."

Joseph turned to Arthur, "Did you bring the contents of the tin?"

Arthur nodded, "Twenty-five pounds, and some change."

Jonah ventured a wry smile, which both Joseph and Arthur caught.

"Mr Baldwin, there is a van outside which I can put at your disposal when you are ready, and I can offer you a small advance of twenty-five pounds towards your initial cost."

After a pause, Jonah asked, "Is there any chance I can deal directly with this Cotes fellow?"

"If you wish I will ask Mr Cotes to call on you to arrange any other details; can you help by housing these men from Wales?"

Jonah smiled and stood up, "You'll be wanting to see what you are paying for, if you follow me I'll show you what I have here then you can take it or leave it, but I shall have to work out a rate later on when I have a better idea of the extras your men will be needing."

Joseph and Arthur viewed the available rooms and the cellar; the cellar would fit in perfectly with Arthur's idea for a place the men could wash away their pit dirt, after they checked on the suitability of the rooms Arthur gave old Jonah the twenty-five pounds petty cash. Jonah, cash in hand, told his wife to show them the short path from the rear cellar of The Bell to the road.

Arthur waited for the woman to go back indoors before saying, "Joseph, that old devil thought he was playing you like a great big fish."

Joseph laughed, "I know," he said, "But what he didn't know was that your niece had taken the hook off his line, and speaking of which," Joseph indicated towards Isabel Green scurrying down the front path to meet them.

"Uncle Arthur," she gasped, "What's going on, he's just paid me two weeks wages and says he wants me in seven days a week if possible until further notice, and asked if I know another girl looking for work, and a cook besides, what's going on?"

"Well Issy, sounds like you have got yourself a regular job for a bit; let's just say you had something to do with it by giving me the tip about your boss feeling the money squeeze. Do you know of anyone looking for work?"

"Cook, no, but almost every girl is looking for work as soon as she leaves school. I walked down with Ruth Winters this morning; Stan Smith at the Boar told her he doesn't want her after today, I'm popping up there now to ask her if she's interested."

"Excellent choice," Joseph heard himself say.

Slightly shocked, Isabel looked inquiringly at him.

"Sorry, didn't mean to butt in, it's just that I came across that particular young lady the other day, she seemed a good worker and very obliging."

Joe Harris took advantage of the gates being open and turned the van around at the drive to Highfield Hall, "Pull in at the Ironmongers on the way back Joe," Arthur told him.

"OK boss," Joe said, "Could do with a gallon or two of petrol anyway, alright if I fill up while you're in there?"

"Fine," Joseph said, "Tell them to add it to the order we're putting in now, and you will need to take some things from here up to The Bell later."

The two managers left Joe at the pump; he would be a while, the hand cranked petrol pump was slow to deliver the fuel.

Still a little shocked by their success, Arthur said, "How many tubs do you think we should have Joseph?"

"Depends on how many they've got in stock, there are three boilers in that cellar, but it will be tight to get more than six of the big bathtubs in there, definitely no more than six."

Chapter Seventeen

Robert Davies, chauffeur to the Cotes family occupied his time by wandering up and down the platforms of Rolleston railway station, and by drinking endless cups of tea in the station buffet, he had been there since ten minutes to five, and it was now approaching seven fifteen. His orders had been explicit, to meet the five o'clock train on which Henry Cotes hoped to return from Pontypridd, and if Cotes was obliged to catch a later train, to wait at the station until he arrived. Davies had the foresight to enquire of the station staff the arrival time of the next train expected from the so-called 'land of song,' a country from which his own ancestors had escaped generations ago, the train was due in at seven o'clock, and now, even that was late.

Activity from the station staff heralded the arrival of another train, he hoped this would be the one bringing Henry Cotes home; finishing his cup of tea, he straightened his uniform and strode out onto the platform. Henry Cotes was swift to disembark the first class carriage, and a porter was now trolleying Henry's few items of luggage towards the platform entrance.

"Ah, there you are Davies, I have been on slow trains before, but I think that one must have been drawn by shire horses."

Davies relieved the porter of Henry's luggage, and following Henry's instructions, instead of strapping it onto the rear luggage carrier; to save time loaded it into the back of the nineteen fourteen Rolls-Royce 'Silver Ghost' limousine.

Henry loved to drive, however, this dark gleaming green coach painted monster, with its black running boards and mudguards, its silvered headlamps, trim, and distinctive radiator, he had driven only once. Henry's reasons for adding this particular car to his collection when he did, were one, because it was the best, and two, because the factory which made them was very close to his estate, but most importantly, because he believed this was the only machine fitting for a man expecting to be socially elevated soon by the royal honours list. His pride as he took delivery of the limousine had been unsurpassed, but the design of the car and its accepted status was such, that his one and only outing led to an embarrassing faux pas to be made by a village shopkeeper, where Henry stopped in the vain hope of purchasing a few cigars. He never drove it again, leaving The Ghost, driven by their chauffeur solely for the use of the family, although, unbeknown to Henry, sometimes his daughter Antoinette used the car without Davies at the wheel.

When Henry failed to return at the expected time, his wife ordered dinner to be served at eight thirty, a little later than their usual time, Henry was enjoying a well-deserved glass of malt in his library when his daughter breezed in.

Antoinette greeted him, "Hi pops, had fun in Wales have you?"

Henry scowled at her, "Antoinette, I have spent a fortune on your education, why do you persist in speaking in that manner?"

"Don't be so stuffy pops, is there no fun left in you, the days when women were servile and meek are long gone, better get used to it."

Henry's male ego was about to respond, but recollections of his sister's recent revelations, and his encounters with Lydia Morgan restrained him, instead he smirked and grunted in response.

"So I am beginning to realise from some things which have recently come to my attention, but God help us if you women ever get the vote."

"Oh, have no fear of it pops that will happen, and soon, there have been women rulers in this glorious empire of ours, one day a woman will be Prime Minister of England."

"Stop teasing; I have had a long, busy, dreary day, you're just being silly and trying to wind me up, unfortunately, tomorrow promises to be even worse for me than today."

"Don't complain about that pops, I have been bored to death, there is nothing to do here. It wasn't too cold this afternoon so I decided to try out one of those new saddles I bought in America, remember, I told you I liked the style of them while I was over in Texas, but I wasn't sure how they would lend themselves to our landscape, and so under the circumstances I rode gentle Indy. I must say I was surprised to see her still here, you promised to get a stallion for me instead, where is my stallion pops?"

Antoinette Cotes loved to tease her father, and if the truth were told, Henry quite enjoyed the banter with her.

"The mare will be going soon, and as soon as I have time I will find you a new mount, but I've rather too much on at the moment to take time away searching for a horse for you."

"Oh no you don't father," Antoinette's tone, suddenly quasi serious, "This time I shall go with you, that's the only way to guarantee the horse you buy is the one I want, I will choose it, and you can pay for it."

"Hmm, I should have guessed you would come up with that condition," Henry said and laughed, "But if that is to be the case, I expect it will be very expensive and I think you should earn it, if you are so bored with country life there is a little something you can do for me."

Just then, the dinner gong sounded, father and daughter proceeded to the dining room, Rebecca Cotes, Henry's wife and his twin sons Richard and Julian had already taken their places at the table. An addition to the immediate family party at dinner was Rebecca's houseguest, her younger sister Christine, a pleasant, affable little woman to whom nature had not been generous in bestowing feminine attributes; despite her family's fortune and connections, no man had ever shown the slightest interest in her. Christine had long since resigned herself to the title of 'old maid', and to remaining unmarried.

No one seeing this family group together could be blamed if they doubted the validity of their relationship to each other, not even Henry would consider himself handsome, and his wife Rebecca, who originated from a very wealthy and well-connected family in Surrey, was rather plain and quite stout. The twins, though not identical, favoured Henry and Rebecca in both their build and features.

Antoinette, the eldest of the three children appeared not to belong to the family group, she could only be described as a ravishing beauty, a point that had not gone unnoticed and caused much speculation amongst the members of Cheshire's society, an observation generating mutterings of amazement more than anything untoward. To them it was a mystery how Henry and Rebecca Cotes could produce such an exquisite creature, nevertheless, they had.

As a young girl, Antoinette had not seemed at all promising, a gangly creature, preferring the activities of the male sex rather than those normally attributed to the young females of her class. By her early to mid teens she could hunt, shoot, ride and drive, as well as if not better than any man. With maturity came the looks, her figure was exquisite, five feet eight inches of symmetrical perfection, crowned by long blonde hair as radiant as sunlight, her bearing, flawless complexion, facial features and the twinkling mischief in her blue eyes guaranteed that in her presence every male's head would turn in her direction. The feminine social skills she learned from the best teachers at finishing school, now she had every weapon in the female arsenal, which she knew how to use to her advantage. In addition, she had inherited her father's cunning and business acumen; the majority of young women fast approaching twenty-four years of age from her social standing relied entirely on a husband or their fathers for support. Antoinette, by continually invading the male preserves, including over the last three years the world of business had accumulated a small, but respectable investment portfolio in her own right.

Neither Henry nor Antoinette paid much attention to, or joined in to any great extent with the inane chatter around the dinner table. Instead, Henry's mind was ever scheming, especially around the problems arising from the explosion at Tilly Pit, tonight however he was determined to enjoy a decent meal, something the trip to Wales had denied him for a couple of days. Antoinette recognised by her father's earlier tone of voice, whatever he had in mind for her to do in order to earn her stallion could well be mischievous, but nothing obvious came to her, she waited in eager anticipation for the meal to end.

With the main course served the chatter continued, one of the parlour maids entered carrying a large brown envelope precariously perched on a small silver platter.

"Excuse me sir," the girl said addressing Henry, "Mr Carver has just left this; he says it is important and that you are to have it straight away, that you are expecting these papers from Heals End."

Henry glanced up, puzzled for a second, and then realised the probable content of the envelope.

"Yes, I am, but they are not important enough for me to leave such an excellent meal, take it into the library, I will deal with it after dinner."

The girl bobbed, and left the room, Henry shot a glance at his daughter, she was studying him closely, he smirked and winked in her direction.

Antoinette became more intrigued, whatever her father expected her to help with must have something to do with Heals End, naturally, she had read the reports of the accident in the newspapers, but apart from that, mining was something she knew absolutely nothing about.

Dinner concluded, the twins made their way to the billiard room, Rebecca and Christine when they eventually paused for breath would doubtless retire towards the drawing room. Something important had arrived for Henry and it awaited his attention in the library; everyone expected his usual instruction of 'not to be disturbed,' this meant by anyone, until he came out again.

Antoinette seemed to have two choices, to plague and tease her boring brothers, or to be bored silly by her mother and aunt's talk of insignificant trivia, neither appealed to her, she decided instead to go to her room and read.

"Antoinette," her father called as she strolled towards the main staircase, "With me in my library."

Mother and Aunt looked at each other in utter amazement, Antoinette smiled, maybe there was some fun to be had this evening after all, she followed her father into his library.

"What are you cooking up pops, I hope this is about my stallion?" she asked cheekily as she closed the door.

Henry laughed, "Partly, yes, just give me a few minutes to read through these papers Carver has left."

Antoinette settled herself by the fire and picked up a magazine from the table.

The wage bill figures were approximately around the amount Henry expected, the prospect of lodgings already found for all the Welshmen pleased him, but he was not amused by the comment that Joseph Shaw thought it necessary for him to deal directly with Jonah Baldwin. However, on reflection, he knew Shaw well enough to believe he had a good reason for the suggestion, tomorrow would need an earlier start than normal, there was much to do, and he needed help.

"Now young lady," Henry said laying the papers aside, "Just how bored are you?"

"Very," his daughter replied tossing the magazine back onto the table, "I am toying with the idea of going back down south for a while, London maybe."

"I never thought I would ever say this, but, due to certain complications which have recently developed, there is something pressing here which may appeal to you. You think I do not, but I know you have been trespassing and dabbling in business ventures on your own. That is work for a man, not a woman; I always knew you have more wit than the boys, but recently a certain someone pointed out to me, that in her opinion you have been playing me for a fool for years."

Antoinette frowned; somebody had tipped her father off to her antics, getting her own way might prove slightly more difficult now.

Henry continued, "My eyes have been opened in the past few days; for instance, I have learned that some members of your sex can be persistent and cunning, definitely not to be underestimated, and that we men who believe we are in charge, quite often are not. If Ly—, if the person who brought the matter to my attention is right, even though I still think you should be seeking a husband and providing me with grandchildren, I believe, mainly because you are a woman, you are the ideal person to help me solve this little problem. I think you will find some fun in it and enjoy the challenge, and if you succeed, you can name your price."

Antoinette was suspicious but intrigued, "Well, I'm listening, go on."

"Firstly; I must have your word that if I involve you, no one else will ever know what you are doing, just the two of us."

"OK pops, you have my attention, so long as it's fun, and it doesn't have anything to do with getting married and settling down, I'm not ready for that yet, when the right man comes along I will let you know, but he hasn't appeared yet."

Henry laughed, "Really, not even your cousin Charles?"

"What?" Antoinette screamed, "Are you out of your mind?"

"I'm teasing; it's just that the same person who pointed out you have been running rings around me for years also informed me Anne always hoped you and young Charles would marry."

"Phew, thank God you're not serious about that, I am well aware Aunt Anne has ideas along those lines, she has dropped enough hints over the years. But honestly pop, quite apart from us being cousins, Charles Heath is the very last man on earth I could ever consider marrying, true, I haven't seen him for years, but back then I never could stand him even when I was forced into his company."

"I am very pleased to hear it, now moving to the little task I have for you, I spent a small fortune ensuring you have all the social skills necessary to move in society, I would like you to pass on a few of those to a young lady of my recent acquaintance."

Antoinette looked quizzically at her father; this request was the last thing she would have expected.

"Father, I hope you are not telling me you have found yourself a young mistress?"

"Don't be silly child, I gave all that up years ago, the young lady in question is the daughter of a farmer at Heals End. I confess I found her to be a beautiful creature and she possesses a lovely nature, however, she is sadly in need of grooming, no fashion sense to speak of, which is not surprising when you consider her background, but I am sure you will like her. Anyway, she is soon to be married and I need to keep both her and her fiancé sweet to lessen the stigma of last Saturday."

"The explosion at that pit you mean?"

"Yes, precisely, her name is Florence Oldfield, and at the moment she is doing a little job for me at her father's farm, she is caring for those poor ponies that survived the explosion. You told me to sell the grey mare I bought for you, actually, I am giving it to young Florence as a reward for the work she is doing with those ponies, I don't think I have ever seen an animal in such a sorry state as they were when they were brought back above ground. Florence will need to learn to ride her, and encouraged to adopt more of the fashionable social graces, because, the man she is to marry comes from, shall we say, good stock, do you fancy taking her under your wing and teaching her enough for her to mix comfortably in society? I will cover any expenses, clothes etcetera if she needs them. If you take on the task you will need to be careful, she is very proud and anything you do must not look like charity."

"Difficult,—what if I don't like her?"

"You will, I guarantee it, it's impossible not to, I shall be going to Heals End tomorrow, come with me, see for yourself, we could take the Rolls if you like."

Antoinette giggled, "What, you drive 'The Ghost,' you haven't driven that since that poor shopkeeper mistook you for our chauffeur."

Henry frowned, "No, I know, I'll never drive it again, and before you suggest it, neither will you, Davies can take us."

"No good,—I will come with you, Lord knows there is nothing to do here, but I think mother and Aunt Chris need Davies and the Rolls tomorrow. If you take one of your other motors, just in case you need to stay over there longer than I do, I will follow you in my Lagonda, what time do you want to leave?"

"Oh, it will have to be very early, no later than ten o'clock."

"Pop, that's not early by my standards, I will meet you half way, shall we say nine, one thing, if I come with you there is one condition."

"What now?"

"Nobody away from home ever uses my name in full, to everyone else I am Toni, not Antoinette, and I prefer it, don't you dare introduce me as Antoinette, O.K with you?"

Henry did not like it, but he agreed, "OK, Toni it is, but you will have to reciprocate and cut out this pop and pops business in the presence of people we employ, it isn't a fitting term for a young lady of class to use."

"Deal," laughed Toni, "Which do you prefer, father or dad, just don't expect me to creep like Rich and Jules, there is no way I am calling you sir."

"I never thought for a minute you would, that habit of theirs annoys the hell out of me as well sometimes, it makes them appear weak. I thought boarding school would be good for them but it seems I was wrong, they've picked up too many servile ways, if it wasn't for this war, a military academy might toughen them up a bit."

"You know father, the more I think of this, the more it appeals to me, but just for clarification, if I take to this girl and think I can help her, you said you would cover the expenses, have I got carte blanche to do everything my way?"

"You have, I wouldn't have asked you otherwise, but don't give her any of those stupid suffragist ideas, leave those things down south."

"She lives on a farm you say, if we have finished here I had better go and check my wardrobe for something suitable to wear, Oh, and the new horse you promised, I am thinking possibly 'Arabian,' black by preference."

Antoinette rose to leave the library, at the door she hesitated and turned, "In a minute, I've just realised, you implied the person who told you about Aunt Anne's hopes for that nitwit Charles Heath and me eventually getting hitched was a woman. You started to say her name, but didn't, so it must be someone I know, are you going to tell me who it was?"

"Good grief girl, you were sharp to pick up on that slip of the tongue, it is someone you knew quite well and liked, but there are very, and I do mean very complex reasons why I can't tell you who it is, that is one thing you will never know from me. All I will tell you is that she has a razor sharp mind, she spotted your little game years ago, unfortunately, I didn't."

"Now you have given me something else to do, I'll bet you I can figure out who she is, I will you know dad, after all, I have to thank her for making my life more difficult."

"No she hasn't, if anything she has alerted me to which of my children is most likely to be successful, the boys as yet have shown no talent for making money, but you have, up until last week the only thing I hoped for you was to make a good marriage. But let me give you a valuable piece of advice my girl, carry on playing the scatty blonde because no man of substance will take on a wife who is smarter than he is, it came as a great shock to me to learn how manipulative you women can be, now get along with you, busy day tomorrow."

Friday 18th January, dawned bright, clear and surprisingly mild for the time of year, by nine o'clock Antoinette's Lagonda 11 Tourer, was fuelled and waiting at the front of the hall. Not to be outdone by his daughter, Henry decided to use his three litre Sunbeam, it was six years old but had a definite sporty feel, and Henry liked it, although it was not a model he considered suitable for winter driving, but in no way was he going to allow Antoinette's fast little motor leave him behind. This also had been brought to the front of the house along side the Lagonda.

Henry, having taken the precaution of breakfasting early was rather surprised by his daughter's appearance as she entered the room; she had replaced her usual sumptuous attire with a plain blue, conservative styled dress, the hem of which reached about an inch over the top of the knee-high ornately embossed Texan styled leather boots she brought back from America. For everyday wear, Antoinette preferred an elegant wedge-heeled shoe, which, with the shorter skirts of today emphasized, and flattered the quite often-visible curves of the leg. Those dreadful high-buttoned boots she had to wear as a child, and still worn by many women repulsed her, she had not put on a pair of those since her mid teens. Initially this morning she had selected a pair of low shoes and flesh coloured silk stockings, until she remembered, her father had said the girl Florence lived on a farm, and therefore she decided the Texan ranch boots would probably be more practical. Her hair, although it was becoming the fashion of the day, she refused to cut into the modern bobbed styles, instead, as today, she often wore it up, and forsaking all other jewellery, her neck was adorned by a single string of pearls.

"Well father," she said, emphasizing her use of the word father, "Is this the kind of thing your young friend might wear?"

"How on earth am I expected to know that?" blustered Henry, "Probably not, your outfit is plain enough I admit, but too continental and modern for an ascetic girl from these parts. Oh, I think I understand; you're dressing down from your usual style so that you don't intimidate her on your first meeting, very clever."

"Will we be going straight to the farm or have you somewhere to go first?"

"I have a lot to do Toni," Henry smirked, as he emphasized the requested diminution of his daughter's name, "If we went to the farm first, you have your own motor, once you and Florence have been introduced I can leave you to your own devices, farm first I think."

Henry's journey to Heals End proved to be much quicker than normal, he drove a larger vehicle, but Toni was a skilful driver and a dreadful tease, knowing most of the route they took she overtook him at every opportunity, and then slowed to a crawl allowing her father to move in front again. Less than a half hour had elapsed since they left home, Henry was leading as they passed the gates to Tilly Pit, and Henry knew Toni would not risk damage to her Lagonda by driving at speed along a farm track.

A little after ten o'clock, father and daughter parked their cars just through the farmyard's gates.

"You little madam," Henry scolded, "You will kill yourself driving like that."

Antoinette laughed, "Oh no father, I won't, I have another toy which moves a lot faster than a car."

Henry's look was inquiring, but his daughter did not elaborate.

Antoinette studied her surroundings, "Very quiet here father," she said, "This place looks deserted."

"Someone will be around; it's the biggest farm on the Highfield Estate, did you happen to notice that old Ford car with milk churns strapped to the back just before we turned into the lane?"

His daughter nodded, the old wreck had nearly scraped her beloved Lagonda.

"That was George Oldfield, the present tenant here, Florence's father, and he can be awkward, he has very old fashioned ideas so watch your step with him."

Edith Oldfield emerged from the house and came across the yard to greet them.

"Good morning Mr Cotes, I'm afraid my husband is out on the milk deliveries, you find me all alone this morning, but can I help you?"

"Good morning to you Edith, I have not called on business, we were in the neighbourhood and I was telling my daughter last night about the ponies Florence is caring for, she is very fond of horses and has come to see Florence and the ponies."

Antoinette stepped foreword and extended her hand, "Good morning Mrs Oldfield, a pleasure to meet you."

Edith took the proffered hand, "Good morning Miss Cotes, I can show you the ponies, but Florence and her fiancé left for Castleton on the nine o'clock train this morning, they have some shopping to do and I don't expect them back until three this afternoon."

"That is a pity Mrs Oldfield; I especially wanted to meet your daughter after the things my father has told me about her, rather than put you to any trouble, would it be convenient if I called later, say after three. I have spent a great deal of time travelling abroad, now that I have returned home I really should spend some time with my Aunt at Highfield, she has been quite ill, but you probably know that."

"I am sure my daughter would be delighted Miss Cotes, by all means call whenever you like."

Edith could not understand the reasons, but this young lady of quality expressing a wish to meet her daughter filled her with pride.

The visitors returned to their cars, "Quick thinking young lady," Henry whispered, "Anne will be pleased to see you."

Antoinette smiled, "I'm sure she will, so long as Charley boy isn't around I shall be pleased to see her, but that is not my only reason for spending some time at Highfield."

"I think you can guarantee Charles will not be at home, I haven't been able to catch him there for days, what else is it you are after?"

"This girl Florence has spent all her life here, right?"

Henry nodded in confirmation.

"A bit of background gossip that you can't supply won't hurt the cause any, servants pops, the housemaids at the hall, girls talk you know, but on second thoughts you probably don't."

The Cote's cars reached the bottom of Tilly Lane, Henry swung his Sunbeam onto the pit bank, Toni tooted and waved as she passed catching the attention of the gate-keeper and several bank's men, his daughter had purposefully toned down her usual appearance, nevertheless, every male's eye followed as she drove past, Henry guessed their comments to each other.

Much to Toni's surprise when she arrived, Anne Heath was in the courtyard of Highfield Hall talking with one of the gardeners, recognising the Lagonda's driver; Anne dismissed the gardener immediately and came over to the car.

"Antoinette my dear, what a lovely surprise to see you, so thoughtful of you to come and spend some time with your old aunt, such a pity Charles is away, you know how very fond he is of you, I'm sure he would have loved to see you."

"Cousin Charles is not at home, yes, such a pity," Toni said, trying to disguise her sarcasm, "Never mind, it is you I have come to see aunt, and perhaps have a wander around the old place." After the briefest pause, she added with sincerity, "I am so sorry I missed Uncle Charles's funeral, but America is so far away, the last time I called with Mother our visit was too brief, I thought I could spend an hour or two with you today to try and make amends."

"You will stay for lunch of course, in fact if you stayed the night I believe Charles will be returning late this evening; it would be so nice for you two to catch up with each other, you do seem to keep missing one another, it must be a year or so since you were together."

Antoinette grimaced at the prospect, "It is longer than that Aunt, it's five years, nearly six, but Aunt Christine is at home and I must return this afternoon, I will need to leave here at about three o'clock, the weather may take a turn for the worse."

"And you drove here yourself, I quite understand my dear, but it is so very nice to see you, come now let us go inside and you can tell me all your news."

Antoinette had her mind upon the task her father had set for her, nevertheless, conversation with Anne she found very pleasant, except for her aunts continued efforts to reassure her of Charles's affection towards her, they talked of finishing school, travel, social occasions, and friends, nothing to task the mind of either woman. Antoinette was relying on her aunt being a creature of habit; she would need to rest soon, which would give her the opportunity to execute the true reason for her visit.

Their lunch was concluded by half past one, Toni noticed her aunts' eyes begin to appear heavy.

"Do you still rest each afternoon Aunt?" Toni asked.

"Normally I do my dear, but it would be rude to do so when I have a visitor."

"Aunt Anne, now you mustn't be silly, don't worry about me; think of your health, if you need to rest I shall be quite content to wander around the house and grounds."

Anne smiled, "Oh, you are such a sweet girl, so thoughtful, the man you marry will be fortunate indeed, perhaps if I rested for an hour we could talk again later, if you want to go out for a walk around the grounds I will not go to my room, I can stay here."

Antoinette left her aunt in the drawing room and made her way back towards the dining room; Hannah Wilkins was just finishing clearing the table.

"You're still working here then Hannah, I thought you would have found yourself a husband by now."

"No such luck Miss Antoinette, I came pretty close though but he got himself killed in France, this war is taking all the men, and that accident at the pit last Saturday took even more."

"Yes, I read about that, it must have been dreadful, I left father down there this morning after he took me to some farm near there to see the state of the ponies which came out. I think he said the name of the farmer is Oldfield, but the girl who is caring for them had gone into town early this morning."

"Oh, that will be my friend Flo; we sat together every day at school."

"You know her and the family well?"

"As well as anyone, it was her brother I was walking out with, but Flo has done very well for herself, mind you Miss, she always was clever, always top of the class at school, and now she has just got engaged to the most eligible young man around here, lucky madam."

Hawkins appeared at the doorway, "Hannah you chatterbox, Miriam is looking for you and she is on the warpath, Oh, beg pardon Miss Antoinette, I didn't realise it was you Hannah was talking to."

"Quite alright Hawkins, Miriam Mason, I remember getting the rough edge of her tongue for pinching cakes when I was a girl, she's not still here is she?"

"That she is Miss," Hawkins scowled, "Only one person ever got the better of Miriam, well that is to say of us servants anyway, even Miriam wouldn't dare talk back to people like you Miss Antoinette."

Antoinette smiled, Hannah was half way through the door, she turned and quickly bob curtsied before disappearing.

Hannah had provided a little helpful information, but Toni would have liked more, chatting to Hawkins proved unproductive, and so she went in search of Hannah again, too late, Miriam Mason had sent her to the village on an errand, and apart from Miriam, no one else, except her dozing aunt seemed to be in the house. In desperation, she took a little walk around the back of the hall in the hope of finding someone who might talk, unfortunately, there was no one to be found, but the sound of horses in the stable attracted her attention.

Toni's heart leapt with joy as she entered the stable, there, in the first stall stood Pickles, the grey pony on which her uncle Charles first taught her to ride as a young girl, she spent a few minutes with Pickles becoming reacquainted, he was old now, but she was pleased he was still alive. In the next stall, a fine chestnut mare stood quietly, Toni judged the mare was about to come into season, there were an assortment of working horses, but the noise was coming from a separate room at the far end of the stable.

She remembered there were two more stalls in that little room, gently she opened the door, there before her eyes, rearing, fighting with its tether was a huge jet-black stallion, a magnificent beast, and from the look of it, somewhere in his close ancestry there was Arabian blood.

"Whoa boy," she said softly as she approached the stallion, "You feeling frisky with that young lady at the far end of the stable being how she is? Where did Charlie boy find you? You deserve better than him, there is no way that fop will handle you."

Antoinette definitely had a way with horses, instantly the stallion began to calm down and within a few minutes, a bond formed between them.

As she stroked the horse she said, "There, there boy, I don't know your name, or where you came from, but if you're not in my stable within a month my name isn't Toni Cotes. Your being here will save pops having to look anywhere else, you will be coming home with me my lad, even if I have to spend time with Charlie boy to get you."

Armed with the little information she had managed to glean from Hannah Wilkins, Antoinette took her leave of her aunt at three o'clock precisely, and made her way back to Valley Farm.

Zack and Florence returned to the farm a little earlier than Edith had predicted, excitedly Edith relayed the news of the morning's visitors, and that Miss Cotes intended to return to see Florence and the condition of the pit ponies in her care after three o'clock on her way home.

Florence began to panic, "Mother, you are scaring me, Mr Cotes and his daughter coming here, should I be worried? The ponies are much better now than when they arrived but they are still far from well, why would she want to come here to see them? What is Miss Cotes like, is she very ladylike, they are very rich people why would she want to come here?"

"I cannot answer that, but she seemed friendly enough, put me at my ease straight away, I liked her."

Zack, up to now had not said a word; he sat by the fireside with a broad grin on his face, which Florence eventually spotted.

"What are you grinning at Zack, it's me who will be for it if she doesn't like what she sees, what is so funny?"

Zack's grin gave way to a mild laugh, "Miss Antoinette Cotes is back in this country is she? She was the other side of the world when the old squire died and so she could not attend her uncle's funeral. Don't worry love, our paths crossed when we were children, and I have heard mother talk about her since, she says Miss Cotes is headstrong and rather wild, but she has one weakness. Miss Antoinette Cotes has a passion for horses and is reputed to be able to tame even the wildest of them; by all accounts, she rides extremely well. Stop getting so worked up, your mother just told you she is coming to see the state of those ponies, and that is all, if she does come back, which I doubt, just relax and be yourself."

"Well if you're sure Zack," Florence said, still apprehensive, "I'd better get changed quickly just in case, the stables are no place for Sunday best clothes."

Edith was quick to intercede, "I wouldn't, you look as pretty as a picture as you are and first impressions go a long way, Miss Cotes is a very beautiful young lady, but you can match her, stay as you are my girl."

"That she can," agreed Zack, "Anyway, I am going to leave you to it, I need to find your father Flo, he was out with the milk when we left this morning and I have some news for him."

Edith and her daughter set about preparing their evening meal; Edith had decided, because this was a special day for her daughter, to cook a large joint of Silverside Beef, Yorkshire Puddings and all the trimmings.

Edith basted the joint, and as she was going out to the root cellar to collect the vegetables, Antoinette's Lagonda pulled into the yard.

"Florence, she's here, that's her car coming in now, quick, run a brush through your hair and straighten your dress."

Edith began to fuss, members of the gentry were coming to call, she went out and met Antoinette halfway up the front garden's path.

"Good afternoon Miss Cotes, I see Mr Cotes has not returned with you this afternoon, my daughter is home, she is just upstairs, do please come in."

Antoinette followed Edith into the kitchen, the aroma of the roast hit her nostrils, she rarely ate breakfast, usually she started her day with just a cup of coffee and a croissant. Lunch at Highfield had been very light indeed, her business here may take quite a while and then she had the drive back to the next county before her next meal, suddenly she felt hungry.

Florence, having quickly followed her mother's instructions, joined them in the kitchen.

"Miss Cotes, may I introduce my daughter Florence to you," Edith said, observing the proprieties.

Florence still felt a little nervous. It was customary when people of differing social orders met, the senior would wait for the lower to approach them, Florence was surprised when Antoinette, hand outstretched walked across the room to her.

"Miss Oldfield, I have heard much about you from my father, delighted to meet you at last," Toni said in a warm, disarming tone.

Unaccustomed to such things, and unsure of the expected protocol, Florence took Toni's hand; bob curtsied and said, "Thank you ma'am, I am told you wish to see your father's ponies."

Antoinette let out a little sigh, "Oh please, let's have none of that class structure nonsense between us, my name is Toni, and that is what I would like you to call me."

Florence looked puzzled, "Tony, isn't that a man's name?"

"It is indeed, I was christened Antoinette Isabella, but I prefer the shortened version, Toni, with an 'i' instead of 'y', and you I understand are Florence, or do you prefer Flo as an old school-friend of yours called you this afternoon?"

Florence, in disbelief, replied awkwardly, "Either, I don't really mind."

"The ponies you are looking after for dad, yes I would like to see them because I am told they are in a sorry state, but that is not the main reason for my coming here to meet you. My father promised you my grey mare Indy as a reward for caring for the ponies from the pit did he not, but he tells me you never learned to ride?"

"He did, yes, but I would have—."

Antoinette did not allow her to continue, "Well Florence I do ride, and dad has asked me to teach you, so we should be seeing a great deal of each other, and hopefully, we can become friends."

Edith Oldfield watched and listened, she could not believe what she just heard; here in her kitchen was a young woman of position and consequence, offering friendship to her daughter, two beautiful young women of a similar age, one fair, and one dark, but apart from that, in looks and dress, there was little to choose between them.

Florence began to relax, "Shall we go out to the stables now, while it is still light?" she suggested.

"Lead the way Flo; let's have a look at these animals shall we," Toni followed towards the door.

"Florence," Edith began, "With it being so mild today, I released the tethers on those ponies and left the door to the back meadow open so they could go outside if they wanted to, is that alright?"

"Should be mum, if any are outside, they are so weak catching them shouldn't be a problem."

The two young women were about to leave the kitchen when Edith had an idea.

"Miss Cotes, your father did us the honour of taking lunch with us the other day, would you care to eat with us, or do you have a previous engagement and have to return home?"

"Mrs Oldfield, if that is roast beef I can smell, I would be delighted to sample your cooking, father did mention you fed him the other day and that the meal was memorable, but please, not Miss Cotes, as I said, I prefer Toni."

"Then that is settled, and you must call me,—"

Antoinette interceded, "I will call you Mrs Oldfield if I may, Florence is my age and so familiarity is acceptable, but for you, your age entitles you to seniority which I respect."

Edith's chest swelled with pride, this young woman who she had not met, or even heard of before today she liked immensely, and Antoinette

Cotes had expressed the wish of becoming a friend of her daughter, this day was getting better and better.

Only three of the ponies were grazing in the meadow, Florence called to them as she and Toni approached, none of them attempted to bolt and the girls each led one indoors by its halter, the third followed of its own accord.

"These poor creatures are in a dreadful state Florence," Toni remarked compassionately, "They are no more than skin and bone, how could anyone allow them to get into this state?"

"If you think their condition is bad Toni," Florence used her present companion's name warily, but with a smile and reassuring nod from Toni, she finished her sentence. "You should have seen them when they first brought them up here, once they go down a pit, if they are lucky, they are brought back to daylight only one day a year, I don't know if it's true but I have heard if they die down there, they are dragged into a disused tunnel and just left to rot."

Toni's face turned crimson with rage, picking up the grooming brushes from a nearby bench she said, "You feed Flo, I'll start the grooming, and, I shall have a few well chosen words to say to pops when I get home."

"It is said it isn't much better for the men who work below ground," Florence said lifting a sack of feed, "Oh, perhaps I shouldn't have said that."

"Why? Because my father owns half of your local coal mine. I very much doubt if he has any idea how things are done in those places, but I do know he was disgusted when he saw these poor creatures, if you know how to handle him he can be a big softy at times."

"And you do?" laughed Flo.

"But of course, don't you do the same with your father?"

"Oh no Toni, my dad is very strict."

"Really, something else I will have to teach you, all men think they are the boss, but in fact women are, and men are quite content if we never let them know that women have an iron hand in a velvet glove. Speaking of gloves, I heard this afternoon that you have just got engaged to be married, but you don't wear a ring, why not."

Florence astounded, stopped her task, "Who told you that?"

Toni laughed, "Hannah, one of the maids at Highfield, is it not true?"

"Hannah Wilkins, I should have guessed, she always was a gossip, but how she knows so soon I cannot imagine. Yes, it is true, that is where I went this morning, to choose a ring. I have it here in my pocket but I wouldn't dare to wear it when I am working, it was so expensive, but I fell in love with this one and my fiancé insisted I should have it, but for my part I would have been happy with something much cheaper."

Toni stopped grooming the pony she was attending to, came over to Florence's stall, and waited.

"Well, come on Flo, don't keep me in suspense, let me see it."

Slightly embarrassed, Florence produced a small box from her pocket and opened it.

The ring nestling in the split of the tiny red velvet cushion was gold, at its centre it had a sapphire set in white gold, surrounded by eight small diamonds.

"My fiancé says the centre stone matches my eyes," Florence said, blushing.

Toni examined the ring closely, "Your fiancé has taste, even I would be proud to wear this, but I am afraid he is wrong."

Florence was startled, "Wrong, how do you mean?"

Toni smiled, "It was the first thing I noticed about you Flo, there is no jewel on this earth which could do justice to those eyes of yours, I am really rather envious of them."

Both girls laughed, and with the ring safely back in Florence's pocket continued their attention to the ponies.

Toni asked after a while, "Flo, are these the only stables you have here, they are in need of some work, where are you thinking of keeping Indy when she is brought over to you?"

"This is the only stable at the moment, but father has promised he will make the necessary provisions, I still feel bad about that you know, you're father giving away your horse, it doesn't seem right somehow."

"From what I have seen of you with these animals, Indy will have an excellent new home, she is a lovely mare, not overly big, but very fast and brave, never refuses anything you put in front of her, and her nature is so steady she will suit you down to the ground."

"Have you had her very long?"

"No, pops bought her for me while I was in America because of her speed and the way she handles over fences, I have other horses besides, but

I have set my heart on a big black stallion, I rode a magnificent animal when I was in Texas, it was an Arabian stallion and I fell in love with it."

"I have heard about those, quite rare aren't they, won't it be hard to find one that's big and black."

"I thought so, almost impossible, but that's half the fun, or so I thought, pops doesn't know it yet, but by sheer accident, I have seen the stallion I want. Flo, it has just occurred to me, if your father is going to make somewhere suitable for your mare, see if you can get him to make room for two horses and then I can bring one of mine over, I shall need a good mount if I am to come here and teach you to ride properly. Anyway, see what you can do to persuade him, if he moans about the cost I will cover that if you're stabling one of my horses."

It could not have been more than three quarters of an hour, nevertheless, all tension between Florence and Toni, regardless of their social differences had disappeared, both young women felt as if they had known each other for years. Henry had been correct, it was impossible not to like Florence Oldfield; Toni was sent here to do a delicate job for her father, but instinctively she knew, she and Florence would become close friends and remain so for the rest of their lives.

The daylight was fading as the two girls chatting and laughing left the stable, suddenly Toni stopped.

"Good grief," she exclaimed, "What the blazes is he doing here."

Florence looked around; the only person in sight was George Oldfield.

"That is my father Toni," she said rather baffled.

"Yes I guessed that, not him, the younger man who was with your father, he just went back into that building over there."

"Oh, that will be my fiancé, he will be staying for dinner as well, he wants to give me the ring formally in front of my parents, and now you as well, you don't mind do you?"

Toni gasped, "You don't mean to tell me you are engaged to my cousin Charles Heath."

Florence burst into laughter, "No of course not, I know it's getting dark and the valley mist is forming, but for you to mistake my Zack for the new squire is quite a good joke."

"Zack, Zack who?" Toni asked.

It had been five years since Toni had seen her cousin, but she was convinced she was not mistaken.

"Zack Morgan, he lives with his mother in a cottage near to Highfield Hall, his mother Lydia used to work there, and sometimes at other great houses as well. When his mother was working away Zack used to live here with us, that is how we first met."

"Oh, my mistake then, sorry it must be this fog that confused me, but then, it is over five years since I saw Charles, and my aunt has been talking about him all afternoon. I suppose he was still in the back of my mind," said Toni, and a shudder went through her at the thought of Charles being on her mind.

Zack re-emerged from the building and continued talking to Florence's father, Toni watched him as unobtrusively as she could, the mist did not help, nevertheless, his mannerisms, features, and hair colour were very much as she remembered Charles to be when she last saw him, but this man was thicker set, obviously much stronger.

"Perhaps, as it is going foggy, I should apologize to your mother and make my way home," Toni said as they made their way across the yard back to the house.

"I don't think you need to worry about fog Toni, it isn't, and it happens a lot in the valley here. By the time you get to the end of Tilly Lane everywhere is clear, it just seems to settle in this valley at this time of day, and I would like you to stay; I think Zack said he has met you before at Highfield."

"Very well, if you're sure about the fog, you are most definitely better company than I would have at home," Toni agreed, trying to pass over her apparent error.

Edith Oldfield was putting the final touches to their dinner while Flo and Toni laid the table when George and Zack walked in.

"George my dear," Edith said as they entered, "We have another guest for dinner; this is Mr Cotes's daughter Antoinette."

Toni moved towards George, "A pleasure to meet you Mr Oldfield," she said as they shook hands, old George was taken off his guard, and mumbled something in response.

Florence dragged Zack from hiding behind her father, laughing as she did so, "Toni, this is my fiancé Zack, I hope it's light enough now for you not to make the same mistake."

Toni studied Zack closely, "Yes Flo, I can see I was mistaken, sorry but he looked familiar, I thought I knew him."

With a broad grin on his face Zack said, "You did years ago Miss Antoinette, you chased me around the courtyards at Highfield often enough."

"Did I, I don't recall, wait a minute, not kiss chase, no it can't be, you're not that little ginger lad that used to work in the stables, my, my, how you have changed, you're a lucky girl Flo, no wonder Hannah was so peeved this afternoon."

"We all grow up Miss Antoinette, if I am allowed to say, you have change somewhat yourself from that wild little girl who preferred the rough boy's games, but I think your preference was the chasing more than the kiss forfeit."

Toni winked as she replied, "Still is Zack, still is."

"Playing kiss chase were you," Florence said and gave Zack a playful thump, "Did you ever catch her?"

Zack blushed.

"No he didn't," laughed Toni, "He was the one doing the running away, and yes, I did catch him quite often, but I promise I won't do it again, he is all yours, lucky girl Flo, lucky girl," and she gave an exaggerated wink towards Zack.

"If you young people have finished reminiscing and teasing each other, dinner will get cold," Edith scolded, "Will you all come and sit down?"

George pulled out a chair from the table, "Miss Cotes, would you sit here?"

"Thank you Mr Oldfield," she said as she took her seat, "But please, call me Toni everyone else does, same goes for you Zack, drop the Miss Antoinette, you're not in service now."

Florence began to move to the table but Zack caught her arm and whispered to her, "What did you mean by it being light enough, what mistake?"

"Oh, it was nothing my dear, with it being a bit misty and going dark when we came out of the stables; she mistook you for someone else, her cousin Charles, you know, the new squire, silly isn't it."

Zack visibly paled.

Throughout dinner, Zack was aware Toni's eyes were focussed in his direction watching his every move far too often; he was by no means naive enough to think this could be the result of a physical attraction. Considering whose daughter Toni was, and his strong recollection of her manipulative prowess from when he knew her as a girl, unlike the others around the table, he was not convinced by her show of affability, she was up to something. By her own admission, she was here at Henry Cotes's instruction, however, Zack's knowledge both of her, and of her family led him to believe her mission was far more than teaching Florence to ride the horse Henry had promised her, a feasible story, but in Zack's mind rather lame. Antoinette Cotes, was, at present, convincing everyone else she was an amiable, modern minded young woman with absolutely no regard for social rank, blonde she may be, but he recognised she was another exception to the accepted concept of a blonde, like his own mother, Antoinette was very clever indeed.

Eventually the conversation turned to the subject of travel, Antoinette regaled everyone with stories of the places she had visited.

With disappointment in her voice Florence said, "You have been very fortunate Toni, apart from the occasional trip into town like this morning; I have never been away from this farm."

Toni replied in shock, "What, never?"

Flo shook her head, "No, never, this is all I have known."

"Well," Toni immediately snapped back, "We can soon change that, come and spend a few days with me at Kirkleston, the weekend at the very least, your mare is there and it's time you got to know her, I will send a car for you in the morning."

"That is kind of you to offer Toni," Florence replied, "But I'm afraid it is impossible, I have my work to do here, don't I father?"

Edith Oldfield kicked her husband under the table, both she and George were delighted with the way the two girls seemed to get on together.

George's face was serious, "Yes child, you do, and impossible it would be to manage without you, but Zack here has arranged for some local lads from the pit to come up tomorrow for a tryout with a view to my employing them. If your mother can manage without you, they can do your other chores for you; go with Toni if you wish."

Florence leapt up and ran around the table to hug her father, "Thanks dad," she said with a tear of joy in her eye, and then she remembered, "Oh, what about the ponies, Mr Cotes entrusted me with caring for them."

Zack was quick to speak up, "You go love, I looked after them as best we could below ground, I'll take care of them for you."

"It seems to be settled then," Toni laughed, "Zack is a big softy and will do anything for you Flo, no wonder dad was impressed, what was it he said now, oh yes, 'about to marry a young man from good stock.' Father aggravates the life out of me with that, always trying to pick out a potential beau for me and talks about them like breeding stock; he does so want a grandchild, but unlike you, I'm not ready to settle down yet and start producing children, too much to see and do."

Zack's eyes shot in Toni's direction at her reference to his being from 'good stock,' a reflex action that was observed by Toni and by Florence, as indeed was his expression of unease, Florence, eager to come to her fiancé's aid, and to change the subject asked.

"Toni, didn't you say it was your uncle, our old squire who first taught you to ride when you were about six?"

"He did, and I had a pleasant surprise this afternoon to find the first pony I ever rode is still in the stables at Highfield, he is looking his age now but he is still there, no one there will have a use for the little fellow, I thought my cousin would have let him go years ago."

"Pickles," chirped Zack, "They did, to my mother, I learned to ride on him as well, mother treats him as a pet now, you aren't the only one to have a way with horses, my mother loves them as well. She won't part with the little fellow, always says he will end his days in comfort, he is at Highfield because our little stable at Hawthorne Cottage is being repaired."

"Remember Toni, I told you Zack's mother used to work at Highfield," Florence interrupted.

"Did you, who is your mother Zack?" Toni inquired, and she looked him straight in the eye.

Zack was wary, but to his dismay, Florence answered.

"Lydia Morgan, do you remember her?"

Toni thought for a moment before answering, "Oh yes, but that was a very long time ago, she was lovely, always found time for a game or two, I haven't seen her there for, Oh, ten years or more, about the time I last clapped eyes on you Zack."

Zack was suffering now, but his fiancé remained in full flow.

"She was sort of there all the time, well, that is, up to the time your uncle passed away."

"Sort of?" reiterated Toni, "What do you mean by sort of?"

"Quite often they loaned her out to work at other great houses, didn't they Zack?"

Zack did not like where this topic was leading, he chose discretion and did not answer.

"Unusual," Toni continued, "It must have been a nuisance for you Zack, being moved about so much, I found it unsettling when father packed me off to boarding school, especially the first time, all that packing and unpacking every term. When I came home, we were always visiting here, and there, for days at a time, funny thing though, I loved Uncle Charles, but whenever mother and I came to stay at Highfield, he always seemed to be away on business. Were you like me Zack; was it a case you had to get used to it?"

Again it was Florence who was quick with the answer, "No, no, Toni, don't you see, that is how Zack and I became so close. People needed his mother's services, but it wasn't convenient for Zack to go with her, so he used to live here with us when his mother was working away, isn't that right Zack?"

Before Zack could answer, Edith confirmed her daughter's statements, "Yes Toni, that's the way it was, Lydia must be very good to be in such demand, and she must have been paid very well for her work, she always gave me more than enough for Zack's keep. He was here so often he became part of the family, and these two became closer and closer as the time went on, I could see a marriage coming years ago, but my George here was not so quick."

Toni laughed, "Now that is a plot worthy of any Jane Austin novel, in fact, I rather think it mirrors one, but the title of it eludes me for the moment, perhaps someone else wrote the one at the back of my mind."

Again, Toni's eyes held Zack's gaze, and she smiled warmly.

The hour was getting late; Toni thanked her hosts and took her leave, Zack and Florence accompanied her to her car, but Edith grabbed George's arm preventing him from going outside.

"How much money have you got in this house?" Edith asked as soon as the young people were out of earshot.

"Not a lot, why?" he replied.

"Go and get what you have, and I will do the same, if our girl is going to spend a day or two with the gentry, she isn't going with only a few coppers in her purse, now move before she comes back in."

George understood, and did as he was told; between them, they found eight pounds, seventeen shillings and four pence.

"Is this the best we can do?" Edith said in despair, "I suppose it will have to manage."

"Manage," retorted her husband, "There is a heck of a lot there, we aren't made of money like that young lady who has just left you know."

"It seems you were right about the fog Flo," Toni said as they went outdoors, "It seems to have almost cleared. Now then, either I will collect you in the morning, or I will send our chauffeur Davies, can you be ready by nine o'clock?"

Florence laughed, "Oh, I think I can manage that, this is a farm, I am usually up and at work by six."

Toni shuddered, "Now that is an unearthly hour to be up and about, until tomorrow then."

Zack and Florence watched the Lagonda as it sped through the gateway.

"Zack, my love, I think I have found a new friend, and at last I shall see how the other half lives," Florence said in delight.

"Perhaps you have my dear, perhaps you have" Zack replied, almost cynically, "Take this with you just in case you need it, money is no object to your new found friend, and I'll not have you embarrassed."

He took his wallet from his pocket and handed to Florence his last three five pound notes.

Chapter Eighteen

There were few direct passenger trains from the various surrounding towns and cities passing through Heals End in the early mornings. Before writing letters to her daughters Elizabeth and Evie regarding Jim Porter's funeral arrangements, Eve Swindon had the foresight to study the train timetables; she enclosed suggestions of the possible trains, which, if they caught, should ensure they arrived home well before ten o'clock, a note containing similar travelling suggestions she also sent to Emily.

Elizabeth's route would be more direct, however, both Evie and Emily would need to start their journeys in an opposing direction to that of their eventual destination, and they would need to change trains at the biggest railway station in the area, Potterton, there, they could catch the only early train taking the branch line passing through Heals End.

As her own train pulled into Potterton, Evie could see her eldest sister Elizabeth dutifully waiting at the prearrange place on the station platform.

Joining her sister Evie asked, "You managed to get time off then Liz?"

"As you see," replied Elizabeth, "But I'll have to get back as soon as this sad affair is over, any funeral is bad enough at the best of times, but I only met our Emily's Jim the once, so I came for her sake really."

"That is one way of looking at it, it's the same for me, with not getting home much I hardly knew Jim either, true, Emily will need any support we can offer, but, if we are honest, we are both here because mother ordered it, in her letter to me she even told me which trains I must catch."

"Same in mine," Elizabeth confirmed, "I was glad she did, I always get panicky if I have to try and work out which train connects with which, and which you have to catch to get you where you want to go."

Evie smiled, although Elizabeth, born just nine months after their mother and father had married in October eighteen ninety-three was the eldest of all the children, nobody could accuse her of being either handsome or bright. However, at her workplace she was highly valued, she would diligently undertake all the dirty, menial jobs no one else wanted to do, unfortunately, thinking was not one of her strongest points, and in addition, she was extremely gullible and very easily led astray.

Evie, looking around the station began to feel concerned, "Have you seen anything of Emily Liz, according to mother's letter, the train we are to catch home is due in ten minutes."

"Not seen her, no, I have been watching out for both of you though, ever since I got here, no not seen her," replied her sister.

Their train arrived, the sisters waited as long as they dared before attempting to board, anxiously looking along the station platform towards the subway from which they expected Emily to appear.

"Perhaps she is already at home," Elizabeth said offering simple logic, "After all; it is her fiancé's funeral we will be attending."

"Maybe so," Evie agreed, "Anyway, the guard is checking the doors and he is about to wave this train out, we had better get on now."

The train arrived at Heals End as scheduled at nine-thirty; the sisters now had the half-mile walk up the bank to reach home, time was pressing, but their out dated conventional floor length black mourning skirts were never intended for hurrying.

"I hate these long skirts," complained Evie, "The new shorter styles are much more practical, I put one on this morning but then thought better of it."

"Good job too, bearing in mind the reason we were sent for, mother would go berserk if she saw you wearing anything which revealed even so much as your ankle," Elizabeth rebuked, "If you have been buying clothes like that, it's a good idea not to come home in them unless you want a good telling off."

"I know, that's why I changed again this morning into this damn thing, I only wear it when I come home if there is a likelihood I shall be going to chapel."

From Heals End Congregational Chapel, the bank grew much steeper; both girls continued without another word as they hurried to reach home by ten o'clock as instructed.

"I see mother's following tradition," Evie said as they rounded the corner by the church and their home came into view.

Snapped from her silent daydreaming, Lizzie now paid attention, "What?"

"The curtains," the younger girl pointed towards the house, "Upstairs are fully closed, and downstairs are only open a slit."

"Oh yes," Lizzie agreed, "We have passed a lot of houses like that as we came up the bank, I didn't know Jim Porter was so well known."

In dismay, Evie sighed and gave a despondent shake of her head, "Lizzie, we are going to a funeral service at Knolsend, which means of course, we shall have to walk back again the way we just came, and on top of that close to another couple of miles to get there. There were a good many men who died last Saturday, not just Jim, you can bet there will be other funerals taking place today, and some of them here in this village."

Elizabeth asked distractedly, "Did they, how many?"

Rather disgusted Evie snapped back, "Oh never mind, we're here now," standing aside, she allowed her sister to climb the front steps first.

Fanny sat sullen faced at the back kitchen table when her elder sisters entered by the back door.

"And what's the matter with your face today madam?" Evie asked.

"Mother's locked the piano," complained the youngster, "She says I can't do my practice for a week, not fair, there's nothing to do now."

Liz and Evie, smirking, looked at each other with satisfaction.

Concealing her slight amusement, Evie said, "Think yourself lucky Jim was not close family, if he was, mother would have locked that piano up for a twelve month at least; you will just have to find something else to do."

"Like housework Fanny," Lizzie taunted, "Still fighting shy of getting your hands dirty are you?"

Fanny Glared at her sister, jumped up, peevishly stuck out her tongue and stomped off into the front room.

Eve, hearing her daughter's voices hurried downstairs, "Good, you've made it on time," she said.

"We have mother," Evie replied, "And we're a bit warm to boot rushing up the bank in all these black clothes, it's too mild today for January, I could have done without wearing woollies."

"Ner' cast a clout till May be out," Eve quoted the old saying, "Emily in the privy is she?"

"No," Lizzie answered, "It's just the two of us, not seen our Em, she wasn't at the station was she Evie."

"No, we thought she would be home already."

"Oh dear what a to do, and there are no more trains now until midday, she won't be home for Jim's funeral."

Sam and Lijah, dressed in their best clothes and wearing black neckties and armbands customary for such a solemn occasion, joined them in the kitchen.

"What's the matter?" Sam asked a little confused to see his wife in a state of mild panic.

"It's our Emily Sam," Eve said tearfully, "She has missed her train, we will have to go without her, Jim was her fiancé and now she won't be there when he is laid to rest."

Consoling his wife, Sam said, "Don't upset yourself love, I'm sure she didn't mean to, perhaps her connection from Bursley was late getting in at Potterton."

"Dad," Lijah interrupted, "I think she might possibly have missed the train intentionally. What was that Victor Wickersby said to you we couldn't understand, 'don't leave home without her,' maybe Emily isn't coming home by train after all, I think we should wait a while, if we went across the fields we should be able to make Knolsend easily in three quarters of an hour."

"We could wait a bit I suppose, its pleasant enough out, yes we will go that way."

"In this get up, are you kidding?" Evie stupidly vocalised her thoughts and received a scuff round the ear from Eve for her trouble.

"Time for a cup of tea then," Lizzie said filling the kettle, and whispering to Evie added, "You asked for that, you know as well as I do how uptight mother gets at funerals, best we watch our step."

The mantle clock struck ten, everyone, except Fanny sat apprehensively around the back kitchen table, just as the clock's chime cocked to sound the quarter hour, Fanny burst in.

"Mum," she screamed, "There's a huge black motor car pulled up outside, Emily was in it with a man in uniform, they are coming across the road now."

Emily came in by the back door, followed by Jenkins, the Wickersby's chauffeur; Eve leapt up and ran to hug her daughter, Sam rose to greet Jenkins.

"Good morning Mr Swindon," Jenkins said as they shook hands, "Mr Wickersby has put a car at your disposal today; I am to drive you wherever you need to go."

"But Mr Jenkins, there are seven of us, will there be room enough for everyone, it may be rather cramped."

Jenkins smiled, "I haven't brought the Cowley you rode in the other day Mr Swindon, the master has sent the big Rolls Royce today, and yes, everyone will fit in comfortably."

Eavesdropping on her father and Jenkins, and never before having been inside a motor car, Fanny charged into the living room and irreverently threw open the curtains to look at the shiny black machine standing outside.

"Fanny," her mother screamed after her, "Close those curtains," the girl obeyed, but instead of rejoining them in the back kitchen, she sneaked into the front room, Eve guessed why, and was about to follow her.

Lijah pleaded, "Leave her mother, she's excited now and it makes a change from her sulking."

"What is she sulking about now?" asked Emily.

Evie sniggered, "It seems mother has locked the piano Em, taken away her escape and excuse not to do anything."

"Mother, was that really necessary?" Emily asked quietly, "I know it's a time honoured custom when there has been a close family death, but Jim wasn't family yet."

"It wasn't your mother, it was my idea," Sam said, "Fanny is becoming a handful these days. The older she gets, the worse she gets, she's plenty old enough to help out around this house, but the little madam always scampers off into the front room and avoids doing anything useful, and besides, we have only locked the piano for a week to try and teach her a lesson."

Jenkins stood grinning broadly, "My youngest girl is just the same Mr Swindon, just the same, finds any excuse to be idle."

Sam smiled, "Glad to hear I'm not alone, and please, call me Sam."

"Very well, my name is Arnold."

"But everybody calls him Arny," Emily chirped up giving the chauffeur a playful dig with her elbow.

Checking his pocket watch, Arny asked, "Do we have far to go Sam?"

"That depends on Emily, if we go to the house, about two and a quarter miles, straight to the chapel it's only two, Emily, you choose."

"I think it is more fitting as a mark of respect to follow the cortège from the house dad."

"House it is then Emily," Jenkins said, "The only thing is, I'm not too familiar with the roads around here and the car has a separate enclosed rear saloon, it will be a help if someone who knows the way could ride up front with me."

Evie was quickest to volunteer, but Elijah countered her proposition, "No Evie, considering the occasion you should ride in the back; I will sit with Mr Jenkins and direct him to the Porter's house."

The family prepared to leave home, but Elizabeth held back and caught hold of Evie's arm holding her back.

"Evie," she whispered, "Mother is in a right mood, I don't think she has noticed yet, but I reckon she will explode soon, have you seen what our Em is wearing, definitely not what mother regards as suitable chapel clothes."

"Nah, she won't say anything to upset Em, not today, and I know she has noticed because I saw her face when our Em first came in. I wish I could afford clothes like that, Emily must be earning a lot more money than she lets on to us, in that outfit she makes us look dowdy doesn't she."

Once Sam, his wife and daughters were safely settled in the back of the Rolls, Jenkins closed the door and opened the front passenger's door for Lijah.

Lijah, intending to be helpful asked, "Would you like me to swing the starting handle for you first Mr Jenkins?"

Arnold Jenkins smiled back at him, winked and replied, "If you want to put your shoulder out lad you might try it, but I prefer to press the start button, it's a bit easier that way."

"Your name's Elijah isn't it?" Jenkins asked as he climbed behind the steering wheel.

"It is Mr. Jenkins, but most people call me Lijah."

"OK, fair enough, call me Arny, your sister always does when the Wickersby's or the housekeeper aren't around, well Lijah, which way do I go?"

"There are two routes by road Arny, one is about a mile shorter than the other, but the old track over Crack Hill is twisty and very narrow, and this is a big motor car."

Jenkins glanced in his rear-view mirror, "This is one of the biggest motor cars that there is lad," he said smiling, "Let's take the longer route and give your little sister a proper treat."

Lijah turned around to see what instigated Arny's remark; Fanny's face was beaming with pride and excitement.

Within fifteen minutes, the Swindon family were in Knolsend, a group of friends and neighbours had congregated on the narrow pavement outside the terraced house of Andrew and Gladys Porter. Never before had such a vehicle come down their street as the one that now slowly turned into it, someone called Andrew and Gladys out of the house to witness the sight. Residents of the little street watched in awe as the luxurious motor car stopped next to them, Jenkins got out, opened the rear door, and to the accompaniment of gasps from the gathering, assisted Emily out of the car.

"Emily," Gladys Porter exclaimed pushing through the little assembly to greet her, "What a way for you to arrive."

Up to now, Emily Swindon had held strong, but now her emotions welled up, and a tear formed in her eye.

"Jim," she asked, "Is he,—"

"He is in the parlour my dear," Gladys interrupted, "Come, you will no doubt want a few moments alone with him."

Gladys led the way into the parlour of her little house; there was no fire, and Jim's coffin stood open on two trestles by the fireplace.

"Join us in the kitchen when you are ready my dear," Gladys said leaving Emily to say her final goodbye.

Emily stood a while by the coffin holding her fiancé's hand; she spoke softly to him before finally kissing Jim's forehead.

When Emily joined Gladys and Andrew Porter in the kitchen, her strength had returned and her emotions were once more well under control.

That morning Charlotte Wickersby had spoken at some length to Emily, her advice, 'at all costs, try to remain strong Emily, in such cases as these someone must appear to be strong, if you break down into tears, just think of the additional grief it could bring to your fiancé's family, stay strong today, grieve later.'

The atmosphere in the kitchen amongst Jim Porter's closest relations, was, as would be expected, one of sorrow. The gathering was not large, Andrew and Gladys Porter, Andrew's mother Martha, Gladys's younger sister Nora, her husband Wilfred and their three children.

"You arrived in style this morning young lady," Andrew observed in his droll manner.

Emily smiled bashfully, "There have been houseguests at work so it has been very busy Mr Porter, there were no trains this morning and so the master allowed Mr Jenkins the chauffeur to bring me home. Mr Wickersby is a very thoughtful, kind man, well, he is at home anyway, I think he is different in his business dealings, if he wasn't I don't expect he would be so rich."

"So your mother led me to understand Emily, I presume that huge motor car has gone back now?" Gladys added.

"Oh no Mrs Porter, Jenkins and the car are to remain here all day in case it is needed, the master has other vehicles that he likes to drive himself, and the mistress didn't need Jenkins or the big car today."

Nora Wright had a tendency to be vicious; her puritanical suspicions were aroused by this uncommon act of generosity by a member of the upper classes, cynically she asked.

"Is your employer so generous towards all the young women who work at his house Emily?"

"He is kind, yes, but not usually to this extent, when Mum and Dad came last Sunday to tell me what happened, I requested leave to return home with them, but with the visitors expected this week, the mistress asked me to stay because all the household staff was needed. The master told me last night that he had ordered Jenkins to bring me home today and to stay with me; Mrs Quint the housekeeper and my friend Sarah were there when he told me, Sarah thinks he did it just to annoy Mrs Quint again.

Nora persisted, "Really, being a housekeeper is a senior position in service, why would your master want to annoy her?"

"I believe Mrs Quint was a servant with Mrs Wickersby's family before she and the master were married, but the master is not overly fond of her because she can be so very fierce, he does all sorts of things just to tease and aggravate her."

Suddenly, Gladys realised behind her sister's questions there were implications of improper conduct on Emily's part, she scowled at Nora putting an end to the interrogation.

"Emily, I invited your mother and family, we must not leave them outside," Gladys said, and began to usher Emily towards the door to bring her parents indoors.

Sam and Lijah, by this time had been waylaid by the local men and were deep in conversation, Emily presumed they were discussing the explosion, her mother and other sisters stood chatting on the pavement. Fanny, up until now, refused to get out of the car, but as Emily reappeared in the doorway, she jumped out and ran to her.

"Em," Fanny said, "Can I see Jim and say goodbye, I liked Jim, I know he is in there, I heard his mother tell you, I want to say goodbye to Jim."

"Don't be silly Fanny," Eve snapped at her, "No you can't, your not old enough for such things, come and stand by me."

Gladys Porter, overhearing Fanny's request intervened, "Eve, considering the circumstances, I know what you must be thinking, but it will be alright, my sister's children have said there goodbyes, if the child wants to see Jim, it is quite safe to let her."

Eve understood her meaning, although Gladys had not actually put it into words, unlike the majority of those lost on Saturday, her son's body had not been mutilated by the explosion.

"Very well then Fanny, Emily can take you to see Jim, but you must not let go of her hand, is that understood?"

Rightly assuming no one inside would be known to them, the two remaining sisters declined the invitation to go indoors. Fanny grasping Emily's hand was led into the parlour, Eve and Gladys followed, but chose to remain near the door whilst the sisters moved closer to the coffin, Fanny looked down at Jim, Eve, ever watchful, saw Fanny's grip on Emily's hand tighten at her first glimpse of a corpse. However, the child's reaction was far different from that which her mother expected.

"Em," Fanny said, "He's waiting now, he's not gone forever Em, he's just asleep and waiting. They teach us at Sunday school when we die it isn't the end; we just fall asleep and wait for the last trumpet to sound on judgement day calling good people to rise again, your Jim's waiting now."

Overcome, Gladys Porter turned to leave the room and choked out the quotation, "Out of the mouths of babes and suckling's shall come forth wisdom."

After a few minutes, Emily and Fanny joined the other family mourners in the little kitchen; Gladys introduced Fanny to the three Wright children, Jim Porter's cousins. The eldest boy, Steven, although twelve months older, he, and his two sisters were all smaller than Fanny, however, with Fanny's gift for senseless chatter it was not long before they all behaved as if they had known each other for years.

Emily had grown very fond of Jim's grandmother Martha, the old woman sat alone in a corner of the kitchen watching the youngsters, and listening to Fanny's story of how she had rode to Knolsend in a huge motor car, she smiled at Emily and nodding in Fanny's direction said.

"Your young sister is a little chatterbox, is she always like that?"

Emily went over to her, "Pretty much Gran, pretty much, how are you keeping, how are those leg ulcers of yours?"

"Bad child, bad, weeping all the time, but if it kills me I will walk after that hearse and see our young Jim off."

Emily thought a moment before asking, "How about if you could ride instead Gran, would that be better for you?"

"Aye lass, it would, but I'm not climbing up on old Dennis's hoss cart if that's what you mean, wouldn't be right, family follow a coffin, not ride up front."

"That isn't what I had in mind, I was thinking of the master's car, Arny is staying over here all day, I'm sure he would drive you to the chapel."

Instantly the children were silent, and four pairs of young eyes were focused upon Emily, Andrew Porter overheard Emily's suggestion, and also noticed the youngster's reaction to it, forcing a smile he indicated in their direction.

"Aye up Emily," he said, "Little pigs have big ears, I think they would like to ride as well."

"Would you?" Emily asked, smiling at the children.

"Oh yes please Emily," Steven replied, "We've been on the charabanc, but never rode in a motor car, could we?"

Emily, wary of Nora's glare and expecting her sharp-tongued rebuke, began hesitantly, "If it's alright with you're—."

Wilfred Wright interceded, "It is, they are all too young to walk in a cortège, never mind what Nora says, if the driver doesn't mind they can ride with Gran, and tell him to come into the schoolroom afterwards for something to eat with us."

Bored with sitting in the car and not knowing anyone else present, Arnold Jenkins had wandered over to Sam, Lijah and the other men.

The distinctive sound of horse's hooves on cobblestones heralded the arrival of the undertaker, Dennis Oliver; the hearse drawn by two black horses drew everyone's attention towards the top of the little street.

"Better drop the car down a bit Arny," Sam said, "Let old Dennis get the hearse close to the house."

"No problem there Sam, at least I have a reverse gear on the car to get it out of here again, it will be easier than expecting those horses to back up to the main road."

Elijah overheard, and he followed the car as it moved about three house lengths down the street.

"Arny," Lijah said as the chauffeur climbed out again, "From here this street looks like a dead end, but it isn't, if you will walk with me to the bottom I will show you the way round into the next street, and that will take you back onto the main road."

As the two men walked towards the end of the narrow street, Arny asked, "Are you expecting the service to take long?"

"About an hour to an hour and a half for the ceremony and internment I would think, the cemetery where Jim will be buried is just behind the chapel."

"Chapel, the services are not at that church we passed on the way here then?"

Lijah smiled, Arny must have noticed the Anglican Church as he drove through Broughton.

"No, from here only half that distance, do you remember seeing the water pump and a road to the left as we climbed out of that big dip, just before you turned the car into here?"

The chauffeur paused, "Oh yes, I think so."

"If you turn right by that pump, Knolsend chapel and cemetery is down that old road," Lijah paused a moment for thought before continuing, "Not that I use them myself, but there is a nice little public house just above the chapel, you could wait there while we are at the service if you like. I'm pretty sure you will be able to get something to eat there, and I will come and find you when it is all over, that is if you are going to stay."

"Got to stay Lijah, Mr Wickersby's orders were to support your sister today and to help out in anyway needed, I know she won't take advantage of it, but just for today, I take my instructions from young Emily."

"Arny, I can't say I have had any close contact with the toffs myself, you know, the money folk, but this Wickersby chap, he appears to be a lot different than we imagine them to be, all the people of consequence I know of treat the likes of us as if we don't exist."

Arny laughed, "I know just what you mean lad, in my job I come across loads of people like that. The sorts you are talking about are usually those who have made a few quid out of the blood, sweat and tears of the working classes, but, unlike the master, they don't have the background or breeding to be classed as true gentlemen, the majority of them are just social climbing vermin, want folk to think they are important."

"Aren't you being a bit severe there Arny?"

"I don't think so, over the years I have developed a sort of sixth sense, I can spot the ones you need to be careful around a mile away. Have to say though, I find it amusing, when I am waiting for the master outside those big boy's clubs of theirs after they have held one of their boozy functions, the way some of them suck up to, and fawn over Victor Wickersby is embarrassing, both for him, and for us drivers to watch."

Elijah was confused, there was a sort of boy's club at Augers Bank Wesleyan Chapel, 'The Brotherhood,' and he had been a member since his late teens. He had learned some surprising things recently about Emily's employer, but for him to be associated with a Methodist temperance brotherhood he found hard to believe, no, it could not be that, Arny had used the word, boozy.

Lijah, trying to understand, queried and repeated the phrase, "Big boy's club?"

Arny winked at him, "Masonic Hall Lijah, that's where the big money boys play."

Emily stood waiting by the Rolls when Elijah and Jenkins returned; she explained about Jim's Grandmother's bad legs, and made her request for the old woman and the children to use the car.

"No problem Em, the car is yours for today remember, anything you say ma-am," Arny said and jokingly touched the beck of his cap.

Emily dug him in the ribs with her elbow and scolded, "Cut that out Arny, stop playing the idiot."

"Come on Lijah, hop in," Arny said, "We need to get this mechanical beast around to the back of that hearse, and while we are about it, if you think there is time you can show me where the road to this chapel is."

"You will have plenty of time Arny," Emily reassured, "It won't take you more than a couple of minutes to go round and come back into this street. They are bound to follow the custom of having all the family present, to say goodbye to Jim before Mr Oliver's men screw down the coffin lid, and load it onto the hearse."

Arny Jenkins drew the car away from the people gathered on the pavement before remarking to Lijah.

"Young Emily is coping very well considering it's her fiancé who is about to be buried."

"Not the first time we have been through this kind of thing Arny, and yes, our Em is strong. If she cracks at all I reckon it won't be until the coffin is in the ground and the Minister gets to the 'Ashes to Ashes' part of the internment, I intend to make sure I am close by her for that."

"Maybe so, I don't think I have ever seen anything unnerve her, she is physically strong as well, tried arm wrestling with her once and she tanked me."

Lijah laughed, "I know, she can beat me at times, I have no idea where she gets that strength from, you wouldn't think it to look at her though would you?"

"Definitely not, anyway, she was telling me on the way here this morning that the mistress gave her some good advice before we left and she intents to take heed of it, didn't say what it was though."

"She has been fairly lucky so far today Arny, I'm flabbergasted mother hasn't rounded on her about the length of that dress and coat she's wearing, or more to the point, the lack of it. There is no way Evie and Liz would have got away with wearing those low-heeled shoes, silk stockings and a skirt just over knee length, I'm afraid mother is old fashioned about chapel clothes, but I have to admit, Em looks very smart in that outfit, and she is brave to wear it."

Arny began to snigger and Lijah looked at him in confusion, "What's so funny?" he asked.

"Funny, nothing's funny except that you're implying style hasn't reached out here into the sticks yet. Actually, Miss Alex had me taking her shopping on Wednesday afternoon, and she took your Emily with her. I rather think it was Miss Alex who picked out that outfit for Emily, and if I am any judge of Miss Alex she most probably paid for it too."

"Who is this Miss Alex?"

"Alexandra Wickersby, the master's daughter, seems everybody Emily comes into contact with, thinks well of her, well everybody except the housekeeper, that old trout Quint, she always hated any attractive girl and she has got worse since her husband absconded with a barmaid more than half his age from one of our local hostelries."

Lijah was stunned, "Oh," he exclaimed, and was about to add he had spoken to Mrs Quint once on the telephone, but as they re-entered the street, Dennis Oliver was waving his black staff at them indicating Arny should stop a little way up from the Porter's house, the car came to a halt and the undertaker approached them.

Somewhat aggravated, Dennis said, "Mrs Porter has just told me some people will be riding to the chapel in this contraption."

Arny confirmed the fact, "That's right, some old lady who has difficulty walking, the lad's grandmother I think, and some of his young cousins."

"Immediate family then," Dennis said, "Just as long as I know, relationship to the deceased is important when forming up the procession," and with that he walked off.

"Strange bloke," Arny commented.

"Very strange," Lijah agreed, "But he is well thought of around here, always treats every funeral as though it is something extra special, he's very thorough when it comes to following protocol."

The moment had come; in silence, Jim Porter's coffin was carried out of the house and reverently slid into the hearse, which, then drew down about a length and a half from the house. Dennis Oliver waved to Arny to bring the car to the front door, and organised the family mourners to form up behind the hearse in order of their relationship to the deceased, Emily he placed at the head with Jim's parents. Dennis and Arny assisted Martha Porter into the back of the Rolls, Jim's young cousins Dennis also ushered into the rear of the vehicle. Fanny, not being family, Dennis instructed to take the seat she had secretly hoped for, with Arny in the front of the Rolls.

Other members of the community attending in order to pay their respects, formed up in a column behind the Rolls, when he was satisfied that the cortège was formed up as it should be, Dennis took his customary place three yards in front of the hearse. Adjusting the positioning of his shiny top hat, his well known badge of office, making sure the long, wide, black silk ribbons were flowing behind his back, rapped his staff twice on the cobbles, and walking slowly, led the procession off to the chapel.

* * *

Henry Cotes scowled angrily at the surface workers ogling his daughter as she sped past the gates of Tilly Pit on her way up to Highfield Hall, all but the gatekeeper disappeared into some building or other. With some trepidation, Henry sought out Joseph Shaw, whom he eventually found in the lamp-house.

"Good morning Joseph," Henry greeted, "Who is this person that wants to see me today?"

Joseph smiled, and with a warning inclination of his head towards the back of the lamp-house, cautioned Henry not to continue any further in front of Len Holding the lamp-house attendant. Henry understood, and waited for Joseph to finish copying into his notebook details of the anticipated locations of the men still lost below ground.

Satisfied he had all the data he required, Joseph left the lamp-house closely followed by Henry, once outside Joseph began to apologize.

"I am sorry about that Mr Cotes, I didn't mean to seem disrespectful, but Arthur and I are finding we have to watch everything we say if anyone is around. There has been much speculation while you were away; any snippet that is overheard is in danger of being misconstrued, not to mention the papers getting hold of it."

"Quite so, quite so Joseph, my mistake, I have had a few distractions this morning, perhaps my mind wasn't properly focused, I didn't notice that chap in there skulking about at the back, so think nothing of it."

The two men crossed the yard towards the offices, as they did, Henry glanced around, the surface workers had re-emerged from their hiding places, and several had positioned themselves within easy eavesdropping distance of the owner and manager. Henry smiled as he realised the validity of Joseph's concern, and made use of it, speaking clearly and a little louder than normal.

"My thoughts have been with you while I was away Joseph, I do hope you are going to tell me that more survivors have been rescued in my absence."

Joseph was confused, before Henry left for Wales, they had reached the conclusion no one in the pit at the time of the explosion could possibly be found still alive.

"Survivors, no Mr Cotes, no more survivors, but we have located three more fatalities, which still leaves fifty-five men still unaccounted for."

Behind closed doors in the comparative security of Joseph's office, both men seated themselves, one each side of Joseph's desk.

"Don't think I am loosing it Joseph," Henry said, "But when I spotted those men trying to eavesdrop on us I thought I would give them something to spread around."

Joseph sighed with visible relief, "I did think it was rather a strange thing for you to say Mr Cotes, but I can see the logic now in your saying it."

"What is that you were copying from those ledgers in the lamp-house, you seemed to be engrossed," Henry inquired.

"I am trying to make preparations for when the men from Wales arrive."

"How so?"

"The way Arthur and I figure it, there are still fifty-five men still unaccounted for down below, we cannot guarantee where they actually ended up after the blast, but the ledgers tell us approximately where they should have been working, including their names and their lamp tag numbers.

All but one of the remaining districts where they should have been working are still blocked off, we had the idea when the new men arrive, Seth and some of the local miners could take them down to familiarize them with the layout before they actually begin the operation. Once that is done, we supply details of how many men we expect them to find in each district and precisely who they should be, and continue working like that until we have accounted for all fifty-five."

"And all will be brought to the surface sealed in their coffins with the identity of the occupant marked on the outside?"

Joseph looked rather uncomfortable, "Exactly, Dr Thomas has ordered the coffins are not to be opened again once sealed below ground on public health grounds, he considered the condition of the last three bodies brought out posed too much of a risk to the public."

"I could see that one coming, which is why I instructed some coffins were sent here without cloth lining," Henry said, confirming his agreement with the proposal, "Has there been much opposition from Seth Fuller and the like to strangers being brought in to undertake this work?"

"Some, yes, but we have leaked the information that the men we are expecting are highly skilled in this type of operation, and they travel around the country to wherever there expertise is needed. A bit of an exaggeration, but if the majority of them do not speak English, Arthur and I thought it would be an acceptable risk. Seth and most of the old hands know they have done all they can to find anyone still alive, they know it is vital for this community as a whole that the mine be brought back into production again, and that has to take priority now, too many families are going hungry without a pay packet coming in."

"You believe they have accepted the situation, regarding men still lost?"

"Rescue squad, yes, nobody ever speaks of it, but they all know if the bodies of men are not found intact after an explosion below ground, on rare occasions the bodyweight for the coffin is made up to give comfort to the deceased's family, I don't know if that is the way the Welsh work."

"Ah, I see where you are going with this Joseph; I will not condone any shortcuts, rest assured Gethin Jones and his men, will, quite literally leave no stone unturned in their search, and bring out of the mine those they are sent in to find. Every family will have mortal remains of some kind to bury, having said that, if you take my meaning, every one of the Welsh lads knows the score, if there is, as you imply some other age honoured custom amongst miners, officially, I don't want to know about it."

Joseph Shaw remained silent, disconcerted by what he perceived to be a reprimand, judging from Henry Cotes's remarks and actions since the accident, he had been convinced, he and Henry Cotes were reading from the same page, that they held the same views regarding future actions, cautiously, he began to elucidate.

"Mr Cotes, I did not intend to imply we should follow any disreputable procedures regarding the recovery of the lost men, I apologize if I have offended you."

Henry sighed audibly, shook his head and replied.

"Joseph, Joseph, you have not given any offence, I have every confidence that you and Arthur Cleaver will do all in your power to bring this matter to a satisfactory conclusion, for my part, I will do all I can to assist you. Let us be honest now, between you and Arthur there is more knowledge than I could ever hope to learn about mining coal, about the customs and traditions of those people who live and work in communities such as this. However, for men like me, there is a two-word phrase, borrowed originally from the world of those men who run this great empire of ours. When there is any possibility that the things they do may be construed by some as unlawful, immoral or shady, they ensure their own position is safeguarded and that they are able to use a protective two-word phrase, that phrase Joseph is, 'Plausible Deniability,' and this is one of those instances where I must have it."

Joseph began to understand, the old squire had always been content to talk about many things, but he could never be persuaded to commit anything to paper, there was never anything that could be produced to incriminate him, if this was how they worked, Joseph resolved to adopt a similar method himself.

Henry had been watching Joseph's facial expression turn from one of confusion, to one of enlightenment.

"Right Joseph," Henry continued, "I believe we understand each other on that point, now who the hell is this guy your message last night said I must see?"

"His name is Jonah Baldwin Mr Cotes, he runs; well actually I think he owns 'The Bell,' at Augers Bank. At first, he was adamant he could not help, but eventually he agreed the Welshmen could all lodge there. A niece of Arthurs works there and she let it slip the old man is short of funds. When we implied you had instructed us to find lodgings 'at any cost,' he changed his mind. I hope that it is all right with you, but I'm afraid I had to advance him the money from our petty cash that he needed to buy groceries and other items he would need. He claimed he wasn't able to set a rate there and then, but he requested to deal with you face to face."

"Why would he want that, I have never heard of the man?"

"He said something to the effect that he had heard of you from Stan Smith, you remember, the landlord at The Boars Head where we had lunch the other day."

"Oh yes, I remember, Charles was being his usual lecherous self, and I was rather generous to the landlord in order to get that girl away from the place and upset Charles's scheming."

"I recall the incident sir, you said the girl was doing some errands for you, but I was not aware you paid the landlord for her services."

"It seemed like a good idea at the time, a bit of a joke, but if this Smith fellow has been talking it may backfire on me. You referred to this Baldwin as the old man, how old would you say he is?"

"I have never been much good at guessing a person's age, but possibly early to mid seventies, I would think."

"And he still runs this Bell place?"

"Just the bars in the evening I understand, as a whole the place is in need of a great deal of restoration work, verging on the derelict in fact, but Arthur and I checked the accommodation, if the Welshmen are prepared to rough it the rooms will be more than adequate, and at least they will be together."

"In that case, I suppose I had better go and see for myself, and find out what your Mr Baldwin is up to, if he thinks he can put the squeeze on me he will find he is mistaken."

Joseph looked despondently at the amount of paperwork piled on his desk; nevertheless, he made the offer, which he hoped Henry would refuse.

"Would you like me to come with you, and introduce you Mr Cotes?"

"No, that won't be necessary, you obviously have things to do here, just tell me where the place is and I will go up on my own."

Joseph was about to draw a little sketch map for Henry when he remembered, at The Bell, there were standing instructions not to open the door to anyone who could be seeking settlement of overdue accounts. Joseph acquainted Henry with these facts, and it was decided that Joe Harris, being known to Jonah Baldwin would show Henry the way and make sure the door was opened to him.

A gentle tap upon, and the opening of the office door heralded the arrival of Arthur Cleaver.

"Ah, Arthur, just the man," Joseph said as his deputy entered the room, "Do you happen to know where Joe Harris is at the moment?"

"He has just gone into the smithy to have his snap early, says he has a run to do at mid-day."

"To where?" Joseph inquired.

Arthur, while he was speaking had been concentrating on some papers laid out on a side table, only now, when he turned did he realise Joseph was not alone.

"Oh, Mr Cotes, good morning, I wondered who the car in the yard belonged to, you seem to come in a different one each time we see you."

"Good morning Arthur," Cotes said without raising his eyes from Joseph's notebook.

"Be a good chap Arthur, go and fetch Joe, I need him to show Mr Cotes where The Bell is," Joseph instructed.

Henry intervened, "Let the man finish his lunch, I'm in no hurry, is there any of that malt left, if not, a mug of tea would be welcomed."

Arthur managed to catch Joseph's eye, "I'll just pop over to the smithy then, and tell Joe to come here before he does **that** run," Arthur over emphasised the word 'that,' "It's the one you arranged for him to do yesterday, remember?"

Arthur had held Joseph's eye, and was pointing alternatively to Henry, who searching through the cupboard had his back to them, and then indicating in the direction of Augers Bank, Joseph at first could not understand, until Arthur mouthed the word 'shopping' to him.

Henry located the bottle of malt, barely half a dram left, at which he looked mournfully, "Ah well, tea it is, stick the kettle on Joseph."

Joseph put the kettle onto the stove and found a glass which he offered to Henry, who declined it, "Nah, you finish it off sometime Joseph, no point in waking my taste buds up for that piddling amount; I'll just have the tea when it's made."

Joseph, knowing Joe Harris to have as much tact as a herd of stampeding cows, and taking heed of Arthur's warning, decided it would be better if Henry knew from him where Joe was going, rather than from Joe himself.

"Mr Cotes, when Arthur and I called upon Jonah Baldwin, after he agreed in principle for the men to lodge with him. He still raised the protestation that to feed twelve men tomorrow would take a lot of food that he did not have, and that he would not be able to buy enough in time, in addition, carriage of the supplies would be a problem. It was then we clinched the deal by giving him the twenty-five pounds in advance, and we also offered the use of the pits van to collect the supplies they need, do you approve?"

"Whatever Joseph, you're the manager here; there is no need to keep seeking my approval over trivia, but you have my thanks for the statistics on the state of the old boy's finances, which will probably be useful."

Whilst they awaited the arrival of Joe Harris, Joseph Shaw elaborated on the possible timetable, and methods the new recovery squad would be instructed to implement, Henry listened closely, occasionally nodding agreement, but said nothing. After thirty minutes, they were interrupted by a heavy knock at the office door; Joseph answered the knocks summons.

"Been told to report here boss before I go and do that daft job you are sending me on, bloody woman's work snapping shopping," Joe Harris complained in his normal cheerless manner.

"Yes that's right Joe, come in," Joseph said in his normal voice, and then under his breath added, "And mind your manners."

"Joe, this gentleman is Mr Cotes, one of the mines owners," Joseph said.

Joe Harris grunted, "How do."

"Mr Cotes needs to speak to Jonah Baldwin, and considering the problems we had in getting any reply when we called, I want you to go up with Mr Cotes and do the same as you did for us, get them to answer the door to you."

"Got yer boss, no problem, thought you might be letting me off going shopping, not my bloody luck that."

Henry found Joe's gruff manners quite amusing.

"Have I got to bring yon big boss back here before I go for snapping?" Joe asked hopefully.

Henry answered, "Oh no Joe, I will follow you in my car, I wouldn't like to deny you the opportunity of learning how a woman does the weekly snapping shop."

Joe Harris realised Henry was joking, he sniggered, "Ready when you are then, vans just outside."

Joe pulled the van well off the road outside The Bell, leaving ample room for Henry to pull his car in behind, which he did, directly in front of the entrance gateway. Before he climbed out of his car Henry sat at the wheel and studied the building for a moment, he realised he must have past the place many times, but as it was situated well back from the road behind earth retaining loose stonewalls, which were topped with very high Privet hedges, he had never noticed it before. Apart from the restricted view through the gateway he now had, all that would be visible from the road, was the top of one gable end to the right of the 'L' shaped building, and what appeared to be an old brick stable in front of the hedges to the left, and a rough track leading around to the rear.

Joseph Shaw had been right, the building was a dismal place and certainly in need of attention, from the front view alone, which he now had, Henry could see The Bell was easily three times the size of The Boars Head, which he estimated to be less than fifty yards higher up the bank.

Joe Harris stood waiting for Henry at the edge of the cobblestoned yard.

"Why are all the curtains closed?" asked Henry, "Ten windows at the front here, and not a one with an open curtain."

"That'll be for two reasons boss," Joe answered, "One, because old Jonah hasn't used most of the place in years, upstairs, in his living quarters on the end there the curtains are usually open, but they are closed out of respect today like, because of all the funerals going on. Closing curtains when somebody you know is being laid to rest is the custom round here, them being buried are either friends, or customers of Jonah."

The curtain to the right of the door twitched, both men saw it.

"Aye, aye," Joe said, "We've been spotted."

"So it would seem, after you Joe."

To the amazement of both men, Joe had only taken a couple of steps along the yard, and the huge door swung open wide, nevertheless, Joe gave his customary heavy knock on the open door and called out.

"It's Joe Harris, anybody in there?"

"Yes, we know" a girls voice replied, "Come in Mr Harris, Mrs Baldwin over did it yesterday and made herself ill, Isabel will be coming with you, she has just popped to the kitchen to fetch her coat and things."

"I'm not alone, there's someone here to see Jonah," Joe called back.

"Oh, alright, I'm coming."

The owner of the voice appeared from a side room along the main corridor, recognising Joe's companion, she bob curtsied, smiled and said.

"Good afternoon Mr Cotes, any little errands for me today?"

"Not today Ruth," Henry responded in astonishment, "I thought you worked at The Boars Head, not here."

"I did, until yesterday, Mr Smith finished me because I was only a casual worker, but for once I had a bit of luck, Issy came up yesterday afternoon and told me Mr Baldwin was looking to hire people, I started here this morning."

Joe Harris stood watching and listening open mouthed, a local serving wench, and the owner of the mine chatting as if they were old friends, he couldn't believe it.

"I've got a nice fire going in the bar Mr Cotes, if you would like to wait in there, I will go and find Mr Baldwin for you."

Isabel Green came along the corridor from the kitchen, carrying sheets of paper, and struggling with several bags and a basket.

"I have been told to come with you Mr Harris," she said, and waved the sheets of paper, "I've got my instructions here, if you are ready, we can make a start."

Henry strolled into the bar, apart from the firelight it was dark, instinctively, he went to open the curtains, but changed his mind; Joe had said something about a tradition of paying homage to the dead.

There was the sound of someone shuffling along the corridor, and an elderly grey haired man appeared in the doorway.

"Mr Henry Cotes I believe," the elderly man said as he entered, moving to the windows, he opened both sets of curtains just a little to allow some light into the room, "My name is Jonah Baldwin, thank you for taking the time to call and see me."

Neither man offered to shake hands, Henry out of caution, and Jonah because his hands were filthy.

"Apologize for the state of me," Jonah said, "But I've just been taking them tubs down the back cellar, and trying to clean it up a bit if your blokes are going to use it as a bath-house."

Henry had no idea what Jonah was talking about, he ignored it.

"I received a message you wanted to deal with me face to face Mr Baldwin, however, my managers would be more than capable of making any necessary arrangements regarding payment for the men's lodging."

"Aye, I'm sure they would," Jonah replied, "Still haven't been able to work a rate out yet, until I know the cost of things nowadays and how much I have to pay for staff, not had people staying here for ten years or more, but my price will be fair, I'll not try to fleece you Mr Cotes."

Henry was taken aback by this, "If it's not your fees you want to discuss Mr Baldwin, why did you ask to see me?"

"Jonah, Mr Cotes, everyone, except youngsters calls me Jonah, let's sit down a bit, my ruddy back is killing me after trying to sort out back cellar."

"Very well Jonah, why did you ask to see me?"

"Well, blame Stan Smith from up the road, he told me what you did for him, and when your blokes were here, they sort of implied you can be very helpful and generous to people if they help you out. So it occurred to me, there is something you need that I can help you with, just maybe, a man like you, with all the contacts you must have would be able to help me in return."

Henry was wary, but curious, "In what way?"

Jonah, for once, found he was struggling for the necessary words; he got up and went to the bar, swilled his hands in the bucket of water Ruth had taken in to clean the floor, and began to draw himself a glass of mild.

"Can I offer you anything to drink while we talk Mr Cotes?"

"I'm not a great lover of ale without a meal Jonah, but you carry on."

"Got a bottle of that malt stuff the old squire used to like somewhere, how about that."

Henry smiled, "That will do nicely, thank you."

Jonah bought himself enough time to gather his thoughts by fumbling about pretending to look for the whiskey, which was exactly where he always kept it. He eventually brought the bottle and a glass, together with his own ale over to the table by Henry, who poured himself a generous helping of malt.

"Well man, come on, out with it, what exactly do you think I can help with?" Henry said as he settled back in his chair.

Jonah paused, "It's this place, it was a good business once but I'm getting too old to run it properly, there's only me and the missis and she's not well. We've got no family to leave it to, so I thought you might, or at least know somebody, who might want to buy it, there's a five acre field as well as the buildings."

"You're never too old to make money Jonah, if the work is getting too much to do yourself, hire staff."

"Had to do that to accommodate the men coming to work at your pit Mr Cotes, it will be nice to see the old place alive again, but truth be told, I've lost interest. My only daughter and her husband are both dead, my two grandsons lost in this bloody war, nobody left now. I did mention only last year to the old squire I was thinking of selling up, he said he wasn't interested himself, said he was too ill, but he knew someone who might be soon."

"Perhaps he meant my nephew Charles, the new squire?"

"Him, no way, I've had dealings with him before. I don't want to offend you Mr Cotes, seeing he's your nephew an all, but I couldn't trust him to even settle a bar tab, he owes me money from years ago, and I know a good many more he owes money to as well."

Henry smiled and shook his head, "You don't offend me Jonah, I am well aware of my nephew's reputation."

"Any chance you would be interested in this place Mr Cotes, I wouldn't want top price, I know the place needs a lot of work doing on it."

Henry thought for a moment, "Personally, no, true I do own hotels, but this one is in the wrong place, if it were on the coast or in a town it would be a different matter."

Jonah's expression was dejected.

"However," Henry continued, "I think I have an idea as to the party whom my brother-in-law may have been referring, if they are not interested, I also know of a young person who would probably be very interested in buying your hotel here, either to run with a manager in place, or to convert into dwellings. In short Jonah, once the Welshmen leave again, I am sure I can find a buyer for you if your price is right."

"It will be, at my age and with things as they are I will take any reasonable offer."

"You know the men are arriving tomorrow, or Sunday, how are your preparations going?"

"Pretty well, beds and rooms are ready and have fires in being aired, still looking for somebody to do the cooking though, as I said, my missis isn't too well these days, if not, for the time being, young Isabel and that Ruth girl will have to manage. Have you any idea how long the men will be staying?"

"That I don't know, perhaps until the end of the year, maybe less."

"The two chaps who came up to ask about them staying here, Issy's uncle and the other fellow said the mine is paying for their board, is that right?"

"Yes Jonah, Joseph Shaw will pay you for room and board, anything else they spend at the bar is down to them."

"What about their washing if there is any, you know, their laundry?"

This was something Henry had not thought of, "I suppose you had better include that with their board, we will pay for that, but only the essentials mind."

"Fair enough Mr Cotes, all bills to Mr Shaw, but do you mind if I ask you something?"

"You can ask, I won't guarantee to answer though."

"People are asking, well some were talking in the bar last night anyway, why are these men coming here when almost all the men around here are miners who could do everything these Welshmen can do?"

Henry immediately saw a propaganda opportunity, and also for him to appear philanthropic, undoubtedly, anything he now said Jonah would relay to customers in the bar, from there, the ripple effect would come into being spreading word throughout the whole neighbourhood.

"That I can answer Jonah, true, local men could probably do the same work, but we need their knowledge of this pit to re-open the mine and get it producing coal again, if the mine does not come back into production soon, almost all the men who worked there will be out of a job. Surely, it is better for this community for as many men as possible to stay employed, which is why I decided to bring in this team of experts to do the more dangerous work, they are used to it."

"Yep, I can see the sense in that Mr Cotes, but it is going to cost you a fortune."

"I know, I shall lose a fair bit of money, but unlike those men last Saturday, not my life, that is the material point, wouldn't you agree?"

"Put like that, I would be a fool not to agree."

Henry's face did not flinch, nevertheless, he felt satisfied his last observations had done his position some good.

"Is there anything else Jonah, or are we done now?"

"Think we are about done Mr Cotes, you will keep an eye out for a buyer for this place?"

Henry rose to leave, "I will Jonah, and you have my word on that."

Jonah accompanied him to the door, this time they shook hands.

"There is just one little thing Jonah, I don't know if Shaw and Cleaver mentioned it, only two of the men from Wales are fluent in the English language, the rest speak mainly welsh."

"Now that may be a bit of a bugger Mr Cotes, still if they can't ask for what they want, they can draw pictures of it, we'll manage somehow."

Chapter Nineteen

Elijah Swindon's prediction of the time, if any, his sister Emily's resolute courage would be most likely to fail her proved to be correct, only when Jim Porter's coffin was lowered into the ground did any of the emotions permeating throughout her being become evident.

The funeral service concluded, Jim's coffin was borne at shoulder height by eight of his closest friends along the lane to the cemetery behind the chapel, the family and other mourners followed to the awaiting open grave. Andrew Porter and Wilfred Wright, irrespective of their own feelings now had to support their respective distraught spouses; during the procession to the grave, Elijah, stealthily edged forward through the mourners to be close to his sister Emily.

Arnold Jenkins, although not family or in anyway connected to the deceased, seized an opportunity by taking it upon himself to lend a supporting arm to Martha Porter, assisting her as she struggled to walk the gravelled lane to the graveside, by so doing, he also ensured he was near the head of the column. Therefore, at the graveside before the internment began, Lijah and Arny had skilfully positioned themselves one each side of Emily, each standing alert and ready for any eventuality. Just as the minister began the committal ceremony, Emily, suddenly overcome with grief, swooned and staggered slightly towards the open grave, immediately a strong arm on either side caught her, keeping the girl steady on her feet until this anticipated, overwhelming burst of emotion passed from her and she regained her composure.

His spiritual duties concluded, the minister led the mourners away from the graveside, the men, as they filed past the grave; each took a handful of earth throwing it onto the coffin, as was their custom. Martha Porter once again sought Arny's arm for support, Emily however, remained motionless at the foot of the grave giving no indication of leaving.

"Lijah," Arny said, nodding in Emily's direction.

"Yes, I know," whispered Lijah, "I'm not leaving until she does."

"I'm alright now bro," Emily assured him, "Leave me here alone a minute, please."

With the exception of the gravediggers hovering in the background waiting to close the grave, everyone vacated the cemetery and adjourned to the schoolroom, suddenly; Emily realized someone's hand had grasped hers.

"Waiting now Em, Jim's waiting now, you'll see him again one day."

Fanny, realising her sister was not amongst the assembly making their way to the schoolroom, had returned to her side.

Emily smiled at her, "Sometimes Fanny, I wish I still had your faith that all will come well in the end, but alas, as you get older that belief seems to go away."

"I'm right Em, I'm right, I know I am, anyway, everyone else is in the schoolroom now, if we don't hurry there won't be any funeral bread left for us, and I like funeral bread."

Bewildered, Emily repeated, "Funeral Bread?"

"Yes," insisted Fanny, "Funeral bread, with fruit in, and lots of butter on it, the sort we only seem to have after a funeral."

Emily had to think for a moment before it dawned upon her what her sister meant.

"You mean Currant Bread Fanny; it's called Currant Bread not funeral bread, but you are right, at a funeral tea you can guarantee that it will be on the table, something to do with its slightly bitter taste I think."

The mourners' refreshments concluded Victor Wickersby's Rolls-Royce was put to good use, before taking the Swindon family back to Augers Bank, Arny Jenkins cheerfully transported home anyone who had travelled more than a comfortable walking distance.

No one would consider the events of this day to be joyous, however tragic the reason, this was the first time the whole Swindon family had been at home together for quite some considerable time. Hopeful all the family would be able to stay long enough for everyone to have a meal together, yesterday, Eve had taken the precaution of preparing a ham shank, the vegetables would take hardly any time to cook.

They arrived home at four-thirty, Evie, and more especially Elizabeth, having been granted only sufficient time off work to attend a family funeral, and both having a tedious return train journey were opposed to the idea when Eve suggested they stay for a meal. Arny Jenkins, who by now was quite at home with the family, overheard their conversation and interceded.

"Hold on a minute you two," he said, "Catching a train, that isn't necessarily a problem, and your mother is looking forward to you all being together for once, which I can understand. My instructions were that this car is at your family's disposal all day, and I am to drive you wherever you need to go, obviously you both need to return to your places of employment, but you don't have to bother with trains, I can take you back."

"Settled then," Emily agreed, "Arny can take you back in the car, it'll save you walking down to the station, and then having to change trains at Potterton, It should take a good hour and a half off your journey."

Evie asked, "Are you planning on staying home a day or two Em?"

"I have permission to stay if I want to," she replied, "But then somebody is bound to use my absence against me,"

Arny and Lijah looked at each other, and both, at the same time said, "Quint."

"Exactly," Emily said, rather astonished by the two men chorusing the name, "The old trout doesn't like me."

"She doesn't like anybody lass, except for the mistress that is," Arny laughed.

Sam was please to see all the fires in the house were still alight and smouldering slowly, before they left he had banked them up with dampened slack, a little coaxing with the poker and with the dampers fully opened, they soon sprang back into life.

Sam, Lijah and Eve, all needed to change out of their chapel clothes, nevertheless, they took turns to entertain their guest while the three elder sisters set to work preparing their meal.

Eve, the last to change, was partway up the stairs when there came a knock at the front door, which she answered to find Albert Beech on the doorstep.

"Afternoon Mrs S," Albert said, "Is that lad of yours in?"

"He is Mr. Beech, he's in the kitchen with Sam and a new friend of ours, go on in to them."

Eve continued upstairs, Albert entered, took off his cap and opened the kitchen door; the first person in his line of sight was Sam.

"Eh up Sam, you come into money or something and told nobody, what's that bloody monster doing sitting outside?" was Albert's greeting.

Sam grinned, "The car you mean, don't be so soft Albert, we've not long been back from young Jim Porter's funeral, Arny here brought our Emily home in that bloody monster as you call it, it belongs to Emily's boss."

"Oh aye," Albert said, shaking hands with Arny, "Come up here an hour or so ago, when you weren't in, with the curtains being drawn, I guessed you'd be at some funeral so I popped up to cousin Gerty's, save making two trips like, wish I hadn't though now."

"How's that?" Sam inquired.

"Well Sam, I knew Gert's husband Ted, and the two lads David and Bill were down pit last Saturday, and I knew they didn't walk out. Any road, seems they thought they'd found young David, Gert's been in a right state since pit blew so they sent for the eldest lass Ethel to come home, and it was her who tried to identify Dave."

"All three lost then?" Sam asked.

"Aye, all of them, any road, seems Ethel thought she recognised that goitre thing on young Dave's throat, but you saw the state of them what come out, badly bruised, puffed up and rotting fast most of them."

Sam nodded.

Albert continued, "It was a lot to ask of young Ethel I know, and seems she got it wrong. While I was there, some woman from Libsley called with the police in tow, you know, that new chap Constable Gregory. The lad Ethel thought was Dave, turns out to be this woman's son, definite, she recognised him from his clothes, and what was left of some birthmark. Young Ethel had got all the arrangements made as well for a burial on Monday."

Lijah asked, "So, what's happening now Albert?"

"Burials going ahead, this other woman has taken it on for her lad, paying our Gerty back what she has laid out; turns out it would have been a new grave, so there's no family already in there."

Sam shook his head, "Can't say I'm that surprised Albert, after seeing the state some of those men were in when they were brought out, I half expected mistakes like that to happen, but you didn't call to tell us about that, I heard you ask Eve if Lijah was in."

"Aye, that's right, it's Bull's funeral tomorrow at Harding End, and because he died trying to get our lads out, Shaw and Cleaver have arranged transport for any of us who wanted to go, pay our respects like, and with Lijah being with Bull when he copped it, I thought he might want to go."

"I am supposed to be on shift in the morning Albert," Lijah said, "But yes, George Sanders was a brave man, I would like to pay my respects, yes, I'll lose a days pay and go with you, do you know if there are many going from here?"

"Quite a few lad, Seth, me and some others who've been on rescue squads with Bull, you just need to be at the pit bank by ten o'clock in the morning, we're all leaving from there."

Emily appeared in the doorway, "Lijah," she said, "Can you slide the table leaves in please, we need the extensions in to seat eight of us."

Albert rose, "That'll be my cue to make tracks and leave you to your dinner then."

"Do you have far to go?" Arny asked, "Would you like me to run you home in the car?"

"Kind of you mate, but no thanks, there's a rumour going round that this new gang bloody owners are bringing in will be staying at The Bell, thought I'd go up and see if I can get any joy out of old Jonah Baldwin, that old bugger might know something we don't."

* * *

In comparison to her father, Antoinette Cotes was an early riser, and to Henry's mild annoyance, her recently acquired habit of taking only a continental style breakfast, denied him the time to consume his usual morning feast before Toni was ready. All he had managed this morning was three rashers of bacon, a fried egg, and half a slice of black pudding. He had called at the farm and at the pit, in addition to which he had spent a little over an hour at The Bell with Jonah Baldwin, now; with the time pressing on he was beginning to feel the pangs of hunger again. Normally when he was in this area he would call upon his sister at Highfield for lunch, but today, Antoinette would be there, and he did not want to obstruct her in the task she had undertaken on his behalf.

A couple of large glasses of malt with Jonah on a relatively empty stomach had not been such a good idea. Henry stood by his Sunbeam outside The Bell, pondering, whether or not to try one of the village shops for a pie of some kind, or to drive the four miles into Castleton, where hopefully, he could take a late lunch at a hotel. This minor quandary found an unexpected resolution when a car passed him going down the bank and immediately came to a halt, the driver; the familiar figure of Dr Thomas disembarked and walked over to him.

"Back from Wales I see Henry," greeted the doctor, "Did Joseph Shaw pass on the bit of intelligence I left with him?"

Henry smiled, "About the inspector, yes, he did, but I'm afraid I've never heard of him."

"In that case, consider yourself fortunate, the name didn't register with me immediately either, until old Tommy Farquhar jogged my memory that is, but I have come across the man seeking the appointment before, years ago, twice in fact."

"Who reminded you?" asked Henry, not familiar with the name.

"Tommy Farquhar, my best friend from my school days, he is at the Home Office now but we still keep in touch. I had quite a shock when he turned up here yesterday unannounced with one of his seniors who had other business in the district. Called as they were passing so to speak, their intention, and reason for them breaking their journey was to speak to the mine's owners, I knew you were in Wales somewhere, and I took the liberty of discouraging them from trying to locate your nephew."

Henry frowned, this sounded ominous, "I can do without bad news on an empty stomach, have you had lunch Patrick, we could try The Boars Head again if you haven't."

"Actually, I haven't, today is my housekeeper's day off, and as I need to call at Tilly. I am heading there now to kill two birds with one stone; I plan to take advantage of those caterers you engaged being entrenched in the smithy by calling in for a snack."

"They're not still there are they; I had those brought in just to cover the initial emergency."

"They were yesterday, and proving to be very popular by all accounts since they dispensed with serving conventional fiddly snacks, but then I don't expect someone like you has ever tried a toasted tea-cake, or a breakfast butty."

"If I had the slightest idea what you are talking about, I might be able to answer you," Henry admitted, bewildered.

"Thought so," Patrick answered with a mischievous snigger, "Come on then, let me introduce you to the dubious culinary delights the simple folk around here live on, after all, in this instance, you are paying for them."

When they arrived at Tilly Pit, Dr Thomas led the way into the smithy; apart from one rather wan young man sitting near the smallest forge, the room was empty, the slightly built fellow rose as they entered.

"Good afternoon Dr Thomas, your usual is it?"

"Afternoon Stephen, yes, and one for my friend here, and a couple of large mugs of tea, from a fresh pot if you don't mind, none of that stewed muck," the Doctor replied with a smirk.

The young man smiled, "Of course not Doctor, wouldn't dream of it, be about ten minutes."

Dr Thomas ushered Henry to a table in the far corner of the room where they could talk in relative safety.

"Well Patrick, what is it I am getting for lunch?" Henry asked as he watched Stephen vigorously attacking a side of bacon with a large knife.

"Wait and see Henry, it will probably look disgusting to you, but it's filling and the taste, though some may say acquired, is out of this world."

"A taste which you I presume have acquired?"

"I have, but if my father ever learned of it he would disown me as being a class traitor."

Henry looked bemused, "I don't understand, why would he consider you a class traitor?"

Dr. Thomas laughed, "There is absolutely no reason why you should Henry, and perhaps it's time for some kind of explanation. The name under which I practice medicine, Thomas, is in fact my second Christian name. I grew tired of the social life, that endless parade of parties and all the ensuing mindless chatter I came to regard as a pointless lifestyle, and so to escape it I chose medicine as a career. No one around here is aware of my true family name, and I don't see why you should be an exception, but in truth, I am the second son of a viscount of this great nation of ours.

My family's lifestyle and title mean little to me, anyway my elder brother is the heir to that, I was merely the spare who is no longer needed now that I have two strapping nephews."

Henry's eyes widened, association with the second son of a viscount could prove most advantageous when it came to finding a single man in possession of such a title as a prospective husband for Antoinette. It was with some trepidation that after so short an acquaintance with Dr. Thomas, Henry asked.

"Is it because of your family connections that you learned the identity of this person who has been appointed as a Home Office Inspector?"

Dr Thomas frowned, "Indirectly, I suppose, yes, but mainly because it is customary for the nobility to pack their offspring off to boarding school at their earliest convenience, if my father hadn't done so, I would not have come across George Walklate so early. Walklate was appointed as a junior master the year before I left, the older boys regarded him as something of an oddity and out of place, that was the first time our paths crossed, and then again eight years ago after a huge explosion in a coal mine in Lancashire."

Henry recalled, "Ah yes, I remember reading something about that, well over three hundred men lost I believe, this Walklate fellow led the inquiry there?"

"Heavens no man, but he was there in a very menial capacity. That particular coalmine in relation to yours, as I said is huge, and unlike this and most other mines had a conglomeration of owners and many investors. Where there is only one, or maybe two owners it is a different matter, in fact, my father owns a couple of pits the size of Tilly as do a good many of his very good friends, if you take my meaning."

Henry remembered their first meeting and the revelation of the doctor's handshake, a slight nod of his head assured the doctor he understood his intimation.

Stephen was paying no attention to them as he tended the makeshift steel hotplate, which one of the blacksmiths had made to fit over the small furnace, and the aroma coming from it was beginning to make both men salivate. Patrick Thomas observed Henry watching the young man working, and realised Henry was ill at ease speaking with Stephen in the room.

Reassuringly Patrick said, "Don't worry about Stephen, he is a patient of mine, the lad is hard of hearing."

Nevertheless, Henry proceeded with caution.

"So you are telling me this Walklate is one of the—,"

"The Craft, Lord no!" exclaimed the doctor, "But he would very much like to be, however, he is not considered suitable material, every time he tries he ends up blackballed, his family, or rather his father is in trade, a grocer or something of the sort."

"But surely that does not preclude him, we, or, our ancestors all had to start in a small way, I understand he has been honoured with the 'Commander of the British Empire,' so he can't be that bad."

"True, he has the C.B.E, and if he possessed more vertebrae than jelly in his spine he could be an asset to any organisation, as it is, my visitors yesterday informed me he is still so eager to please everyone, pushing for this or that appointment, he actually exudes an air of desperation. Tommy and I were seniors at the time he was appointed to our school, it didn't take long for everyone to see Walklate was ambitious, but ambition on its own is a vicious mistress. All my close friends there were from similar family backgrounds to my own, and we used to look upon Jittery George, as we called him, not so much as a social climber, but more of a mountaineer."

"I take it you did not like him very much Patrick, but I'm afraid your reference to jelly eludes me."

"Like is not the word I would choose, trust would be better."

"I see, and the jelly?"

"Bone is stronger than the jelly between the vertebrae, as a schoolmaster he had very little in the way of backbone, even the young boys soon figured that out, and took every opportunity to use it to their advantage."

Henry still looked bemused, "Still a bit lost here Patrick," he admitted.

"Let me see, an illustration as an example," continued Patrick, "Ah, I know, think of this, when two opinions are totally opposite, can you possibly agree with both?"

"Wouldn't have thought so, no," Henry responded shaking his head.

"Nevertheless, he does, whenever called upon to make a decision, he would seek everyone's opinion and support the majority view, however, the minute their back was turned, straight away he would scoot over to the opposition and cover himself by promising to support the other side."

"Dangerous tactics," observed Henry.

"Precisely, that is the reason the craft will not admit him, nobody's identity or dealings would be safe, the C.B.E was arranged as an appeasement for small services rendered, and to give him a little more credibility whenever it became necessary to use him again. In other words, in the corridors of power he doesn't amount to much, men like him with the ability to talk convincingly for hours without actually committing to anything, seem to have their uses, and as I learned yesterday, he has been used many times. Fortunately, he is so vain and naive he now considers himself important and indispensable, when actually, he is regarded by those with the power merely as a nobody who wants to be a somebody."

"Hmm," Henry pondered, reflecting upon his own ambition, his long awaited inclusion in the honours list, "I believe I know what you mean, but from what you say, is he the right man to conduct an inquiry of this kind?"

"I asked the same question yesterday when Tommy called. Tommy's superior who could easily have stopped it even though it is a lower department's responsibility, confirmed, against his own better judgement, and Walklate's insistence he is the right man for the job he has been tentatively selected, nevertheless, now he thinks he is indispensible, he is being a bit difficult and stipulating his terms of acceptance. He will be the figurehead only, flirting here, there, and everywhere as Tommy told me he still does, by all accounts he can be convincing enough to the general public, because he is such a verbose man, the problem is he honestly believes he is always right, even when he is obviously wrong."

"I have a nephew rather like that."

"If you mean your new partner, I know, nothing like his father is he?"

"Sadly no, but I thought you came to this district after my brother-in-law passed away."

"I did, I never knew the late squire, but I know of him and his rank, a highly respected man I am told."

Henry was silent a moment, the protection of the powerful people he hoped for, now seemed to be forthcoming.

"I appreciate the advance information Patrick, but I am still dubious of the outcome of an inquiry."

The doctor reiterated, "Henry, there are many men like yourself who could be affected by an adverse outcome of the forthcoming inquiry, but, the investigation could, and no doubt will take several months, however, a great number of people already seem to know the outcome. Friend Walklate, like on the previous occasions, will be flanked by at least two of their men to feed him ideas and keep him on track preventing him taking off on his customary wild tangents. Tommy is of the opinion; Walklate's naivety has increased to such an extent since my last encounter with him he will not notice their control, Walklate is expected to, and no doubt will ponce about giving his usual impression of being in charge, hence his selection."

"Did your friend have an input on choosing this fellow and making the appointment because of his ability to talk?"

"Lord no, that came from much higher; how high I have not been told, quite possibly confederates of the old gentleman who came up to Staffordshire with Tommy who have considerable holdings in the mining industry."

"What did you say the older gentleman's name was?"

Patrick smiled through his beard, "I didn't, and as you weren't here to meet him I am not permitted to say, doubtless at some future date he will make himself known to you."

"He is of high rank?"

Again, Patrick smiled, "In both definitions of the word, yes, extremely, Tommy is to be the contact and messenger instructed to liaise with us up here."

"I am amazed an incident up here is receiving so much attention in the capital, not that I am complaining, one never knows what can emerge once an inquiry begins."

The doctor's face took on a serious expression, "Don't let me mislead you Henry, in such circumstances as we have here a full and very thorough investigation has to take place, and be seen to do so. However, if the person leading that investigation has a self obsessive nature and poor judgement, someone who sees and hears only things already in his head, any safety omissions common to the industry are more likely to be missed."

"I appreciate that Patrick of course, and I know it's hard to tell someone his judgement is completely off, I keep trying with my nephew, but arguing with him is like talking to a mollusc, pointless, but surely someone, at sometime has had a quiet word with this Walklate fellow?"

"I was given to understand people have tried, but every time, jittery George goes into a peevish sulk, whimpering that if he isn't doing the job properly he will quit and somebody else can do it, so nobody bothers anymore, now, they just play along and make sure he is guided in the direction they want him to go."

"He sounds a very curious and complex character, dangerous even," observed Henry, "I will have to be on my guard when I have to deal with him."

Stephen called to them, "Doctor, your snaps ready, do you want me to cut it in half, or leave in one piece before I bring it over?"

"One piece for me Stephen, but you had better bring cutlery over, my friend has never seen a breakfast butty."

Henry stared at, and with his fork gingerly examined the contents of the plate the lad set in front of him. Beneath an inch-thick slice of bread sat a fried egg, nestling upon two sausages sliced in half, these in turn lay on four thickly sliced rashers of bacon, and based by another inch of bread.

"You were right Patrick, it does look disgusting, and how are you expected to eat this?"

"Please yourself, but don't knock it until you try it, the first one I had here, I tried to be genteel and used a knife and fork, until I noticed one of the old miners sniggering at me, he shouted to me, 'you're loosing half the taste like that mate, pick the bugger up and bite it,' he was right."

Henry observed the way his companion cradled the concoction in his huge hands, and emulated his movements, clumsily at first, but he soon acquired the knack. This method of eating did not allow further conversation between them until the monster sandwiches were devoured.

"Well?" asked the doctor, "What did you think?"

Henry smirked, "Dented the hole in my stomach a bit, and you were right, they are delicious, especially when you have all those flavours mingling in your mouth at the same time stimulating the old taste buds, there could be money to be made in the right areas by providing such food quickly like that."

"Our class loses out on so many simple pleasures by following etiquette," Patrick said smiling, "One of the reasons I was happy to quit my old life and live as I do, can you manage another?"

"That I could," Henry replied, and turning to Stephen called, "Hey there young man, two more of the same."

Stephen did not move, which annoyed Henry.

"He didn't hear you Henry, I told you he is hard of hearing, I'll go."

Stephen once again busy at his hotplate, Henry and the doctor were safe and free to continue their discussion.

"We have known each other a very short time Patrick and I really appreciate you sharing with me the points you have, but surely some of the information you have past on should be considered highly confidential, is it safe for you to have told me?"

"There has been a terrible accident here Henry, which will doubtless have a lasting effect on this community, but everyone in anyway connected with the winning of coal knows those deadly pockets of methane can appear anywhere, and at anytime, not quite an act of God, but more a freak of nature instigated by man interfering with mother nature herself. By your actions since the explosion, you have demonstrated an eagerness to aid the people here. Needless to say, I am fully aware that like any man of business, you are also trying to protect both your investment and your reputation, not to mention the reputations of others like yourself who have similar investments.

Your handling of the situation so far has been closely watched, certain people hold the opinion, if you meet with personal, social or financial disaster here because of the conditions the men work in below ground, others, by association might also. Therefore, the particulars I have passed on would have been given to you direct, but you were in Wales and we didn't know when you were due back. My visitors needed to be back in London this morning, my instructions were simple enough, to make you aware of certain factors when you returned, anything you have been told is intended to guide you, and make evident the fact you are not alone.

For my part, I was impressed when you removed that pretty young serving girl away from your nephew's clutches the other day, and the speed at which the coffins you promised arrived at the pit. There is however one recommendation to ensure the support I have outlined, keep your nephew out of your plans as much as possible, he is considered dangerous and unreliable. His birthright bestows his position in life as the local squire, but he could never aspire to take his late father's rank, although, I have heard talk of grandchildren born the wrong side of the blanket, perhaps one of those may inherit the late Charles Heath's better characteristics."

"You are remarkably well informed regarding my family Patrick, it saddens me, but I would have to admit, as did his father towards the end, my sister's son has proved to be something of a disappointment to us all, well, apart from to his mother, as for his producing illegitimate children, you cannot expect me to comment on that point."

"Of course not Henry, I would not expect you to do so, forgive me, that observation was ill advised and unacceptable."

Henry chortled, "On the contrary Patrick, it is quite acceptable, in fact, I have every confidence that a descendant of the Heath family from the wrong side of the blanket as you so discerningly put it, will have a far greater effect on this world than my nephew, after all, the way young Charles behaves it will not be difficult."

Patrick Thomas was, to say the least a little mystified by Henry's reply, however, he decided it would probably be better not to pursue this subject any further, the task his visitors delegated to him yesterday he regarded as concluded. Henry Cotes should be in possession of enough detail to assess probabilities, and to enable him to make adequate preparations for the investigation to come.

The doctor left the pit bank just before half past three, and when Henry located Joseph Shaw in his office, Joseph had nothing more to report, Henry couldn't find any legitimate reason to stay much longer himself. By now, Antoinette should be back at Valley Farm, and Henry had estate business at home, however, before he left the office he decided to telephone Highfield Hall to see if his elusive nephew had returned home.

It was Hawkins, who answered his call, and informed him the master was still away, and the mistress had retired for her afternoon rest. Henry, was not really surprised, and by four o'clock, with his mind more at ease than it had been for a week, he pulled his Sunbeam off the pit bank and headed home to Kirkleston Manor in Cheshire.

Antoinette arrived home just as the hall clock struck half past the hour of ten, apart from the servants, it appeared everyone had retired for the night; she began to climb the stairway when a voice from the library called to her.

"Well young lady, have you had an enjoyable day, I expected you home long before this," Henry, seated in his favourite chair, a decanter of his favourite malt at his side had purposefully waited up until his daughter's return.

"I have indeed pops," Toni replied as she joined him and helped herself to a generous draft of his malt, "Although, I have to say the air is developing quite a nip now, but this will help."

"You met with young Florence I take it?"

"I did, and you were right, it is impossible not to like her, I have never felt a bond develop with anyone as quickly as it seems to have done between Flo and I, she will be arriving here in the morning to stay for a few days, I presume you have no objections?"

"None whatsoever my dear, the company will do you both good, and with your aunt here, the house could do with livening up a bit."

"Pops you are a cunning old blighter at times, I hope you aren't matchmaking for one of the twins, if you are, you can forget it," Antoinette mischievously probed.

"Not at all, I thought I told you the girl is soon to be married."

Toni smiled, "That's right, you did," she agreed.

All the way home she had been devising some method of extracting information from her father, for this purpose the hour, and the malt were working in her favour, Henry was too relaxed and clearly off his guard.

"You know pops, when this escapade started and you asked me to help, I agreed because I was so bored, but I couldn't figure out why you would be so interested in a country girl if it wasn't for the delights of the flesh."

Henry retorted, "Can't a man help someone for the sake of it these days?"

"They can pops, but you wouldn't."

Henry was about to protest indignantly, but Antoinette continued speaking and stopped him.

"It was a pleasant change for me to enjoy convivial company without having to be worn out with civility, to be able to talk and laugh whilst enjoying an excellent meal, by the way, did I mention that Flo's fiancé Zack was at the farm and had dinner with us."

Before she laid her trap by mentioning Zack's name, she held Henry under intense scrutiny, she knew her father well, with the decanter at his side, he would be mellow, and the flash of Henry's eyes at Zack's name added some weight to her suspicions.

Henry recovered quickly, "Was he?" he said as innocently as he could, "What did you make of him?"

"He's changed a bit since I used to chase him around the grounds at Highfield; grown into rather a fine figure of a man, Flo is a lucky girl."

"High time you found yourself a husband young lady, or have I got to do it for you, I made a contact recently that could be very helpful to those ends."

"Pops, don't start that again, when I find the man I will accept, you will be the first to know."

Henry scowled, but conceded.

Toni set her trap deeper, "I thought when Flo gets here tomorrow I would take her into town to find her some riding gear, and maybe some fashionable clothes if she needs them, which you are paying for pops, right?"

"Yes, I said I would cover any expenses, but she is proud, do you think she will accept things like that from you?"

"Leave that to me, anyway, she will need a wardrobe to match the quality of the engagement ring Zack gave her today."

"Quality," queried Henry.

"Oh yes pops, it is beautiful, I would be proud to wear it myself, but then if I remember correctly, you did say the man she is to marry came from good stock."

With a jolt, Henry remembered Lydia's observation that Antoinette had manipulated and ran rings around him for years, somehow she must have stumbled upon, or suspected the truth of Zack's parentage and was skilfully seeking confirmation.

"Did I," Henry flustered, "If I did, I must have meant he was a very good worker, or something like that, actually I don't remember saying anything of the kind."

Toni giggled, "Of course you don't pops, of course you don't, however, my eyes don't lie to me and his features are too distinctive for me to be mistaken, if there is something you don't want to share with me now, one day it will come to light. Changing the subject, you don't need to look any further for a stallion for me, quite by accident; I have found the one I want, how to get hold of it though is the problem."

Henry, with some relief Antoinette had dropped the delicate subject for the time being asked.

"Really, where?"

"In the stables at Highfield of all places, he is a magnificent animal."

"Oh, now I come to think of it, Anne did say Charles had acquired a couple of horses along with other things on the strength of his expected inheritance, and I am fairly sure she said he hasn't paid for them yet."

Antoinette smiled with delight, "Now that could be lucky," she said gleefully, "All I have to do is find whoever Charley boy owes the money to, pay him first and that stallion is mine, or rather you can pay him first, can't you pops?"

"If your heart is set on it I suppose I will have to."

Antoinette arose from her chair, went over and kissed her father's forehead, "Thanks pops, by the way, there is another little matter I wanted to discuss with you."

"And what pray would that be?"

"Considering you have just promised to obtain that stallion for me off Charley boy, this may not be an appropriate time to fall out with you."

Fall out, over what?" Henry was too mellowed by the malt and the news he received today to be angry.

"The pretence of my calling at that farm was to see for myself the condition of those poor ponies, was it not?"

Henry sighed, "Here it comes, I have been expecting this."

"Then you will not be disappointed will you pops, how on earth could you allow any creature to be so neglected as those poor beasts?"

Again, Henry sighed, "The answer to that is, I did not know. Do you seriously believe I would condone such a thing if I did; I was just as outraged as you, possibly more so, you didn't see them when I did, and by now with young Florence's care their condition should have improved. When you are the owner of a coalmine, there is no call on you to go grubbing about underground, I realise now, to the men who do, ponies are just another tool for them to use."

"They are tools that are mistreated if that's the case," Toni retorted angrily.

"Were, not are," Henry corrected, "If it will make you feel happier child, I took time out to venture below ground while I was in Wales, specifically to see the underground stables."

Still irate, Toni snapped, "And?"

"The ponies there are in a little better condition than the ones you have seen, nevertheless, I gave orders that an alternative, possibly a mechanical method to bring the coal out must be found. Until a new method is installed, each beast is to spend no more than four weeks at a time below ground, and not sent back before it has breathed God's fresh air for at least another four weeks. There, will that placate you somewhat?"

"Well, it's a start I suppose, anyway, time I was off to my bed, quite a bit to do tomorrow, not counting the challenges laid at our door."

"Challenges, what challenges?"

"Pops, you seem in better humour tonight, but for the past week you haven't been yourself, I can understand it with the doom and gloom legacy for you and those poor village people left by that gas explosion. I can sympathize with them, but it is a coal mine that caved in not the sky, the world is still turning, life goes on."

"True enough, it has been a long gloomy week."

"It's gone now pops, no one can turn time back to last Friday, come on pops, there is still life to live, fun to be had."

Henry frowned and refilled his glass.

"None of that now pops, this time last week you had ambitions and objectives, get them back. You have given me the challenge, amongst other things, of turning a farm girl into a lady, and I have given myself an even bigger one. You would like to be Sir Henry and have grandchildren, although pops, preferably without my involvement in that one, finish that drink, get of to bed and wake up fighting the Henry Cotes way, I do, night night pops."

"I do wish you would stop using this slang talk of yours," Henry scolded.

"Only do it to wind you up pops, but if you insist," she paused by the library door, turned, bob curtsied, and in a mocking tone said, "Goodnight sir."

"Oh you cheeky madam, get off to bed with you, and good luck with your guest tomorrow."

To be continued:—